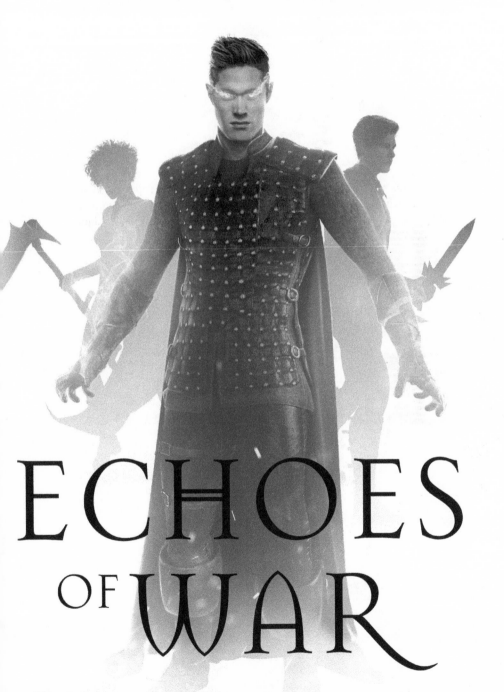

JOHN PAQUIN

ECHOES
OF WAR

Echoes of War
Copyright © 2022 John Paquin

Published by Noctua Publishing Inc.
Orillia, ON, Canada.
www.johnpaquin.ca

First Edition

ISBN: 978-1-7774256-0-9 (paperback),
978-1-7774256-3-0 (hardback)

Cover and interior layout by Miblart.com

Printed in U.S.A.

To Sarah and Melissa,
who encouraged me to finish this project
every time I considered setting it aside.

ACKNOWLEDGEMENT

Many generous and talented people came together to make this book possible. I would like to thank Roxanna at Proofreadebooks.com for her professionalism and editing services. I would also like to thank my AMAZING Beta Readers—particularly Brady Mulvihill, Manda Drake-York, Melissa D'Urso, and Michelle Mulvihill—whose invaluable feedback allowed me to make crucial developmental edits and hone my plot. I would like to give another big thank you to Miblart.com for professionally formatting my book, as well as designing my cover. I would also like to offer a huge thank-you to Cristina at Authors Large and Small, who managed my book launch marketing and connected me with countless reviewers, artists and other professionals that allowed me to bring this book to the world with its best foot forward.

ADD ME ON SOCIAL MEDIA!

@paquinjohn (on most platforms)
OR
Visit me!
johnpaquin.ca

FOREWORD

This book contains gratuitous and graphic depictions of violence and some references to perverse sexual behaviour. Many important cultural and historical figures, places and events will be represented in a reimagined version of our world. If you may be triggered by these kinds of subject matter, DO NOT READ THIS BOOK.

PREFACE

Behind the veil of ordinary perception, there are no epic battles between Heaven and Hell. Angels are not engaging Demons in a war for supremacy over the Earth and neither Angels nor Demons exist in any preconceived form we have ever imagined. They do not battle each other for the same reason that the clouds do not battle the rain and the trees do not battle the soil.

They are two states of the same element.

CHAPTER I

LOST AND FOUND

D aniel awoke to the sound of chirping birds, carried in on bars of sunlight that penetrated the small gaps between the shutters on a nearby window and painted across his face. He craned his head to look out the window, but the shutters prevented him from getting much of a view of the outside.

Where am I?

Daniel tried to gauge his surroundings, but shadows cloaked the corners of the room.

Did one of those shadows just move?

He stared unblinkingly into the darkness, scanning for the slightest sign of movement, but after a few moments, relaxed a little.

The shadows stirred once more, unfolding and approaching the bed where he lay. Daniel screamed with a pitch that sounded alien coming from him.

"Boy, stop screaming. I mean you no harm."

Panic gripped him until the sparse light in the room finally cleansed the darkness away, revealing an old man with a gaunt, bearded face and wispy white hair. The man opened the shutters and doused the room with sunlight.

"My name is Azra. I am a High Priest and a physician here at the Temple of Shamash. We found you on the riverbank."

Daniel stared at Azra, mouth agape.

Azra observed Daniel for a moment and then continued, "Do you remember why you were walking alone, along the Euphrates?" he said, folding his hands over his white robe. Gold tassels danced against intricate gold geometric embroidery.

As Daniel shook his head at the old man's question, a warm, wet droplet landed on his arm, and when he looked down, he realized it was drool. Embarrassed, he quickly wiped his mouth and arm on the blankets, casting a sideways glance at Azra.

An amused smirk cracked across Azra's face. "It's alright boy, don't worry about it."

Daniel sat quietly, ashamed, trying to forget he had screamed and then drooled on himself in front of the old man, who stood patiently observing him.

Azra chuckled and rifled through his pockets while he approached the bed. "I almost forgot. You were carrying something with you. Ah, here it is."

Pulling his fist from his pocket, Azra extended an open palm toward the boy.

Taking the stone, Daniel turned it over and over in his hand, remembering the feel of it. Someone had washed the pendant, and its pure white stone finish shone in the sunlight.

Suddenly fleeting images washed over him; images of a small girl—a familiar face with a wide smile and a small white pendant hanging below it—flashed through his mind. "*Daniel!*" she giggled as she reached up toward him with open arms. Another flash and the girl ran with the pendant carelessly bouncing off her back and shoulder. Then came a man's hands, offering the pendant to the girl. Joy illuminated the little girl's face as she held the polished white stone in her small hands. *"Upon a glad heart, oil is poured,"* a female voice whispered from among the memories.

"Upon a glad heart, oil is poured. From where no one knows," Daniel muttered into his open palm.

"What did you say, boy?" Azra asked inquisitively.

Daniel glanced up nervously, but hesitated before answering.

"The pendant. The words on it are from a saying: 'Upon a glad heart, oil is poured. From where, no one knows'. It means 'a glad heart is anointed by heaven'."

"An old proverb indeed. Where did you learn it?"

"It's written on the pendant. It says *oil* and *heart*, which is a short way of saying it."

"Yes, but *where* did you learn to read it? Who taught you to read the pendant?"

The boy paused momentarily, straining to remember. "... I don't remember. Someone just said it to me once... or around me, I'm not sure."

Azra crossed his arms and continued to stare at the boy with interest as if he were facing a complex puzzle. "Can you at least remember your name?"

"Daniel. My name is Daniel."

"Alright Daniel, until we figure out where you've come from, you're welcome to stay here."

A knock drummed on the door.

"Come," Azra said authoritatively, prompting a young temple slave in a plain brown tunic and sandals to enter.

Daniel noticed the boy was about his age, maybe a little younger than him, with light brown hair and almond-coloured eyes—from what he could tell. The boy resisted eye contact with Daniel, stealing only quick, nervous glances at him.

"Good. Help Daniel get changed."

The boy nodded and moved toward Daniel.

"If you'll excuse me, I have duties elsewhere, but we will talk again soon. Kaleb will attend to you."

Azra closed the door behind him and walked vacantly down the hall.

I'll most definitely have to test this boy for reading and comprehension, but who could have taught him to read? What an unexpected mystery. Could the boy have walked from Mari? It would make sense. Mari is the closest village to where I found him. I will have to send word to the village and inquire further.

Azra had found Daniel face-down along the riverbank, dehydrated and covered in ash. At first, several deep cuts and bruises reshaped the boy's face, but his wounds healed with supernatural speed over the five-day sail to the Port of Enki, in Sippar.

Azra had wanted to examine the boy personally, but his position as High Priest and his other responsibilities had made that impossible. Instead, he assigned Kaleb to look after Daniel and alert him if the boy regained consciousness.

How unexpected... to think I was only checking in for a moment! Such an odd boy, but he is certainly more striking than I had imagined, Azra noted, remembering how Daniel's ice-blue eyes and light brown hair contrasted with his dark olive skin.

"Azra?"

The voice hurled Azra's consciousness back to the present, and it took him a moment to compose himself.

Damn that swine. If it were politically feasible, I would have the man wear a bell for the rest of his life.

Samir blinked as he stood frozen in front of Azra.

Yes. Stare at me with your stupid, beady little eyes, and your fat... everything else. Do you know why your face is always red? It's likely caused by a heart or circulatory problem tied with eating more than your portion at every meal and then towing your gratuitously fat ass around the temple complex. Are you even aware of this?

"Brother Azra, it is good to see you have returned safely from your pilgrimage. What news have you brought from the north?"

"As I told the others, nothing significant has changed about our relationships in the north. The king and his allies are requesting the usual grain and food store supplements, and aside from the odd raiding skirmish, the empire is relatively peaceful at the moment—all of which you would know had you attended the meeting earlier today."

Samir chuckled casually and continued on, sidestepping the obvious dismissal.

What an irritating man.

"Funny, usually a council meeting takes place after *all* of its members have gathered. By the time I had arrived, most of the other members had already dispersed." Samir's grin did not reach his eyes.

"I would think a man of your stature would be more punctual, brother. Was there a petty dispute somewhere that needed policing or maybe one of the young slaves had their feelings hurt?" Azra tilted his chin upward to stare down his nose at the shorter man.

"As a High Priest, like myself, you should know that we handle *all* the affairs of the temple, including the emotional instability of young boys ripped from their families to serve as slaves. We are not just politicians, Azra, we are the wheels that keep the cart rolling. You would do well to remember that if you ever hope to gain an ounce of goodwill from anyone—especially those you expect to follow you."

"You cannot feed a community with good intentions, Samir, just as you cannot lead people if you allow yourself to get wrapped up in mundane details. If you stand too close to the fire, it will consume you."

"It is unfortunate that you believe that. I believe we work for the people first and the temple second. I would even argue putting the community first should be the priority of any man."

"And that is why you provide emotional support for young boys, while I negotiate significant matters with important leaders."

Samir paused, casting a downward glance. "Well, I—I had forgotten that another urgent matter requires my presence. Excuse me."

Undoubtedly. Azra sneered as the other man migrated down the hall.

After the door had shut behind Azra, the boys sat in awkward silence. Daniel spoke first, attempting to break it.

"So... you're Kaleb?"

Kaleb nodded without making eye contact.

"My name is Daniel. I think Azra mentioned that, but he didn't really introduce us."

The other boy continued to stare at different points on the floor.

"So... what do you do here?"

Kaleb paused for a moment and then looked up at Daniel. "I'm a temple slave."

Daniel looked at the boy with confusion. "What's a temple slave?"

Kaleb shot him a look that said: *are you kidding?*

"I can't remember much from before I woke up here."

"I guess they don't have many temples in Mari, eh?"

"Mari?" Daniel arched an eyebrow.

"Right, you don't remember anything. Mari's a village near where we found you. Azra said he thought you might be from there since the next nearest village was a day's walk away and you clearly hadn't gotten there by boat."

"What makes you say that?"

"You were covered in ash. There's no way that would happen on a riverboat."

Daniel contemplated the point for a moment. "That makes sense. So, what do you do at the temple? I didn't even know priests had slaves."

"Priests don't have slaves. The temple adopts us, and then we just work at the temple. The priests tell us what to do, but technically, we're owned by the temple," Kaleb explained.

"How long have you lived here?"

"Probably three or four years, I'm not sure. A while anyway." Kaleb let the information sit, offering nothing additionally.

Daniel looked out the window at the clear sky and then surveyed the room for a moment. "How long have I been here?"

"Well, you've only been at the temple for a day or so, but we found you six days ago along the riverbank. You were sleeping the whole time."

Six days?!

Suddenly, Daniel felt a fierce hunger and nausea wash over him. He put a fist over his stomach and steadied himself. "Do you have anything I can eat?"

"Yeah, I guess you haven't eaten or drank anything in almost a week." Kaleb brought a folded tunic and sandals over to Daniel and held the pile in front of him.

"Here. I was told not to dress you after I bathed you so that a physician could look for any injuries hidden by the ash."

"You bathed me?" Daniel said nervously.

"Yeah. Azra watched me to make sure I cleaned you... as good as they expect me to clean myself. It was gross." Kaleb said with disgust, avoiding eye contact again.

"Sorry about that," Daniel muttered sheepishly.

"Don't worry about it," Kaleb replied hastily. "I'll take you to the kitchen once you put the tunic on."

Daniel threw the tunic over his head and stood at the side of the bed. He faced away from Kaleb as he pulled the lower part of the tunic toward his knees. Then he fastened his belt and sandals and followed Kaleb out the door.

Kaleb led Daniel down the hall. The temple architects mostly made the halls of mud brick with some support pillars made of dark wood, covered with a wax finish. The bricks were all painted in various shades of yellow, green, blue and white to form elaborate, repeating mural designs featuring suns and strange animals. Large tapestries suspended between the wooden supports also carried the solar-themed motifs.

After the boys followed a turn in the hallway, the colourfully painted mud-brick gave way to a dark wood panelling of a similar colour to the support pillars, but with a much finer, smoother grade visible beneath the clear wax coating. Footsteps echoed less loudly in this part of the building, as if absorbed by the walls themselves.

"I like this part of the temple because it's quieter and most people don't spend a lot of time here."

"Why is that?"

"It's the kitchen. There's no real need for anyone to be in the kitchen unless they're cooking. Almost everyone works in the fields."

As they turned another corner, the hallway finally opened up to a large room with several stone ovens— mostly filled with baking bread except for one with a few ceramic pots inside, which clacked with boiling liquids. On the walls hung shelves with suspended vegetables and spices. In the centre of the room sat a sizeable slab-stone table constructed of one polished rectangular stone slab centred horizontally over the top of a smaller rough rectangular slab laying on the floor.

Along the sides of the table, there was a line of stools, presumably for the cooks to sit while they worked. Various vegetables and spices lined the tabletop, both in jars and bundles laid out in what looked like a semi-organized spread.

Kaleb walked over to the far end of the kitchen, where a boy was setting out rows of hot bread, pulled from the ovens by a flat, shovel-like tool. Daniel made his way to a stool while he watched the other boy smoothly scrape the bread off of the blackened stone of the oven and expertly transport it to the table.

"Hey, Zee," Kaleb said, greeting the other boy.

"Just a sec," he replied hastily as he continued to evacuate the loaves from a line of ovens.

Daniel noticed that the bread appeared to be getting darker as the rows of bread grew.

He put too many loaves in at once.

"Do you want a hand?" Kaleb asked.

Zee hesitated for a moment before replying. "Yeah, grab a peel."

Kaleb grabbed another flat shovel-like tool from a rack along one wall and went to work removing bread from the ovens alongside Zee. The smells of freshly baked bread filled the room as both boys darted frantically to save the bread from burning.

Daniel grabbed one loaf nearby; the crust was only slightly warm, but when he bit into it, hot steam escaped, burning his mouth and face.

"Argh—!" he yelled, dropping the loaf.

"Are you fucking stupid?" Zee roared.

"I forgot about the steam," Daniel muttered.

"Give him a break. He hasn't eaten in a week," Kaleb said.

"What? Where did you find this guy?"

Zee removed the last loaf of bread from the oven and then leaned on the counter, eyeing Daniel as he wiped the sweat from his face. "He's that kid Azra found, isn't he?"

"I'm the one that saw him first, but yeah." Kaleb put the peel back on the rack and returned with a cup and a full pitcher of water. "Drink this and don't touch anything else."

"I'm hungry, not an idiot." Daniel glared at Kaleb and then drank the cup so fast it left him out of breath. He refilled the cup two more times and guzzled them down just as quickly.

Zee poured Daniel a large bowl of stew and broke a hunk of bread from a long-cooled loaf sitting on a nearby shelf. "Yeah, well, don't try to prove it until you leave the kitchen. You'll end up cutting yourself on a carrot or something."

A smirk cracked Daniel's expression as well. "I'm going to stab you with a carrot."

Kaleb chuckled.

"Whatever. Shut up and eat this," Zee said, handing the bowl and bread to Daniel.

Daniel ate three bowls of the stew and finished the loaf of bread before he felt satisfied. Zee and Kaleb had eaten a bowl each while they quietly watched Daniel like he was some strange animal that had wandered into their view.

"So, no food or water for a week, eh?" Zee said with an amused but sympathetic tone.

"Yeah, it's easy when you're passed out the entire time."

Zee cocked an eyebrow at Kaleb. Kaleb nodded in confirmation.

"Wow."

"Yeah, it hits you hard when you wake up, though. I was feeling kind of sick until a minute ago."

"I'm surprised the food didn't make you throw up," Kaleb said. "You ate a lot just now. When I first got here, Azra got pissed at me, and he made me work for a week without food. When I finally got to eat, I threw it all up. It was the worst."

Zee laughed.

"What did you do?" Daniel asked.

"He kept making me wash his clothes, and I told him he smelled like a dead asshole," Kaleb explained.

"Kaleb doesn't know how to let his inside thoughts be inside thoughts," Zee said.

Daniel smirked.

"Shut up. Anyway, it was gross, and I told him. I think he's been punishing me ever since."

Zee laughed. "Listen to you. It's like you've only ever done one thing wrong in your entire life."

"I did. I'm a nice guy. You make me sound like some kind of jerk."

"I make you sound like nothing. You get in trouble because of you."

"Like you're so perfect."

"I never said I'm perfect. I just said you haven't done *only* one bad thing ever."

"Well, you've done way worse stuff than me."

"No."

"Yeah."

"No, not *way* worse."

"You have."

"Maybe way funnier, but not way worse."

"What about Yosef?" Kaleb exchanged challenging stares with Zee, each barely holding back a grin.

"Who's Yosef?" Daniel asked.

Zee chuckled and shook his head before turning to Daniel. "Ok, so there was this really old priest, Yosef. He came from up north somewhere and he talked funny, but everyone knew you stayed away from him when he was mad. Anyway, this one time—before I knew my way around—Samir asked me to go do something, and I got lost and ended up in here. I was so hungry, I just started eating whatever I could find. Yosef came in and saw me. He was pissed. I threw some potatoes and bread at him and ran. He chased after me and kept threatening he was going to break me in half and stuff until we got outside. I ran across the garden, and it had just rained, so the whole place was slippery. I ended up sliding as soon as my feet touched the mud, but I didn't fall, so I just kept running. When Yosef hit the garden, his feet slid out from under him, and he landed on his butt. Then, when he tried to go after me again, he flew forward and landed on his face. It covered him in mud, and he smelled like cow dung. After that, we just called him *shit-streak*."

"Not to his face, though."

"Definitely not to his face."

The boys chuckled and then cast sideways glances at Daniel as the moment faded.

"So, you really can't remember anything from your hometown at all?" Zee asked Daniel.

Irritation coloured Daniel's tone. "I get flashes of memories sometimes, but that's it. I don't remember my friends or my family or even where I'm from. That's how I remembered my name. All I know right now is that when I woke up, I was laying in a pile of ashes and when I started walking, I didn't know where I was going. I just didn't want to sit in a pile of ashes. Eventually, I must've passed out again, and that's probably where they found me."

"You don't have to get all mad. I was just asking," Zee said.

"It's just that people *keep* asking me."

"Hey look, it's just weird," Kaleb said. "Everything about how we found you is weird, so people want to know what happened just as much as you do. If you don't want to talk about it, it's fine. We're good. Are you good?"

"I'm good."

"Okay then. We should probably go before someone catches us hanging around in the kitchen, so I'll show you around some more, and you can tell me where you want to go from there, okay?"

"Alright."

Zee sighed. "I should get this bread packed up for the Sun Prayer Ceremony. I'll see you guys later."

Both boys headed out of the kitchen and down the hall. At the first intersection, Kaleb led Daniel to the right and then down a long corridor. Soon, the hallway lost the wood panelling decor on the walls and returned to the mosaic sun-themed designs.

"What's with all the sun stuff? Sun designs on the walls, the Sun Prayer thing Zee was talking about earlier... Do you guys pray to the sun?"

Bitterness coated Kaleb's words. "We don't pray to the sun, we pray to the Sun God, Shamash. The whole temple is dedicated to him. People believe that it's important to keep Shamash happy because they think he controls the harvest and the weather and all kinds of things. A lot of them even say he's the most important god of them all because a bad harvest can mean a lot of people die."

"You don't seem convinced that things work that way."

"I think people use gods as an excuse to do stupid things. That's all. If there's going to be a drought, there's going to be a drought. No amount of prayer or sacrifices or temple slaves change anything like that."

"That makes sense." Daniel wanted to say more, but decided against it.

The hallway suddenly angled sharply to the left. The new corridor had openings along the right wall that exited to the terrace and offered fantastic views of the expansive farmland below.

"Welcome to the Gardens of Sippar," Kaleb said as they looked out briefly over the land. "We rotate the crops every year, and some priests insist on certain crops being planted in certain areas, so most people find it hard to tell from here what we're looking at. Not me though. Grasses are closest to where we're standing. Then beans and vegetables—they go on for a while— and way past that are the oats, wheat and barley. On the southern side of the Garden is an orchard of fruit trees like figs and apples."

Daniel gaped in awe at the scale of the operation before him.

"It's huge," Daniel said.

Kaleb chuckled. "Yeah, it kind of has to be. We supply most of the food for the nearby cities and many of the villages—especially when they have a bad harvest. Everybody farms around here except the Royal Family, soldiers, merchants and some upper-level government guys. You were probably a farmer too, back in Mari."

"Do you know a lot about Mari?"

"Not much. I know that it's used mainly as a trade stop for travelling merchants, but a lot of the people that live there are farmers because it's easy to sell food to a hungry caravan."

Daniel nodded, but the memories of his past remained submerged.

Were my parents' farmers from Mari? Are ashes all that's left of the village now?

Kaleb saw Daniel's expression. "I know we don't have any answers yet, but I'm sure we will. You looked like you rolled around in a fire pit. Whatever happened will be big news, and we'll hear about it soon."

"Yeah."

"Besides, we don't know if you're even *from* Mari yet. We found you by the river, so anything's possible."

Daniel surveyed the Garden. "How many people does it take to run this place—like, how many people live here?"

"There's probably 50 priests and three times as many temple slaves. Three of the priests here are *high priests*. They run things. There used to be more, but they're all old guys, so they get sick, or whatever, and a couple died a while back."

"Why don't they replace them?"

"They replaced one of them, but apparently it's an entire process, and they just haven't found the right guys for the job. If you ask me, they just don't want to promote another priest to their level. They all argue all the time. It'd just be a huge hassle for everyone."

Daniel considered this for a moment, but moved on.

"How do you fit 200 people in this temple?"

Kaleb laughed. "You'd be surprised. The Temple has two main levels that house about a hundred people, a piece. We used to keep the priests separate from the temple slaves, but we don't have as many priests as before, and we're always getting new temple slaves, so the temple's too packed to do that anymore."

"Then how did I get my room?"

Kaleb sighed. "You actually have *my* room. I share a room with someone else right now."

First, he has to bathe me and then he's got to give up his room to me for who knows how long.

"Hopefully, someone finds me sooner than later. Maybe Azra will let me go back to Mari and see if I can find my family."

"He might, but who knows? You woke up from the longest coma I've ever seen. He probably won't let you go right away."

Daniel snickered. "Yeah, you're right. Sorry about making your life suck so much, though."

"My dad left me here when I was little, and I've been a slave since then. Worse things could happen. Don't worry about it," Kaleb said, puffing out his chest a little.

Daniel frowned and looked out over the sprawling farmland. "Hey, can we go look around down there?"

Kaleb glanced at the sky. "Sure, but we can't be too long."

The boys exited the temple and descended the short staircase that connected the terrace to the garden below. From above, human hands had clearly laid the garden out, but at ground level, it felt like more of an untouched valley. Many of the grasses and grains grew tall and wild-looking. The plots that grew both beans and legumes looked as natural as a cluster of wild bushes, and the plots appeared to be more randomly dispersed than they did from above. When the boys arrived at the orchard, it was like a dim forest of trees filled with every colour and type of fruit.

"Some elders used to call this place *Eden* after the old stories. Some still do, but everyone knows it's not the real thing."

Daniel stared blankly.

Kaleb chuckled and shook his head. "So, Eden was a mystical garden where Gilgamesh—the first king—found the fruit of immortality. Azra says Eden was around when the world was mostly jungle, but then it got swallowed by the sea after the gods flooded the world."

As Kaleb finished speaking, Daniel looked up and saw two men in similar robes surveying the fields.

"That looks like Azra with one of the other high priests, Ghali." Kaleb gestured toward them.

Azra glanced in the boys' direction and ended his conversation with Ghali before heading toward them.

"We had better go meet him," Kaleb said.

The boys wove their way through the fields until they reached Azra.

"Daniel, it's good to see you getting some air. Kaleb has been useful to you, I hope," Azra said, peering sideways at Kaleb.

"Ah—yes," Daniel said awkwardly, as he and Kaleb exchanged glances. "He showed me around the temple, and gave me some food and water."

"Ah, so you've seen the kitchens then as well?" Azra said, although he now looked directly at Kaleb. "How were they?"

"Uhh—large?" Daniel said with confusion.

Azra raised an eyebrow at Daniel. After a pause, he aimed a sobering stare back at Kaleb. "Ah, yes. Large indeed. Kaleb, how was Zehariah's progress?"

"He's prepared," Kaleb said, maintaining eye contact.

"Good. Go help him carry the loaves."

Without a word, Kaleb headed back toward the temple.

Azra glanced up at the sky and walked past Daniel in the direction he had come. After about ten paces, he called back toward Daniel.

"It's time for our mid-day ceremony. Do you care to join us?"

Nodding, Daniel jogged toward him.

Priests and temple slaves slowly coalesced into a flowing mass spanning four or five men across. Their bodies collected naturally, like heavy rainfall forming tiny run-off streams that pooled into a flowing river. Daniel wasn't being carried away by this river of bodies so much as he was becoming one with the river itself, flowing along to a natural destination.

The path through the garden snaked around nearby trees and bushes, but it didn't take long to reach the south-eastern side of the orchard. It was no less beautiful than any other part of the temple grounds: earthy greens of moss and tiny saplings shooting upward between the dead leaves and fallen rotten branches and logs. There was mysterious energy about this place for no apparent reason. The birds sang no differently here; in fact, it may have even been quieter than the rest of the garden.

Observing the devotees more closely, Daniel noticed a few humming to themselves, but most were silent. The silence was heavy, but it didn't appear to be fearful or threatening; it was a reverent quiet.

An incomparable and indescribable sense of loss followed their departure from the tree line. The warm sunlight shone brighter and more intensely here, washing over their faces, and Daniel kept his eyes shut during those first few steps away from the protective shade of the grove. When he opened them again, it felt like he had entered a new world.

The procession had emerged onto a large grassy field. This place had a distinct look from the garden but was the same type of land—just wilder. Grass grew unhindered and unkempt here. The only clear evidence of consistent human presence was the dusty path underfoot.

Daniel thought he could smell water, but there was no body of water in sight.

The procession continued to flow westward into the field, and Daniel thought he could hear what he believed to be humming at first. It was actually chanting. The chanting flowed so naturally that it could've been a wave beating against a rock or a few songbirds in the morning, announcing the sun.

The river of bodies divided as the devotees seated themselves in a layered semi-circle around Azra, who sat with his back to the mass, facing a stone slab. His chanting was noticeably more disciplined, but did not overpower the voices of the others. Before long, Daniel found his own voice repeating the chant; the rhythm had swept him up before he realized it. The feeling of community—of belonging—was commanding, but also intoxicating and addictive.

Ghali appeared to be wandering around the crowd now, with a basket. At first, it appeared as if he'd meant to leave the group quietly, but then, as he reached the edge, he snaked back into the crowd. Daniel watched him for some time, trying to figure out what he was doing before realizing the other devotees were placing something in the basket. He weaved closer and closer to the front, arms reaching up to him as he passed, until finally, he stood beside the altar. With a slight bow, he knelt and set the basket down in front of Azra before taking his place to the side.

Azra seemed to say a prayer, bowing repeatedly toward the basket before facing the crowd and removing a small fluffy-looking trinket. The chanting had gained speed now, as if the intention was to fit every word into a single moment. Azra held the trinket over his head with both hands and whispered a few words before placing the trinket into a metal bowl in front of him. Then he held up a simple knife, whispering again. Carefully, Azra squeezed the blade of the knife into his palm, letting the blood drop onto the fluffy trinket he held below it. His face showed no sign of the pain, but there was no doubt in Daniel's mind that it was painful.

Holding his arms out, he looked up to the sky, said a few more words, and then threw something into the bowl, causing the trinket to burst into flames.

As the small fire blazed and burnt out, the chanting slowed and became quieter until it eventually stopped.

Daniel looked over the mass of people all around him and noticed two slaves emerging from the forest a long way off. When they got close enough, Daniel realized it was Kaleb and Zee. Each of them flanked the assembly from a different side, cutting in from the outer edges.

Leather straps layered their bodies with large bags and satchels overfilled with bread, and each boy cradled a basket brimming with what looked like cheese. As they passed through the crowd, devotees were removing the cheese and bread and passing it around until the boys reached the centre of the semi-circle and offered food to Azra. Azra accepted it with a nod, and then they sat on either side of him.

Immediately, everyone shifted and joined new groups in social conversation. Azra waved for Daniel to join them at the front and gestured for Daniel to sit across from him, closing their small semi-circle.

"So, what were your impressions of our ritual?" Azra asked.

Both Kaleb and Zee shot subtle glances between Azra and Daniel.

"I don't know. It was good, I guess. I've never seen anything like that before," Daniel said awkwardly.

"That you remember," Zee said.

Daniel shot him an irritated look.

Zee cracked a grin, causing Daniel to grunt, while Kaleb and Azra both smirked without looking at each other.

Daniel noticed the bandages on Azra's hand as he ate. "So, you guys do this every day?"

"Yep," Kaleb said.

"Same time every day," Zee said.

He didn't have a scar or even a cut on his hand earlier. How is it possible that he does this every day?

"So... you just heal really fast?" Daniel said, gesturing to Azra's hand.

"That's a story for another time," Azra said curtly.

Daniel made a face but let the explanation sit. "What was that fuzzy thing you burnt?"

Azra was chewing when Kaleb jumped at the question. "I don't remember what it's called—"

"An effigy," Azra said, as he choked down a mouthful of bread.

"—Ah right, an effigy. Basically, everyone puts a strand of hair in the basket and then Azra ties it into a doll shape—"

"—Into an effigy shape, because it's an effigy," Zee grinned.

"—Whatever. It's an effigy. I got it. So, it's a doll shaped effigy—"

"It's just an effigy-shaped effigy," Zee corrected, addressing Daniel.

"I swear I will punch you," Kaleb raised his fist.

"Sorry. Just tell us about your doll-shaped effigy," Zee said.

"It's not my—" Kaleb took a deep breath before continuing on. "Azra ties the hair into a doll shape," he said, emphasizing the last two words before he paused and shot a challenging stare at Zee.

Zee only smiled and gestured that he should continue.

"Then," Kaleb continued with slightly too much energy, "I forget what I was talking about."

Azra had just finished eating when he jumped in with thinly veiled amusement.

"Daniel asked what the *fuzzy thing* was. You explained it was an effigy made from the hair of every person at the ritual. I think you were going to explain why we burn it, but the situation got somewhat... confused."

"Only because Zee's an asshole," Kaleb muttered as he picked at the grass in front of him.

Azra's gaze slid over him, but he continued speaking as if he hadn't noticed. "The ritual allows us to give thanks to the sun and recognize our connection to it. Everything used to carry out the day—in any capacity—comes from the sun. Even the food we eat indirectly comes from the sun. The sun warms us and allows the plants to grow. Those plants provide us with food to feed ourselves or feed the livestock, who also provide food for us—like milk, meat, and cheese. That food gives us the energy to build and create great things, or even cultivate more food. In this way, the sun gives us everything we need to live, but how can we depend on the Sun so completely and give nothing in return?"

Daniel frowned at Azra for a second.

Azra smirked and continued on. "Words without actions are lies, empty promises created for selfish purposes. With no follow-through, even a well-intentioned promise will poison a relationship or even destroy it. Actions without words, no matter how great or complex those actions may be, are empty in their own way as well. Without openly crediting our behaviour to a specific purpose, its meaning becomes lost or misconstrued. By openly reaffirming our commitment in chant and giving something of ourselves as an effigy—to honour the sacrifices made for us—we combine words with actions to form a binding pact with Shamash. We believe these practices are the main reason we never experience drought or pestilence when many other places are wracked with either or both."

Kaleb rolled his eyes, prompting Azra to flash an irritated, sidelong stare at him. Zee cleared his throat nervously.

"Why do you give blood while everyone else only gives some hair?" Daniel asked.

"The hair is a gesture of contribution. A strand of hair is the least painfully obtained sacrifice that a person can offer, while blood is the most painfully obtained, but also the most sacred. Everyone is offering a little of themselves, while I guarantee the sincerity of their sacrifices with my blood."

"Then why are you the only priest that has to cut your hand every day?"

Azra cleared his throat before answering. "I do not *cut my hand*. I offer my blood upon the Altar of Shamash, and I am not burdened by performing the ritual each day. I have been entrusted with this task for many years and several reasons... but technically, I suppose any of the priests could offer a blood sacrifice if they chose."

"So, you're the leader here?"

Kaleb mumbled something that caused Zee to snort and suppress a smirk.

Azra narrowed his eyes at Kaleb before continuing. "No. All high priests like myself carry the same authority. This kind of council ensures all decisions are made fairly and wisely, with multiple perspectives in mind."

"It also ensures that there will never be too much power held by any one man except the king." Azra stiffened suddenly before scowling toward the familiar voice which belonged to a chubby man dressed similarly to Azra and Ghali. He had slipped in beside them so quietly that no one had noticed his appearance.

"I'm sorry to have startled you, Azra. I merely wanted to add a minor detail to your lecture."

"Yes, I suppose as a fellow high priest, your contributions are always welcome, Samir."

"Thank you, brother. I have a temple matter I would like to speak to you about. Care for a walk?"

Kaleb's eyes widened as he looked over at Zee. Zee only raised an eyebrow in reply.

"Of course," Azra said flatly as he stood and walked with Samir.

"Another serene mid-day offering to Shamash, brother. Something in your execution always leaves me feeling renewed."

"I have to wonder what made you think I'm interested in your emotional state. Perhaps you are confusing me for one of your lost boys?"

Samir closed his eyes for a moment and took a deep breath before continuing. "The reason I wanted to speak to you is to clear the air about some concerns I've had lately."

"Concerns regarding what?"

"Rumours are circulating that you have been carrying on... inappropriate relations with some of the boys."

"That's ridiculous. Boys create rumours, it's what they do. I'm surprised you're considering any truth in what you've heard."

"Well, ordinarily I wouldn't, but I'm hearing the same names and circumstances again and again. I would prefer to dismiss these rumours entirely, but it's not the first time that you have been accused of such activities."

"Have you spoken with any of the boys named in these rumours?"

"No. No, of course not. They are young boys and it would only embarrass them. I thought it would be more prudent to have this conversation with you directly."

"So, are you asking me or accusing me of this behaviour?"

"Azra, I'm asking you—if nothing else than to set my mind at ease."

"No, Samir, I am not having *inappropriate relations* with young boys."

Samir searched Azra's face as he spoke but gave no sign if he believed him. "Alright, thank you for indulging me. I am sorry to have bothered you."

"Don't be. A concern of yours is a concern of mine."

Chapter 2

Established Legacy

Madius awoke into total darkness. He tried to move, but found himself tied to a wooden chair, sitting upright. "Damn it." he groaned, as he shifted to work his bindings. Every part of his body was sore, and he was pretty sure he had a few broken ribs.

The smell of roasting meat and spices permeated the dark, carrying with it the sounds of men laughing and singing. From amidst the faraway noise of their celebration, grew the sound of footsteps approaching Madius from directly ahead. Suddenly, a door burst open, revealing three torches that flooded the room with light, blinding him momentarily. As the darkness cleared, Madius found himself surrounded by three soldiers.

"Leave us," the youngest man barked to the others. The other two men obediently backed out of the room and closed the door.

Madius searched the young man's face for a moment but could not place him. He probably wasn't any older than nineteen years old. The young man wore leather lamellar armour and carried both a knife and a sword at his waist. His face folded into a snarl that twitched at the corners of his mouth while he stood staring at Madius.

Madius said nothing. Instead, he hung his head and cast sidelong glances around the empty wooden hut surrounding him.

"Let me tell you a story—" the young man began after an extended silence.

Madius let out a low chuckle and sat up to meet the other man's gaze. "I'm a little tied up at the moment, boy."

A million lights exploded over Madius' eyesight as his face connected with a brutal backhand. "Shut your whore mouth. I'm a warrior, you're a fucking lap dog. You do not speak unless I allow it. Nod if you understand," the other man demanded.

Madius spat blood and slowly brought his gaze up to meet the other man's hateful stare.

"Nod if you understand!" he snarled again.

Madius paused for a moment and then yielded a nod.

"Let me explain something to you. Your reign has brought oppression, shame, and death to a proud nation. Before you came with your masters to plague our lands with your Assyrian filth, we were peaceful. Our tribes unified under common law, and our only goal was prosperity, but then the mighty Madius brought an army to Media to end all of that—for just a little more land," he snarled.

"You don't understand the first thing about the politics of war," Madius said in disgust.

The young man punched Madius hard across the face. "I warned you to shut up. I won't do it again." He took a long breath before continuing, "The day you rode into the capital, your men slaughtered everyone—not just warriors, but whole families. They left fathers weeping over their wives and children, and children over their parents. Did you know King Phraortes was out walking with his son when your men cut him down? The boy was only fifteen, and you brought the chaos of war to his doorstep. You killed his family in front of him and razed his entire world to the ground."

"Phraortes was a bold man. He resisted the Empire for many years, and yet, in the end, it made him a man to be feared by kings, and men that kings fear never live long," Madius offered, searching the young man's face for any sign of whether he has earned the man's ear or another strike to the face. The young man made no move, so Madius continued, "Phraortes was a great leader, and a great warrior—and his influence was growing. The attack against Ecbatana wasn't personal, it was political. If your country had become more powerful back then, you could've been standing over me today under totally different circumstances— or maybe not. Who knows? What I know is that we all have our orders, and an ally ordered me to neutralize a threat. In war, you have an objective, and your mission is to complete that objective. You can't concern yourself with every young boy weeping over his father in the street."

"I was that boy!" The man grabbed Madius by the hair and yelled within a handsbreadth of his face. His eyes burned hungrily for vengeance.

"You are still that boy, Cyaxares," Madius said flatly, "and you are naïve if you believe anything you do today is going to rewrite the past or change the future. Even if you kill me, Assyria will send another man to take my place—maybe even my successor in Skuza, but either way—Media will remain a part of the Empire, and none of it will ever bring back your father."

"You're right," Cyaxares said, as he set the torch into a sconce near the door and returned to Madius, "none of it will bring back my father, but it will help me take back my country."

Then, in one swift motion, he drew his sword above his head and drove the tip of the blade down between Madius' neck and shoulder, into his heart. Madius writhed momentarily and then went limp upon Cyaxares' sword.

"And your death will be the first step," he whispered into Madius' lifeless ear.

CHAPTER 3

FRERE JACQUES

"You know I would do anything for family...." A voice whispers.

Daniel opens his eyes and looks around the camp. Everyone is sleeping. He recognizes his brothers and sisters everywhere, huddled together in clusters for warmth.

I need to get some blankets made.

As he looks out, Daniel sees one of his sisters shivering at the edge of a nearby cluster and takes off his tunic, draping it over her. Slowly the shivering stops, and Daniel smiles down at her. The chill forces him to rub his own arms for warmth.

I guess I should make a fire.

As he moves to gather firewood, he notices a shadow shift at the edge of the camp and freezes. Daniel stands silently, looking around and listening for a moment. Soft footsteps circle the edge of the camp, and he catches several glimpses of movement in the darkness.

Is it happening already? Please God, we just got here.

Suddenly, everything is dead quiet, aside from the snores and breathing of his people. Daniel allows himself a sigh of relief, but it's immediately interrupted by screams and gurgled cries. Wide-eyed, Daniel spins around, taking in the chaos before him. Men and women with sharp stone spears and flint knives are stabbing his people in their sleep. The camp wakes and struggles against the attackers, but many of its people have already died.

Daniel runs at one attacker, tackling him just before he lands a killing blow on his brother. Then, Daniel knocks the knife out of the man's hand and holds him up angrily by the throat.

"Why would you do this? These people were innocent. We've never harmed you," Daniel shouts.

"Why? You are Demons! They foretold you would bring about the end of *my* people." The man chokes the words out in fear and disgust.

Daniel boils with rage. "Can't you see? Your people have brought about their own end! We had no intention of harming you."

As Daniel finishes his sentence, every man and woman who attacked the camp immediately becomes engulfed in blue flames. Daniel, unharmed by the flames, drops the man to the ground as he writhes and smoulders.

Through the fire, smoke and screams, another man appears, staring right at Daniel.

"You know I would do anything for family," Daniel says. "Sacrifices had to be made."

The man only stares at Daniel, statue-still, as shadows dance across his face and his eyes glow red despite the light of the dying flames.

Daniel shot out of bed, searching for the red glowing eyes in the relative darkness of the early morning.

What was that? It felt like a memory.

Daniel's dreams had become notably more frequent and intense lately. The strangest part was that they usually included the same group of people travelling through the wilderness. Sometimes they even named places he had read about, but it was all wrong. Many of the places that were lush forests and grasslands in these dreams appeared as desert regions on a map. When he spoke to Azra about the dreams, the old man dismissed them as nothing.

Maybe I'm overthinking it.

Daniel got up and put on a clean tunic.

Several weeks had passed since Azra had found Daniel on the banks of the Euphrates. News had eventually come from the north that the Cimmerians had attacked the village of Mari looking for food, and they burned it to the ground. There were rumours that the Cimmerians themselves were wiped out in the attack by a defending army. Others said that *Adad*, the God of Destruction, had awoken from his slumber and begun wandering the desert, incinerating towns like Mari in his wake.

Daniel had asked Azra about the rumours, but his reply was simple:

> *There is always a truth behind rumours, but that does not make them accurate. Rumours entertain. The Cimmerians had just lost a war against the Lydians—a rivalling neighbour—and it's possible they came to Mari with a weakened army, but they are brilliant tacticians, and it is extremely unlikely that every able Cimmerian just happened to be involved in a raid that turned into a massacre for both sides.*

As for gods roaming the desert, I'm sure you're old enough to know the difference between the truth and a child's bedtime stories.

Azra's words resonated with Daniel and helped him to keep it all in perspective, but despite all the rumours about foreign raids and war, there was no news about his parents. No one came looking for Daniel, and the only thing that had made it easier was the growing bonds he shared with Azra, Kaleb, and Zee.

When he needed advice or reassurance, he spoke to Azra. Azra had become a kind of father figure to Daniel, while Kaleb and Zee became like brothers.

Azra knocked on Daniel's door and poked his head inside without waiting for a response.

"Daniel, do you mind heading to the library and searching for a recipe for Yew berry jam? Apparently, it was Samir's favourite childhood treat. He has made himself useful as of late, and I want to reward his efforts."

"No problem. I'll head to the library right away," Daniel replied.

Azra nodded and closed the door behind him.

Daniel smiled. *I guess I'm going to the library.*

Most of the slaves never learn to read before entering the temple, and then there's no need for them to learn after. But Daniel could. Azra took advantage of this constantly by sending Daniel on errands to the library.

Within a few weeks, Daniel had become very efficient at finding information and even began researching his own topics of interest. Soon he had learned about everything from farming to politics, but he had become obsessed with stories from the past.

Most of the oldest written records disappeared about 500 years ago, at a time Azra referred to as "The

Sundering" when the world seemed to go through some sort of destruction and rebirth. But people kept sharing their stories through word of mouth and eventually recorded those stories again, trying to hold on to whatever ancient knowledge still existed. Some of the oldest tales detailed the wrath of ancient gods or unimaginable creatures, but his favourite ones were about the Djinn.

The Djinn were an ancient race of semi-divine creatures created by the Canaanite god. Some accounts said they were evil creatures that only exist to tempt and corrupt humanity. Other stories claimed a god created the Djinn as guardians. Something compulsively drew Daniel to them, and regardless of their origins, he had to know everything about them.

Luckily, the Library of Sippar held an immense collection on nearly every conceivable topic—including Djinn.

The library encompassed one large room, almost a quarter the size of the entire temple, and at least twice the size of the kitchen. Reinforced shelves lined the walls and strained under the weight of countless clay tablets and rolled paper scrolls. Throughout the room stood tall wooden podiums with square shelves on all four sides, which stored even more records. The tops of these were flat, with tablets stacked on top. In the centre of the room sat a square wooden table covered in maps. Daniel sat in a chair at its side reading a scroll being held open by two tablets he used as paperweights.

Suddenly, the door creaked open, breaking the silence and revealing Kaleb as he entered.

"Hey. Apparently, the Djinn had their own village far west of here called Beit Jinn—*the house of Djinn.*"

"Wow, that's really uninteresting, but it must've been nice, just sitting around, reading about useless facts instead of doing any *actual* work."

Daniel grinned. "Shut up, slave. Shouldn't you be planting something?"

"I figured I'd take a break from hard labour, sort of like you always do, and maybe see what you're up to."

"Whatever. Obviously, that's your favourite joke today. Save it for other people."

"Yeah, I'm actually here because Azra was looking for you. Apparently, you were supposed to look up some kind of berry mixture for him."

"You're a berry mixture."

"I'll berry mixture your face."

"That doesn't even make sense."

"Doesn't it?"

Daniel gave him a flat look that was threatening to crack. "I'll punch you."

"Don't be mad, berry-gobbler," Kaleb said as Zee walked into the library.

"Haha, Daniel's a berry-gobbler," Zee snickered.

"You guys are both dicks."

Zee and Kaleb laughed.

"I actually came by to let you know Azra's looking for you, Daniel."

"Yeah, that's what Kaleb was saying. He must really want this berry mixture recipe."

"I'll give you a berry mixture," Zee said.

"You're lame. Kaleb already made that joke." Daniel sighed as he got up from his chair. "I guess I'll go give Azra this recipe. I'll see you guys later."

As Daniel walked down the hall, he looked at the instructions again:

Remove pits from berries,
crush well,
and then boil pulp for several minutes until reduced

People are ridiculous. We discover a tree that could kill us and still find a way to eat it without getting poisoned.

When Daniel finally reached Azra's study, he was tending the small herb garden he kept potted by the window. Daniel came into the room and sat down on a chair near where Azra was working.

"Why do you keep potted plants indoors when you have a huge garden just outside?" Daniel asked, breaking the silence.

"Several reasons. These are healing and restorative herbs, so I like to have them close at hand. I also don't trust the untrained rabble outside to raise certain species without killing them. It's also very calming to grow plants this way... like I said, there are several reasons."

The pair sat quietly for a few minutes, with only the sound of Azra's pruning shears to break the silence.

Daniel cleared his throat awkwardly and spoke. "Did you still want that berry recipe?"

"The yew berry jam—yes," Azra answered, but made no move to stop pruning or even face Daniel.

Another minute passed before Daniel spoke again. "Did you want me to give it to you... or what should I do with it?"

"If you consider how long you had me wait before bringing me this recipe, I would think you should be able to wait a short time for me to finish what I am doing."

"I'm sorry, I had trouble finding it at first...."

"Nonsense. You had found the recipe ages ago," he scolded with some amusement. "You know, I was a boy once—always lost in stories or obscure facts that seemed to only interest me. I understand the... draw those stories have, but you must understand that time is precious. Everything precious has a cost."

"So, the cost of your time is my time," Daniel said flatly.

Azra stopped to face him with a level stare. "And it is a far better trade than the cost of insolence. I give you a lot of allowances, but do not mistake me for one of your slave friends," he said as he returned to his pruning.

"Why are you always a jerk to everyone?"

Azra put his shears down and turned to face Daniel. "Excuse me?"

"Well... I mean, you do nice things for people sometimes, but you always talk to people like you hate them. Why do you do that?"

The honesty took Azra aback, but he replied calmly. "I don't hate anyone. I hate incompetence, and since most people behave with incompetence, I don't have the patience to concern myself with how my tone affects them."

"But isn't it harder to get people to trust you and do things for you when you talk to them like they're stupid?"

"Have you seen anyone refuse to do anything I've asked in the entire time you've been at the temple?"

Daniel thought for a moment and then shook his head.

"Do you know why?"

Daniel shook his head again.

"Fear."

Daniel frowned, but said nothing.

"There are many ways to rule over others," Azra began as he put the shears away and leaned against a nearby chair, "but two of the most common are by either fear or diplomacy. Some leaders prefer to use diplomacy; they balance *give* and *take* between themselves and their subordinates, slowly building rapport, hoping one day when they need to count on the support and loyalty of those subordinates, they will come through for them rather than rebel or defect."

"That seems like a pretty fair way to convince people to follow you."

"That seems like a fair way to *urge* people to follow you, but life is not fair, and people are even less so. I am not a gambling man, and I do not take chances with things of great importance."

"So, you rule with fear."

"I demand respect and strive for perfection. I do not let failures pass unnoticed or unpunished so that people work harder to be successful. I do not let others speak for me in a conversation, and I certainly do not go into a conversation without knowing how to dismantle the person before me. A man to be feared is a man to be respected, and without that respect, you can never guarantee another man's loyalty."

"That seems really heavy-handed," Daniel muttered.

"You may be unconvinced right now, but if one day you are in a position of leadership, you tell me then if you would rather be a gambling man or a tyrant. Even if they don't realize it in the moment, the ruler people want, the one that will actually lead them effectively, is the tyrant."

"What do you mean?"

"Leading people is not about titles and it's certainly not about benevolence... or *popularity*. It's about influence, and influence comes from leveraging a man's most basic fears."

Daniel could only stare in disbelief.

"You've wasted enough of my time today. Go help Zehariah prepare for the noon meal," Azra said as he turned away from Daniel.

"Wait," Azra called over his shoulder before Daniel reached the door, "leave the recipe on the desk so I can look it over."

Daniel tossed the recipe on the desk beside him and exited the room.

The unexpected philosophy lesson had caught Daniel off guard.

That was weird. Azra never explains himself—especially to me.

Daniel closed the door behind him and then froze.

The world had taken on the silvery grey scale of twilight and a cool silence that had spread over everything. Daniel felt a sudden urge to get outside and hurried through the halls toward the nearest exit.

As Daniel burst through the door, he looked up at the sky and then out across the land; he was standing in an enormous wheat field.

This field isn't a part of the temple grounds.

The clouds and the tall, swaying stalks looked completely ordinary, except for everything being dimly lit and drained of colour. When he turned around, he found more tall grass swaying where the door should be.

Where am I?

Daniel spotted a dark figure shambling silently in the distance and headed toward it. Charred pieces flaked away from the figure with every stiff footfall, and the smell of smoke and burnt hair grew stronger the closer Daniel got.

"Hey, are you alright?"

The figure stopped mid-shamble and slowly turned to face Daniel.

Charred flesh hung loosely over exposed bone on every part of its body. Its milky eyes and slacked jaw hung wide in a permanent scream.

Daniel stood frozen in place, unable to process the image before him, until the blackness slowly started receding up the creature's body, replacing flaked ash with smooth, tan skin. The eyes became unclouded, revealing a familiar emerald green. The jaw muscles rewove themselves and the mouth contracted into a feminine, reassuring smile. As clothes and hair seemed to materialize around the figure, Daniel gasped. It was his mother.

"Mom...." he whispered.

Daniel's mother wore a simple blue dress. She kept her hands folded in front of her as she smiled meekly at Daniel, but made no move to close the distance between them. A little girl in a small green dress darted in from the right and hid behind Daniel's mother. The girl peeked sideways from behind his mother's blue dress, causing the girl's dark brown hair to cascade away from her and reveal a small white pendant hanging around her neck. Daniel's eyes became wide with realization—it was his sister, Elisa.

Before Daniel could call out to her, the little girl dashed back into the field, out of sight. He scanned the area, but there was no sign of her from where he was standing.

"My Daniel," Daniel's mother said, causing him to refocus his attention on her. "It's good to see you. I've missed you, but you can't be here. You should forget about us."

"How could I forget about you?" Daniel replied before a childlike giggle from behind distracted him.

He turned just in time to catch a streak of green, dash into the field out of sight.

"You have once already," said a male voice.

Daniel turned to face the speaker, who now stood where his mother had been only seconds before. He was unusually tall, with a man's head and a tiger's body from the neck down. He had fair skin with dark brown hair, and his eyes were an intense red, but with oval irises like a cat's eyes. He kept his arms folded and casually leaned on a fence post that had not previously been there.

"... I wouldn't exactly say it's a stretch that you could do it again."

Daniel eyed the creature suspiciously as it inspected its nails and licked its paw.

"Who... are you?"

The creature stopped preening and looked up at Daniel. "You can call me Ankl. Well, I guess it might be hard to tell in this form. It looks like you see me as some sort of tiger creature with a human head. You constructed this form, you should know."

Daniel stared in confusion.

Ankl rolled his eyes, landing a level stare on Daniel. "You see me this way because your brain tried to process the form of something it had never seen before, then transposed some familiar images that carried an approximate similarity with what it believed you saw and you have... a tiger-man." Ankl finished with a sweeping flourish.

Daniel shook his head in slight frustration. "No, I mean who... what *are* you?"

Ankl smirked in amusement. "The human understanding of the world is fairly restrictive. In this time period, in this spiritual form, your people would probably call me a Djinn. You can call me Ankl."

"You're a Djinn?" Daniel said in awe.

"*Djinn* is probably the closest approximation to what I am that you would understand, yes," Ankl said flatly. "Technically, I'm just a mass of spiritual energy."

"What does that mean?" Daniel asked.

Ankl sighed and shook his head regretfully. "This is going to be painful, so keep up."

Daniel sighed.

"All energy in the universe behaves the way water does on Earth; it can be generated, directed and recycled, and can even exist in different physical forms—the way water can become solid ice or a misty fog. And, just like water, energy likes to pool, the way rainwater collects into puddles."

"Okay...." Daniel said slowly.

"All living things generate energy through the chemistry of their natural physical processes, and since every living thing has a slightly different *personality* to their behaviour, the energy generated by each life form has its own individual *fingerprint* specific to the life they have lived. Humans call this fingerprint a *soul*. Are you still with me?"

Daniel paused before replying. "I think so."

"*Soul* energy does not differ from any other form of energy. When the body dies, the energy left over becomes a part of a larger pool of *soul* energy, dispersing the *fingerprint* of your personality across the entire pool. Then, when a new life is born, it draws from that pool of souls. The interesting thing is, that *fingerprint* I mentioned earlier never really gets destroyed, it just becomes diluted. So every once in a while, a concentrated remnant of a certain fingerprint re-emerges during birth which influences the behaviours of the new life *so deeply* that it creates a feedback loop, building upon the remnant fingerprint, instead of creating a new one. Humans call this effect *reincarnation*, and whenever a remnant of my Djinn brethren re-emerges, I am drawn to it."

"So, I drew you to me... because I'm a reincarnated Djinn?"

"More or less."

"And you're also a Djinn?"

"Depending on your definition, yes."

"And why are you here?"

"I'm just an observer."

"Why does an observer need to introduce themselves?"

"Well, you were pretty boring until recently. I thought that after all these years you were finally going to get to the interesting part, but then you lost your memories and we're back to boring again."

"So how does that—"

"I'm going to make you an offer. Leave the temple and I will give you your memories back."

"Just leave the temple."

"That's right."

"What happens when I leave the temple?"

Daniel's last words echoed in his mind until he opened his eyes and found himself lying in bed with Zee and Kaleb standing over him, watching intently.

"I think he's waking up," Kaleb said in surprise.

"Hey, welcome back," Zee said as Daniel opened his eyes.

Daniel sat up and held his head in his hands. "What happened?"

"Azra said you opened his door and then just sort of fell through it and passed out right there," Zee replied.

"That's really weird," Daniel said.

"That's what I said," Kaleb said.

"Hey, what do you remember last?" Zee asked.

Daniel remembered running through the halls, the silver plain, his mother and Elisa.... and meeting Ankl. Daniel shook his head. "Not much, just talking with Azra and then going out the door, but I guess that part was a dream because you said I never made it."

Zee made a falling gesture with his hand that ended in a clap. "Down like a pile of bricks."

Kaleb and Zee chuckled while Daniel grimaced and shook his head.

There was a long pause before Zee broke the silence. "Well, if you're okay, I'd better go. Tomorrow I've gotta carry this place on my back, you know, so you have more time to read and avoid chores."

"Dick," Daniel replied.

"See ya slackers." He said as he left the room.

"I had better go, too. You're good though?" Kaleb asked.

"I think so," Daniel said, as he frowned and looked up at Kaleb. "I think I saw my mom, and my sister—I don't remember many details, though. It was weird."

"That sounds pretty weird, but it was just a dream, right? Dreams are weird," Kaleb said.

"I guess," Daniel said quietly. "Kaleb, you've been here a while, right?"

"Yeah, years. Why?"

"I've been thinking about my family a lot lately. I've been here a long time now, and no one's come looking for me. None of the rumours even make it sound like there are any other survivors from Mari—assuming I'm even from there."

"What's your point?"

"You've been here a long time... to me it doesn't seem terrible, you know, to stay here. Do you think I should give up looking for them?"

"I don't know if you should give up on them or not. I think you can't live your whole life in the past. Things that happened, happened. You just have to accept where you are right now."

Daniel took a minute to consider the advice. "Ah—yeah, you're right. Thanks."

"No problem. I'm going. See you tomorrow."

"Yeah," Daniel said, and laid down as Kaleb left the room.

It was evening now, and the relative stillness pressed Kaleb deep into thought. As he made his way through the temple halls, he thought about Daniel's obsession with finding his family.

Why would he bother? Everyone eventually lets you down. He's naïve. He could look over the entire world and finally find them, and they might just drop him back off at a place like this—just like my dad. Even your parents will abandon you if it suits them. All people are selfish. They're just selfish, selfish assholes.

The thought of his dad and the good memories—times when he had felt a strong bond with him—collided with the more recent memories of his father trying to justify giving Kaleb up to the temple. His father had referred to it as *an honour* to the family.

What a load of crap. He abandoned me.

Tears of frustration welled up, but he pushed the weakness away.

I'm not going to cry about it. A man never cries. And I'm better than this place. I'm more than just some slave, and I'll show you someday, dad. I'll show you how I've grown, the man I've become, and you'll regret ever leaving me to the wolves. I'm stronger, and I'm smarter than most of the other guys. Yeah, I've made some mistakes. Every guy has mistakes and things he regrets—especially things he can't control. It doesn't make you any less of a man. You grin and bear it until you can fight back. Because that's what a man does. No matter what, I'm still a man.

He stopped in front of the door to Azra's room.

He took a deep breath and opened the door to find Azra lying naked on his bed, looking annoyed.

"Good, you're finally here," Azra said. "You know I hate tardiness. Close the door and come to bed."

Kaleb clinched his jaw as he entered the room.

I'm still a man, he thought again angrily, and then closed the door behind him.

CHAPTER 4

THE JESTER KING

"My Lord, Skuza would like to thank you—"

"Oh, just stop. Skuza is barely worthy of being considered an independent ally of Assyria," King Ashur sassed from his golden throne. His gold and red embroidered cloak draped heavily across his shoulders, largely obscuring the fine red silk tunic he wore beneath.

The man before him stood in the centre of an immense hall, dressed in a green long-sleeved shirt and trousers covered by an ornate golden breastplate and greaves. A tall, conical, green and gold-trimmed hat sat upon his head.

"You, Bhodan, are a mere shade of the man Madius was, and he was destroyed by a child. Cyaxares has made a fool of your country, and you come to me... with thanks? I find that both presumptuous and pre-emptive. You are not coming to us from a position of strength. Therefore, this is not a negotiation. This is a petition—a plea for your survival."

"Yes, my Lord," Bhodan said, eyeing the two large guards on either side of the king.

"As I am both benevolent and generous, I will grant your plea and allow Skuza to remain a vassal state of the Empire but with the following condition: from now on, the Empire will oversee all Askuzai affairs of state to avoid further incompetence from your military and further unnecessary losses to your people. I will send a Steward with a military battalion to accompany you back home—*where they will* remain—to ensure that Skuza is protected appropriately."

The man stared up at Ashur with an intense fire in his eyes. "But, Sire, Askuzai archers are the greatest archers in the world. How can you simply discard—"

"Askuzai archers? There are no Askuzai archers, there are only Assyrian archers—*my* archers—and I shall use my archers, however I choose."

One of the guards approached the king and whispered in his ear. King Ashur nodded in affirmation, prompting the guard to signal an order to the back of the room and step back again. "Now, it appears that the Empire has lost an allied force and gained a dependant, so there will have to be some recompense to ensure Assyria can afford to extend its continued protection to Skuza. I am going to increase your taxes significantly. I am sure you are capable enough of allocating your own resources to ensure the payments are prompt and consistent, Chieftain? Unless you would be more comfortable abdicating your position to our military leadership?"

"No, my Lord, I am capable," Bhodan responded in a low growl.

A loud crack punctuated the end of Bhodan's sentence as the enormous doors at the end of the hall opened to allow entry to a short man with a gold-tasselled, multicoloured robe and a black and gold tasselled hat. The bells tied to his clothing jingled loudly enough to draw the attention of any casual observer. Behind him, shadowed a large armed guard in black lamellar armour that dwarfed all other men in proximity.

"Excellent. Then I'll allow you to take your leave, Askuzai. I imagine it will take a considerable effort to implement these changes in a timely manner," Ashur replied, waving his hand dismissively.

Bhodan bowed before Ashur and then pivoted and marched away, glaring at the loudly jingling hat and robe of the colourful newcomer as he passed. The large doors closed promptly behind him and silence washed over the hall as the new petitioner waited for the king to speak.

"Kandalanu, how is my King of Babylon?" Ashur said amusedly, breaking the silence.

"My Lord, I am as much a king as any fool—I merely deliver your will to the people of Babylon," he said with a smile and an exaggerated bow.

Ashur giggled and shook his head. "Such dramatic nonsense. You are the King of Babylon. It has been so for nearly 20 years. You are no longer a simple jester. You belong to the people of Babylon."

"My Lord, Babylon is just another of the many diverse provinces in your vast empire, and besides, I've been a fool longer than I have been a king."

"Such humility Kandalanu, if only truer fools would follow your lead."

"Allow me, My Lord, to lead them by example as their Jester King."

"That's rich, my friend," Ashur giggled. "I truly appreciate your timing. With so many disappointments lately, I had nearly forgotten how to laugh. Have young

Ashur and Sin seen you enter the palace yet? I'm certain they have missed you since your last visit."

"I'm sure they have My Lord, I will be sure to see them as soon as I settle my entourage. It seems I've brought almost the entire population of Babylon with me."

Ashur laughed. "Ah yes, my poor, nomadic king. What life have I thrust upon you? Take whatever time you need to get settled. The boys will have to understand. How long will you be staying in the city?"

"I had planned to stay for a few months, but I can always extend my stay, Your Majesty."

"Excellent, it will be good to have you close, my old friend. I have missed you."

"I am honoured, My Lord," Kandalanu said with a sweeping bow.

"Arrange your people then and join me for dinner tonight. There will be a feast in your honour." Ashur said as he stood to leave the throne room.

"You are very gracious, My Lord," Kandalanu said, holding another bow until the king had left the room. He then turned and left the hall himself. As he approached the door, he gave a hand signal to the looming armoured guard at the back of the room, prompting him to follow.

As they walked out of the hall, the guard leaned down toward his ear, "Our messenger has returned from Media. The king is willing to discuss the arrangement further."

"Excellent. And Uma?" Kandalanu whispered.

"She would like to meet with you tomorrow, if possible."

"Tell her I would be happy to. It's been ages since I've seen Ariel."

"Should we prepare for you to attend the banquet tonight?"

"Of course. We are the guests of honour. Ashur will expect us," Kandalanu said with a smirk.

"Then it seems a king and his fool will be reunited tonight, my Lord."

Kandalanu chuckled and patted the guard on the back as they walked. "Nabo, my friend, you may have missed your calling."

CHAPTER 5

THE THREE-FOLD LAW

Gloom had rolled in with the morning across the Temple grounds, like a thick fog choking the daylight out. Some boys had found a body lying face-down in the garden. They had turned it over, discovering blue lips, bloodshot eyes and a familiar face twisted in distress.

It had been Samir.

Samir had always been a favourite among the boys, lying somewhere between a brother and a father for most. His corpse had left a few of the boys shaken, but his death could be felt everywhere. Even Zee and Kaleb had difficulty collecting their thoughts today.

Daniel felt impartial about Samir's death. He hadn't really lived at the Temple long compared to most of the other boys, and his interactions with Samir were relatively short and infrequent, since researching and running errands for Azra dominated most of his time. He felt like the only one untouched by the weight of the loss until he realized Azra didn't appear affected by it, either.

Azra was performing the autopsy on Samir's body to determine the cause of death, and he had asked Daniel to assist him. As they stared down at the naked corpse lying on the table, Daniel felt

the need to break the silence.

"Azra, you've lived at the Temple your whole life, right?" Daniel asked him, as he handed Azra a small knife.

"Nearly, yes," Azra replied curtly.

"Do many people die at the Temple?" Daniel asked, staring intensely as Azra incised the chest.

"People are fragile and our time is short, so yes, all people have the tendency to die."

"But have many people died since you were at the Temple?"

Azra stopped and turned to face the boy. "Why do you ask? What's with all of these questions?" Daniel fixated on Azra's knife, tracing the blood that oozed down over his hands and dripped onto the table as he spoke.

"Uh... I just wondered why you aren't upset about Samir's death like everyone else."

Azra shook his head and returned to his work before answering. "Everyone grieves differently."

Daniel felt the answer was incomplete, but let it sit anyway. "How do you think he died?"

"I'll know once I get under the ribcage."

Azra cut organs out of the body, naming them aloud and handing them to Daniel, explaining which bowls he wanted them set into on the adjacent table.

"And finally, we come to the heart," Azra said, holding the dripping, venous mass before him. "Hmm," he said, as he gave the organ a small squeeze. "Another bowl please Daniel—a large one."

Daniel passed a large ceramic bowl to Azra and watched him place the heart into the bowl and make a cross-section.

"What is it?" Daniel asked.

"It felt tight."

"What does that mean?"

Azra inspected the dissected organ, turning it over and over under the candlelight. "Ah! Here, see this?" He gestured with the knife toward the organ.

Daniel moved in closer to see what Azra was trying to say.

"What am I supposed to see?" Daniel asked.

"The veins in the heart, they're nearly closed up with this thick fluid."

"Isn't that blood?"

"No, my boy. There's blood mixed in it, yes, but it's more like a clotting fluid."

"So, what does that mean?"

"It means Samir literally felt his heart stop beating at some point."

"Oh," Daniel said quietly as he looked between Samir's face and the displaced organ.

Azra searched Daniel's face for a moment before breaking the boy's focus. "Well, a man's heart doesn't simply stop. By all other accounts, Samir appears to be healthy."

Daniel couldn't imagine how Azra could determine a dead man's health while he lay dissected on a table but didn't ask.

"There must be some kind of cause," Azra stated, as he paused and scanned Daniel again. "Let's look at what he ate today. Pass me the stomach."

Daniel passed Azra the bowl he remembered as the stomach. Azra set the bowl on the table and carefully sliced a line into the sack before taking a second knife to open the organ and probe the insides without touching the contents with his hands. The stomach was full of undigested food and brown mucus.

"Why is there so much?" Daniel asked.

"He probably ate just before he died. It looks like it was quite the breakfast."

"Why is everything brown?" Daniel asked as Azra continued to probe the contents.

"Ah, right here," Azra exclaimed as he pried a couple of seeds out on the end of the knife.

Daniel tried not to react to the horrible-smelling brown seeds in front of him. "What are they?"

"Yew berry seeds."

"Why would Samir eat poison berries?" Daniel asked as Azra set the seeds aside.

"He probably didn't intentionally. We'll have to investigate further to determine if it was truly an accident," Azra said.

Why wouldn't it be?

Daniel looked up at Azra's face, but Azra continued before he could voice the thought.

"I'll take a walk in the garden to see if yew plants were growing naturally on the grounds. I need you to check the kitchen and see if we were storing yew berries there for any reason."

"We were," Daniel cut in, "don't you remember that yew berry jam recipe you wanted me to research? I gave you the list."

"Ah... yes, well—" Azra stuttered.

"Actually—" Daniel said as a shock of awareness suddenly set in, "the recipe I found was specific about pitting the berries before making the jam, and you said you found yew berry seeds in Samir's stomach... but I don't think Zee would purposely do anything to Samir."

"Well, intentionally or not, the fact of the matter is that a high priest has died, but I suppose we shouldn't jump to conclusions just yet. We need facts. I need you to find Zehariah and ask him about the jam."

"Ok...." Daniel agreed hesitantly.

"What are you waiting for?" Azra asked impatiently.

"Well... can I wash off first?" Daniel asked, looking down at his blood-spattered clothes and hands.

"Ah. Yes, that's fine, but then straight to the kitchen. There's no time to waste."

After Daniel had washed and changed, he headed down to the kitchen to look for Zee.

How am I supposed to do this? Zee is my friend, and he liked Samir—everyone did. This must be an accident. Once I prove it was an accident, everyone will understand.

When Daniel got to the kitchen, he only found Kaleb making himself a snack. Daniel startled Kaleb at first and he attempted to hide what he was doing, but then bounced back to stuffing some sliced cheese and vegetables into bread.

"Hey," Daniel said, trying to acknowledge his friend casually.

"Hey," Kaleb replied flatly.

"... what's going on?"

"I was hungry. It sucks about Samir, you know? I just figured I'd eat something and forget about it for a bit."

"I get it. I was actually looking for Zee. Have you seen him?"

"I saw him earlier, but he wanted to be alone for a bit."

"... why would he want to be alone? I didn't know he was that close to Samir," Daniel said.

"Yeah, I don't know. I guess he just wanted to do his own thing for a bit," Kaleb said without looking up.

"Alright, no problem. If you see him, let him know I'm looking for him."

"Sure," Kaleb replied.

Daniel wanted to ask his friend if he was ok but thought better of it. Clearly, Samir's death was bothering him, and no one enjoys being cornered into a conversation about how they're feeling.

Instead, Daniel left the kitchen and continued on until he wandered into the dormitory. He was still thinking about how adamant Azra was about investigating Samir's death when he spotted Zee in the corridor.

"Zee!" he called out to him.

Zee stopped for a moment and walked toward him. "Hey, Daniel. Have you seen Kaleb around?"

"Uhh... yeah, in the kitchen. Why have you been looking for him?"

"Yeah, he asked to be alone for a bit, but it's been a while, and I'm kind of worried about him. I mean, I was close with Samir too, but Kaleb's broken up by the looks of it. He never cries or anything, so I've never seen him like this. Why are you looking at me like that?"

"It's just weird. He said you wanted to be alone, but he seems down, and you seem completely fine."

"That is weird, but like I said, he's been weird all day. What are you up to? Did you and Azra find out what happened to Samir?"

"Well... that's actually something I need to talk to you about."

"Me? Why?"

"Well, I wanted to ask you about that jam Azra was asking me to research."

"What about it?" Zee asked suspiciously.

"When I was researching the recipe, it was very specific that the seeds had to be removed from the yew berries before cooking, but we found yew berry pits in his stomach. Are you sure you removed all the pits before you made the jam?"

Zee seemed taken aback for a moment. "No. I know for a fact I didn't."

Zee's answer caught Daniel off guard. "What? Why didn't you follow the recipe? I wrote it really clearly."

"I did!" Zee yelled in frustration. "I can't read, I'm not all fancy like you but I never forget anything I hear. I remember Azra told me specifically to use the whole berries. I'm sure he didn't say anything about removing the seeds, I swear."

"That can't be it. Azra knew they were poisonous, and he knew what happened as soon as he saw them. Everyone forgets things *sometimes*. Do you think you forgot a step? This is important, you have to remember."

"No! No, I'm telling you, I'm certain he said to use the whole berries. If you don't fucking believe me, go ask him yourself."

Zee stomped off without looking back.

What just happened?

Immediately, Daniel went back to Azra and explained what he had discovered.

"I distinctly remember instructing Zehariah to remove the pits because they are poisonous," Azra said.

"Well... clearly it was an accident. He forgot what you told him, and he's too much of a ball sack to admit it," Daniel said with a shrug.

"Accident or not, we can now say with certainty how Samir died."

"That's true... and now everyone should understand once we explain it to them, right?"

"What people understand is that someone has killed their beloved high priest, Samir, and something like this cannot go unpunished."

"Wait, what? It wasn't on purpose, it was an accident, it was just carelessness—a mistake."

"But carelessness is the cousin of indifference. If Zehariah truly cared about Samir, he would have taken extra care to follow my directions, rather than allow such a crippling misstep to occur."

"No, I'm telling you, this is all a mistake. Please."

This is all my fault.

"I cannot control the will of justice. Zehariah will be executed at dusk. I will give you a chance to say goodbye after we have issued the sentence. Until then, I will ask that you stay here in my study until I return."

Before Daniel could protest, Azra left the room and blocked the door from the outside.

Daniel ran to the window and looked frantically for Zee until he saw him walking toward the building. Daniel immediately began beating on the window and yelling at his friend, but Zee couldn't hear him. Then he saw a group of priests approach and surround Zee, clutching him by the arms.

Daniel watched helplessly as Azra approached him and began talking. Zee's face grew slack with shock and then twisted into insult and rage. He screamed at Azra for a few minutes before he hung his head and went still.

As they escorted Zee into the building, Daniel slumped against the wall, slid onto the floor, and cried.

After what felt like hours, Azra returned and let Daniel out of the room. "Zehariah is waiting for you and Kaleb to say goodbye at the Altar of Shamash. You should go now."

Daniel wanted to cry again, but resisted as hard as he could. If this were the last time he'd see his friend, Daniel didn't want Zee to see him cry.

When Daniel arrived at the clearing, he saw Zee sitting on the Altar, feet dangling and a sombre expression as he stared off into space. Kaleb stood with him, staring at his own fixed point on the ground. Several priests and slaves surrounded the boys, with Azra and Ghali standing off to the side, observing.

When Daniel approached, he tried to greet his friend with his most casual greeting, but he barely croaked, "Hey, Zee."

"Hey," he replied.

The three boys sat in silence for a long time before Daniel spoke again. "How are you?"

"Good for now," Zee said, as his face transitioned quickly from a smile to a sneer, and then settled on a pained frown. "I-I'm good."

"I know you didn't do this," Daniel said.

Kaleb looked up immediately and nodded his head in agreement as he looked between Daniel and Zee.

Then Daniel reached out to give his friend a hug, using the proximity to whisper in his ear, "We don't have to do this. If we run right now, you could escape."

Zee pulled back to look his friend in the eye, his own filling with tears. Then he pulled Daniel back into a tight hug and burst into laughter that soon became a strangled cry that lasted a long time.

"Thank you, my friend," Zee whispered, when he was calm enough to speak again. "Kaleb said the same thing, you know. There's no escape from this. It's not fair, but this is my fate."

Daniel only nodded as he released Zee. Kaleb silently put his hand on Daniel's shoulder and squeezed before dropping his arm back to his side.

As the sun sunk into the horizon, Azra approached the boys. "It's time to begin."

Both boys hugged their friend one last time before standing back.

"So, how are we doing this?" Zee asked in Azra's direction.

"The law dictates that we must punish a man in the same manner as the offence he committed."

"So... what? You're going to kill me with jam tarts?"

"No, that would be ridiculous. We have acquired this bowl of yew berries. You will eat them whole until you are no longer breathing."

Zee received the bowl and stared at the red berries for a long time. Then he picked up a handful of the berries and looked up at Daniel and Kaleb.

"I don't want to die," he said and began sobbing uncontrollably.

Ghali looked away, but Azra's face twisted with impatience.

"Be a man and accept your fate! Is this how you want to be remembered?"

Zee only cried harder, dropping most of the yew berries from his hand.

"This is ridiculous!"

In the blink of an eye, Azra stood over the boy, cupped Zee's outstretched hand in his own, filled it with berries, and forced him to cover his own wailing mouth. Zee struggled to remove Azra's hand from his own, but Azra maintained an iron grip until he felt the boy swallow. Then Azra wiped his hand on Zee's clothes and took his place beside a shocked Ghali.

"Keep eating," Azra barked.

Zee's eyes welled with tears and his hands shook so hard he nearly dropped the bowl as he ate the berries. For a few seconds, everyone was blanketed in a heavy silence. Everyone except Zee. His quiet whimpers and muffled chewing seemed to carry across the entire field.

Suddenly his face twisted, and he doubled over, screaming and writhing, first clasping his stomach and then his chest. Eventually, screams became grunting, which then turned into convulsions until finally, his glazed eyes stared toward the evening sky and he stopped moving forever.

"By Shamash, justice is done," Azra snapped and walked away as the priests gathered Zee's body.

Daniel and Kaleb stood in silence as they watched Zee get wrapped in a thick blanket and then carried away.

Eventually, the entire procession of witnesses cleared out, leaving only Daniel and Kaleb below the newly unveiled night sky.

Daniel lowered himself onto the grass while Kaleb stood in front of the altar for a moment and then hopped up onto it, sitting where Zee had been only moments before. Daniel observed Kaleb's vacant survey of the altar, staring as if he could still see his friend lying motionless beside him. After a while, Kaleb lay on his back and Daniel did the same.

Minutes passed before Daniel broke the silence. "When you look up there, at the night sky, what do you see, Kaleb?"

"What?"

"The stars. Sometimes the stars make shapes or look like things to me."

"Ah."

"So, what do you see?"

Kaleb let the question sit for a moment and replied, "Possibilities."

"Possibilities? What do you mean?"

"What are stars?"

"I'm not sure. In the library, I read something once that said they're the souls of the dead watching us, protecting us from harm and lighting our way in the darkness."

"That's an interesting thought."

"Yeah, I thought so too. I don't know if anyone still believes that, but it's definitely comforting."

"Everyone needs to understand the world around them, but more than that, everyone wants to feel comforted," Kaleb said. "People, more often than not, like making things up and smearing everything with religion, rather than trying to understand how something actually works or why it exists. We need answers, but we're too lazy to chase after them. It's all lies, but it's comforting, so who cares?"

Kaleb clenched his jaw for a second before continuing.

"Stars don't have these kinds of dilemmas. You say they're the souls of the dead, but what if they're suns or moons that are really, really far away? No matter what anyone thinks, the stars are what they are, and none of our judgments affect or restrict them—we're the only ones restricted. They just hang up in the sky, shining down at us. They get to be free, and we get... this."

"A lot of people are selfish and shallow, but a lot of people can think for themselves too. Like you and me, right?" Daniel said, twisting toward Kaleb.

"Do you actually believe that?"

"Gotta believe in something, right?" Daniel replied with a weak smirk.

"*Belief*. Beliefs are stupid. I used to believe that I'd never abandon someone I cared about."

"Kaleb, there was nothing you could have done. The Law—"

"Don't give me that shit!" Kaleb snapped as he sat up to catch Daniel's eyes in the dark. "*Oh, the Law is the Law*—another bullshit lie used to excuse *our* failure to do the right thing. You say there was nothing we could have done? There were tons of things we both could have done! There were things *I* could have done days ago," he said and then looked away.

"What do you mean... days ago?" Daniel asked suspiciously, as he sat up to face Kaleb.

"Forget it."

"Forget it? You forget it. Tell me, how could you know about any of this days ago? How?" Daniel demanded, ripping tufts of grass from the ground and tossing them toward Kaleb.

Kaleb sat in silence for a long time, fidgeting, until finally he rubbed his forehead with his fists and answered.

"Because," he said, his tone low and sticky with guilt, "I think Azra has been talking about it for a long time."

"Azra's been talking about killing Zee?" Daniel said in shock, shuddering as he remembered how Azra force-fed the Yew berries into his friend's mouth.

"Well, not recently... I think Zee was just the scapegoat. He always talked about how much he hated Samir, how he wished he would die, and how ironic it would be if Samir died from overeating because he was so fat."

Kaleb's jaw quivered as he finished speaking.

"Wait, so you're saying—"

"Azra killed Zee and Samir."

Daniel couldn't believe what he was hearing.

Zee had been like a brother to me. Azra murdered him? As a scapegoat? It can't be true... but it makes sense. Could it be true? But how would Kaleb know?

"Kaleb, how do you know all of this?"

"I told you, he told me things."

"But why?"

"He just told me things sometimes."

"When though? When would he just randomly meet up with you for a murder plot heart to heart? I was with him every day."

"It wasn't during the day."

Daniel gestured frustratedly for an answer.

"It was at night, ok? He came to my room at night," he yelled defensively, before slumping down. "I guess now he makes me come to his room."

"Wait, what?"

"It started a while ago," he continued quietly, "before you got here, but it became every night after...."

... after I took over his room.

Daniel froze in horror.

"Anyway," he continued after a long pause, "I always fought it at first, but eventually, I stopped fighting it. I guess after a while he realized I never told anyone about it and started telling me his other secrets."

As the revelation sunk in, Daniel felt his heart wrench with every word the other boy spoke. "Why didn't you tell someone?"

"I did. Not at first... but eventually, I did. I've only ever told one person other than you."

Daniel arched an eyebrow. "Who?"

"Samir. I think he knew when I told Samir too, but I don't think he knew it was me. One day, he'll be sick of me, and he'll just kill me too," Kaleb said, devoid of emotion.

Icy fear shot through Daniel and crystalized around his heart.

"We have to run, Kaleb. We need to go right now," Daniel said.

"What do you mean?" Kaleb asked with a frown.

"I mean, we need to run tonight."

"Where? Where are we going to go? This is the only place I've ever known. Technically, it's the only place *you've* ever known."

"It doesn't matter where, we just need to go. We'll figure it out."

"I—I can't. If I leave, he'll just find some other guy to replace me. At least if I'm still sleeping in his room, he won't do this to anyone else."

"There has to be another way. You can't just let him rape you until he kills you one day on a whim."

"What else can I do?"

Daniel thought for a moment. "What if we have *him* put on trial?"

"We can't do that. Azra's the one that puts other people on trial."

"Yeah, but that should be true for all the high priests, then. Azra said it himself: all high priests carry the same authority. That means Ghali should be able to put Azra on trial."

"I don't know."

"Just think about it. You can stay in my room tonight and decide in the morning, ok?"

Kaleb paused for a long time. "Ok," he said.

"Ok."

The boys headed to Daniel's room. When they arrived, they slipped inside and closed the door again as quietly as possible. Daniel felt his way through the dark, searching for a lamp.

"Did you move everything around in here?" Kaleb whispered.

"Just a few things," Daniel muttered.

"Things were fine where they were, you know—gross. Why is it wet over here?"

"Wet? Hold on, I'm trying to find a light."

"Allow me." Azra's voice slid out of the darkness.

Suddenly, a flash of light exploded in the room as every candle self-ignited all at once.

"You're late," Azra said flatly from the corner of the room. Daniel swivelled to see him sitting on his bed, facing the boys with a sneer that curled menacingly at the edges of his mouth.

"Azra... what are you doing here?" Daniel said.

Azra laughed a wicked, feigned laugh that didn't touch his eyes. "What am I doing here, indeed? Is that all you have to say? How shamefully unimaginative."

Daniel's mind went blank and his mouth became so dry he couldn't swallow. "We—um—Kaleb was still upset and—"

"Daniel," Kaleb interrupted quietly, "he knows. Look."

He followed Kaleb's line of sight and found Ghali's lifeless corpse hanging off the wall. Thorned branches protruded through his chest and wrapped around his limbs. A puddle of blood and excrement covered the floor below him.

Daniel stared in shock.

"I got impatient waiting for Kaleb, and then I found you both talking by the altar. I guess I was just in the right place at the right time. I left a little early though, so I have to ask, what was your plan in the end? Let me guess, you boys thought you would sneak out of Sippar in the middle of the night and tell someone all about the evil Azra? Would you, I wonder, have remembered to tell them that this was the same evil Azra that managed a temple for young boys the world had thrown away? The same evil Azra that took you in and gave you a home when he found you alone and injured on the shore of a river?"

"You killed Zee and Samir... and now Ghali." Daniel shouted desperately, "you can't keep killing people!"

"Oh? Is someone is coming to stop me? All I can see are two scared little boys."

Azra watched the boys' expressions for a long time.

"Why won't you just let us go?" Kaleb pleaded quietly, looking down at the floor.

"You would know better than anyone, my boy," Azra said with mock compassion. "It's because you became obstacles—loose ends that need to be tied. I have a grander path than remaining a high priest at Sippar. I can't have Ghali putting me on trial or Samir smearing my reputation. I certainly can't have Zehariah creating suspicions about Samir's death," he said casually, looking between the boys as they listened in horror. "And I can't have you running your mouths to anyone who will listen."

The blood drained from Kaleb's face as he looked at his friend, unable to speak.

"You know, you boys were both so important to me. It's a shame how sometimes the smallest things cause the most pain," Azra said as he threw a pouch at Daniel's feet.

Suddenly Azra's hands twitched as he waved them in front of his body and Daniel found his own hands working against their will, reaching for the pouch on the floor. Panic burned against Daniels's face.

Oh, no! No, no, no, no, no... He can control my movements?

"It's called weaving, boy. You asked me before how I healed myself every day? It's a power only a few know about and even fewer understand. It's also handy in situations like this one, right now."

Daniel tried to resist, but the influence of Azra's weaving was too strong. Kaleb's eyes grew wide as Daniel poured a handful of Yew berries into his palm. Daniel blubbered helplessly.

"Go on, boy," Azra said smoothly. "Give them to Kaleb."

Against his will, Daniel's legs shuffled him closer to his friend.

Daniel's eyes met with Azra's and he shook his head, pleading for him to stop.

Azra only gestured back: *go on.*

Daniel tried to pull away, but could not resist the weaves Azra was using. He covered Kaleb's mouth, forcing berries inside, and couldn't remove his hand until Kaleb had swallowed.

The boys slumped, heads together. Defeated.

"I'm sorry Kaleb. I'm sorry," Daniel wailed.

Suddenly Kaleb screamed and clasped his body the way Zee had only a few hours before. As he flailed in anguish, Kaleb grabbed Daniel's arm and they locked eyes. Daniel clasped onto him while waves of convulsion crashed inside of Kaleb, twisting and warping his body.

Bloody foam spilled from his lips as the spasms subsided and his wide eyes communicated their last unanswered plea.

Daniel felt parts of himself flake away as he stared, horrified, at the sight of his dead friend.

Then he bared his teeth and fired a dangerous stare at Azra, but there was no recognition of any threat being communicated between them.

"Why did you do this? He didn't deserve to die," Daniel yelled.

"What do you mean, he didn't *deserve* death? No one deserves death, boy. People live, and then they die at some point afterwards. Death is just a part of life. Having control over death is having control over life and only those who can do that have any *real* power," Azra said.

Daniel sadly looked over the corpse of his friend.

"Kaleb was always destined to die young, but you, you could have lived a long and happy life. You could've become a high priest one day. Maybe. Instead, you interfered in my affairs and now a lot of innocent people have to die tonight. Even my boy had to die because of you. I will need a new boy now," he said with a slimy smirk.

As Azra advanced on him, time seemed to slow down.

Ankl's voice whispered to Daniel from the back of his mind, *You're pathetic now. What happened to the man I knew? Is he buried so deep?*

Daniel felt a flame inside of him grow and roar through every fibre of his being.

Yes, Ankl whispered, *show him what true power looks like.*

Suddenly, Daniel raised his hands and shouted, "Stop!"

Azra froze. Daniel's face broke into a snarl and his eyes shone with blue supernatural fire. Daniel could now see an intricate web of blue interconnecting threads, pulsing and vibrating as they connected to every physical object, both near and far.

"I will destroy you. You will pay for every crime you've ever committed," Daniel snarled.

Daniel made a crushing gesture with his right hand.

Azra screamed as he arched his back and looked upward, but the scream quickly evolved into a dark, genuinely entertained laugh.

"Just kidding," he said, and with a wave of a hand, he seemed to push the threads aside like cobwebs.

Azra laughed darkly.

"You will never cease to interest me. Unfortunately, your threats are a little less interesting."

Azra splayed and curled his fingers toward Daniel before making a twisting gesture. Daniel began to wretch and cough until he spat his tongue out with a mouthful of blood. Then Azra made sweeping motions in the air, causing Daniel's hands to separate from his arms as if they had been sliced away. An agonizing scream burst out of Daniel while his open, dripping wounds cauterized themselves, and then he fell unconscious.

Draping Daniel over his shoulder, Azra made his way out of the building and into the street. People seemed to take notice of Daniel and eyed Azra with suspicion as he passed.

When Azra reached the city gates, a pair of guards blocked his path.

"Hold on," said the larger of the two, placing his hand on Azra's chest. "What is your business? Where are you taking this boy?"

Azra splayed the fingers on his free hand toward the guard and slowly raised it, keeping it horizontal to the ground. The higher Azra raised his hand, the redder the guard's face turned. Every vein under his skin inflated until the man exploded in front of Azra.

The second guard, horrified, attempted to run. Azra pointed his fingers toward the man with an upturned palm. In one motion, Azra made a fist and yanked sharply downward in front of him. The second guard's head flew backward with a loud crack and hung behind him like a discarded hood. Azra passed through the gates before the body had stopped running and collapsed to the ground.

When they had finally gotten a short distance away from Sippar, Azra laid Daniel on the ground and began weaving thick vines across every wall and every window in the city.

There was a lot of screaming and crying tonight. There's too much blood staining the ground. I can't allow any more suspicion to unravel my reputation.

Every ship in the port was destroyed, and every exit was blocked, entombing the entire city.

There's no future for this place any longer.

Azra reached out to the threads connecting the flames around the city. He felt the intense vibrations that created the heat and increased them exponentially, turning their golden light into a supernatural blue.

Azra continued to weave, coaxing the blue flames to pour out and flood the city, cleansing it in the heat of a thousand suns. The firelight seared his eyes, but Azra could not look away from the devastation.

So beautiful, he thought.

Azra sunk onto the grass with tears streaming down his cheeks, while Daniel lay unconscious beside him and ash rained around them like snowflakes.

Just beautiful.

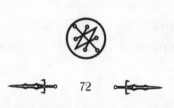

CHAPTER 6

THE BEGINNING
OF THE END

One day I'll make it right.

It was a bright day with few clouds, which always made Daniel feel energetic and positive. His mother had asked him to feed the chickens, but the day was too beautiful to be wasted on chores.

A friend caught up to him as he ran toward the field.

"Dan, where you goin'?"

"Jared," he grinned. "It's too nice a day to get stuck with farm work. I figured I'd escape for a bit. Maybe explore the field."

"I'm pretty sure we've explored this entire field several times over," Jared chuckled.

"What are you up to today?"

"Nothin'. Want some company on your adventure?"

"JARED!!" came a shrill voice, cutting off all other sounds. "Where have you been?! I specifically told you to mind the sheep with your brother."

The voice bellowed from a large, scowling woman in a white and blue striped skirt, hiked over her knees. An awkward bow-legged jog carried her toward them.

"Oh, crap. It's my mom. Change of plans."

"Damn Jared, she's pissed."

"Yep. Looks like I'm going to have to waste the day on herding."

"She's scary today. I say you run for it."

Jared sighed loudly. "No, a real man doesn't run from monsters. Especially ones that know where you live."

"I guess I'll see you later." Daniel laughed.

"I'll see you later," Jared said, waving as he jogged backwards. Jared's mother tried to grab him as she approached, but he evaded, running away from her, and back toward the village with her close on his heels.

Daniel chuckled and shook his head, turning back toward his original destination.

The grassy field became dotted with tall bushes and trees as Daniel journeyed further. In some places, the trees streaked across the rolling countryside in jagged copses. Daniel smiled as he finally entered a shaded treeline at the top of a hill, but his intention was not specifically to find shade.

Finding the perfect climbing tree was always an exercise in patience and careful selection. It had to be close enough to the ground that the branch was thick and horizontal, but high enough up the tree that it gave him a satisfying vantage point.

Everything looks different from above. Everything seems less random, he thought, climbing into a nearby tree. *Everything has a place and a function. Like how a single ant, up close, appears to be carrying on his own little journey, all by himself, but when you stand up and look at the entire ant hill, you see that there's something... ordered about how they all move around. They all have their own plans, but at the same time, they're all working together towards a bigger plan.*

Once Daniel found the perfect branch, he rested his back against the trunk and straddled the limb, letting his legs dangle. The view was as beautiful as it was familiar; a vast and hilly grassland, overlaid by patches of farmland and peppered unevenly with trees and shrubbery. To the east and north, Daniel could see the Euphrates River cutting through the land, and to the west, at the edge of the horizon, was a mountain range, like a pale shadow dividing the ground from the sky. He had seen all of it many times before, but he couldn't help feeling that he had a special connection with the surrounding land. He felt he *belonged* here.

Daniel looked out across the fields around Mari, and within a few moments he had nodded off to sleep.

A horn trumpeted from somewhere in the distance, resonating everywhere. Daniel awoke to it, half-asleep and confused, unable to recognize what he had heard at first.

The horn blew again, long and loud, but this time, the sound of a thousand voices roared up immediately afterward.

Daniel rubbed his eyes and tried to scan the distant horizon. At first, nothing stood out, but slowly, a dark line thickened along the northern border between the earth and the sky. The darkness grew into a thick bubbling mass and then spilled over onto the hill below. It poured over everything until it broke apart into hundreds of pieces, each tumbling down the countryside and morphing into the shapes of individual men. They roared, waving their weapons as they ran toward the village.

Daniel felt a surge of panic, washing away his initial disbelief. He scrambled down the tree, jumped off a low-hanging branch, and sprinted home as fast as he could.

Smoke filled his nostrils, and Daniel nearly choked as he got closer.

Keep running.

Raiders set fire to the straw houses nearby. People screamed indiscriminately. The cries of children mingled with the shouting and laughter of the invaders.

It's only a little farther.

Daniel's lungs were burning now and his muscles ached. He scrambled under an abandoned cart and tried to get his bearings.

Across the entire village, marauders darted from every direction, like a frenzy of botflies over a carcass. And a raider now headed purposefully toward Daniel.

I'm trapped.

He walked up to Daniel's cart... and continued right past him. A muted sigh escaped his lips until the raider returned a few minutes later—this time dragging a young girl by the hair behind him. She screamed and fought frantically to escape his grasp.

There was a moment where her eyes locked with Daniel's. A plea for help flooded their connection, and she reached out to Daniel, sobbing and pleading incoherently. Daniel had known this girl. They had grown up together, and his arm shot out to grasp hers, fingertips brushing in an effort to find a mutual grip, but their fingers couldn't close the distance between them.

Time slowed down.

Daniel watched the girl's face fill with the awareness that he couldn't save her, and then empty of all hope. Despite the surrounding chaos, she stopped screaming. Her face paled, and her outstretched hand fell listlessly to her side while her assailant dragged her away. Daniel hung his head and pounded the ground.

Why is this happening? I'm sorry....

Suddenly she screamed wildly, digging her fingers and heels into the ground, trying to resist the man as hard as she could.

"Shut up, girl," the raider shouted over his shoulder, punctuating the demand with a quick, explosive yank of her hair.

Daniel could not hear a snap over the ambient violence that surrounded him, but he knew there had been one. Daniel's eyesight blurred as he tracked her dragging, lifeless body until it disappeared into a nearby hut.

Daniel squeezed his eyes shut, causing tears to escape them.

I have to find Elisa. I have to find mom and dad. Stay focused.

Daniel rolled out from under the cart and ran toward a nearby blazing hut. He ducked down and evaded a few others from the raiding party jogging by. Then Daniel ran again.

I have to find them.

Then he spotted them in the distance; Daniel's mom and sister lay crouched behind a large wagon, while his father stood protectively over them with his sword ready. Daniel called out impulsively and ran toward them, but instead of elation or relief, Daniel only saw terror painted on their faces.

"It's me!" he yelled, but his mother only squeezed Elisa more tightly, and his father ran at him with his sword held upward. Just as Daniel's father came within arm's reach, he put his hand on Daniel's back and leaped over him, pushing off of Daniel so hard the momentum threw him face-first into the mud. Daniel heard the clang of metal on metal before he even hit the ground and cleared his face to see his father in a sword fight with an invader.

"Go to your mother!" he yelled.

Daniel ran to his mother, and she grabbed him.

"Oh Daniel, my son. My Daniel."

Daniel watched his father wield a sword he had never seen, with a skill he had never realized he possessed.

"When did he learn to fight?"

"Your father wasn't always a farmer."

The swordsmen expertly thrust and parried in response to each other as smoothly as waves lapping against the shore.

Again and again, they came at each other, advancing, retreating and ultimately encircling one another; each movement anticipating and inciting the next, creating a cascade of flashing metal and violence. The duel went on for several minutes like a choreographed dance. Neither man felt a blade despite the speed of their attacks.

Then Daniel's father lost his footing. He tried to regain his stance, but had to improvise a roll to dodge an overhead slice from his assailant. The roll was too weak, and Daniel's father landed too close to his opponent. The raider seized the moment to chop into his enemy's spine at the base of the neck.

Daniel's father fell, snatching one last glimpse of his family. His eyes poured out a silent apology as they clouded over and blood gushed from his wound.

Daniel's mother screamed and howled in despair while the man laughed menacingly and walked toward them. A twisted smile split across his face like a sinister gash.

Daniel looked out over the village for somewhere for them to run.

Raiding parties ran in every direction, trampling bodies that covered the charred and bloody ground. In the distance, Jared cried over his own mother's body, cradling her head in his arms until an arrow impaled him in the eye, knocking him backward.

Daniel's mother and sister continued to wail as another sneering marauder approached.

We're never getting out of this. This is it.

Daniel felt tears running down his face and squeezed his eyes shut as he huddled closer to his mother and sister. His father's glassy gaze weighed over him, judging Daniel's weakness and failure to act. Judging his inability to adapt to a life without the safety and familiarity of the village where he was raised. For 13 years, Mari had been his entire world. Now Mari was being erased.

Daniel's body vibrated with the pace of his heartbeat and his head spun.

Suddenly the world drained of all colour, and time appeared to stop around him. Leaning against an overturned wagon, stood Ankl.

Daniel whirled his head around in shocked disbelief at the frozen horrors all around him.

"Oh no. No, no, no, no, no," Daniel repeated hysterically.

"Keep it together, boy," Ankl said in an even, detached tone.

"What... is... is this real? What are you? Am I dead?" Daniel asked.

"Nearly, or rather, you should be."

"I... I should?"

"Yes, but I'm inclined to help you."

"... Why?" Daniel asked.

"You're too important to die here, but apparently too stupid to survive this particular challenge on your own," Ankl said.

Is this really happening? Am I already dead?

"BOY! Look at me. Focus. I know you have questions. We will cover the specifics later. Do you want to live?"

Daniel stared agape for a moment before he could collect his thoughts. "Can you save me from the raiders?"

"No, but you can. You just have to remember how."

"Ok, so how do I do that?"

"You just... remember."

Daniel thought for a moment. "I don't get it. I don't know *what* I'm supposed to remember."

"So, you're not going to put any energy into saving your own life?"

"It's not that. I need your help. You're telling me to remember something I don't even—"

"Fine, fine. Here," Ankl said, as he approached Daniel and touched him on the forehead, "but next time I'm going to expect some level of effort on your part."

Daniel could feel a surge of power course through him with a bright white light, and his skin glowed until the heat enveloped his entire body.

Wait! Wait, this is too much!

Daniel opened his mouth to call out and howled with a supernatural roar. The light inside of him exploded outward in a blinding, expansive flash that washed over everything and transformed the visible world into ash.

When the light had faded from Daniel, he collapsed onto his back. Time had returned to normal, but the surrounding space had transformed into a barren black wasteland. Bits of ash floated down over him as he watched the sky.

Am I...alone?

Unexpectedly, a crow swooped down and landed beside Daniel, eyeing him with curiosity. Daniel tried to reach out to the crow, but he was too exhausted to move, and his eyelids became heavy.

The loud shriek of the crow was the last thing he heard before the world faded to darkness.

Daniel awoke lying on his back and jostled around at the back of a horse-drawn wagon Azra had picked up along the dusty road to Nineveh. A crow shrieked from just beside Daniel, startling him upright. It was late morning, and there was no one travelling along the road beside himself and Azra, who drove the cart. Azra looked back at regular intervals to either check on Daniel or the road behind them.

Daniel knew he should wonder why, but he just didn't care. Nothing mattered anymore. The memories of their last night in Sippar flooded his mind and submerged him in the new realities of his life.

His family in Mari was dead. His brothers in Sippar were dead. And Azra....

Daniel's mind kept going back to that night, particularly when he unleashed his weaves against Azra.

Daniel squeezed his eyes and pressed his head into his knees.

Azra had a trail of bodies going all the way back to his childhood. I saw everything. When he found me. When he told

Zee to use the pits. All those nights with Kaleb. It was just like Kaleb said. Azra intended to kill him eventually, no matter what. How long until he kills me?

For the first time in his life, Daniel felt completely isolated, defenceless, and alone. The man he had trusted as a father had taken away everything he cared about, and there was nothing anyone could do about it.

The world is unjust. There are no rules that force anyone to behave in any way. Nothing is fair. Nothing matters anymore.

He felt a numbness set in that washed over everything and dulled every sense he had. He slid back down, laying on his side.

I am nothing. I have nothing. Nothing further will ever come from my being alive. How is this better than dying, Ankl?

Daniel curled up in despair.

Daniel felt like he should cry, but he didn't, and his body wouldn't allow it, anyway.

Right and wrong. How can they exist if there's no one to enforce them? Did I kill Zee and Kaleb, or was that Azra? Who's really to blame? Was that my purpose? Maybe my purpose is to suffer forever; just a series of injustices I have to endure, on and on, with no end in sight.

It had been a few days since they had left Sippar, but Daniel had lost track of time. He just laid on the cart, slipping in and out of consciousness, endlessly trying to forget about everything that had happened.

It would just be better if we don't stop... except for food. I'd stop for food. Any food would be good. Daniel curled tighter.

Putting pressure on his stomach made the aching hunger less for a short time, but soon it would be back. Daniel hadn't felt this hungry since he first arrived at the temple, but this time Kaleb wouldn't be here to take him to a kitchen.

It feels like I'm drowning. Even when I'm breathing, it feels like I'm holding my breath.

Daniel willed the thought away.

I wonder where we're going? Will they have food when we get there?

Daniel drooled. He tried to wipe it away on the back of his hand, but the hand was no longer there. Daniel had never been as depressed as he was right at that moment.

"Buck up, Buttercup, the world isn't all bad," a voice barked nearby.

Daniel shot up again and looked around.

That wasn't Azra... who was that?

Daniel popped his head up and swivelled around to see who spoke. He was alone on the cart, aside from Azra, who focused intently on the road, and a crow perched on the sideboard.

Did that crow just... speak to me?

"What, can the devil speak true?"

Daniel frowned.

"Too soon, I guess."

Daniel quickly looked from the crow to Azra and back to the crow again. Azra didn't seem to notice a talking bird had hitched a ride on the back of his cart—and was loudly chatting away within arm's reach from him.

"I constantly reintroduce myself to you; if I were human, I would have serious doubts about the value of our relationship," the crow ranted with irritation.

What is he talking about? Am I delirious?

"Idiot!" the crow squawked. "You're not delirious. Maybe lazy and somewhat incompetent, but not delirious."

Is it reading my mind...? Wait. Is that Ankl?

"Finally, back on the same page," the crow squawked. "Interesting how it's weird for Azra not to hear the talking bird, but somehow the talking bird itself is totally normal."

Why are you here?

"I thought I would try to cheer you up. You're pathetic *still*—or maybe *again?*" The bird paused thoughtfully. "No, it's definitely *still*. I was right the first time."

You're terrible at cheering people up. How are you even here?

"I'm literally always with you. It's less like watching and more like being in the right place all the time."

I shouldn't have asked. It's not like it matters. I can't do anything, anyway.

"Not with that attitude."

Daniel sighed.

"Look, I can't solve your problems for you, but there has to be a better way than this. You're literally crying or helpless or curled up in a ball. You're like a child."

I am a child.

"Well, I still think there's another way. When you want to accomplish something, you have to try harder than not at all," Ankl said.

Daniel looked up at him silently.

"Look, you spend every day sulking right now, when you should be trying to turn that frown upside down, but you can't, because you blame yourself for the deaths of every single person you've ever known. It's a deep pit, but you've seen worse—"

Daniel curled up tighter, staring at the wooden planks running below him.

"—and I'd love to watch you endlessly cycle through your worst moments, but the truth is, you're not responsible for all of this. Well, maybe some of it, but definitely not all of it."

You're fucking terrible at helping.

"How are you so weak and useless? You were *Azazel*. Now you're... this. The Azazel I know would fight his way out of this situation."

So I should attack Azra, then? Right here on the cart? Am I going to instantly feel better? Am I going to bring him to justice? I failed once, but you know what? I'm at a severe disadvantage. Right now is obviously the perfect time to try again.

"Failure is a part of growth."

And what could I even do to him now? Stub him to death?

"Stub him to death," the crow chuckled unnaturally, "that's fantastic."

I'm serious.

"That would be incredibly ironic."

Daniel scowled in confusion for a moment and then shook his head.

Whatever. All this talking is a waste of time. There's no escape from Azra.

"You'll find a way. You set your own limitations."

Daniel sighed in despair for a moment.

Just go away.

Daniel rolled to his other side and curled up, facing away from the crow.

The crow tilted its head unnaturally to each side, observing Daniel for a moment, and then flew away to a passing tree.

Anyone that had ever met both Sin and his brother Ashur commented about their identical appearance. Shumu, their guardian, had once told them that this was partly because they had both received their mother's looks; dark brown hair and green eyes with olive skin. According to Shumu, she had been a strikingly beautiful woman.

Sin had never met his mother, because she had died in childbirth, and he often wondered what she would have been like. He often wondered what it would be like to have a mother at all.

After her death, his father never remarried. Sin had asked Shumu about it, but the answer only created more questions,

No one knows why your father never remarried. All I can say for sure is that your father once told me that your mother was the only woman that ever captivated him the way she did. Don't overthink it.

He's right. I was definitely overthinking it. I'm always overthinking everything.

The thought made him chuckle.

How long have I been wandering these halls today, thinking about the memories of stuff I've already thought about?

Sin embraced his thoughtfulness because it was one of the few things that made him distinct from his brother. Ashur was stubborn and assertive. Sin thought of himself as more reserved and analytical, but sometimes he felt like people treated him differently because of it.

It's like they think I'm less capable than he is, like I'm weaker.

Sin turned a corner.

It doesn't matter. Ashur is Ashur and I am me.

Suddenly, a servant whipped around the corner and collided with Sin, knocking their heads together. They grappled eachother before falling together on his back. Sin tried to touch his forehead because of the pain and entangled his fingers in someone else's hair. He opened one eye and found the most beautiful girl he had ever seen staring back at him.

Sin immediately froze and felt his face turn red. The girl went completely pale as she realized who she had run into.

"Oh no. Oh, no-no-no. I'm so sorry, my lord. Please forgive me," she panicked, climbing off of him.

"Hey, it's ok. Really. I mean, my head hurts, but nothing's broken. Are *you* ok?" Sin asked, standing up.

Very smooth.

"What? Me? Yeah—I mean yes, I'm ok thank you, Your Highness," she said, averting her eyes.

"No, just call me Sin. I'm not the crown prince, you— uh, you don't need to be that formal with me," he said, studying her face.

Ask her name! Do it! Do it now or you'll miss your chance!

"What's your name?" Sin blurted.

"Miriam," she said hesitantly, with a weak smile.

"Miriam," Sin said, smiling despite himself. "Wait, did... did you use my body to break your fall just now?"

Not smooth! Not smooth!

"Ugh," Miriam groaned as she knelt down and picked up bouquets of dried spices from the floor that Sin had only just noticed. He knelt beside her and stacked the empty pots into his arm that were strewn across the floor alongside the spices.

"Um... thanks," she said as they stood, looking at the stack of pots in Sin's arm.

"Hey, I can help you take these wherever you're going—if you want?" Sin asked.

"Um... no, it's ok. I can do it," she said, reaching out and prompting Sin to transfer the stack into her arms, "but thanks anyway... uh, Sin?"

"Well, where were you headed, anyway? I'll walk with you."

She looked down at the spices and pots in her arms. "... the *kitchen?*" she said, arching an eyebrow.

"Ah—yeah. Yeah, I guess that makes sense," he said, embarrassed.

Miriam shook her head.

"Sin, you seem like a nice guy, but it's my first day and I'm already late because I ran over a prince. I really have to go," Miriam said, turning to walk away. Then she stopped and turned back toward Sin again. "I'm really sorry I ran you over, though."

"I'm not. I mean, it's really no problem," he said.

Miriam nodded with a smirk and began walking away again.

"Wait!" he shouted after her.

Miriam stopped and turned around again. "What?"

"Uh... Can—can I talk to you again sometime?" Sin said.

"Um... sure?" She said.

"Ok! Thanks!" he yelled back before running down the hall in the opposite direction.

Miriam let out a short giggle and then shook her head as she turned around again and headed for the kitchen.

CHAPTER 7

INTO THE LION'S DEN

The sky was bright and overcast, making the clouds seem to glow white with their own soft luminescence as the cart finally came to a halt. Daniel felt an unexpected sense of relief wash over his entire body when the violent rocking ceased, but Azra quickly replaced it with an intense sense of panic as he dismounted the cart.

Oh, no! he's coming for me! I have to run!

Before Daniel could will his body to push off the back of the cart, it tilted forward abruptly. The momentum forced him to slide forward, somersault over the front of the box and then land face-first into a pile of ash. Daniel coughed and struggled to stand, repeatedly attempting to put weight onto his amputated forearms and falling, trapping him in a painful cycle of failure.

A large pair of hands gripped him under the arms, lifting him. Daniel screamed and thrashed in terror until Azra spun him around and slapped him in the face, knocking him to the ground.

"Now you listen to me. We've arrived at Nineveh. I will not allow you to embarrass me like this when we meet with the king. I'm going to pick you up, and then you are going to keep a brisk pace behind me all the way to the palace. If you scream again or cause me any further difficulties, I will use my fist to strike you instead of my palm. Do you understand?"

Daniel looked at the ground, attempting to avoid eye contact.

"Nod, if you understand," Azra commanded.

Daniel nodded, continuing to stare at the surrounding ashes. As Azra lifted him, Daniel realized for the first time that the leather straps used to tie the horse to the cart had singed edges, and the animal was nowhere to be seen.

There are no tracks, as if the horse just disappeared.

Daniel could feel Azra's eyes on him as he surveyed the ground.

"No animal in the world can travel for days without stopping, boy. There is a consequence for every miracle. Come, it's time to enter the city."

As they travelled the road into the city, Daniel found his gaze lifted skyward toward the pointed crenelations that peaked along the cerulean walls of Nineveh.

These walls are enormous.

"Come, boy. We must not dally here."

Daniel nodded reflexively and followed Azra with wide eyes, taking in the sights all around him.

The city air carried the spicy scents of cooking while it swirled and mingled with the aromas of strange perfumes, incense, and human occupation. Hundreds of simple cloth canvases shielded market stands below, providing paying customers a temporary relief from the midday sun. Most people milled about the overcrowded streets shoulder to shoulder in every direction. Nearly everyone shouted over the bustle of friends, customers, and hawkers.

Daniel felt weak from hunger and overwhelmed by the constant waves of smells and sounds crashing against him from every direction. Bodies collided with him repeatedly, tossing him from side to side, and airborne dust made it harder and harder to breathe as he walked. He had lost track of Azra, but instead of relief, panic electrified every inch of his body as he struggled to see over the endless sea of bodies.

Where am I? Should I run? Which way is out?

Suddenly, Daniel tripped and fell, knocking the air out of him. He tried to get up, but the relentless crowd kicked and stomped over him without realizing. Daniel struggled to crawl despite being trampled. He coughed, but couldn't catch his breath through the dust.

I'm drowning. I'm going to die down here.

Black, muddy tears streamed down his face, clearing his eyes enough to look around for any means of escape.

Out of the haze, a hand reached out and grabbed him firmly by the arm, lifting him up. It was a girl about his age. The hood of her white cloak obscured her face, but her voice was clear and confident.

"Let's go," she said.

Daniel nodded and stumbled alongside the girl as she guided him by the arm toward a large blue building in the distance.

Two life-sized, seated lion statues greeted Daniel when they arrived at the building. An immense bronze door sat between the lions. The girl grasped a thick bronze ring that hung from the centre of the door and used it to knock loudly three times. The echoes caused Daniel to take in his surroundings more carefully, fixating on the bronze lions embossed on the door.

The door creaked open, revealing another girl around Daniel's age with fair skin and loosely braided red hair. A short white tunic with embroidered blue squares along the trim wrapped around her body, and a wide blue belt held it closed.

Is she a guard? Daniel noticed the staff she held at attention.

"Who are you?" the red-haired girl demanded.

"Ariel, come on. I brought him here," the cloaked girl said.

Ariel looked Daniel over and grunted. "Fine, but you're telling Uma."

"Don't worry."

"Today, Eva."

"Ok, fine, I'll tell Uma today. I promise."

Ariel sighed and let them pass.

"Thank you," Eva said cheerfully.

"Whatever," Ariel said, rolling her eyes.

Women and girls, each with a unique braid and all wearing the same white tunic as Ariel, stood at every entranceway and patrolled the halls, glancing at Daniel as they passed.

The hallways shared a similar layout to the Temple of Shamash, except that here, they covered the walls in lion-motifs and blue tapestries. Daniel couldn't help staring at the lions and paused in front of one of the statues guarding the hall.

"The Lion represents the ferocity and cunning of the goddess. She has many faces, including war and fertility, so a lioness is fitting." Eva explained from the shadow of her hood. "Let's keep going. I'll get you something to eat."

Daniel nodded and tried harder to keep up.

The warm smells of cooking and sweet incense wrapped themselves around Daniel as they walked. Eva led him further down the hall until eventually, they reached the kitchen. It was like what Daniel had seen at Sippar, except in one corner there was a small table with benches on either side.

"Please, sit," Eva said, pointing to the benches.

Then she pushed back her hood and removed her cloak, draping it across the back of the table. Eva wore the same white tunic as Ariel, and her earthy brown hair wove into an intricate braid that snaked across her scalp and rested over her shoulder. Her glistening hazel eyes punctuated her round, girlish face and dark caramel skin. Daniel stared at her, open-mouthed.

She's the most beautiful girl I've ever seen.

"Please... sit," Eva said, more bashfully. Her face flushed.

Eva prepared a bowl of stew and a few chunks of bread for Daniel on a plate. After setting the food in front of Daniel, Eva sat across from him at the table. He grinned in anticipation until he tried to lick his lips.

All of Daniel's anticipation capsized into despair and he plunged his head onto the table and cried.

"What's wrong?" she said, reaching out to him.

Daniel fought to push the tears back down and rolled his forehead back and forth along the table.

"Oh! Oh my gosh, I forgot. Let me help you," she said, taking a seat beside him.

Daniel pounded his head on the table and hummed a note out of key until his breath ran out.

Eva stroked his hair gently and sat quietly with him for a moment.

"Hey, look. Look at me," she said, tilting her head to make eye contact as Daniel slowly lifted his head. "I'm going to help you, ok?"

Daniel hesitated and then nodded weakly, prompting Eva to place one arm around his torso. "Let my hands be your hands."

Daniel turned to look her in the eye and found himself inches away from her face. A swell of mixed emotions caused him to look away, but Eva made no indication if she had noticed.

Eva picked up the bowl and brought it to his lips, whispering, "Slowly now," before carefully pouring the stew into his mouth.

Daniel instinctively raised his arms, attempting to prop the bowl up and empty it faster, but it was spilling along the corners of his mouth and eventually, it caused him to cough.

Eva pulled the bowl away a little.

"Slowly, slowly," she repeated gently.

Daniel allowed Eva to try again, while he tried to pace his eating better.

Eva patiently fed him multiple bowls of stew until he gestured he was finally full.

Daniel leaned back, closed his eyes, and smiled. For the first time in almost a week, Daniel felt satisfied.

Am I happy? Maybe...

When Daniel opened his eyes, Eva smiled back at him.

"Hi," she said with amusement. "By the way, my name's Eva."

Daniel closed his eyes and gave an appreciative nod.

Eva laughed. "This is where you tell me your name."

Daniel frowned and shook his head. He opened his mouth and showed her the void where his tongue used to be.

"Tongue too, huh? We can figure that out later. That is, if you plan to stay with us for a while."

Daniel nodded vigorously.

Eva laughed. "Ok, that's good. There's one last thing we need to do before I show you to your room."

Eva led Daniel back through the temple, and then into a room that he didn't remember from Sippar—it was a heated bath. The priests and slaves bathed at Sippar, but the water had to be prepared beforehand and poured into a tub. Here the water appeared to be heated from underground somehow and there was much, much more of it.

Daniel felt his clothes being tugged at gently and then spun to face Eva in horror.

"It's not like that," she reassured him. "I'm just washing you."

Daniel still felt anxious, but he allowed her to undress him and remove his bandages anyhow. Once Eva finished, she guided him by the shoulders, down some steps and into the bath, bringing with her a cloth and a stone to scrub with.

"Keep your arms up. I need to wash around your wrists, but I don't think you should put them underwater just yet."

Daniel was nervous at first, but Eva seemed to be very comfortable, often humming while she washed him and it put him at ease.

"Your pendant," she said as she scrubbed his chest. "Have you always had it?"

Daniel shrugged.

"It's pretty," she said, pausing thoughtfully, before scrubbing Daniel again. "You know, in the village where I was born, there's an old story about pendants like that one. They say that many years ago, when the world was still new, there was a magician king named Solomon. He was so powerful he commanded an army of Djinn. One day, the magician king ordered the Djinn to find the most beautiful women in the land and bring them back to his palace. So, the Djinn went out in search of the most beautiful women any man had ever seen—and they found them—but along their journey, the Djinn had fallen in love with the women. Instead of bringing them back to the magician king, the Djinn settled down at the base of a nearby mountain. Eventually, the women gave the Djinn many sons and daughters, and the Djinn loved their children so much that they made small pendants to protect them. In my village, they say that those who wear the pendants today are descendants of those beautiful women and the Djinn of King Solomon."

Eva's story made Daniel miss the Library in Sippar. Daniel missed Kaleb and Zehariah. He missed Jared. And his parents. And Elisa... Thinking about everything he had lost crushed his heart against his chest.

I'm sorry. I'm so sorry.

Daniel hung his head to hide his face as it twisted in sorrow. His chest shuddered as he inhaled.

Eva had begun quietly humming again, but he had never heard the tune before. He found it strangely soothing, but instead of helping him bury his sadness, her song gently coaxed it out of him until he sobbed uncontrollably.

Reflexively, Daniel wrapped his arms around Eva as he cried, startling her. She stood frozen for a moment, arms held stiffly at her sides, looking down at the naked boy crying over her shoulder, but then she gently wrapped one arm around his waist and placed one hand behind his head, firmly pressing it against her shoulder. And she continued to hum as they swayed gently from side to side.

When Eva finished washing Daniel, she dressed him again with a fresh tunic and escorted him to his sleeping quarters.

"This will be your room for the next few weeks. No one will disturb you here," Eva explained, gesturing for Daniel to enter the room.

Daniel nodded and went in. The room was plain and undecorated, with no windows. In the corner was a single bed with an adjacent table. An unlit oil lamp sat on the table and someone had left him a plain brown blanket with a simple pillow at the head of the bed. Daniel walked over to it and sat down, looking at Eva.

"You should sleep. I have to speak with Uma, the high priestess, but I'll come back soon. Ariel and I will come find you for meals and to make sure you're comfortable. You met Ariel at the door. She's actually a softie, but you'd never know it."

Daniel considered this for a moment and then nodded before laying down.

"Sleep well," Eva said.

Daniel closed his eyes as the door closed and fell asleep before Eva's footsteps faded completely down the hall.

CHAPTER 8

DAUGHTERS
OF THE MOON

The busy sounds of the day transitioned to quiet as the temple wound down for the evening. Ariel had always enjoyed the late afternoon patrol. It was usually uneventful, and it gave her a chance to take a breath and reflect.

Ariel caught sight of Eva walking towards her. Eva's hand twitched purposefully as she approached, communicating a brief message to Ariel: 'dog' and 'smell'.

"Did you just call me a smelly bitch?" Ariel said, resisting a grin

"I didn't hear anything," Eva smirked. "Maybe it was Nina."

"*Nina* isn't even in this wing of the temple," Ariel said, while her fingers furiously signed out 'boat', 'raider' and 'sex'.

"Hey! *You're* a dirty pirate hooker," Eva replied.

Ariel broke into a giggle. "I never said dirty."

"It was implied."

"Pirate hookers are people, too."

"I guess you would know."

"You bitch!" Ariel shouted as she attempted to swat at Eva.

Eva dodged before Ariel could touch her.

"Ohhh, too slow." Eva giggled, making a face.

Ariel seized the moment to slap her arm and run away.

"Hey!" Eva shouted, chasing after her. The girls ran down the hall, staves in hand, dodging and weaving around the few temple slaves that were still milling around. Ariel made a face at Eva over her shoulder and suddenly found herself deflected backward onto the ground, sitting beside her staff.

"Should you girls be running down the halls?" Azra asked, staring down at Ariel.

"You could have moved aside, so I didn't bounce off of you," Ariel muttered.

"Excuse me?" Azra said.

"You could at least help me up," Ariel said.

Azra rolled his eyes before begrudgingly extending his hand.

Ariel instead stood up quickly and brushed herself off.

"Don't worry, I got it," she said, picking up her staff.

"Excellent," Azra said flatly. "Since I have you here, maybe you can help me track someone down. I'm looking for a boy."

"We don't do that here, but you're welcome to leave and never come back," Ariel said.

"Watch your tone, girl," Azra sneered.

"I don't have time for this," Ariel said, attempting to push past him.

"Wait," Azra said, grabbing her arm.

Ariel shook herself out immediately and glared.

Azra exhaled loudly and continued. "This boy is my travelling companion. He came with me from Sippar and he's injured. His name is Daniel. I'm wondering if you may have come across him today. I know Eva has a penchant for adopting strays."

"That she does," Ariel said, as she exchanged glances with Eva.

No, Eva signalled.

Ariel turned back to Azra, arms crossed. "What does this boy look like?"

"Light brown hair, blue eyes. A little shorter than you. His hands are injured."

Try missing.

"Nope. Never seen him. Why are you travelling across the empire with an injured boy, anyway?"

"The king summoned me. I will not explain myself any further. Just make sure—"

"No, of course. It all makes sense. The king summoned you and your first choice of travel companion is a gimp boy, because of your deep, spiritual need to help vulnerable young boys wherever you go. It all checks out."

"You insolent—" Azra seethed, moving toward Ariel.

"Azra," Eva said gently grasping his arm with a smile, "Ariel seems to have gathered an appropriate description from you and I realize you're worried about this boy— what was his name?"

"Daniel."

"Daniel. Right. So how about first thing tomorrow? I will do a patrol around the city, and if I run into a boy matching Daniel's description, I will send word to the palace. Alright?"

Azra breathed deeply, recomposing himself. "Yes, I suppose that will be acceptable."

Another temple guard now stood at attention beside Ariel. "Fatima, please escort high priest Azra out of the temple."

The guard gestured for Azra to lead the way.

"Goodnight, Eva. Ariel." Azra nodded to each as he left.

Ariel waited for Azra to travel out of earshot before letting out a disgusted grunt.

"He's a dick," Eva whispered, glancing over her shoulder as she led Ariel away, "but sometimes diplomacy can go a long way."

"So can my staff."

"I'm sure Uma would love to deal with that mess."

"I'm sure she would appreciate my decision-making process."

Eva nudged Ariel playfully. "Great! You can tell Uma all about it when we go see her."

Ariel shot a questioning look at Eva.

"We've been summoned."

It had been almost a week since Sin had met Miriam. He thought about her every day and what they might talk about—if he ever built up the nerve. Sin knew he was being a coward, but he didn't know how to approach her again.

Technically, she approached me that first time.

Sin considered trying to recreate the situation again, but he didn't know how to do that without accidentally hurting her.

Even if I did, I don't know where she'll be. It's not like I can just wait in the kitchen. Or just outside of it... can I? No, I can't. Well, technically I could... but—No! What am I thinking? That's weird. Don't be weird.

"Ugh," Sin groaned as he lay on his bed.

"What?" Ashur said, entering the room. "What are you thinking about?"

"Nothing."

"Yeah... That sounds like something you'd do," Ashur smirked, draping himself over a nearby armchair.

Sin sighed and rolled over to face his brother. "Hey, have—do you ever, like, uh, talk to girls?"

"Do I talk to girls?" Ashur said, raising an eyebrow. "You mean like, do I walk up to random girls and have a conversation?"

"I mean, like... are there any girls you like?"

"Well, yeah, I like girls, but here at the palace, there aren't really any girls I'd try to talk to. Unless we had like a hot serving girl or something, I guess."

Sin narrowed his eyes at Ashur, making him tilt his head.

"Look, I don't really get to talk to girls... like that," Ashur admitted. "I mean, there was a girl at that big banquet dad had last year, but I froze and messed it all up. I never really got a chance to talk to her."

"Ah. Ok, never mind then." Sin rolled onto his back again.

Ashur thought for a moment. "Man, were you asking me like, 'how do you talk to girls?'"

"Yeah, I guess, but you basically said you don't know."

"Yeah, I don't know. Sorry," Ashur said. "Is there a girl you like?"

"... it doesn't matter, I was just wondering if you knew how, you know, in case."

"Ok," Ashur said, unconvinced. "Anyway, it's basically time for our lessons, but Shumu has some sort of business with dad, so he sent me to get you while he does whatever he's doing. We should get going."

"Alright," Sin said, rolling off the bed.

The boys travelled through the halls of the royal living quarters, passed the guard barracks, and continued into a large courtyard.

The courtyard bustled with people. Over the years, Sin had seen his share of the foreign officials and palace administrators that often met here to discuss politics or to wait for an audience with the king. Today, an enormous crowd accumulated outside the northwest corner, near the main entrance to the throne room.

"There are a lot of people here today," he said, nodding toward the crowd.

"There are a lot of people here every day," Ashur replied.

The boys crossed the courtyard to the northeast corner, passed a guardroom, and followed a long hallway into a large ballroom.

"Shumu wants us to meet him in the library," Ashur told him as they entered.

"Alright."

Three entrances lead to the smaller rectangular dining hall that paralleled the ballroom's north wall. The kitchen and the library both had entrances off of the dining hall. As the boys passed through it, Sin strained to peek into the kitchen from a distance before following Ashur into the library.

The library was almost the same size as the dining room. Sturdy wooden shelves lined the walls with clay tablets and stacked rows of smaller scroll racks filled the spaces in between.

"I guess Shumu's not here yet." Ashur walked toward a table in the centre of the room.

"Well, I'm going to get a snack then. I'll be right back," Sin said.

"I'll come with you."

"No," Sin said hastily, "I mean, someone should stay here in case Shumu comes."

"... I guess." Ashur eyed Sin with suspicion.

"I'll be right back. I'll bring you something."

Ashur sighed. "Ok, just hurry."

Sin worked his way back to the dining room and poked his head into the kitchen.

She's not here. Should I go?

"What are you looking for?" a voice asked from behind.

Sin yelped and whipped around with his arms held up defensively. Miriam giggled and shook her head as she walked past him into the kitchen and unloaded several heavy bags from her arms onto a countertop in the centre of the room.

"Nothing! I'm looking for nothing," Sin said.

"So... then, what are you doing here?" Miriam repeated with a smirk.

"I—I was going to grab a snack."

"Ah. So, you weren't looking for me?" Miriam asked.

"Well, I hoped—I mean, I wasn't sure if you would even be here."

"I didn't think you were going to talk to me again after you ran away." Miriam put a hand on her hip, looking him up and down.

"Ran aw—oh, right."

You're an idiot. Why did you run?

"Yeah, I wasn't running," Sin lied.

"You weren't running?" Miriam asked, frowning.

"Yeah... I just remembered I had to do something important."

"Okay?"

"Yeah, and then I left."

"Ok." Miriam began clearing and organizing her counter space for some kind of baking task.

"But, like, very fast."

"And then you left very fast."

"Uhh, yep." Sin nodded.

"That's called *running*," Miriam said, walking past him to add some ingredients from a shelf into a bowl.

"Ah, yeah. I guess that's... true," Sin mumbled.

Miriam walked past him again and placed the bowl on the countertop.

"So, you never tried to talk to me like you said you were going to," she said, carefully pouring flour from one of the bags on the counter into the bowl. "It's been a week. What happened?"

"Well, I didn't really know how to find you." Sin rubbed the back of his head.

"You knew I work in the kitchen though."

"Yeah, but I didn't want to wait for you all the time in and around the kitchen. I thought it would be weird."

Miriam stopped pouring flour and nodded thoughtfully. "You're right, that would've been weird."

Yes! Good!

"*But*," Miriam said, inspecting a nearby pitcher before filling it with water, "technically, lurking by the door is how you found me today. Right?"

"I—I guess so," Sin said.

"So," Miriam said, setting the pitcher of water down on the countertop, "you waited a week to avoid being a weirdo, but in the end, you decided to be a weirdo anyhow—"

"Well, not—"

"—just for a chance to talk to me," Miriam finished with a smirk, turning to face him.

What?

"Yes...?" Sin replied uncertainly.

Miriam's smirk grew into a smile and she looked away, trying to hide the redness in her cheeks. "Ok, weirdo. Come over here. Have you ever made bread before?"

Sin shook his head and walked toward her.

"Ok, let me show you what I'm doing," Miriam said.

Ariel and Eva arrived at Uma's sleeping quarters just after her servants had redressed her and they waited patiently by the door.

After a few moments, the temple slaves dispersed and Uma emerged from an opaque privacy screen across the room in a simple plum nightgown that clung flatteringly against her buxom frame and accented her midnight skin. Uma's attendants had freshly braided her greying hair in an intricate style that whorled around her scalp and cascaded into a single thick tail resting over her shoulder.

"I heard Azra was in the building. Was there any trouble?" Uma asked, reclining on a nearby couch.

"No more than we expected," Eva said.

"Maybe slightly less than we expected," Ariel said.

"Good," Uma said.

"He will probably want to talk to you tomorrow about Daniel's—the boy's—whereabouts," Eva said.

Uma smirked. "I'm sure he will. For now, keep *Daniel's* location guarded. Ariel, make sure the other girls understand that they have never seen this boy."

"Yes, mother," Ariel said.

"Was there anything else?" Uma asked.

Both Eva and Ariel shook their heads in unison.

"Then I think it's time for you both to get some sleep—actually, Ariel, I have something important I need to discuss with you if you could wait a moment. Eva, you may go."

Eva exchanged a questioning look with Ariel, who appeared equally confused.

Talk later, Eva signed as subtly as possible.

"Goodnight, Mother," Eva said, closing the door behind her.

Uma patted the seat beside her. "Come sit with me."

Ariel came over and sat beside her. Uma angled herself to face Ariel and clasped her hands.

"When I was young, I lived in a foreign country where our neighbours had invaded us for over 100 years. During that time, we only knew peace for short periods while we were subjugated under foreign rule. Finally, my people found support in one of the most unlikely places—Assyria. They had always considered us a vassal state, but they never paid much attention to our politics as long as no one threatened their sovereignty over our lands. My father was the one that finally convinced the king to end the instability and name a ruler. Although he didn't respect our right to govern ourselves, King Ashur's father respected our ancient royal bloodlines and installed my father as a governor of the region. And although my father wanted to avoid war with King Ashur, his new appointment gave him an opportunity he couldn't ignore. My father was a great man with many allies, and he believed that we should have the right to rule ourselves independently. It did not take long for my father and his allies to make those dreams a reality. Unfortunately, our neighbours to the east and south still saw us as weak and began positioning themselves to invade my country once more. My father, now the pharoah, knew he had to strengthen his position with these neighbouring countries as quickly as possible to avoid any further bloodshed. So, he sent my sister to Thebes in the south, and me here, to Nineveh, each to become a high priestess in the capital of a neighbouring nation. My father hoped that by doing this, he could finally establish our country as a strong *independent* nation, capable of *choosing* our allies —and it worked."

"Okay, why are you telling me this?"

"Ariel, I have received some... interesting news from your father."

"Okay?"

"To strengthen his relationship with Media, your father has promised you to Cyaxares' son Astyages."

"... What? How could he just do that without even telling me?"

"He believed he had no other option that would secure lasting peace and independence for your people."

"Hmm. Just like your dad. So, it's like that I guess," Ariel said.

"I understand what it's like to have another person make important decisions about your life. Nothing makes it okay, but knowing you will make hundreds of other people's lives significantly better makes it a little easier to accept."

"Yeah, well, *you would know*. It's a good thing I conveniently found out how similar we are just a minute ago, otherwise I'd be pissed about how completely fucked up this is."

"Ariel, I'm not your enemy."

Ariel breathed deeply.

"Ugh, I know I'm sorry. I just—this isn't something he would have just decided in the moment. It's not like he didn't know how I would react once I found out, either. Which, I'm realizing, is probably why he asked you to be the one that tells me." Ariel sighed.

Uma draped an arm around Ariel and gently squeezed while Ariel laid her head on Uma's shoulder.

"Listen, life is almost never fair—especially for us. Men constantly decide for us and try to speak for us. They forget we make strong, intelligent allies if they don't treat us like servants and commodities. What Kandalanu did wasn't fair, but there are worse fates than marrying the heir to a powerful country."

"You're right." Ariel sighed.

"You know," Uma said, "Astyages is also supposed to be good looking too."

"Really?" Ariel asked.

"I'm actually not sure. It's probably too soon to tell. He's still only a little boy."

"So, you heard it from Azra?"

"Come on now." Uma smiled down at her.

Ariel chuckled. After a moment, she looked up at Uma. "Do you think he's an asshole?"

"Who, Azra?"

"No. Well, yes, Azra—of course, Azra—but no, Astyages."

"Astyages? I told you, he's only a small boy."

"Right. Sorry," Ariel said.

Uma sighed. "Don't be. I heard he actually *is* a bit of an asshole."

"Oh, my god! You called a *child* an asshole. You actually said *asshole*, that's crazy. Am I dying?"

"Laugh while you can." Uma squeezed Ariel a little.

"Right. Because my future husband's an asshole and a child."

"Aren't they all?" Both burst into laughter that settled into a comfortable silence.

"You would've been a good mother, you know."

"I like to think I *am* a good Mother."

"Tch, you know what I mean." Ariel sighed.

Uma chuckled. "I know what you mean, but somehow, I feel like I'm exactly where I'm supposed to be."

CHAPTER 9

SNAKES AND LADDERS

Three years later.

B eads of sweat dotted Daniel's forehead and rolled along the side of his face. In a fluid motion, he wiped the sweat away with his bicep and slipped out of the leather strappings that enabled him to use a wooden stirring spoon, leaving it on the counter.

This stew seems to be done, assuming it didn't burn to the bottom of the pot.

He walked away from the stove, toward a large, polished countertop in the centre of the room.

The countertop had a few jars of dried spices strewn across and a large, covered bowl near the middle. Daniel cleared the jars away and then dumped some flour on the counter before returning the bag upright and setting it aside with practiced ease. Daniel then pushed the lid off the bowl, revealing a fluffy ball of rising dough.

Pulling the bowl towards him, he slid his wrist into the leather straps of a modified knife lying nearby and set to work, slicing off a portion of dough. In one motion, Daniel laid the knife back on the table and slid easily out of the straps, allowing him to pinch the sliced dough onto the table between his wrists.

Eva entered the kitchen and smiled as she watched Daniel knead and manipulate the dough adeptly with his wrists and forearms.

"Where's my bread?" Eva said, giving him a slight shove as she approached him. "Oh, you're getting pretty good at that, eh? What's your secret, huh? Who taught you this amazing skill?"

Daniel shrugged his shoulders and then shot a smile toward Eva.

"Yeah, you know who did," Eva said, walking over to the stove. "Hey, what's going on with this stew?" she asked, giving it a stir.

Daniel got up and joined her, repeatedly looking into the pot and back at her.

"What...?" Eva asked.

Daniel gestured into the pot, causing a few flakes of flour to float into the stew.

Eva looked more closely into the pot before turning back toward Daniel. "I don't—" Eva stopped mid-sentence.

Daniel had wiped flour from his wrist onto her nose and spun around behind her, laughing, before she could react.

"I can't believe you did that! Just you wait—" Eva said, lunging toward Daniel, but Daniel ducked and wove around her, allowing him to get behind her again.

Daniel laughed.

"Oh, you're so going to get it when I catch you." Eva grinned, running after him.

Daniel scrambled around the countertop where he had been kneading the bread, positioning it between them. Eva chased Daniel once around the table, but he kept his distance.

They were at a stalemate. Daniel stood, knees bent, ready to spring in either direction, while Eva attempted to fake him out at random intervals.

"Who do you think even taught you those moves?" Eva said.

Daniel straightened up and pointed behind her. Eva narrowed her eyes and spun around to see Ariel standing by the door, smirking at them.

"What are you guys up to?" Ariel asked, walking towards them.

Eva crossed her arms and glanced at Daniel. "You should ask him. This little dick thinks he's funny. Don't you?"

Daniel made an expression of shock and insult that cracked almost immediately, freeing a brief chuckle.

Ariel laughed. "Yeah, he definitely does. Anyway, Uma sent me to get you both."

"Okay... did she say why?"

"No, all she said is that she needed to talk to the three of us alone. It just seemed important."

"Weird. Well, we can't just leave the bread and stew like this."

"Nina should come any time to finish things up here. It'll be fine," Ariel said.

"Okay... that sounds important. I guess we shouldn't keep Uma waiting."

"So, Ashur, when are you going to introduce me to your girlfriend?" Miriam asked, leaning forward. The regal purple couch where she sat lay parallel facing its twin, with Ashur reclined across it. Both couches sprawled lengthwise along an enormous rug that centred the polished stone floors of the royal living quarters.

"You mean *us*, right?" Sin asked, glancing at her back from his position beside her.

Miriam leaned back into the couch, where Sin had his arm draped, and gave him a level stare. "I meant *me*. You don't care about who he's dating.... *do you?*"

"Well, I mean, he is my broth—"

Miriam broke into a wide smile and gave him a playful shove.

"Just so you know, you're the worst," he said, leaning in for a kiss.

Miriam reciprocated and put her head on his chest.

Ashur smiled at them and rolled his eyes, resting his gaze on the ornate wooden carvings and tapestries affixed to the walls. Even after all of these years, and despite the fact every room and hallway was similarly decorated, he still found it all very...distracting. Although, at times like this, the distraction was hardly unwelcome.

"So?" Miriam said, continuing to stare at Ashur expectantly.

"So, what?" Ashur replied.

"So, you're obviously holding out on us," Miriam said plainly.

"How do you figure?" Ashur smirked.

"Well, you're way less of a weirdo than this guy, and he did pretty well for himself," Miriam said.

"I *did* do pretty well for myself." Sin chuckled.

"Hey," Miriam said, glancing up at him, "could you focus here?"

Sin smiled and shook his head.

"So, spill it. Where have you been hiding her? When do I get to meet her?"

"Never," Ashur said bashfully. "She doesn't exist."

Miriam's expression told him she was unconvinced. "Yeah. *Okay*. Seriously, when?"

"When, what? I told you there's no girl."

"That's disappointing—and not just because I expect more of you. It's been just the three of us for way too long. I feel outnumbered."

"So, you want me to get a girlfriend... for you?" Ashur smirked.

"Actually, yes. That is what I want. But she has to be hot. I want a hot girlfriend. Sin, you don't mind if I have a hot girlfriend, right?"

"Well—" Sin rubbed the back of his head and turned bright red.

"See? He doesn't mind. So, where's my hot girlfriend, Ashur? Where?"

Ashur chuckled. "You're so dramatic. I'll tell you what, as soon as I get a girlfriend, I'll give you first crack at her."

"I'm going to hold you to that," Miriam said, crossing her arms.

Ashur sighed. "The truth is, with father being so sick, Shumu has really been increasing my workload. He says that he wants me to be ready... it's just a lot right now. Honestly, I don't know if I *can* be ready."

"I don't think any king is actually ever ready when they take the throne," Sin said. "Just look at those records in the library. On paper, sure, there's usually a plan for succession, but mentally? Emotionally? Our father and his father both ascended after *their* fathers died tragically in battle. You can't really prepare for that."

"That's true," Ashur said.

"But," Sin said, raising his finger, "one thing they all have in common is strong advisors supporting them while they adjust. You have that. You have both me and Shumu. You also have almost the entire court supporting you, which rarely happens."

"Yeah, I guess. That's surprising though, since some of them still can't tell us apart," Ashur said.

The three of them laughed.

"Listen, you will be a good king. Trust yourself."

"Thanks, but if you ever want to wear the big boy robes and switch places for a couple of days, you just say the word, *King Ashur*," Ashur said with a wink.

"No deal," Miriam said flatly. "Where he goes, I go, and I don't want *that* kind of reputation."

"How do you know we haven't already secretly swapped identities before?" Ashur said.

Miriam looked between them. "Wait, you haven't, have you?"

Ashur looked at his brother, suppressing a grin. "You never told her?"

Miriam looked up at Sin. "You wouldn't."

Sin smirked down at her with a shrug.

"You perverts!" she yelled, throwing a pillow at Ashur and slapping Sin repeatedly.

"We're kidding!" he yelped, shielding himself with his arms. "I swear, we never did that! I give, I give!"

"You're still perverts," she said, throwing one last backhand into Sin's chest. "You better not have swapped."

"We didn't." Sin smirked.

"You better not have," Miriam said, pointing up at him.

The smells of cooking meats and spices wafted into the room, causing Ashur's stomach to growl.

"I wonder what we're having for dinner tonight," he said.

"Crap. I should have been helping prepare the meal. I'm super late, I have to go." Miriam stood up and then she leaned down to Sin and whispered, "I'm sorry," as she kissed him.

"It's fine, go." Sin smiled.

"I love you," Miriam whispered. "Bye Ashur," she shouted as she ran out of the room. Suddenly, she poked her head back into the room and pointed at Ashur. "Don't forget, she has to be hot. And interesting. I only deserve the best."

"Got it. I'll get us a hot, interesting girlfriend. Any preferred flavours?" Ashur asked.

"Flav—ugh, pervert. You ruined it," she said in disgust. "I'm leaving."

"Bye, Miriam!" Ashur called after her.

Sin chuckled from his seat. "I can't believe you almost convinced her we swapped identities without telling her."

"Well, after all that girlfriend talk, I couldn't let her win the *entire* conversation."

"*Win the conversation*, eh?" Sin shook his head. "I wouldn't worry, though. I'm sure when things calm down for you, you'll meet a girl like Miriam."

"Ha, no thanks, brother. I'm pretty sure you found yourself the most ridiculous girl in the world."

"Yeah, but she's my ridiculous girl, you know?"

"I'm really happy for you. I'm glad you ran into her."

"Me too," Sin said contentedly. "I think I might marry that girl."

"You should marry that girl. Just remember that if I come to the wedding and you *say* there's going to be a banquet, and then there *isn't*," Ashur paused dramatically, "that will be the second time your loyal brother had to starve for this relationship."

Sin chuckled. "I've seen you eat. You don't starve for anyone."

"You make it sound like I'm taking the food out of *your* mouth."

"Put it this way, the food never has the chance to *get* to my mouth."

"Oh, then let me make you a sandwich right now... made of my knuckles!" Ashur shouted as he ran and dove at Sin on the bed.

Sin rolled out of the way and onto his feet. "You think you're fast?"

Then Sin mimicked the dive maneuver Ashur had just launched at him.

Ashur evaded as easily as his brother had a moment ago. "You think you've got better moves than me?"

Sin jumped off the bed to face off against him. "I guess we'll see," he said as they circled each other, both anticipating the other's attack.

Ashur stopped circling once he blocked Sin's path to the door.

"What are you going to do?" he goaded. "Where are those moves?" and then faked a lunge that caused Sin to move back a step.

Sin countered by pushing off toward Ashur's right side, but stopped short, allowing him to evade his brother's grasp, spin, and then dive to Ashur's left. Sin landed into a roll, using his momentum to stand and keep running without stopping.

Holy shit, what was that? Ashur thought, turning to see Sin jog down the hall.

"Let's see you try that again!" Ashur yelled, chasing after him.

118

"Eva, Ariel, Daniel," Uma began, welcoming each of them with a gentle smile, "thank you for coming so quickly."

"Mother, what's this about?" Eva asked.

Uma paused while a novice attendee poured a hot cup of tea nearby and then signalled for her to leave the room.

"I would like you and Daniel to escort Ariel to Babylon with an entourage of your sisters, to prepare for her first meeting with Astyages," Uma said, sipping the tea.

"That doesn't make sense. The meeting is months away. And why am I bringing an entourage of temple slaves?"

"Bo Dancers," Uma corrected.

"Wha—? Bo Dancers? You're serious. How many?" Ariel asked.

Uma took another sip and answered quietly, without making eye contact. "All of them."

Eva and Daniel stared in shock at Uma before sharing a glance between themselves.

"All—wha—All of them? Why? Who is going to protect the temple? Who is going to protect you?" Ariel insisted.

"This is the Capital, I will be fine," Uma said, holding the cup in her lap.

"No, something else is going on here," Ariel said, pacing.

"Ariel, listen, I just need you to trust me," Uma said, reaching out to her.

"Wait, you're scared. Something big is about to happen," Ariel said, and then her face smoothed with realization. "Shit, it's King Ashur. He's about to die."

Uma paused thoughtfully and sipped her tea, speaking into her cup. "You're right. The king has been very sick for a long time—"

"Well, we've been poisoning him for years," Ariel said.

"Yes. Well, regardless, he does not have much time left. He could literally leave us any day now, and when a king dies, there is always a period of chaos before they crown a new king and he earns the trust of his people. You haven't seen it, but the streets become dangerous—even during the day," Uma said.

"No, something still doesn't add up. If it's so dangerous, then why are you sending me away with an army of Bo Dancers?" Ariel asked.

"Azra," Eva said quietly, stepping forward to meet Ariel's gaze. "It's Azra you're afraid of, isn't it, Mother?"

Uma averted her eyes but stayed silent.

"Holy fuck, it is," Ariel said. "But why? Why are you so afraid of him?"

Uma set her tea on the table beside her. "Ariel, listen to me. Azra is powerful. I'm certain he destroyed Sippar, and I can't be sure of what he will do after Ashur is dead. If the plan I developed with your father is successful, then everything will be fine, and I will call you all to return to the temple. But I won't gamble with your lives."

"And what about the temple slaves we leave behind? Those girls will be defenceless," Ariel said.

"I have already sent many of them to other temples under the guise of deliveries or other errands. Only a few at a time—I can't evacuate the entire temple at once because it would be too obvious. I'm trying to save as many lives as I can in the best way I know how."

"And what about your life? I don't want you to die." Tears rolled down Ariel's scowling face.

"I don't want to die either and I'm going to do everything I can to prevent that, but the most important thing to me is that all my girls are safe. I can't keep myself alive if I'm also protecting all of you. Go to Babylon. Be safe, please. I will send a message to you when it's time to come home again." Uma wiped away a few of her own stray tears.

"Yes, Mother." Eva choked on the words.

"Yes Mother," Ariel said, "but I am taking the rest of the temple slaves to Babylon, and they are leaving tonight."

"No, Ariel, it's too risky." Uma pleaded.

"You want me to go to Babylon? Fine, but I'm not leaving any defenceless girls behind for that monster to do... who even knows what? No, the temple slaves can leave tonight—Nina can lead them—and I'll take the Bo Dancers with me in the morning as my official entourage."

Uma nodded. "Alright. Nina will leave tonight. I'll leave you to brief her at your discretion, Ariel."

"Yes, Mother."

Walking around the palace always made Azra unusually sentimental. Even now, after three years of walking the same halls, he hadn't become numb to it. Every corner held a memory of his childhood—his last truly happy memories—and Ashur was often a part of them. Something inside of Azra nagged at him incessantly, urging him to feel something for Ashur.

It was another life. I can't allow myself to be distracted by meaningless illusions of a world I was never really a part of.

Admittedly, some of the familiarity and closeness had resurfaced between himself and Ashur, but it differed from when they were children. Ashur was the king, and he was only a physician, and the lines did not blur between their relative stations.

You were always going to die this way, my brother. It's only by a strange twist of fate that I happen to be here to witness it.

Azra approached the door and knocked, waiting patiently for the king's voice. After a long wait, Azra finally heard a voice shout, "Come," but it was a young male rather than the king.

Azra entered the room and saw both princes, Ashur and Sin, sitting on the bed on either side of the king. The boys' bodyguard, a retired general, Shumu, stood at the edge of the room watching over them.

"Azra—" the king croaked dryly, triggering a long coughing fit. "Azra, please... could you give us a minute? I'll have them send you in as soon as we are finished."

"Yes, my lord." Azra bowed and left the room.

Azra waited in the hall.

It won't be long now, maybe a day or two at most. He's probably saying goodbye to his sons right now.

Before long, the door opened, revealing Sin and young Ashur. Grief and emotional strain were plainly visible on their faces. Shumu nodded to Azra and followed closely behind the boys, scanning for any obvious threats ahead.

Azra let himself into the room and closed the door behind him. "Lord, are you ready for your treatment?"

"Of course, Azra. Please, help me sit upright."

Azra carefully helped Ashur sit up and helped him sip the solution he had prepared for his nightly treatment. Once Azra realized the cause of the king's illness, Azra had planned for his "treatments" to contain an additional dose of poison to help speed along the deterioration. Despite himself, Azra instead developed a solution that genuinely eased the king's suffering.

"I am sorry that my treatments haven't been more effective, my lord."

"No, please, your treatments are probably the only reason I have lasted as long as I have."

Azra nodded. A short chuckle burst out of Azra, breaking the silence. "Do you remember when we were children—"

"Azra, I've told you before. I can't talk about our childhood. It's... it's just too painful." Ashur broke into a long cough.

A pained twitch arced across Azra's face and then disappeared just as quickly. "Ah, yes. I'm sorry, my lord, it was thoughtless of me."

"I think I would like to rest now. Please leave me."

"Goodnight, lord," Azra said.

Nightfall had come and the darkness that spread over the land was thick and heavy. To Ashur, it felt like the setting sun had allowed the weight of the universe to collapse upon its people as it sunk into the horizon.

Why did I come out here?

Shumu's voice rang out in his mind with the answer:

Your father has summoned you and your brother. The king believes he might not last the night.

Ashur had thought the fresh air and sunset would give him peace of mind, but they did not. The view from the terrace had only darkened his perspective.

... he might not last the night. I guess now is as good a time as any.

Ashur entered the palace and made his way to the king's chambers.

Soon to be my chambers, I guess.

He met up with Sin and Shumu in the hallway in front of the doors to his father's room.

"Where's Miriam?"

"I haven't been able to find her all day," Sin said.

"This isn't really the place for a royal consort, my lord," Shumu said gently.

Sin nodded, staring at the floor.

Sorry, brother. I want to reach out to you, but I barely have enough strength for myself.

Horror gripped Ashur at the thought of breaking down in front of his father.

Shumu trained me to be his successor my entire life. A strong leader can't be seen sobbing like a child. I want you to know that when—when it happens, I won't let you down.

"Are you ready?" Shumu asked, searching each of their faces. The boys nodded, prompting him to open the door.

"My lord, your sons have arrived," Shumu announced.

"Ah," he said, briefly interrupted by a cough, "Ah, thank you. Please, let them in."

Shumu bowed and stepped aside, allowing the boys to enter.

"My sons... my beautiful sons. Please, sit with me. We have much to discuss."

The king patted the bed on either side of him. As the boys sat, King Ashur grasped their hands and looked them over.

"It is so good to see you, you've both grown into strong, handsome young men."

"Thank you, father," Ashur whispered.

Sin, wiping a tear, moved his lips to echo his brother, but no sound came out.

"Your—" The king choked and started again, struggling against another cough and the flood of emotion threatening to bare itself from just behind his eyes. "Your mother would be so proud of you."

The king grimaced at each of the boys again and patted their clasped hands on either side of him, allowing the moment to stretch.

After a few minutes, he cleared his throat and took on a serious expression. "I've summoned you both here to inform you of your roles after my passing."

He might not last the night.

Ashur took a deep breath and squeezed his eyes as tight as he could until his father spoke again.

"Ashur, as you are already aware, I have chosen you as my rightful successor upon the throne of Assyria. I have left you with a heavy burden. This Empire was built by my father, and my father's father, and so on, going back to its foundation. But now, as we speak, our enemies have begun to circle, and our allies threaten rebellion. I had hoped to leave you a peaceful nation, but instead, I must leave you with a nation blanketed by unrest and turmoil. I ask you, my son, to draw upon the strength of your ancestors to build and protect this great empire as we have for generations. I ask you to bring peace to our people so that you may pass to your son, the nation I had intended to pass onto you."

"I will, father," Ashur said.

"I know you will, my son, and you will not be alone. I have asked Shumu to act as Regent until your eighteenth birthday, at which time you will fully assume the throne. Under his guidance, I am absolutely confident you will become the king I hoped you would be."

"Thank you, father," Ashur said, as his face twisted and strained against him.

A loud knock came from the door. The king attempted to call for the visitor to enter, but a coughing fit overtook him and lasted several minutes. When he had finished, he gestured for Ashur to call the visitor in while he composed himself.

"Come," Ashur called.

Ashur and Sin both turned when Azra entered the room. Ashur noted he appeared to take in the scene as soon as he arrived, but still seemed distant from it.

How does he remain so unaffected?

The king coughed. "Azra, please... could you please give us a minute? I'll have them send you in as soon as we are finished."

"Yes, my lord," Azra said, bowing as he left the room.

It's time for father's treatment. We shouldn't stay much longer.

"Sin," the king said, "you have grown into as capable a man as your brother. Although I realize you have no desire for the throne, I must ask that you rule Babylon in the name of your brother, as my brother once did for me, and my uncle did for his brother. These will be difficult times for Ashur. He will need your wisdom to advise him and your strength to help protect our borders. I ask that you travel to Babylon and train there under Kandalanu until your eighteenth birthday, at which time you will assume the Babylonian throne."

Sin nodded. "Yes... I will do this for you, father."

"Also, I understand that you have become very close to a young servant girl."

Sin looked up at him in shock, causing the king to laugh.

"I *am* the king, boy."

"Uh-y-yes. Yes, father."

"Do you love her?"

"Yes. I do, father."

"If I have learned anything worthwhile from your mother, it is that during your life, you will love many people to varying degrees, but true love may only come once. Search your heart, and if you truly love this girl, make her your queen in Babylon. Do this knowing you have made your father proud."

"I will, father." Sin choked.

"I am more proud of you—both of you—than words can express. When I am gone, in your times of deepest doubt, remember that my only regret is being unable to spend more time watching you grow into the men you have become."

The boys nodded and sat quietly with their father for a few moments until Shumu broke the silence. "We should go so the king can get some rest."

The brothers walked, lost in thought, allowing Shumu to guide them through the hallways to their rooms.

"You need to get some rest tonight. Anything can happen over the next few days and you need to be ready," Shumu said.

When Ashur finally got into bed, he had intended to sleep, but instead, hours slipped by as he thought about his father.

I promise I won't let you down.

His father's words carouselled in his mind.

... Draw upon the strength of your ancestors to build and protect this great empire...

What does that mean?

Ashur tried to remember anything he could about the kings that came before him.

Why didn't I pay attention? Sin would've paid attention.

The itch to learn more bubbled up inside of him until he couldn't think about anything else.

I need to go to the library. It's almost morning anyhow. I'm definitely not getting any sleep tonight.

When Ashur reached the courtyard, the night wore an eerie quiet, aside from distant yelling or the odd animal call that rang out in the distance.

The heaviness from earlier still hung in the darkness and made him feel uneasy, so he hurried toward the ballroom entrance.

The distant yelling became louder and more intense with every step, but Ashur couldn't clearly make out what was being said until he entered the ballroom.

"Answer me! What were you doing?!" a man roared.

"I-I'm just a cook. I don't know anything," a girl sobbed.

Those voices... sound so familiar.

"Tell me!" the man boomed again. The girl only sobbed harder in reply.

Finally, Ashur turned a corner and found himself in the kitchen, staring at Miriam, crying on the floor as Shumu stood over her demanding answers.

"What's going on here?" Ashur demanded.

"This *traitor* was tampering with the king's food. I knew it was poison. I *knew* it, but I would have never imagined it was you," Shumu shouted at her in disgust.

Miriam pleaded between sobs. "Ashur! Please, Ashur, I don't know what he's talking about. I don't know about any poison. Believe me. You—You have to believe me...."

"I don't know, Shumu," Ashur said doubtfully. "How do you know it's a poison and not an ingredient you saw?"

"I've seen my share of poisons, and this," Shumu said, producing a small vial of liquid, "is a poison."

"I swear it's not. Ashur, please, it's not. You know me. I'm just a cook. You *know* me," Miriam said.

Father told Sin to marry this girl. She's been like family over the last three years. She loves Sin, she would never hurt him like this. I have to convince Shumu that she's telling the truth.

"Shumu, you said you definitely saw her pouring from the vial into father's bowl?" Ashur asked.

"Yes," Shumu answered.

"What kind of meal did you prepare for father's breakfast?"

"Porridge," Shumu replied before she could answer.

"Okay, so Miriam, you were making my father's porridge, right?"

"Uhh—well, yeah. Yes, I was."

"Okay, and so the vial was just filled with some sort of ingredient for it, right?"

"Yeah, I was just making porridge—"

"I believe you. Okay?"

"Okay," Miriam said, brushing hair out of her face and regaining some of her usual composure.

"So, what's in the vial?" Ashur asked.

"Umm... it's—it's just a seasoning blend," she said, clearing her throat. "It's just a few spices to give the porridge flavouring, so it's not so plain."

"Okay, that's a pretty reasonable explanation. Isn't it, Shumu?"

"Well, it would be, except this vial isn't filled with some fucking *seasoning blend!*" Shumu roared at her.

Miriam winced.

"You know what, if it has such a delicious flavour, why don't you eat some?"

"*What?*" Miriam said in shock.

"Come on Shumu, this is getting out of hand," Ashur said.

"No, I think it's time for a taste test." Shumu frantically scooped some porridge into a bowl.

"No! No, Ashur—" Miriam said.

"No, you said you're just a cook—" Shumu poured the contents of the vial into the bowl and stirred.

"No, I don't want to," she repeated.

"—and that this is just some *delicious seasoning*—" Shumu brought the bowl towards her, spoon in hand.

"No, Ashur, he's being crazy—" Miriam said, pushing away from him until her back pressed against the wall.

"—so have a bite of this delicious, *flavoured* porridge—" he said, holding the bowl within an inch of her face.

"No! I'm not going to."

"Why?" Shumu demanded.

"Um... Because you added way too much... it'll be gross. It won't taste right." Miriam's eyes darted between the bowl and Shumu.

"But it won't kill you, right? I mean, if it's just *spices*." Shumu leaned closer with the spoon held beside her mouth.

"Miriam," Ashur said carefully, "just eat it. If you eat the porridge, then we can prove this is just a misunderstanding."

"That's right Miriam, eat the fucking porridge. Show me how wrong I am."

A drawn-out silence blanketed the room.

"... I can't," she whispered finally.

"What was that?" Shumu asked, withdrawing the bowl and spoon from her face.

"I—I can't," Miriam said.

"What?" Ashur said in disbelief.

"I can't eat the porridge."

"... Because...?" Shumu prompted cruelly.

"Because," Miriam sighed, "it's poisoned."

"... From the vial?" Shumu asked.

Miriam nodded.

Ashur stood frozen in horror, unable to process what Miriam had just said.

"Three years. You lied to us for three years. You listened to us prepare ourselves for our father's death. Meanwhile, you were the cause all along. We thought of you as *family*. Sin was going to *marry* you. Did you even give a shit? Was all of it just a lie?"

"No, I care about your brother. I care about both of you—" she said.

"Then why? How? How could you do this?"

"I wanted to tell you so many times. I never expected things to go this way. I never thought I would care about him... but then I did. But by then, I was in too deep, and I had this job, but—"

"So, murdering our father, the king of the Assyrian Empire, was just a job to you?"

"No, that's not what I meant—"

"I know what you meant. It's pretty clear that you'll say whatever you have to say, and manipulate anyone you have to manipulate, to get what you want," Ashur said.

"No, it's not like that—" Miriam pleaded.

"You know what? Just save it for my father. You can explain everything to him."

"Wait, no! You can't," Miriam said.

Shumu grabbed her by the arm and dragged her to her feet. "We definitely can."

"But what about Sin?" Miriam asked.

"He can't be a part of this," Shumu said. "We don't know how he will react."

Ashur looked at Shumu in surprise but soon nodded in agreement as the realization washed over him.

I assumed he'd just be with us, because he's always with us, but Miriam's betrayal will be bigger to him. We don't know how he'll react. What if he took her side instead of ours? Will he try to help her escape? Would he fight us?

"I know... It'll be too difficult," Ashur said.

"He'll never forgive you!" Miriam said.

"Probably not, but you literally poisoned a king to death. You must be judged by a king, Miriam," Ashur said, and the three of them left the room.

"Good morning, lord," Azra said as he entered the bedroom. "I have your morning treatment."

"Excellent, Azra. Please, would you...?" Ashur asked, gesturing for his assistance.

Azra carefully helped him drink the liquid, which Ashur finished with a cough.

"Lord, as your physician, I would strongly advise you to settle any outstanding affairs."

"I appreciate your concern, Azra."

"If I may speak freely, lord?" Azra paused.

"Go on."

"These last few years, I have truly appreciated the time we have spent together. It has reawakened a lot of memories from... a happier time in my life. I would like to pledge myself to your sons as their guardian—as a token of my appreciation to you."

"Token of appreciation?" Ashur asked, arching an eyebrow slightly.

"For allowing me to experience, one last time, what it is to have a brother," Azra said.

"We are not brothers, Azra. Our mother was a whore and a disappointment, and your father was a traitor. You should not exist. That is why my father demanded that you become pledged to the temple. He wanted to erase you," he finished between coughs. "You are here, Azra, because I recognize you as a capable physician, nothing more. No, Shumu has always been the boys' guardian, and he will be their Regent-guardian when I pass."

Ashur's response took Azra completely aback.

We're... not brothers? But, I cared for you like a brother... didn't I?

Azra felt sick, and he could feel his chest tightening.

What is this feeling? I can't breathe.

Suddenly, the door burst open, allowing five guards to pour into the room, followed by young Ashur, Shumu, and a young girl Azra had never seen before.

"What is the meaning of this?" the king demanded weakly.

"Father, Shumu found this girl, Miriam, adding something to your porridge today. When Shumu confronted her, she said that it was a cooking ingredient, but refused to eat it," Ashur told his father.

Shumu thrust Miriam toward King Ashur. "Tell him what you told me."

Miriam cried and struggled against him. "I don't know what you're talking about. I don't know what he's talking about. Please let me go."

"Tell him what's in this vial!" Shumu roared.

"I don't know. I don't—" she repeated frantically.

"Tell him!"

"I really don't know. I really don't. Please. Please."

"Tell. Him," Shumu said, pulling her within an inch of his snarling face.

"Okay! Okay. Okay. Okay, I'll tell you. I'll tell you," Miriam sniffed, wiping her face. "It's... a poison."

"Poison? Where did you get such a thing?" the king asked.

Miriam searched each of their faces, the desperation plain on her own. Suddenly, her eyes glimmered with faint hope.

"It was him," she said, pointing towards Azra. "He said he would hurt me if I didn't do it. I swear, I had no choice. He said he'd kill my entire family."

Horrified shock spread across Azra's face as he looked between the girl and the king.

"All this time, it was you," the king croaked. "I should have known. I should have known a traitor's son would grow up to be a traitor."

As Azra processed the tangled scene around him, he suddenly felt the nagging demand for empathy inside of him flake away. Relief washed over his entire body, and he remembered what it was to be at peace once more.

A dark laugh burst from his lips that silenced the rest of the room.

"Young lady, you are a despicable liar, but somehow you were exactly what I needed."

Azra flicked his wrist in Miriam's direction, and her head twisted backwards with a loud snap before she fell to the ground. Then he gestured towards Shumu, forcing him to draw his sword. In seven fluid strikes, Shumu stabbed young Ashur in the heart, slit the king's throat open, and then killed all five guards. Shumu looked over the carnage, horrified and covered in blood.

"Hold on just a moment," Azra said calmly to Shumu before he yelled into the hallway. "Help! Guards! Someone, please! Shumu has killed the king and his son! Guards!"

Shumu stood frozen, unable to move.

"Just another moment," Azra said quietly as he calmly knelt on the bloody floor in front of Shumu.

Shumu raised his sword above his head as if to cleave Azra's skull. As soon as the first guards entered the doorway, Azra released his weave on Shumu and began whimpering and pleading for his life.

"Stop! Drop your sword!" a guard yelled, and then rushed toward Shumu.

Shumu dodged the attack and launched himself into the hallway, engaging a stream of guards as he ran. The guards in the room immediately chased after him.

Azra rose, calmly wiping his bloodied hands on his robes and appreciating the surrounding carnage.

I should have done this years ago. We could have skipped the poison entirely.

Chapter 10

Behold a White Horse

A riel's footsteps echoed as she walked, disturbing the empty halls with a lonely reminder of the bustling community that occupied this space only a few hours earlier.

It's sad seeing the temple become an empty shell like this, but it's better than leaving my sisters to die—or worse.

Ariel had made one more attempt to convince Uma to leave tonight with Nina's group, but Uma refused.

My place is here, Ariel, at the temple.

I hate leaving you behind, but you're not exactly letting me weigh in on this. I'm surprised you even agreed to let me evacuate the temple slaves. Obviously, you know this is the right thing to do.

Ariel had lived at the temple for nearly her entire life, and she had become one of Uma's personal attendants as a child. She knew how stubborn Uma could be once she had decided on a course of action.

Hopefully, you forgive me when you find out I sent half of the Bo Dancers with Nina to keep them safe as well.

Ariel knew it was the right choice as soon as Nina suggested it.

They're going to need protection as soon as they leave the city.

Now Ariel made sure the rest of her sisters could also get to Babylon safely. Although they rarely saw actual combat as temple guards, the Bo Dancers were highly trained fighters. This also made them disciplined enough to follow orders or take action without hesitation.

And now I guess they're trusting me to lead them. None of them even asked why we're leaving or when we're going to return. I hope their trust isn't misplaced.

A strange scream broke the silence, jerking Ariel's attention away from her thoughts.

What... was that?

The scream rang again.

Daniel? Oh no, Azra!

Ariel sprinted faster towards them.

You fucking piece of human garbage! We've kept Daniel safe—from you—for three fucking years, and that's not going to change today!

"What are you doing, Azra?" Uma demanded.

"As I'm sure you know, the king is dead. I watched him die, less than an hour ago—a sword got to him before the poison could—but I had to wonder, who would send a young girl to assassinate a king?" Azra slowly approached her while dragging Daniel by the ankle behind him.

"Azra, release that boy. He has nothing to do with—"

"You know, she accused *me* of the poisoning—almost had me executed for assassinating the king—and at that moment, I stared into her eyes and I instantly thought of you. So I came here to ask you myself, and look who I find." Azra said, gesturing lazily to Daniel with his free arm.

"I demand you release the boy. Now."

"No, I don't think I will. I've had the most fantastic day. I literally got away with murder. Several, in fact. Look, I'm still wearing some of the royal family," he said, gesturing to his blood-spattered robe, "and no one stopped me on the way here. Do you know why? It's because I've become the only viable heir to a vast empire. I have the power to kill a group of people in the middle of the day. So why—especially now that I'm reunited with my long-lost boy, who *you* have been hiding—why do you think you can demand his release?"

Suddenly, Eva came sprinting from behind Uma with two Bo Dancers. As Eva reached Azra's position, she slid under Azra's arm and released his grip on Daniel with her staff before resting alongside Daniel. The other two Bo Dancers stopped in front of Uma, crossing their staves in front of her. Azra glared behind him at Eva with unmasked hatred.

"You are standing in *my* home, Azra. Do not forget your place," Uma said.

"You forget *your* place, woman. As long as I carry equipment that you are forever lacking, you would do well to show some restraint and obedience."

"It seems at least two of us are living to regret that unfortunate circumstance," Uma said, disgusted.

Azra scoffed. "I refuse to play with you any longer. I am your king. Return the boy to me and move aside."

"I don't think you heard me," Uma said, projecting her voice. "You will not dismiss me in my own house and you will not molest that boy. I forbid it."

Azra laughed. "You forbid it? Oh Uma, your beauty is so great, and truth be told, it has enabled you significant power over men—power that may have even become *unequalled*, if Psamtik had married you to a king rather than sending you away to devote yourself to a foreign goddess. But there is one man who will not be swayed by your beauty—me."

"We get it, you don't like women," Ariel said, taking stance a few steps behind Azra. "It's just too bad you never tried adults. Unlike young boys, some of them might actually be willing to have sex with you—you know, if you play your cards right."

As Azra turned, he seemed to notice for the first time that Daniel had escaped further down the hall with Eva. Azra's face twisted with rage.

"Impressive Uma. You've kept your brothel so well stocked, the whores ooze out of the walls," Azra said.

"Wow, what a mouthful," Ariel said, drawing Azra's attention fully onto her, "and here I thought you had a thing for dainty portions."

"You must get all the boys with that bashful charm," Azra said.

"I was just thinking the same about you. Maybe we should swap stories later."

Go with Eva and Daniel, and take the Bo Dancers. Uma quickly signed.

Ariel stayed in place.

Go with Eva, Uma insisted.

Ariel shook her head.

Go!

Ariel hesitated and then ran back down the hall toward Eva and Daniel.

Uma breathed deeply.

"Azra," Uma said, drawing Azra's attention back to her, "this has gone on long enough. You need to either calm down and respect where you stand or leave. Decide now."

"What I've decided, *Princess,* is that you have outlived your usefulness to me," Azra said, making a crushing movement with his fist towards Uma.

Uma immediately reacted, fluidly sweeping her arms in front of her and then spinning away from Azra, landing in a low stance.

"Interesting," Azra said with a malicious grin.

The Bo Dancers guarding Uma rushed forward, attacking him in unison. Together, they brought their staves down on Azra, forcing him to retreat backward a few steps. Both Bo Dancers spun counter to each other, positioning themselves on either side of Azra before extending their weapons. Azra ducked just in time, causing their staves to shear the air above him. Seizing the moment, Azra directed weaves against their legs.

Both fighters noticed Azra's outstretched hands and kicked his arms away before cartwheeling from him. They landed in a ready stance on either side of the hallway, surrounding Azra.

Azra cast his weaves like a net, dodging and ducking to avoid contact with the Dancer's staves. The swirling, fluid forms of Uma's guard evaded and dispelled every weave.

Uma ran at Azra, launched into a high dive, and then somersaulted in the air, soaring gracefully overhead for a moment, before landing behind him. Uma spun low, sweeping Azra's ankle with her staff. Azra crumpled as his ankle crunched and folded. Azra rolled over and sent weaves at Uma. Uma dispelled them and thrashed one of his hands with her staff. Azra recoiled, clutching his mangled hand. Both guards pinned his shoulders against a wall with their staves.

"Azra," Uma said, "this has gone on long enough."

"You're right, princess," he said breathlessly, raising his uninjured hand in surrender. "I would like to end this peacefully."

Uma considered for a moment. "Peacefully?"

Azra nodded.

Uma signalled for the Bo Dancers to escort Azra away.

The Bo Dancers cautiously released him, slowly edging forward. Azra extended his hand as if requesting help to stand but made a swiping motion instead. One fighter saw the motion and fluidly waved it away; the other fell to the floor with her head twisted unnaturally to the back. The lone Bo Dancer used her momentum to spin around and pin Azra to the wall with her staff.

"Run, Mother!" she yelled, turning to face Uma. Azra smiled and touched her ribs. The second fighter fell to the ground, face already turning blue, as Uma fled the temple.

Daniel's chest burned, and the world blurred past as he and Eva dashed through the empty blue streets of the lower city.

I don't know if I can keep up this pace much longer.

"Just a bit further," Eva shouted behind her.

Daniel saw a tall mast poking up above the nearby buildings.

Finally.

As they reached the docks, a line of Bo Dancers appeared to be climbing the ramp onto the ship. Eva led Daniel onto the ship behind them.

"Eva!" one girl called.

She was one of the squad leaders.

"Fatima. I'm glad to see you. Is everyone here?" Eva asked.

"I think so. After Ariel gave the order, it didn't take long to evacuate everyone."

"Has anyone seen Ariel yet?"

"Not yet. We assumed she would arrive with you," Fatima said as they stepped onto the deck.

"I'm going to find the captain. Can I leave Daniel with you?"

"Of course," she said.

"Thanks," Eva replied, turning to Daniel. "I'll be back. Don't go anywhere."

Eva disappeared into the crowd of ship's crew and passengers, leaving Daniel to look over the enormous ship. Bo Dancers were everywhere shouting roll call, while sailors and slaves wove around them, preparing the ship to depart.

There must be hundreds of people on this ship.

Eva re-emerged from the crowd and pulled Daniel to the side, away from everyone. Daniel could see the docks below and the lower city sprawling beyond, from where they stood.

"Ariel hasn't arrived yet," Eva whispered. "I told the ship's captain to leave... without her."

Daniel leaned on the rail and hung his head.

"I feel like I'm abandoning her. She's been there for me since the day we met. Do you think—" she said, meeting Daniel's gaze. "Never mind," she said, allowing her shoulders to slump as she sunk onto the rail.

"I know Ariel's tough. And I know everyone's trusting me to keep them safe. I just hope Ariel can still escape. I hope I'm making the right choice."

Daniel draped his arm around Eva and pulled her in toward him, prompting her to lean her head on his shoulder and rock with him gently as they watched the sailors raise the ramp and prepare to leave the port.

Echoes struggled to fill the empty throne room under Azra's disapproving gaze.

I asked the guards to restrict petitions to affairs of state. I set this time aside to ensure the empire is properly maintained, and yet they slap my hand away. I could have better used the time to search for that used-up whore of Ishtar. No doubt she's already on her way to Babylon or Egypt by now. I could have taken care of the lot of them from here, but you can't weave an enemy you can't see. Even the power of a god has its limits.

"Guard!" Azra shouted to the end of the hall. "You, by the door."

One guard by the door looked around and then stepped forward. "Y-yes, sire?"

"Did I not request for all affairs of state to come forward?"

"Uh-yes. Yes, sire."

"Then where are my petitioners?"

"Well, sire, there are none in waiting."

"Ah, excellent. Let it be known that within a day of my ascension, I, King Azra of Assyria, have achieved undisputed peace across the empire."

"Yes. Yes, of course, sire." The guard replied, staring blankly at Azra.

Azra rolled his eyes.

"This exchange has been underwhelming. Say nothing and return to your door duties. I will have someone speak to my governors who is actually qualified to do so."

"Y-yes, sire," the guard said, returning to his post.

Azra gave the man a flat stare and shook his head, shifting casually to one side of the throne.

I'm finally the head of the mightiest empire in the world, and somehow, I still have to do everything myself. I'm drowning in idiots.

"Who is the highest-ranking man in this room right now?"

Dead silence swept through the hall.

"Hmm? Anyone?"

An immense guard knelt beside the throne.

"My lord, I am General Ballit."

"Ah, yes. General Ballit. I remember you. You advised King Ashur until his death."

"Yes, sire."

"I would like you to reach out to my governors and appropriately... express my insistence that they make arrangements—as soon as possible—to come *here*. Remind them it is customary to renew their loyalty to the empire when a new king ascends the throne. Oh— and while they are here, a report on the situation of their assorted regions would also be appreciated."

"Yes, my lord."

This man appears to be competent... so far.

"How adept are you at finding people?" Azra asked.

"Are we speaking about locating lost children or tracking and eliminating traitors to the throne?"

"Both possibly. Does that affect your ability to complete the task?"

"I serve the throne loyally, lord."

"Even if you had a personal relationship with the target?"

"My lord, General Shumu was a legend and a mentor to nearly every man in this room, but he killed the king whom he swore to protect. That betrayal cannot go unpunished, even for a general. Even for a prince."

Azra smiled. "Excellent. Then I will leave the matter with you. Please ensure you give any other *conspirators* travelling with him equal care."

"Consider it done, my lord."

Uma leaned against a building, still cloaked in the blue light of early morning, hoping to remain hidden from any early risers in the Lower City market. Uma had traded her priestess robes for a plain brown tunic and face covering, but she still felt danger looming everywhere.

I have to find somewhere to hide until I can escape from the city.

Peaking carefully at the street, Uma calmed somewhat.

No one seems to be following me.

Uma glanced in the opposite direction and peered deeper into the shadowed alley where she stood. On either side, smooth walls rose to the sky, pitted only by a few doors and windows.

Heading deeper into the alley, she carefully peeked into windows and jiggled latches on doors. Eventually, she discovered an open window and peered inside. The room had a few chairs, a table, and a bed with no access to the floor above. Snatching a look over each shoulder, she carefully climbed into the room. Dust puffed up from the floor as she landed and she swatted the air, but to no effect.

No one has lived here for a very long time, she thought with a sneeze.

Uma put her scarf over her mouth and continued to survey despite the dimness, taking inventory of the stove and any supplies left behind. Suddenly, the room darkened, and Uma heard a soft scuffle near the window. She whirled around and pounced toward a shadow standing behind her. The figure put their hand out, allowing Uma to grab their wrist, spin them around and pin them against the wall.

"Who are you?" Uma demanded.

"Wait! It's me, Mother."

Uma spun the figure around to face her. "Ariel?" she said, blackened tears forming around her eyes.

Ariel pulled her scarf away, revealing her familiar red hair and fierce expression.

Uma cried and hugged Ariel. "Oh, Great Mother, you've returned to me."

Ariel pulled away to replace her scarf over her mouth for a cough.

"Why are you here? Did your sisters make it to the ship?" Uma asked.

"Yes, Mother. Eva passed the order to the squad leaders, and I swept the temple for anyone left behind. I didn't find anyone, so I came back to find you, but all I found were... bodies."

"You shouldn't have come back! You should be on a ship to Cutha right now."

"I know, but I couldn't leave you."

"Oh, Ariel."

"It's too late anyway, the ship is long gone by now."

"Where's your staff?" Uma asked, looking her over.

"Oh," Ariel laughed, "I left it just outside the window when I climbed in."

"I would have recognized you better if you were carrying it," Uma scolded.

"Sorry, Mother," Ariel smiled, reaching outside the window to pull her staff inside. "What is this place?"

"It's just an abandoned house. It seemed like a fair place to hide, but it's all dusty."

"I feel like that is the least of our problems right now. We should leave the city immediately."

"I suppose that would be a better option."

Ariel studied Uma's face for a moment. "Ok. Stay here for a bit. I'll go to the market and get some supplies and see if we can still leave the city easily."

"I'm coming with you," Uma said. "Maybe together we can pass as a mother and daughter going about their business."

"Mother, my skin is so fair, it's pink. Yours is as dark as the midnight sky."

"Maybe you were adopted? I mean, technically you were, so it's not a complete stretch."

Ariel flattened her expression. "Mother, come on. Having passable justifications is not the same as being inconspicuous. So far no one has recognized me without my temple robes, because I was just a forgettable temple slave. But you're the high priestess. It's safer for you to stay hidden until we have a better idea of Azra's next move."

"I'm going and that's final. We're safer together. If anyone asks, just tell them I'm your stepmother."

"Fine, but you follow *my* lead, Mother." Ariel moved toward the door on the opposite side of the room.

"We'll see," Uma smirked.

"You know, maybe it's not that suspicious if we go together. You could be anyone."

"Exactly."

"You could be a senile old woman. That I found—"

"Oh, come on now."

"—just wandering around the city. If not for me, who knows what would've happened to that poor, old, witless—"

"Ok now, let's *go*."

Rapid footfalls echoed through the alley and past the window above Sin. The icy darkness wrapped around him as he sat curled up against the wall, while Shumu stole nervous glances of the street from the corner of the room, to the side of the window.

This is it. This is my life now. Just me and Shumu, running from the empire forever. Somehow, that monster took the crown and now we're the fugitives.

"I still don't understand why we're running," Sin muttered.

"I told you. Azra has framed us... for many deaths."

"I wasn't even there. How could I be responsible?"

"Azra has framed me to take the throne. He would've noticed by now that I helped you get out of the palace, so you're undoubtedly marked as a co-conspirator."

"... as if I would have my father killed. And my brother... and Miriam," he finished, with a croak.

"I'm sorry, Sin. I worried about your safety. If I had left you in the palace, Azra would have had you killed also, and I couldn't allow that to happen. You and your brother... were like sons—" Shumu stopped abruptly, unable to finish.

Sin could sense Shumu's pain, but it was a quiet hum in the background of his own roaring grief.

"I'm just sorry, Sin," Shumu said quietly. "But we should be safe here until we can get out of the city."

"How do you know? Where is *here?*"

"This was the house I grew up in. I don't believe Azra would know about it. Most people who would remember me from back then are dead now."

Sin always forgot that Shumu had retired as a decorated general before becoming his bodyguard. Sin thought this was partly because he had never known Shumu as a general, but it was also because Shumu looked the same for as long as Sin could remember.

Shumu could literally be any age and I would never know. Am I being protected by a feeble old man?

Sin eyed Shumu with suspicion.

Shumu noticed Sin glance at him and responded with a frown. "You can trust me, Sin. I will protect you. I don't know if I can return you to your rightful place on the throne, but I will protect you."

I'm suspicious of the only person in the world who isn't trying to kill me. How did everything get so fucked up?

Sin curled tighter.

I miss you, Miriam.

"Get some sleep, Sin. I'll keep watch."

Sin lay on the floor, thinking of Miriam until he fell asleep.

Sin woke up to the sound of Shumu's snoring. He sat up and saw Shumu had pulled a chair up to the window and somehow fell asleep leaning back into it.

You were on lookout and somehow you managed to fall asleep, sitting up.

Sin's stomach growled and peered out the window and saw the blue light of dawn settling across the buildings and walkways. A few people seemed to mill about, but the streets weren't bustling by any means.

I'm not hiding in here all day, Shumu.

Grabbing the large plain cloak and scarf he had used to escape the palace, he covered his face and headed out onto the street.

CHAPTER 11

PATH OF THE DYING
LIGHT

The red morning sky greeted Ariel as she and
Uma made their way to a gate in the Lower
City market. Aside from a few of the merchants
setting their stands, the streets were mostly empty. The
women made their way to the gates easily, but the
large doors remained closed. Ariel led Uma to a nearby
merchant.

"Wait here," Ariel whispered.

"Excuse me, sir. My mother and I are hoping to travel
back to our home in Calah today. Would you happen
to know if the road from this gate will take us there?
It's so easy to get turned around." Ariel asked sweetly,
approaching a guard.

"Isn't it dangerous for two ladies to be walking the
roads alone?"

Ariel giggled. "In Assyria? No, this is the safest empire in the world, and we're only travelling less than a day's walk. But if you're worried for us, we'd be happy to have you escort us as far as you're willing to go. We just need to head home."

The guard eyed her suspiciously and then sighed. "I'm sorry, miss. You and your mother will have to stay in the city a while longer. No one can pass today."

"Even two helpless ladies?" Ariel asked.

"No one. By order of the king, the gates stay sealed until further notice."

"Alright, I'm sorry to have bothered you," Ariel said. Uma was carrying a basket of bread and assorted produce when Ariel returned to her.

"I bought some more food," Uma said as Ariel led her down a nearby alley.

"Looks like we're not going anywhere just yet," Ariel said.

"The merchant told me as much. They've sealed the city gates until the kings' assassins are found. It seems they're believed to still be in the city."

"No shit, it's Azra. He's probably sitting on the throne as we speak. I doubt they're even looking for him."

"Judging from our interaction with Azra earlier, I'm certain they believe someone else is responsible. Knowing Azra, he has likely shifted the blame onto us."

"Ugh, figures." Ariel sighed. "Well, we need to leave the city before they start searching door to door. Any suggestions?"

Uma paused thoughtfully. "Maybe one."

"Lead the way." Ariel smiled.

Swirling dust devils whipped past Ariel's cheeks as she stared over the walls of Nineveh and traced the Khosr River as it carved its way to the Tigris.

"When I first came to Nineveh," Uma said, "I often stood along the southern walls of the citadel to watch the Khosr flow through the lower city. I guess it reminded me a little of home," she finished, following Ariel's gaze.

Grazing cattle lazily made a meal of a small field between the river and the citadel.

"So, we follow the herd out?" Ariel asked.

"Most of the way, yes. We can pose as herders initially to avoid suspicion and slowly make our way up the pasture. We still have to row a kuphar across the moat before we're out of the city, but this way, we can bypass the city walls."

Ariel scanned the riverbank in both directions. "I guess we'll have to backtrack east and recross at the bridge. Depending on the time of day, it shouldn't be too hard."

"The guards don't appear to be stopping pedestrians inside the city as yet," Uma agreed.

"Alright. Let's get you back to the house and I'll gather supplies. We can leave this afternoon." Ariel said.

Climbing down, Ariel felt the weight of eyes following her as she and Uma made their way back to the abandoned house.

What's wrong? Uma signalled her.

Possible tail, Ariel signed back. *Keep walking, stay hidden. I'll follow from behind.*

Ariel ducked into a side alley and waited quietly. After a few moments, a boy with dark hair and olive skin emerged from the shadows, following the path Uma had taken only a moment prior. Ariel silently tailed the boy until she saw an opportunity and then leaped at him from the shadows. The boy let out a short squeak that was muted by the layers of Ariel's scarf being pressed into his mouth.

"Listen to me. You're going to calm down and stop struggling, then I'm going to remove the scarf. If you yell or scream, I will break your jaw. Do you understand?" Ariel said.

The boy nodded, wide-eyed with fear.

Ariel removed the scarf, but maintained her grip on the boy. "Who are you? Why are you following us?"

"I-I wasn't. I mean, I was, but we—a friend and I— are trying to find a way out of the city and I saw you were too. At least you seemed like you were."

Ariel frowned at the boy. *He's obviously not a guard or a soldier.*

"I can't decide what to do with you."

"Does that mean you're going to let me go?"

"No, it means I'm going to take you to see someone who *will* decide."

Staring at the door, Uma waited nervously in the darkness for Ariel to arrive. Uma hated everything about this situation.

She had been in danger many times throughout her life, but those situations had been isolated and quickly dealt with. She had never been a fugitive before, forced to look over her shoulder at every stray sound.

When Ariel slipped through the door, it had been so silent that it caused Uma to jump and take a ready stance.

I brought a guest, Ariel signed.

Uma relaxed a little and watched with interest as

a boy materialized into the darkened room from behind Ariel.

"Mother, this boy was following us. He claims he's trying to escape the city with someone else." Ariel closed the door behind them.

Uma inspected the boy and immediately recognized him from his green eyes and dark features.

He's one of the king's sons, but will he admit as much to me?

"What is your name, boy?"

"Uh—it's Sin, ma'am. I wasn't going to harm you or your daughter. I'm just trying to get out of the city with my, uh, dad."

Ariel shot a frown towards Uma.

Your dad, hmm?

"Ah, I see. And where is your father?" Uma asked.

"We're at a house here in the lower city. I need to get back before he notices I've left."

He's been mostly honest so far. I should let him escape back to whoever is claiming to be his "father" and leave here with Ariel... but he's also here because of us. Because of me. I had never intended for him or his brother to be harmed, only for someone else to assume the throne in their place for a short time.

Uma looked over Sin.

I owe it to him to help him escape.

"Alright, Sin, we will accompany you back to your father and then we will help you both escape the walls of the city."

"Ok, thank you. Thank you," Sin said, leading the women into the alley.

I think this is a mistake. Do you think we can trust him? Ariel signed.

I believe so. Let's give him a chance. Uma signed back.

Ariel nodded.

They pulled on their hoods and entered the busy street.

The darkness of the house contrasted heavily with the bright afternoon sun, forcing Uma into temporary blindness as she entered the house.

"Where were you?" an older man demanded.

Shumu. He was the boys' guardian, if I remember correctly.

"I was hungry."

"Who are these women?" Shumu's face somehow hardened further than Uma had previously imagined possible.

Ariel offered Shumu the food goods they had purchased that morning. "Here, please. My mother and I mean you no harm. We only want to help you and your son."

"They said they're trying to get out of the city. Maybe we can help each other," Sin said.

Shumu observed the women and assessed Sin's face.

"Why do you need to leave the city so urgently?" Shumu asked.

"I wouldn't say we're trying to leave *urgently*. We're just trying to get home now that our business here is done," Uma explained.

"Where is home?"

"Calah," Ariel answered.

"And what exactly was your business here in Nineveh?"

"My sister has devoted herself to the temple," Ariel said.

"It's a tremendous honour to our family," Uma beamed.

"And your husband?" Shumu asked, "Why did he not accompany you?"

"My husband was killed by raiders a few years ago," Uma said, eyes downcast for a moment.

Uma thought Shumu seemed only partly convinced, but it was all she needed.

"I'm sorry for your loss," Shumu said.

"It has been hard, but you know, you push forward," Uma said.

Shumu let out a steady stream of air as he scanned their faces. "So, how do you plan to escape a city on lockdown?"

A gentle breeze whipped past Daniel's face, causing his head wrapping to flap momentarily, but it did little to ease the oppressive heat of the midday sun.

At least we don't have to walk, Daniel thought as he and Eva swayed in stride with the donkey below them.

"We're lucky I could find this donkey," Eva said.

Well, we could have ridden on a horse or inside a covered wagon if we would have left Cutha with the others.

Then he shook his head and sighed.

No, I was worried about Ariel and Uma, too. I'm glad we waited, just in case... it just sucks being out here, with no shelter from the sun, for hours.

"We're almost there," Eva sighed, "almost there."

Nothing seems to grow very well outside the cities.

Daniel took in the dry, grassy landscape. Trees grew here and there, and bushes dotted the plain, but it wasn't *lush* by any means.

Maybe it's the rivers. Most of the cities I've read about were built along either the Tigris or the Euphrates. Even Nineveh had its own canal system...

"When I was a young girl... before the raids... our village used to have the freshest water anywhere. My father used to say that the waters of Beit Jinn flowed down the mountain from heaven. Obviously, that's just a story fathers tell their silly girls, but there was something about that water. It just tasted different, you know? I don't know how to describe it, but it definitely tasted nothing like the water in Nineveh. I remember when I first got to the temple, I couldn't drink the water without boiling it a hundred times." Eva chuckled a little. "It probably wasn't even water by the time I was drinking it, but Ariel would help me boil it, anyway. She was always there for me, you know? Always."

Daniel hugged Eva tightly and laid his head against her back, and he heard Eva's breath quiver for a moment as she inhaled.

Eva rubbed her eyes and cleared her throat. "We're almost there. We're almost there."

"So, what do you think of our escape plan?" Ariel asked. She tilted her head playfully, allowing the dim candlelight to compliment her face.

"I think it's good." Sin said, letting the silence sit between them.

"What's going on?"

Sin glanced at her, but said nothing.

"We honestly aren't planning to kill you or your dad."

"I know."

"Oh, you know, and yet... you're still being weird."

Sin searched her smirking face. "I knew you wouldn't kill us when you first caught me in the alley."

"Oh yeah? And how did you know that?"

"It was obvious that you hadn't noticed me watching you until we were in the alley."

"And what if we were following you and we lost sight of you? How did you know we weren't looking for you on that rooftop?"

"I heard your conversation. You were planning your own escape. You didn't even know I was there. You weren't searching for me."

"What if we were?"

"You weren't," he said flatly.

"What if we were?"

"You weren't."

"How do you know?"

"Because when we were in the alley, you had the upper hand and the questions you asked weren't the kind people ask when they're searching for someone."

"Oh?" Ariel said, narrowing her eyes.

"They were the kind you ask when someone's searching for you."

Did she just tense up?

"Well, technically you *were* following us, so it all seems pretty appropriate if you ask me. A guy your age rarely follows a mother and daughter into an alley with good intentions." Ariel leaned back.

"Yeah. Yeah, I get that."

"So?"

"So what?"

"Why were you being weird just now?"

"I know you aren't planning to kill us, but I still don't understand why you're helping us."

Ariel sighed. "To be honest, I'm not even sure myself. My mother has a soft spot for strays, I think."

Strays?!

Ariel glanced at him and chuckled gently.

"What?"

"You're just... you're kind of cute sometimes."

Cute?

Sin felt his face burn as he registered the comment and turned away.

Shumu felt a smirk creep across his face as he watched Sin talk to the strange red-headed girl from the next room.

He seems happy when he's around her.

Shumu shook his head and felt the warmth of Uma's gaze upon him as she traced his line of sight to the next room.

"Your daughter reminds me of someone that was close to him," Shumu said.

"What happened to the girl?" Uma asked gently.

"She died. Tragically," Shumu said, allowing his smile to fade.

"I'm sorry to hear that," Uma said.

Shumu noted the genuine sadness draping Uma's features.

"Have we ever met? You also seem so familiar, but I can't place where our paths would have crossed."

Uma giggled, looking him over. "They wouldn't have. I would've remembered a man such as yourself. It's probably a passing resemblance."

"Maybe. Have you been in the city long?"

"No, we only came for my daughter. Now that the temple has taken her in, we need to head back home."

"To Calah."

"Well, probably not. More likely, we will keep moving west."

"So, you are planning to break out of a city on lockdown and then, instead of returning home, you will continue west?"

"Truthfully, I heard some girls talking at the temple... they were saying something terrible happened at the palace. In my experience, that's usually a good time to be anywhere else."

"You're not wrong. Did they mention anything specific about what may have happened?"

"No. Nothing. But I've been alive a long time and my intuition is rarely wrong," Uma said.

"Fair enough," Shumu chuckled. "Your accent; it's faint, but I swear I've heard it before."

"Oh," Uma laughed, "it's Egyptian. No one has taken notice in years. I thought it had disappeared entirely."

"Well, it's incredibly faint, but I have an ear for accents. Still, it must have been years since you've been to your homeland."

"More like decades."

"I imagine you haven't aged a day in all that time."

"I can see where your boy gets his way with the ladies."

Shumu chuckled bashfully. "Yeah, he has become quite the ladies' man."

"I should tell my daughter to keep an eye."

"Don't worry about Sin. He's a good man, but he has dealt with a lot of loss lately. I doubt he'd allow himself to get too attached to anyone right now."

"Ah," Uma said patiently, "And how about you? Are you married?"

"... No. Sin is... all I have."

"I understand."

"Let's all get some sleep, and we'll regroup in the morning."

"See you in a few hours."

Loud coughing and sputtering drew Sin's attention into the night, but the darkness shrouded its faraway source.

"What? Am I not enough for you?"

"Wha—? Oh, no sorry. Sorry Miriam," Sin said, shaking his head, "It just sounded like someone was dying or something out there."

"So, I have to be dying for you to pay attention to me, then?" Miriam smirked.

"No, of course not." Sin paused and then added, "But it might help if you were hotter."

"Hmm, I was thinking the same thing about you earlier when I saw the new stable boy."

"Really."

"Yeah, I mean look at me and look at... well, you," Miriam said gesturing, "I really married down."

"We're not married yet."

"Yet. That basically means married."

"I guess I never considered there were any other options." Sin wrapped his arms tightly around her.

"There aren't," she said, resting her head on his shoulder.

Stars poked holes in the moonless night sky above Sin and Miriam, and the memories of a thousand conversations danced quietly around them as they contentedly observed it. Sin smiled as he took her hand and gently laced her fingers into his.

An animal sniffed and snorted hoarsely nearby, causing Sin to peer around them into the darkness again.

"I wish we could just say like this forever," Miriam said with a sigh. "Don't you?"

"Yeah. I wish we were the only thing in the world right now," Sin replied, kissing her on the head.

An argument broke out between a man and a woman, punctuated by shrill yelps that ripped Sin's attention into the night.

"Sin," Miriam whispered to him, "Sin, just stay with me."

Sin looked between Miriam and back into the darkness again.

"What? What are you talking about?" Sin asked.

"Just stay here with me. Just stay with me, Sin."

Sin felt drawn to the argument, and the voices seemed to become more familiar to him as he listened.

"Sin, please, don't go. Please, just stay here with me."

"I—I'm sorry, my love. I have to... I have to—" Sin's hand fell away from hers and he rose to follow the sounds into the night.

Sin awoke in darkness, filled only by a soft dripping noise and a dim stream of light trickling in through the curtain dividing his room from the next. A shattering roar erupted from the next room, causing Sin to jump to his feet from the bed, but he slipped on the floor and landed backward. When he recovered, Sin realized the floor was slick and slimy. He quickly rubbed his hands on his clothes, leaving his skin feeling sticky and dirty.

He attempted to stand again—this time, successfully. Soon his eyes adjusted, allowing him to take stock of his surroundings and easily trace that lonely bar of light from the next room, across Ariel's limp body and over the glistening gash on her throat.

Sin touched his face, and the iron smell of blood wafted strongly into his nostrils.

Oh, no. Ariel...

"I knew we had met before, *Uma*," Shumu roared.

Sin moved to the doorway and slid the curtain aside. When he entered the room, he found Uma lying on the ground, bruised and bloody, tears streaming down her face.

"I never wanted to see the princes hurt. I never wanted that. Believe me," Uma pleaded.

"Azra is an ambitious madman who just happens to be the king's half-brother. What did you think was going to happen?" Shumu said, pacing.

"Kandalanu was supposed to take the throne. Kandalanu, not Azra. We thought we had everything under control."

"You can't control a man like Azra. He's too unhinged. How could you not consider that?"

"How could we anticipate a *massacre*? Ashur was a tyrant and our only hope for a better future–the country's only hope–required removing him from the throne. We had planned that Kandalanu would relinquish his power back to the young princes after a period of appropriate change."

"Appropriate change?"

"—AND I was counting on *your* training and counsel to guide young Ashur to be the *righteous king* that his father never was."

"Flattery? Really?"

"It's not flattery. It's the truth."

Shumu directed a stony stare down at Uma. "I don't want to hear your 'truth'. You sent a young girl to assassinate the king."

"She was well trained and able. She knew what—"

"What did she know?" Shumu shouted, his voice trembling with pity. "It was a death sentence. She was a child, Uma. A child. Don't you see that? She was somebody's daughter, entrusted to your care, and you allowed her to throw her life away before it even started."

"No!" Uma yelled. "Miriam was young, but she knew the risks and she completed her mission bravely. I forbid you to diminish her sacrifice."

Miriam...? Sin thought, staring dumbly at Uma from just inside the doorway.

Uma tried to sit propped up against the wall and noticed him.

"What could you possibly know about sacrifice, *priestess?* I have led armies of men—barely old enough to drink—to their deaths against enemies who would otherwise destroy our way of life. Those boys gave their *lives* to protect yours. *That* is sacrifice," Shumu growled.

"We are not so different, *general.* I also trained my girls as warriors, and they are *also* willing to sacrifice their lives to protect our people. I think the difference is that you lost the stomach to do what needs to be done."

"How dare you?"

"I think the question is, how *do* you go from being a general in the world's largest standing army to the nanny of two young boys? They didn't demote you as a matter of discipline, otherwise, you wouldn't have remained as the king's advisor. So how does that happen, hmm?"

Shumu turned away from Uma to avoid the question and noticed Sin standing by the doorway, covered in blood. "Sin...?" he whispered.

"It doesn't," Uma continued, "There are two reasons a general retires... and you haven't died in battle."

Shumu hung his head. "I was tired of seeing all the death, Uma," Shumu said quietly. "I was tired of all the death."

"Is that why you killed an innocent girl in her sleep?" Uma hissed.

Wait... No....

"You... killed Ariel? Why would—" Sin said.

Shumu's face twisted with emotion as he looked between Sin and Uma. "Ariel was hardly innocent, you witch. I couldn't let you live once I knew who you were, and she was your bodyguard. No doubt she would have killed me and Sin before we left here. I had no choice."

"No choice." Uma said in disgust, "Like you had no choice when you killed Miriam?"

Sin's eyes were downcast, lost in shock.

Shumu turned on Uma like a beast circling his prey. "I did *not* kill Miriam."

"Then tell me, *general,* how did you survive that room when Azra supposedly killed everyone?" Uma asked, narrowing her eyes.

"It was Azra—"

"And yet, Azra didn't kill *everyone,* did he? He left you alive. Why would he do that? He used his power on you, didn't he?"

Shumu stared at Uma but said nothing.

"Wh-What power? What power does he have, Shumu?" Sin asked.

"Azra has the power to bend people to his will, like a puppet master," Uma said acidly.

"Like... puppets...?" Sin said. The words rolled around his mouth like it was a foreign language. The realization built-up pressure slowly until it foamed out of him. "*You killed everyone?*"

"I didn't want to."

"You killed Miriam!" Sin roared.

"No, Sin. It was Azra he—" Shumu tried again.

"—and Ashur! You killed my father. You killed everyone I've ever cared about."

Shumu backed into the windowsill and sat, shoulders slumped.

"Were you going to kill me? After you killed Uma, were you going to kill me?"

"Of course not. I'm trying to help you survive. Don't you see? Uma deserves to die."

"Why? She was trying to help us escape—they both were."

"They were killing your father! They stole your birthright!" Shumu shouted.

Shumu hung his head and said nothing. Sin fought to see through an increasing blur, fought to hold on to the anger that allowed him to keep his composure all this time. But the anger was giving way, and tiny fissures in his composure began to crack apart. Tears rushed out of him, carried by the howl of irredeemable loss.

"I always wanted you and your brother to live through this," Uma said sadly. "After Ariel found you, she cautioned me about getting involved in your escape, but I thought I owed it to you. Shumu's right, I am at least partly to blame for your suffering, and I thought... I thought that if I could help you escape, it might ease my conscience a little."

"And how's that working out for you, priestess?" Shumu grumbled.

"I should've never gotten involved," Uma whispered.

Sin's crying died down when he heard Shumu clear his throat.

"You should...," Shumu whispered breathlessly, with his head still hung. He was so quiet it was barely audible.

Sin looked up at Shumu's face. Shumu seemed to mouth something, but only blood came dripping out from his lips. Sin tried to lift Shumu's head and saw that his eyes had gone blank. Sin recoiled, allowing Shumu's body to fall to the floor.

"Uma...?" Sin began, turning to face her.

"Sin, watch out!" she cried desperately, pointing toward the window.

Sin spun in the direction she was pointing, but it was too late. A man dressed fully in black, tightly wrapped clothing leapt onto Sin and plunged a dagger deep into his chest. With one fluid motion, the assassin dislodged his knife and sliced Sin's throat below his voice box.

Sin writhed in agonizing pain, coughing and sputtering as he gasped for air.

Suddenly, he heard Uma chuckle and strained to look up at her from the floor as he bled out. The assassin casually advanced on her.

"So, he sent Ballit's assassins. You tell Azra—" Uma began, but the assassin lunged at her before she could finish. In two more fluid strikes, Uma fell to the floor beside Sin, staring back at him as the blood drained from her body. Coughing turned to sputtering, and sputtering turned to a hoarse animal-like snorting until all breathing stopped.

The world slowly darkened around Sin until he no longer could remember where he was or what was going on.

I wish we were the only thing in the world, a familiar voice whispered.

Then the pooling blackness overtook him, erasing his smiling face from existence.

CHAPTER 12

THE WHITE CITY

The afternoon sun set the air on fire. Every breath made Daniel shudder as if it contained a mouthful of flames, and the sunlight baked his eyes when he opened them. Even his clothes felt as if they might ignite at any moment.

Eva handled the reins with one hand and grasped Daniel's wrists with the other, forcing him to lean against her back while they rode. He felt Eva shudder and gave her waist a small squeeze. Daniel felt a weak squeeze on his wrists in reply. This was how they had communicated over the last few hours, suspended in the endless heat as they were carried along, semi-conscious, to their destination.

Are we going to die? Did we survive Azra only to be killed by the Sun? Maybe Shamash really was on his side.

Suddenly, Daniel chuckled.

"Daniel?" Eva said weakly. "Are you... laughing?"

Daniel shook with laughter, contagiously drawing Eva into it.

"But why?" She asked between breaths, "Why are we laughing? What's happening?"

Eva gasped and stopped laughing. "Daniel, look!"

Daniel opened his eyes and straightened his back to look beyond Eva. The horizon looked like a moving liquid in the distance, distorting everything. Daniel squinted at the liquid horizon until shimmering white walls rose out of the ground and shone out to them like a beacon.

"We made it Daniel," Eva whispered.

As the city grew, the vegetation became lush again, and the air smelled wet from the nearby Euphrates. Black geometric designs with a dragon motif materialized along the top of the walls, and guards appeared between the triangular crenellations, keeping watch over the city. Over time, the road widened, allowing a growing throng of travellers to pour into the city like a river. Daniel found himself comforted by the buzz of other people after the long silence of their journey.

Soon the road carried them through the main gate, where the walls flanked them on both sides and guards peered down at them, inspecting the crowd. They drifted forward, under a second gate and then into an open marketplace that lined the road on either side. Large alabaster stones paved the road beneath them, similar to those used to build the city walls, but they were hardly visible from the heavy foot traffic.

Ahead, Daniel saw the dense crowd divide and make way for two lines of women carrying staves and walking towards them.

Eva unwrapped her face as they approached. "Nina, Fatima, it's good to see you both."

"Ariel never made it?" Fatima asked.

Eva only shook her head in reply.

"The king allowed us to escort you to the palace in place of his guards," Nina said. "We brought you some water, too."

"Thank you. It's good to see you all again. Did everyone else arrive safely?" Eva took a few gulps of water from the waterskin.

"Everyone except Ariel and Uma," Nina said.

"Well, that's something I guess." Eva wiped her mouth and twisted slightly toward Daniel, supporting the waterskin with her shoulder. "Drink it all."

Daniel gulped the water down in an instant and tapped Eva to let her know when he had finished.

Fatima smiled at Daniel, taking the donkey's reins. "I'm glad you both survived the journey. The king is eager to meet with you. We shouldn't keep him waiting."

Nina flanked their other side, and the others fell into a double line formation behind them.

Finally, Daniel thought, as they approached the palace gates.

The palace was a relatively short ride from the outer walls, but when you factor in the ride from Cutha and the boat ride before that, the journey had been a feat of endurance.

If I remember correctly, the temple was one of the first permanent buildings here and the palace beside it was the second. The rest of the city formed around them on every side, although no one is really sure when, since everything written prior to The Sundering was destroyed. It's a city as old as recorded time.

A brief laugh escaped Daniel's lips.

"He's happy," Fatima said over her shoulder.

"He's delirious." Eva's smirk transformed into a gasp as they passed under the flowering vines that draped the white gates of the palace.

The vines climbed the walls and wove along a wooden lattice overhead that shadowed the alabaster path from where they stood to a pair of enormous palace doors. Pink flower petals naturally fell from vines, carpeting their path below. Flower beds and benches dotted the grassy lawn that flanked the walkway on either side, and a tiered flower garden framed the enclosure.

Nina giggled at Eva's reaction. "I know. That was my reaction when I first saw it. According to the guards, the king has always kept a garden."

Ahead, Daniel heard the immense doors creak open as they approached, allowing them to enter without stopping. Daniel couldn't help but appreciate the intricate wood carvings on the doors, clearly depicting people celebrating with wine and dancing.

Out of the hall, a voice boomed toward them. "Welcome! Welcome to Babylon."

Daniel sat up to crane around Eva's shoulders.

A small, older man headed toward them, beaming, with arms outstretched. Black and silver robes with tassels hung loosely from his body, and a multi-fingered hat with bells jangled as he walked. "Welcome all to the Palace of Babylon."

A worried-looking administrator in green robes wrung his hands at Kandalanu's left while an enormous bodyguard in black lamellar armour smirked and shadowed silently from the right.

The administrator nervously approached the king. "Sire, allow your humble servants, such as myself or your personal guard, to announce your... well, everything for you. It is... unheard of for you to speak for yourself when not strictly necessary."

"Nonsense. My voice works perfectly well. Maybe better than yours."

"But sire—"

"Do you mean to lecture the king in front of his guests?"

"Well, no—"

"Do you have prior experience lecturing a king in public?"

"No, sire."

"What about in private?"

"Sire? I—I don't—"

"That actually seems less enjoyable."

"Yes. Well, no. It's not—"

"What are you saying? I can hardly understand you."

"Apologies, sire."

"Tavis, I'm getting the impression that you may, in fact, be inexperienced in public speaking. Fear not, we will get you practiced in no time. Just maybe not today."

"Yes, sire."

The king began to walk away and spun in place, facing the administrator. "However, if an occasion arises where I cannot speak for myself, I will let you know."

"Y-yes sire."

"Excellent." The king nodded and spun back towards his guests. Suddenly, he circled back to the administrator. "I forgot to mention that you are doing a wonderful job in your new role, Tavis."

"Uh, thank you, sire?"

The king looked up towards the guard, who nodded with a smirk and then back towards the administrator. "Excellent," he said, whirling back toward Daniel and the others once again.

The guard snorted in amusement as he exchanged glances with the confused administrator.

Eva had climbed down with Daniel and passed the reins to Nina, who walked the donkey out of the garden as the king approached them.

"Eva," he said, "it's always a pleasure to have a rose such as yourself in the palace."

"Thank you, your highness," she replied with a giggle.

"And who is this?"

"His name is Daniel, your highness." Daniel bowed toward him.

"Ah, Daniel! And what brings a young man like yourself into the company of these lovely ladies?"

Eva giggled and shook her head. "Daniel is mute, your highness. He can't speak."

"Ah, that's unfortunate. Well, Daniel, allow me to introduce myself as King Kandalanu of Babylon." Kandalanu delivered a bow with a flourish, before cocking his head toward Tavis, who now appeared to be in visible distress.

"Tavis? Are you alright?" Kandalanu straightened and pivoted to face him.

"Sire... kings don't—"

"Tavis? What are you mumbling?"

Tavis opened his mouth to speak, and then noticed the guard slowly shaking his head at him, prompting Tavis to nod silently.

"I apologize for Tavis. He's a competent administrator, but he's still adjusting to his position. He's very rigid. Not enough flex." Kandalanu illustrated with an awkward noodling movement while everyone stared in varying degrees of amusement and confusion.

"Forget about that. It must have been a long journey for you both. You could probably do with a warm bath and a cup of wine."

"We appreciate your hospitality, your Highness," Eva replied with a bow.

"Is there any news of Uma or Ariel?"

Eva pursed her lips. "Regretfully, no. I wasn't able to confirm if they even left the city. I'm sorry, your Highness."

Kandalanu's eyes reddened with sadness, but he only nodded in response.

"Please," he said, breaking the silence, "allow my bodyguard Nabo to show you around the palace and let him know if you need anything."

"Thank you," Eva said.

Daniel offered another curt bow in gratitude. As he lifted his head, he paused in shock.

Is that... Kaleb? How?

"Eva!" the boy said in Kaleb's voice as he jogged toward them.

"Hey, little man," Eva said, ruffling his hair somewhat.

The boy made a face and tried to groom his hair back to its previous state. "Hey, come on. I'm not a little kid anymore, you know."

"I know. It's just an old habit, Nebu. I haven't seen you since you were *so* little."

"Yeah, I guess. Who's this?"

"Oh, this is Daniel. Daniel, meet Nebuchadnezzar."

"Hey," the boy said, lowering his voice somewhat and extending a hand. "Call me Nebu."

Daniel slowly revealed his amputated wrists and made a small bow.

"Holy crap, what happened to your hands?"

"Nebu!" Eva scolded.

"I was just asking. You don't have to tell me if you don't want to."

"He couldn't either way, son. Daniel has been mute for many years. He lost his hands and voice in the fire that—in a terrible fire," Nabo choked on the last few words.

Realization crept across Nebu's face. "You knew Kaleb?"

Daniel nodded slowly, glad for the first time in his life that he couldn't speak.

"Ah," Nebu said.

"Let our guests get settled and you can meet them properly later." Kandalanu gently tapped Nebu on the back.

"Uh, yes Uncle."

"Yes, *Your Majesty*," Tavis corrected. Nebu only made a face at him and ran back into the castle.

Nabo smirked and shook his head. "Shall I show you to your rooms?"

The evening breeze carried the sweet smells of flowers on notes of cooking and incense as it gently swept past Eva's face. Eva closed her eyes to breathe it all in.

This garden is so... serene.

A full moon illuminated the entire garden for Eva as she walked in its silvery light. A particular flower caught her eye, and Eva knelt, gently cradling its delicate petals in her hands.

So beautiful.

A thorn caught her fingers as she withdrew, and when she investigated, another thorn pierced her skin.

"Roses," Kandalanu said from behind her. "They're beautiful and some even say they have healing properties, but they have quite a sting for those who underestimate them."

"I'm sorry. I didn't mean any harm."

"I know you didn't, Eva," Kandalanu smirked and knelt beside her.

"You know, my wife loved roses. When King Ashur appointed me king of Babylon, it was her only request that we have a small rose garden."

"Small? But it's so large!" Eva laughed.

"Well, it *was* small. But you know, as the years went on, she had more requests and I loved her, so no request really seemed too unreasonable. And I am a king, after all. I *should* have an immense display of beauty somewhere in the palace. That was her argument, at least." He chuckled.

"What did you say to that?" Eva smiled, turning towards him.

"Well, you know, I always told her she was the only beauty that I ever cared about. She thought it was flattery, but I'm telling you here that it was true. After she died... I guess you could say this is the one place I could still feel her presence, so I just kept it alive for her."

"That's beautiful," Eva said, wiping her eyes quickly. A pause settled between them.

"You know, Ariel always loved this garden when she was little," Kandalanu said.

"I think I used to know that. I knew she loved flowers, but she never really talked about her life before she came to the temple."

"Temple life... is hard on relationships. Devotees often feel abandoned, and parents, well, we feel like a part of us has been scooped out and displaced somewhere. You know, there are two kinds of people who typically become devotees, orphans, and the children of unwilling nobles. Politics plays a big part in temple life, as you know, but it starts right from the beginning."

"I'm sorry I couldn't bring Ariel back with me," Eva said sadly.

"I know you are. Sometimes, I wish I had set aside more time to be a better father, but I have more families to be responsible for than just my own."

Eva stroked Kandalanu's arm. "I know, and I think Ariel always knew, even if she wouldn't admit it."

"I'm not so sure, but I appreciate you for saying so, my dear," Kandalanu said, patting her hand.

Eva let the silence linger between them for a moment and then asked, "Do you think they're still alive out there?"

Kandalanu paused for a moment in consideration. "You know," he began carefully, "they're warriors, her and Uma. I would like to believe my daughter is ok, but the world is a dangerous place and a warrior's heart craves battle. Only time can reveal their fate."

CHAPTER 13

REBIRTH

S in opened his eyes.

"Miriam!" he croaked, shooting up from the bed. Sharp pain stabbed at his throat and between his ribs, causing him to groan.

A soft palm lay against his chest, pressing him gently backward. Sin turned in surprise and saw a smiling, gentle face staring back at him.

"Lay back down, dear, and try not to speak. You're not ready to get out of bed yet."

Her voice and face are so familiar...

"Do I—," Sin began.

No, that's not what's important right now.

"Where am I?" Sin croaked, making a face.

The air burns so much.

The old woman smiled. "You're at my house. You're still in Nineveh."

Sin stared in shock and it took a moment to compose himself. "Sorry. I have to go right now."

"No. *I'm* sorry, you're too injured to go anywhere yet, but you're safe. No one knows you're alive except for me and my granddaughter."

"You know who I am?"

"Of course. I took care of you for years after you were born."

Sin tilted his head in query.

"It's ok, you and your brother were very young," she said kindly. "Your father knew Shumu wasn't really suited to care for toddlers on his own. He was always there, but when you scraped your knees or woke up with a nightmare... well, that was me."

"... Rooroo?"

"You always called me Rooroo," she laughed. "I guess it was too hard to say Roohangiz."

"How--," Sin paused with a grimace, "How am I alive?"

"I was a physician before I was your nursemaid. That's why your father chose me for the job. They used to say I was as close to a Weaver as you can get without the gift, but then my granddaughter was born and I guess I just felt it was my time to retire. That girl, so mischievous," Roohangiz said, shaking her head, "but I guess you're lucky she snuck out that night to see what was going on in that house. You're alive, thanks to her."

"Is Shumu...?"

Roohangiz shook her head. "Shumu and the other women were dead when I arrived. You were barely hanging on by a thread, but sometimes a thread is all you need."

Sin turned away from her.

Shumu's dead. I'm alone now.

Sin touched his neck. The wound had mostly healed on the outside. It was just tender.

"How long has it been?"

"Maybe a couple of weeks? But that's why you still need your rest."

Weeks. I've been asleep for entire weeks and every day I'm here, I'm putting Roohangiz and her family in danger. But where could I go? I have no home. I have no family... what am I going to do?

A cool breeze filtered through the garden, gently caressing Eva's cheeks and tossing the hair along her shoulders as it carried the sweet floral perfumes of the garden into her nostrils. She took a deep breath, savouring the peace.

Eva frowned.

What is that boy doing?

Nebu was sitting on an out-of-the-way bench where a growing nest of shavings piled onto the surrounding lawn.

"Hey there, little man," Eva said.

"Hey Eva," Nebu said, absently.

"What are you working on?"

"I had an idea." Nebu set aside a long, curved piece of sharpened wood.

"Oh, yeah?"

"Yeah, I've been cross-training between your style and the Babylonian style for a while now, and I realized that Bo Dancers are really powerful. It's probably a better overall combat style."

He picked up a staff and carved into one end.

"I can definitely agree with that."

"But I feel like Bo Dancers are also at a sort of disadvantage."

"How so?"

"In the field, the enemy is trying to kill us, but you can only disarm someone or knock them out with a staff. That means that our losses are permanent, while the enemy's losses only last as long as it takes to wake up again."

"They don't always wake up."

"I'm sure a lot of them would, though. Even if half of them do, that's a lot of enemy forces we have to put down twice."

Nebu blew shavings out of the deep notch he had created at the end of the staff.

"Ok, where are you going with this?"

Nebu fitted the wooden blade into the slot on the staff and wrapped the joint tightly with leather. "Bo Dancers are experts at disabling their opponents because they know how each hit affects the body. What if we gave them a blade? Like, what if we added a blade to their weapon? Just like this?" he said, presenting the altered staff to Eva.

"Let me see?" Eva said, accepting the weapon.

She tested the blade joint and then stood up and balanced the staff in her hand.

Seems pretty well balanced still, although a metal blade would need a counterbalance.

Eva looked around and then whirled the blade around in the familiar forms of her style. The staff still felt like an extension of her body despite the modification.

"Hmm, not bad. You have to be aware of the blade positioning, but otherwise, yeah, it would actually work pretty well," Eva said.

"I mean, you still have a blunt end, but there are times when having the blade would help, right?" Nebu asked.

"Yeah... that's true. What do you want to call it?"

"I think I'll call it a Scythe."

"A Scythe... Hmm, Can I keep this?"

"Yeah, sure. I was making it for you, anyway."

"You're cute."

Nebu growled. "I'm not trying to be cute. I mean, I'm a warrior. If I can do something that makes our army stronger, isn't that what I *should* be doing?"

"You're right. This is really great. Thank you."

"Eva," Nebu said.

"What's up?"

"Do you think people take me seriously?"

"What do you mean?"

"Like, do you think people see me as a warrior or as a kid?"

"Well, technically you *are* a kid," she said, ruffling his hair a bit.

Nebu recoiled gently.

"Hey, look at me. You are not an adult yet. That's just a fact—"

"Forget it."

"BUT," she said, pulling him back towards her, "you're smart, you have great reflexes, and you're a great fighter. If you would have asked me if I thought you'd have my back in a fight, I would've said yes. Without question."

"Really?"

"Absolutely. If you're serious about your training, it doesn't matter how old you are or what people think. All anyone cares about is whether they can depend on you when the time comes."

"Well, you can depend on me. I think I'm a warrior, so I guess I am one."

"No 'I guess'. Say, 'I'm a warrior'."

"I'm a warrior."

"Maybe one more time like you actually believe it."

"I'm a warrior!" he said more fiercely.

"That's what I thought," she said with a gentle smirk. "I'm going to take this prototype to the blacksmith and see what it looks like with a metal blade."

"Thanks, Eva!" Nebu grinned.

The blinding white walls of Babylon seemed to repel Sin as he walked along a nearly vacant road to the city.

It feels like I'm walking upriver, but there's literally no other path for me.

Sin pulled away the cloth covering his mouth and took a waterskin from under his cloak.

Sin lifted the waterskin to his mouth, higher and higher, until he held it over his head. Only a drop came out.

Shit, I ran out just in time, I guess.

The glistening white walls loomed above Sin as he reached the gates of Babylon.

It's been so long since I was last here.

"Stop where you are!" a guard shouted.

Sin jerked his attention forward and saw two guards materializing from the shadow of the gate.

So much for entering unnoticed.

"What brings you to Babylon?" the guard demanded as he stopped in front of Sin.

Think, think, think... why would I need to talk to Kandalanu?

"I—uh, have a message—an urgent message. From King Azra," Sin said.

The guard grunted. "Alright. What is this message?" he said.

"It's for the king's ears only."

"Your message will never meet the king's ears if I don't approve it."

Shit. I shouldn't have picked Assyria. I don't know anything about what's going on in the court right now. Why would Azra send a messenger here? He won't wait much longer for an answer. I can't think of anything. I blew it. I blew my only chance to survive.

Sin jumped as the guard placed a hand on Sin's shoulder. "Look at me. How old are you?"

"Uh, seventeen."

"Ok. I've heard of... *King* Azra. Judging by the look on your face, this message is going to mean life or death for you or someone you care about. Am I right?"

Sin nodded.

The guard sighed, looking around at the landscape. "Alright. Alright, here's how this is going to happen. I will escort you, you will say your piece and when the king is finished with you, I will escort you back to the gates."

"Thank you. Thank you, sir."

"If you do anything suspicious, I will kill you on sight. Do you understand?"

Sin nodded.

The guard grunted and shook his head. "Ok let's go," he said to Sin before directing the guard beside him. "You're with me."

Relief and anxiety ebbed and flowed inside of Sin as he processed the interaction that just occurred and prepared himself to meet Kandalanu.

This guard... it doesn't make sense for him to agree to help so suddenly. He definitely didn't appear to recognize me. Does he fear Azra for some reason? No, it felt more like pity. Maybe he has a son my age? Will Kandalanu be as willing to help me?

As they walked, more details of the city sparked a collage of near-forgotten memories from Sin. A stack of empty barrels sat along a wall beside a fruit preserve vendor, shaded by the colourful canopy above. A lid leaning up against the pile rocked slightly with a sudden gust of wind, drawing Sin back to a moment of surprise as he discovered his brother's hiding place in a long-finished game of hide and seek. Sin passed a sweets' vendor he and Ashur frequented, and then a shadowed alley nearby where a group of boys once tried to rob them of their treat. Sin remembered their victory over the boys and then Ashur's disappointment upon finding their treats now covered in dirt on the ground. So many places where he and his brother hid when they snuck away from Shumu. Places where they fought or played with other children. Sin found it oddly comforting to return here and wade through his childhood memories. Everything was the same as he remembered, except slightly weathered.

"Wait here," the guard said, as they stopped a few paces from the palace gate.

He spoke with the men guarding the entrance, prompting one to go inside. When he returned, he signalled Sin and his escort to approach.

The garden, it's so nostalgic. It's hardly changed either since the Queen was alive. Maybe it's a bit bigger? I think there were different flowers... and definitely different guards.

Women carrying staves lined the walls and walkway.

Emotions bubbled up from him as he spotted the familiar multi-fingered hat ahead, it's bells jangling with every movement. Kandalanu faced away from Sin while he talked to a boy and girl both around Sin's age, and Nabo stood to one side.

Ashur and I loved you. We called you uncle... but after everything that happened, can I trust you? Should I?

Nabo directed his imposing stare toward Sin, but it melted into surprise. Nabo whispered into Kandalanu's ear and he turned and stared at Sin with an unreadable expression before gesturing for him to approach.

Every step was heavier than the one before it. Sin's ears burned and his scalp prickled, forcing him to completely remove his headwrap.

A long silence filled the distance between them. Sin shifted uncomfortably and fiddled with the scarf in his hand.

"Come, sit with me," Kandalanu said, gesturing toward a pair of cubic stones. The two sat facing opposite one another. "How many years has it been since you visited the city?"

What?

"I—uh, I don't know. I think maybe ten?"

"Ah yes. You were still a boy then. Is it the same as you remember?"

"Yeah, mostly, I guess."

"A lot has happened—probably more than even I know, judging by the look of you."

Sin nodded, reflexively reaching for his neck.

"One question is burning at me, though, my boy. Why are you here?"

"I—I don't know," Sin said, as his gaze sunk to the ground.

"Do you want the throne?"

"What? No. I've never wanted the throne. It was always supposed to be Ashur—"

"Do you want to kill me?"

Sin gaped at Kandalanu's directness. "Wh—why would I want to kill you?"

"Well, you're here, without Shumu, which tells me he has probably been killed and judging from that nasty scar on your throat, he probably died protecting you. Obviously, *someone* tried to kill you. The question is, do you blame me?"

Sin shook his head. "I'm pretty sure it was Azra. When we were going to leave Nineveh, we met a woman that was travelling with her daughter."

"A woman?"

"Yeah. She was going to help us escape before—before we were attacked. She said some things... about you and what you were planning. It didn't sound like you wanted me or Ashur dead. She seemed to think everything was Azra's fault."

"Do you believe her?"

"I don't think you're completely innocent, but I don't think you expected Azra to kill everyone."

Kandalanu nodded. "That is a fair analysis," he murmured. "Do you remember this woman's name?"

Sin paused for a moment. "Shumu called her Uma."

"Do you know where she is now?"

"Probably the same place as Shumu," Sin said.

Kandalanu nodded carefully. The girl he had been speaking with earlier sniffed and cleared her throat.

"Oh, Eva?" he said, turning to the girl, "I've kept you long enough. I know you have something urgent you need to do right now. We'll speak again later?"

"Y-yes, thank you, your highness," she croaked faintly. The boy beside her watched with concern.

"Go with her, Daniel," Kandalanu said.

Daniel nodded and jogged after Eva.

Kandalanu leaned backward, folded his arms, and exhaled deeply. "Sin, you don't want the throne. You don't want to kill me, and you clearly don't have a message from Azra. I don't understand why you're here. What should I do with you?"

"I—I don't know. When Shumu and I were on the run, it never really mattered *where* we would go specifically because I still had one person in the world that cared about me. But then he died. Now I'm alone and everyone that knew me considers me a traitor for crimes I never committed. Everyone, apparently, except you."

Sin met Kandalanu's gaze.

"Maybe you're partly to blame for everything that happened, but you were always kind to Ashur and me. I have to believe that you never wanted either of us to die. And I guess I need to believe that some part of you still wants me to survive now."

Kandalanu felt his face tighten into a grin. "You know, Nabo, there's something uniquely satisfying about walking through the grass in bare feet. I know, without a doubt, that if I were sitting at my throne and someone rubbed my feet with pads of grass, I would hate it, and yet I find this uniquely comforting."

"That is quite the mystery, my lord. Although I would caution you against demonstrating too much mystery in front of the nobles when our allies are so few," Nabo said.

"Nonsense, this is my garden," Kandalanu said, waving him off. "Besides, there is no one here that has met me for the first time. The king made it very well known he chose his jester to be the king of Babylon after his brother's betrayal. I'm sure that even outside of the empire, very few have not heard of the jester king. No, their reactions are measured. They're reacting in a way that they believe is appropriate to their station, but make no mistake, when you peel away all that pretense, they know what to expect of me and me of them."

"Yes, sire."

"I'm an old man, Nabo, and I've spent almost a quarter of my life quietly improving the lives of the people he sent me here to shame. If I want to walk around barefoot in *my* garden, I'm going to."

"I agree, sire."

Kandalanu surveyed the garden thoughtfully for a moment. "Nabo, we've known each other for a long time."

"Yes, sire."

"And yet you still doubt me."

"Is it not my job to be critical and advise you accordingly?"

"It is, but it's interesting which times you feel compelled to speak up and when you choose to stay silent."

"Understood."

Kandalanu turned and placed his arm on Nabo's shoulder. "My friend, I don't think you do. I'm not asking you to give me less advice. I'm asking you why you would put *so much* effort into advising my choice of footwear and none into my decisions regarding recently dethroned monarchs requesting asylum."

"Truthfully," Nabo sighed, "I don't know what you should do with Sin, or even if you made the right decision. In moments like these, I've always found its best to say less, and trust your judgment to carry us through."

"I appreciate that. I guess we'll have to see if I made the right choice."

A brief silence passed between them until Nabo spoke again. "I'm sorry that Ariel didn't make it out of Nineveh."

Kandalanu nodded and cleared his throat. "Me too. I said she would get herself killed doing the right thing.

I just never expected how *accurate* that would be." Kandalanu shook his head, putting his sandals back on.

"Sire, that road won't bring you peace."

"No, you're right. You're right," he said, pretending to appreciate the interwoven vines and lattice above. "I agree with what you were saying earlier about taking advantage of the current instability and carving out new alliances from the slighted and the vengeful."

"Assuming we can also convince them to ally with each other."

"I am a firm believer that there is no grudge a political marriage can't solve—at least temporarily."

"We will see. The hatred between Media and Skuza runs deep."

"Have faith, my old friend," Kandalanu said, patting Nabo on the back. "Speaking of which, I've actually been thinking for some time about a way to renew our own bonds with Media."

"Oh?"

"Adoption," Kandalanu said, motioning for them to head back into the palace from one of the nearby side entrances.

"Adoption, sire?"

"Yes," Kandalanu said. As he turned into a side room, he waited for Nabo to follow and shut the door. "I would like to adopt your son and betroth him to Cyaxares' daughter, Amytis."

Nabo stood in shocked silence.

"Come, sit," Kandalanu said, gesturing to a small table in the centre of the room with chairs. "I believe it would strengthen our position with Media considerably and give us a way to maintain their loyalty without oppressing them."

Nabo moved the chair so that he could face Kandalanu with his back against a wall before he sat down. "Why Nebu and not Sin?"

"Sin would be better suited I'll admit, but he doesn't want it." Kandalanu knelt and rummaged through a series of nearby cabinets.

"One could argue that you ended up being a capable leader despite not wanting the throne."

"Yes, yes, but there is a time for a thoughtful leader, and there is a time for an assertive leader. Sin is incredibly compassionate and thoughtful, but I feel that will make it difficult for him to be an effective leader at a time like this."

"With a civil war on the horizon, you mean?"

"Is that not what I said?" Kandalanu asked, over his shoulder.

"So your first choice in succession—during a time of war—is a 12-year-old boy with no prior training?"

"He's had plenty of training."

"He's had combat and weapons training, not diplomatic training."

"Is it not the same? On the battlefield, you learn to size up an opponent, execute negotiations, adapt to unexpected change, and make tactical decisions on the fly. There's no better place to learn diplomacy in a hurry."

"That's frightening. I fear for both my son and the empire."

"That was very melodramatic. Are you taking this conversation seriously?"

Nabo peered at Kandalanu's back.

"I can feel that stare, Nabo. Your son will be fine. He will have the royal guard and an army of Bo Dancers. And he will have wise council from both you and Sin. He will be fine."

"Could you at least consider the possibility that Sin is the stronger choice before you make any official decrees?"

"If it makes you feel better, I promise to sleep on it. Alright?"

"I would appreciate that very much."

"Alright then, consider it tabled."

"So your plan for Sin—currently—is that he trains my son to be king?"

"Currently. Eventually. Down the road. Did you not say you trust my judgment?" Kandalanu asked.

Nabo nodded.

"Excellent." Kandalanu pulled a jug of wine from a cabinet.

Nabo sighed. "So why have you decided all of this now?"

"So we have a plan in place before we leave, of course," Kandalanu said, moving to a side table and sniffing a bottle of wine. "Where are those cups?" he muttered to himself, searching in an adjacent cabinet.

"Leave? Leave where?"

"I've been thinking it's about time we negotiate an alliance with Egypt. Ah! Here they are," he said, pouring a mouthful into a cup.

"That's interesting. Eva was thinking the same thing when she and I spoke last," Nabo said, suppressing a grin.

Kandalanu emptied the wine into his mouth, swished, and then spit. A moment passed before he shrugged and began pouring two cups. When he looked up, he noticed that Nabo's grin had tightened into concern.

"Relax, it's not poisoned. Probably. I have many years of experience testing wine for poisons, so *very* probably," Kandalanu said, handing a cup to Nabo.

"Yes, but," Nabo said, taking the cup, "the fact we're having this conversation leads me to believe you've never tasted poisoned wine."

Kandalanu sat down beside Nabo. "You don't know that. And either way, I've drunk plenty of *unpoisoned* wine in my lifetime. Enough, one could say, that I could detect the slightest note out of place."

"One could say." Nabo stared forebodingly into his cup.

"Well? Drink up!"

Nabo shook his head. "Here's to good health!" he said too loudly, and then raised his cup and emptied it in a matter of gulps. When Nabo set his cup down, he sat motionless for several moments with his eyes shut.

Kandalanu leaned in close to his face. When Nabo finally opened his eyes again, Kandalanu threw himself back dramatically and let out a relieved hoot before refilling their cups. "What a relief! For a moment, I thought I was going to die alone."

"Hilarious."

Kandalanu suppressed a grin and sat back thoughtfully. "Going back to Eva, though, she has some powerful arguments in favour of strengthening our ties in the south. I'm not afraid to say that woman is a force of nature, just as Uma was. She comes in like a gentle rain and moves you like an ocean wave."

Nabo chuckled. "Yeah, I've experienced that myself. There's no disagreeing with her."

"No, there is not. She keeps herself in the know, and she can back up anything she throws at you."

"That she can."

"Have you seen her fight?"

"We've sparred a few times. I have to say, I'm not sure if I could best her on the battlefield. She doesn't fight with a blade and she could easily outmatch any of my swordsmen, any day."

"Actually, Nebuchadnezzar has been working on a prototype staff that includes a blade," Kandalanu said, taking a sip.

"You're kidding."

"I'm completely serious. He's calling it a *scythe*."

"I don't even know what to say to that. I guess we're lucky they're loyal to Babylon."

Nabo took a long swig from his cup.

Kandalanu laughed. "Don't worry. They'll *bolster* your forces, not replace them."

"Let's hope." Nabo grinned.

"Would you say she has the respect of your men?"

"Without a doubt. She's young, but my men definitely accept her authority before they step off that field. It's spooky. I've tried to observe it directly, but it happens silently. Something just clicks and seasoned fighters want to prove themselves to her. Her approval has become the bar they all aspire to."

"Good. Promote her to general and make sure everyone is aware of the change. I want her input about how we expand north."

"Consider it done." Nabo raised his cup, emptied it, and placed it in front of him.

Kandalanu smirked and refilled his glass. "So that's it? You're just going to let me place a child in a high-ranking advisory position? Your only topics of contention are adoption, footwear, and food poisoning? As a royal advisor, you should consider how your advice would appear to an outside observer."

"We literally just agreed that she's earned it. Your feet are dyed green from prancing around the garden and you worked really hard to get me to drink this poison wine with you. As an elderly person in a dubious position of leadership, I advise you to consider how your *decisions* appear to an outside observer."

"As a *stable* and just king, beloved by the masses, I am taken aback by your comments and I feel I have no other choice but to relieve you of your royal duties," Kandalanu said, emptying his own glass.

"I'll drink to that." Nabo held out his cup as Kandalanu offered more wine.

"Most people in your position would be devastated right now."

"Most people haven't advised you."

"How hard can it be to advise a king?"

Nabo rolled his eyes and shook his head.

"What about Sin? I'll bet Sin could advise me."

"Maybe with some training."

"So, you think you could train Sin to do your job?"

"Gaining a casual understanding of what a Royal Advisor does is easy: you advise the king," Nabo began as he grabbed the pitcher and refilled their cups, "but gaining the sheer discipline required to carry out that duty... takes years."

"It takes years?"

"Years."

"And discipline?"

"Yes, so much discipline."

"And in this *discipline*, how would you describe your primary philosophy?"

"How would I describe it? I would describe it as... ok, imagine being the advisor to an important person. Like a king, for instance."

"Ok."

"And imagine you have to go in with the best intentions for your king, every day."

"Ok."

"So that means you critically analyze all situations from multiple angles—"

"Ok, I'm with you."

"—so that you can construct and provide the most meaningful advice to your king." Nabo emptied the pitcher into his cup, prompting Kandalanu to search the cabinet for more wine.

"Seems reasonable."

"All the while," Nabo began with a chuckle, "you maintain perfect, unreadable fucking emotional control—"

"Perfect control. I've noticed that," Kandalanu said with a grin as he returned with a fresh jug.

"Yes. Perfect emotional control. Which you will need—and get this," he said laughing disruptively, "You will need perfect emotional control when you provide all that carefully crafted advice because the king... will ignore... all of it," Nabo whooped with pure uncontrolled laughter.

"Because the king will ignore it." Kandalanu laughed.

"All of it," Nabo said between breaths, "It's like—it's like, 'Sire, I don't think you should do cartwheels in the corridor'."

"Cartwheels?"

"Cartwheels, like full-on cartwheels. I'll say, 'Sire, I don't think you should do cartwheels. You're the king. You know what he says?"

"What does he say?" Kandalanu grinned.

"Because I am the king, I can do cartwheels anywhere I please." Nabo finished with a mock flourish, almost falling off his chair.

Contagious laughter ensnared the two of them until they were both out of breath.

Kandalanu's chest and ribs burned from howling. "You-you're unbelievable. Do you realize what you just—" Kandalanu winced and then shook his head while he tried to catch his breath.

Neither could speak again for another few minutes.

Nabo stared into his cup with a lopsided smile, eyes glazed with wine. "You know, you are the most ridiculous person I have ever met, but you are also my favourite person," he said, pausing for a hiccup. "I don't keep you alive because you're my king."

"No?"

"No. Not really."

"Then why bother protecting me at all?"

"I keep you alive because I would be sad if you died." Then Nabo looked up at Kandalanu, raw emotion straining his face.

"I would be sad if you died too," Kandalanu said, pausing thoughtfully, "but the truth is, my friend, you are a warrior and I am a king. Long life and a peaceful death are two things we swore off when we became who we are."

"That's easy for an old man to say."

"Are you jealous that I've somehow managed to get a couple of extra murder-free decades over you?"

"Yes, when you put it that way, I have to agree," Nabo said, gesturing with his cup.

"Well, there is a secret to living as long as I have," Kandalanu said, peeking up at Nabo from the pitcher as he refilled his friend's cup.

"Get a good bodyguard?"

"Oh, no. Nothing like that."

"Really?? I think it's 'get a good bodyguard'."

"No, the secret is to get a good night's sleep and a well-balanced diet."

"So, you're telling me, all of these years, you never expected anyone would make an attempt on your life?"

"Of course I did. That's why I hired a good bodyguard," Kandalanu said, struggling to suppress a grin.

Nabo snorted. "You... You're—someday people are going to read about you and they will never believe you were an actual person."

"It's always when you've made the biggest impact that people will invariably doubt you've done anything at all."

CHAPTER 14

BLOOD AND ASHES

A familiar voice echoes in the darkness: "It's not that we've done anything wrong, Azazel. I think it's just that we're here at all."

Daniel clasps his head and screams. Bodies of his brothers and sisters lay everywhere. Blood pools into rivers that paint streaks across the ground. Everything fades to darkness again.

"This place is beautiful," the female voice says. "We can make a home here."

Images of a lush green valley in the shadow of a mountain flash intensely. Houses. Gardens. People laughing. Bodies. Bodies bleeding everywhere. Darkness.

"The people call this place Beit Jinn," the voice giggles.

Daniel screams again with tears in his eyes, looking down at his blood-soaked hands. The blood converges into his right hand and then forms itself into a scarlet blade.

Daniel roars. Every vein in his body threatens to explode.

And he charges. Slices. Impales. He screams in the faces of the dead.

Daniel shot out of bed, panting.

Was that a dream... or a memory?

Daniel sat for a moment trying to collect himself when he saw something move in the night. He held his breath and listened. He was sure he could hear something, but his heart still pounded against his ears.

Daniel rolled out of bed, narrowly escaping a knife attack. A quick glance over the shoulder revealed a man dressed completely in black standing over the bed. The assassin lunged at him again, but Daniel dodged. A barrage of swipes and thrusts sent Daniel into a flurry of dodges and spinning misdirects that gave him the opportunity to kick the other man and make a run for Eva's room.

I have to make sure she's ok.

Daniel ran down the long, brightly lit corridor, thankful for palace lighting standards.

Where are the guards?

Daniel's breath was loud and hoarse, but he kept running at a full sprint, shifting his weight to take corners without slowing down.

They can probably hear me coming if they've already made it to Eva's room, but if there's any chance I can beat them, I have to try.

Just as Daniel made the last corner, he saw someone slip into her room. Daniel threw his weight into the door before it closed. A man grunted, staggering backward as the door swung open.

Daniel charged at him, shoulders down, slamming into the man's chest. The man brought his elbow down onto Daniel's back and a knife flashed upward, running through Daniel's ribcage. Daniel screamed in pain, waking Eva. Eva immediately rolled off the bed, grabbed her staff, and landed in a defensive stance.

The assassin struck Daniel again before Eva leapt forward. She used the downward momentum to break her attacker's collarbone. Then she pivoted, knocking him in the side of the face hard enough to send him flying. Eva waited for her assailant to get up, but he stayed motionless on the ground.

Daniel groaned and crumpled against the wall for a moment. His side seared in agony, and the wound gurgled when he breathed.

Not good. It feels like only one side is pulling in air.

Eva ran to him. "Daniel! Are you ok?"

Daniel nodded, but he could feel the warm wetness leaking out. Eva hastily tore a strip off a clean tunic laid out for her by the palace servants and wrapped it tightly around Daniel's chest.

"This will have to do for now. Can you walk?"

Daniel nodded weakly and stumbled towards her. Eva watched him carefully, and then grabbed her staff and checked the hallway for other attackers. "Stay close to me, okay?"

Daniel nodded again as Eva pulled him into the hallway after her.

The fight supercharged Eva's senses. She felt like she could see in the dark, and her body jerked to a halt at the slightest sound of movement. The constant stopping didn't seem to affect Daniel, though, as he hobbled a few paces behind her, trying to stay close. Eva checked the next corner for any movement and then waited for Daniel.

Eva looked back to check on Daniel for a moment and heard soft footsteps quickly coming toward her. As she swivelled around, she came face to face with a human wall of black lamellar armour. Instinctively, she whirled her staff upward, and it connected with an alabaster corner as the man in black dodged.

"Eva, it's me," the man whispered. Nabo slowly poked his head around the corner with his hands held upward. Eva lowered her staff.

"Where is Kandalanu?" Eva whispered.

Kandalanu grinned as he appeared from behind Nabo. "I've been hiding in the shadow of a mountain."

"Where is Nebu? Is he not with you?" Nabo asked.

"Not yet. We were just attacked, and I decided the best option was to find you and Kandalanu."

Nabo nodded. "Ok. We need to find my son. Let's split up—"

"Dad!" Nebu shouted as he and Sin ran down the hall towards them. Nebu hugged his dad when they reached the group.

"Are you ok?" Nebu asked.

"Yeah, but me and Sin had to fight like 10 guys. I was a warrior, Eva!" he said, flexing.

"Good job, buddy." Eva smiled.

"He fights really well," Sin said.

"Yeah, and Sin is on a whole other level. He might be as good as you, Eva."

"Really?" Eva asked, peering sideways at Sin.

"Yeah, it was crazy. Where did you even learn to fight like that, Sin?"

"I uh—it's a long story," he said, rubbing the back of his neck.

"Yeah, well, it was really lucky we were together, right?" Nebu beamed.

"Definitely."

"We need to move. We've stayed here too long and something tells me the palace is missing an entire guard detail," Eva said.

"Agreed. We have to escape the palace and blend into the city. Then we'll regroup to figure out our next course of action. The most direct route to the city, however, is through the garden," Nabo said.

"Through the main gate?" Eva asked.

"Through any gate. All exits out of the palace pass through the garden. The builders walled the city in three layers but they built the palace less... tactically."

"It's unlikely that the city's founders expected this kind of attack to penetrate the outer defences," Sin commented.

Nabo grunted in agreement. "If we're going to meet any resistance, it'll be waiting for us in the garden."

"Whoever did this had specific knowledge of the palace security," Kandalanu said.

"Would Azra know those kinds of details?" Eva asked.

"General Ballit would, and he commands a legion of assassins and spies from Nineveh. With Azra on the throne, he now has command of Ballit's men," Nabo said.

Eva nodded hesitantly and quickly took stock of the group, ending with Daniel. *He's looking worse.*

Eva locked eyes with Nabo, and he nodded as if reading her mind. "Okay, let's go."

Eva followed Nabo and Kandalanu, while pulling Daniel by the wrist, closely behind. When they reached the garden, the twilight still shadowed it heavily.

Nabo signalled for them to stop and survey the area.
It's so quiet and still.

Nabo signalled for them to move again, but Eva grabbed his arm. "Wait. I don't hear any crickets."

Nabo draped Daniel around his shoulders like an injured lamb and then exchanged glances with Eva and Kandalanu. "Okay. We're going to make a run for it. Expect a fight, and no matter what, just keep going." Then he placed his hand on Nebu's shoulder. "No matter what, you run."

Nebu nodded hesitantly and hung his head, but Eva clasped his hand, drawing his attention. When he looked up at her, she smiled. "You're a warrior."

Nebu nodded and readied himself. "I'm a warrior."

Nabo surveyed the grounds one more time. "Okay, RUN. Go, go, go!"

The five of them took off in a hard sprint for the gate.

Three men, all dressed in black, immediately lunged from the shadows. Eva and Nebu whirled, evading a pair of knives in unison. As Eva assessed her surroundings, she saw the body of one of their black-clad assailants fly off to her side like a doll.

Did Nabo just throw a man across the garden?

Eva spotted five more men approaching from the front. She spun and wove her way through the first two, disabling them without stopping, but a third forced her to block. Eva disengaged, pushing the man backward, but he came again. Eva parried his lunge and whirled behind him, knocking him out with a thrust of her staff.

Suddenly another grappled her from behind with a basket hold.

Dammit!

A loud crack vibrated the air behind her and his grip released. Eva spun in time to see the man collapse beside her, revealing Nebu holding a staff.

"Where did you get that?" she asked.

"Over there," he smirked, pointing to his side, where Kandalanu stood with three bodies sprawled around him.

"Kandalanu! Where did you learn to fight like that?" Eva asked.

"I've lived a very long life, my dear, and I didn't fill it wholly by playing the fool." Kandalanu winked.

More shadowy assassins flooded the courtyard, encircling the three of them, forcing them back to back.

Sin burst out of the mob, vaulting upward and landing in a low stance between Eva and Kandalanu, facing the assassins.

"Wow, Nabu wasn't joking about those moves," Eva said.

"Told ya," Nebu shouted over his shoulder.

"You've fought with a staff before?"

"Once or twice," Sin replied, spinning the weapon adeptly into his other hand.

"Good, I'm counting on it. Are you ready, little man?" Eva asked.

"Like you even have to ask," Nebu said. "Did they have to bring an entire army, though?"

"They probably thought they needed to," Kandalanu said as he readied two knives. "Your father's strength is... well known."

Grunts and stifled yelps sounded as bodies flew across the garden.

"No kidding." Eva gaped as Nabo plowed his way into the circle, using a corpse to shield himself. When he reached Eva and Kandalanu, he casually tossed the body away and set Daniel down between them.

"I thought you said to keep running no matter what," Eva said.

"I did, but you stopped. They've cut us off from the gates either way, though. We're going to have to make a stand here." Nabo drew a sword with each hand and readied himself.

Running and being carried had ground Daniel's wounds to the bone. Pain vibrated throughout his body like a low hum. As the enemy closed in, everyone tightened their formation around Daniel. His heart drummed heavily against his ears as he struggled to stand, and he felt light-headed.

"Stay awake, Daniel. Keep your eyes open," Eva shouted.

The first group of combatants ran at Nabo. Nabo lifted his sword with both hands and slashed through three of them like stalks of grain. His sword lodged itself firmly into the spine of the last man, and he had to dislodge it by pushing him off with his boot. Blood splattered onto Daniel as Nabo raised his sword again for another swipe.

Kandalanu reached into slits at the back of his robes and then launched knives from his palms with shocking pinpoint precision.

He's cutting them down almost as well as Nabo.

Suddenly, something crashed into Daniel and he toppled against Nabo's back. Daniel turned to catch Eva bracing against her opponent, while he bore down on her with an overhead attack. Eva struggled for a moment and then launched him backward with a leveraged kick.

"Sorry about that!" she yelled over her shoulder to Daniel. Two more black-clad assassins ran at Eva before he could sign a reply.

Eva's bo blurred left and right, crunching wrists and cracking jaws, causing her opponents to fall backward unconscious.

Even Nebu stood his ground, using his speed and size to evade and create openings. Bodies piled onto the ground around them, but enemies continued to materialize from the shadows. And they were slowly closing in.

Kandalanu whirled, bells jingling, as he sliced and whipped knives into his opponents. Eva fluidly spun and feinted, thrusting and blocking, dancing through the attacks, sometimes maneuvering in tandem with Nebu or Sin. Nabo leveraged his enormous size to cleave multiple attackers with every swipe.

Waves of bodies flew or crumpled in every direction as they fought. The air became saturated with the scent of iron while sweat and blood fell in every direction like crimson rain.

Blackness covered Daniel's vision for a moment, and when he came to, he found himself slumped over Eva's back.

"Daniel!" she screamed. "Wake up!" Eva attempted to fight while keeping Daniel from falling over.

Daniel pushed off of her unsteadily, causing Eva to look over her shoulder at him, but Daniel nodded to her as he wheezed and regained his balance.

As he followed Eva's movements, he realized they had become slower and less dynamic than before. Even the others moved more sluggishly.

Nabo swatted at an enemy, but he evaded completely, and the unchecked momentum threw Nabo off balance. Another combatant nearby slashed Nabo's hamstring and carved open his leg, but Nabo brought his arm down for a crushing blow. Then several men flanked Nabo's uninjured side, swarming him completely.

Eva exploded into a tidal wave of thrusts and spinning sweeps that disabled them, but then another man leapt at Eva from behind. She tried to evade his wooden clubs but lost her footing and the connecting blow brought her to her knees. He seized the moment and whipped a double blow at the side of her head. Eva went limp and fell to the ground, but Daniel dove, catching her as she landed.

The club-wielding attacker laughed darkly and advanced on Daniel.

Shit! Where is Nabo? Nabo laid on the ground beside Daniel, gashes glistening in the dim morning light.

Suddenly, Kandalanu appeared behind Eva's assailant, stabbed him several times, and kicked his lifeless body away. Daniel's mouth went wide in awe, but Kandalanu only chuckled between breaths and threw himself back into battle.

Wave after wave poured in on them. Kandalanu spun and sliced and whipped his knives in a fluid dance that held the enemy back, but the dance slowed with each passing moment. Movements that were dazzling before now revealed openings. A knife made its way into Kandalanu's back. Kandalanu grunted and threw two more knives as he fell into a kneeling position, chest heaving. One blade sank deep into its target, but the other missed. The assassin seized the moment and dove at Kandalanu, thrusting his dagger into the old man. Kandalanu pulled it out and shot it into the man's eye before crumpling to the ground.

Sin and Nebu continued to fight, nearly back to back, circling Daniel and Eva. Black figures inched closer, like shadows pooling around a dimming flame.

A laugh erupted from Sin that slowly transformed into a primal cry that emptied his lungs. He inhaled and screamed into the faces of his enemies again. Nebu joined him, screaming toward the enemy until his voice cracked. Shock blanketed the enemies' faces. Sin and Nebu dove back into battle, spinning and clubbing the enemy, but their fatigue caught up with them. Enemies crowded over them, stabbing and impaling the boys until they collapsed onto Daniel, pinning him to the ground.

Everyone is dead now. This is it....

Colour drained from the world, leaving a silvery sheen over everything. All movement stopped, leaving Daniel alone in a frozen hellscape.

"*This is it!*" a voice mocked. "That's you. That's how you sound every time something interesting is happening."

It's just like in Mari.

"Good job remembering this time," Ankl said flatly as he towered above the frozen attackers beside him.

Daniel carefully wiggled out from under Eva and tried to set Eva's head down.

"I wouldn't do that if I were you."

"I'm just laying her head down so she doesn't fall."

"Yes, but, everything that happens right now will happen in an instant, which means, if you actually make contact between her head and the ground, the speed that they'll make contact—and the *force*—" Ankl paused, arched his eyebrows and inhaled sharply, "I just wouldn't do it."

Daniel shook his head and carefully stepped around Eva, leaving her suspended where she lay.

"So, I couldn't help noticing how good you've gotten at letting your friends die." Ankl gestured to the scene around them.

"Wh-what?"

"Look at this. It's a masterpiece. Blood raining down from the sky. Bodies scattered across the ground like a basket weave. And here you are, at the centre of it all, just standing around like a spectator. You can't even find paintings this dramatic for another couple of millennia."

Daniel growled. "Are you fucking kidding me? This isn't art, this is a massacre! I'm hardly even a part of it. I couldn't physically pick up any of these weapons if I tried. I can't punch or club someone using my arms because it would literally break my bones while doing no damage to my opponent. There is nothing I can do in this situation to affect any of these people. Nothing."

"Ok, so then you're just a useless drag on everyone around you?"

"Ahhhh! No!" Daniel roared. "You just accused me of letting everyone die, and then you acknowledged that I'm useless. Why are you torturing me? Why are you here? Why am *I* even here?"

"Remember when you finally cornered Azra back at the temple?"

"... In Nineveh?" Daniel asked.

"In Sippar, obviously."

"Oh. Ok."

"The day he killed all your friends."

Daniel frowned. "Ok, yeah. Yes. I said I remember."

"Technically, you said *ok*, which means nothing, but that's fine. Please, go on remembering things how they never happened."

Daniel shook his head and looked away.

"We're here because when your adrenaline spikes, it alters your sense of time *supernaturally*."

"Wait... what about all those dreams?"

"Well, your dreams are something else entirely. Your adrenaline doesn't exactly spike during sleep, does it?"

Daniel only narrowed his eyes at Ankl.

"I'll save you the brain trauma—it doesn't."

"Ok," Daniel said hesitantly.

"Think back to your little showdown with Azra."

"Ok. I remember."

"What do you remember?"

Daniel thought for a moment. "I remember... being so angry. I just wanted him to pay."

"Good. And then what happened?"

"I felt really hot like it filled my veins with fire."

"And what did you see?"

"I saw... I saw—it was like a web of blue threads that connected everything."

"Good. What you saw were lifethreads. Tiny, invisible threads connect everything in the universe—that's why it's called *weaving* when people manipulate the lifethreads. When something is alive, it gives off a certain vibration that gets sent along its connecting threads. All objects at either end of the lifethreads vibrate at their own frequency, either amplifying or cancelling each other out. Ultimately, this is how the universe interacts with itself. The frequency of these vibrations determines everything from how brightly a star will shine to how long a person will live and even how healthy they are."

"Why can't I see them anymore?" Daniel asked.

"It's not that you can't see them, it's that you aren't *used* to seeing them. Instead of trying to see them, you just told yourself that you couldn't anymore."

"So, you're saying I should try harder?" Daniel narrowed his eyes.

"That summarizes all the advice I've ever given you."

"Yes, and it's all been very helpful so far."

"It would be if you actually listened to what I'm saying. Let me ask you, that first time when you saw the threads, what did they feel like?"

"Well... they felt hot."

"Yes, but how did they feel against your fingers?" Ankl asked.

Daniel thought hard for a second. "I don't remember. I don't think I ever touched them physically with my hands."

"That's right, you didn't. So, if your fingers never touched the threads when you wove them, why do you need hands?"

Realization washed over Daniel. "I could've... I—"

"The only person holding you back is you. It's amazing you've made it this far, to be honest, but you can think about all of that after you save yourself from these guys," Ankl said, gesturing to the swarm encircling Daniel.

Daniel appraised the remaining enemies surrounding the courtyard as colour was slowly returning to the world, thawing it into motion. When he turned back around, Ankl had disappeared.

Figures.

Daniel closed his eyes.

I have to see the threads. I have to remember....

White-hot fire coursed through Daniel's veins again, like it did in Sippar. Strips of flesh emerged from Daniel's mouth and from the ends of his forearms, like tendrils, sensing the world around him. The tendrils grew and multiplied, entwining one another until they became three tangled, pulsing knots. Each tightened around themselves until they fused into a pair of hands and a tongue.

Daniel opened his eyes. Movement had sped up almost to normal, but something else caught his eye. Fiery blue threads interwove and blanketed everything like a thick web suspended in the air. Daniel could clearly see the lifethreads connecting everything around him. Daniel felt the heat of the threads connecting the men to himself. He felt their stories pour into his mind. Their successes and failures. Their motivations. Their loved ones.

It's so loud. Daniel pushed past the cacophony.

He felt the wounds of his friends, felt their faint vibrations, and amplified them, coaxing wounds to close and tissues to strengthen and regrow themselves.

The intense light-filled Daniel again, but when he looked down at Eva, he took a deep breath and exhaled, keeping it just below the surface.

I want to save them. I'm not going to kill everyone again. Just the enemy, focus on just the enemy....

Daniel took another deep breath and went to work, pouring his fire into the veins of every intruder in the garden, just as time returned to normal.

One by one, the black-clad warriors paused in shock as they discovered Daniel standing before them, uninjured with blue flames engulfing his hands and eyes. Then shock quickly turned to fear as the first of them exploded into a bloody pile, blue fire dancing across the remains.

Another exploded.

Then another.

One man shouted and pointed at Daniel. "Demon!"

"It's Adad! He is here!" shouted another. "He has come out of the desert to punish us!"

Enemies exploded as their comrades tried to run. Waves of bloody explosions swept outward from Daniel until the garden was devoid of movement. Then the blue flames around Daniel extinguished themselves and he collapsed into the blood-soaked earth.

Daniel awoke to streaks of sunlight painted across his face from the nearby window. He groaned and rubbed his eyes.

Wait... what? My hands! I have hands again!

"That was the guards' reaction as well," Nabo chuckled.

Daniel shot upright to face Nabo and the two guards standing behind him with anxious expressions.

"Nabo!" Daniel shouted happily, "I'm glad you're ok."

"And you can talk now, apparently."

"Oh... yeah. Are Eva and Kandalanu alright?"

"They're both fine. The four of us were all found lying together, unconscious. They thought we were dead at first." Nabo smirked.

"I can imagine," Daniel replied quietly.

Nabo studied Daniel for a moment before he broke the silence. "The king has requested your presence as soon as you awoke. I realize you're still... adjusting... but—"

"No, it's ok. I understand. Is there another tunic I can wear?"

"Of course," Nabo snickered, handing Daniel a fresh tunic, "we had to destroy your old clothes, but no one expects you to meet the king naked."

Daniel chuckled nervously and threw the tunic over his head before leaving the bed. "I'm ready when you are."

As Daniel followed Nabo down the halls, he realized they were in a part of the palace he had never been before. It smelled of must, and distant yelling echoed off the stone walls. The hallway around Daniel was long and ornately decorated with alabaster and obsidian, like the rest of the palace, but there were no windows. Guards lined both sides of the hallway until it ended in front of a large wooden door. As they travelled down the hallway, the yelling grew louder.

Wait, is that... Kandalanu's voice?

Kandalanu was yelling from behind the door, but none of the guards were reacting. Daniel looked up at Nabo with concern.

"Don't worry," Nabo chuckled, "this has been going on all morning. You'll see."

Guards opened the door as they approached, allowing Daniel to see Kandalanu in a nightgown, surrounded by a team of puzzled physicians.

"No! I feel fine. In fact, I feel 20 years younger. I don't need more rest. What I need is space," Kandalanu yelled.

Two of the physicians looked at one another, while a third spoke, "Sire, we're just concerned—"

"You're concerned that the mystery of my good health is too much to accept?"

"Well, frankly... yes, sire."

"Isn't that why you're *here*—to keep me in good health? Now you're telling me you're concerned that you are doing *too* good a job?"

"Well, not exactly—"

"So you *weren't* doing a good job and now you feel suspicious about my health?" Kandalanu said, cocking an eyebrow.

"Well no, that's not—"

"Is it guilt, then? Because I can assure you, I am healthy through no fault of your own."

"Sire."

"Yes?"

"Sire, if it pleases you," another physician spoke up, "we would like to consult with other healers and return with better answers."

"Yes, please take all the time you need, but in the meantime, I am going to run my country."

The physicians bowed and then filed out of the room.

Nabo frowned. "My lord, they don't always know when you're joking."

"Yes, yes, I'm aware," Kandalanu said with a smirk and a wave, "but you would think that after serving me for decades, they might catch on, eventually."

"You would hope. I've brought Daniel as you requested."

"Ah yes, Daniel. I'm sorry to keep you waiting. It's these physicians, you understand," Kandalanu said, gathering clothing items from around the room, "Old men are supposed to be frail and sick, and here I am, healthier than yesterday."

"I understand," Daniel smirked.

Kandalanu turned to peer at Daniel under a furrowed brow, before tossing his tunic and replacing it with a clean shirt, "It doesn't matter in a private conversation like this, but remember that in public, you refer to me as sire or my lord. Your highness is also acceptable."

"Yes, uh... yes," Daniel said.

"It will get easier," Kandalanu smirked as he stepped into a pair of pants.

"Ok."

"Come help me get dressed," Kandalanu said. "Hold this."

Kandalanu handed Daniel three thick sheets of leather sewn together along the top, with rows of sheathed throwing knives inserted along the edges.

Holy crap, it's heavy. There must be 30 knives in this thing! Daniel thought as Kandalanu fed his arms through the buckled shoulder straps of the weapon holster.

Daniel helped Kandalanu tighten the straps and noticed that the three layers dangled loosely from his mid-back, making a dull jangling when he walked.

"Robe next. I was dead, you know. Nabo and the others, too. And you definitely should've been dead."

"Ah, yeah."

"And now we're all alive, and you can speak. And you seem to have freshly grown hands."

Daniel looked nervously toward Nabo, but the man's face was unreadable.

Why am I here?

Kandalanu finished tying his belt and turned to face Daniel.

"I'm very interested in not only knowing how any of this is possible but also understanding how we all became *healthier* than we were before the battle. Fighters usually don't end the battle with fewer injuries than they had going in."

"Well, we definitely didn't die, but we were all really badly injured." Daniel began.

"Yes, but *what happened?*" Kandalanu insisted.

"I—it's hard to explain," Daniel said, looking away.

Kandalanu peered at Daniel for a moment, and then walked to the edge of the room and poured himself a drink.

"I've known Uma for probably the better part of my life. She was originally from Egypt. Did you know that?"

Daniel only shook his head.

Kandalanu sat at a nearby table and motioned for Daniel to join him. "Well, she was. Uma was a magnificent woman. As regal as they come. And she had a sharp mind. Very little happened around her she was not aware of—and if she knew about it, she knew whom it impacted and what to do about it."

Kandalanu took a sip from his cup, staring off for a moment in memory. "Her perception was unmatched, that's for sure. And I could tell she really liked you."

Daniel reflexively cocked his head, and his face tightened into a frown.

"But more and more, I find myself wondering, *why?* One could argue that she protected you because she suspected Azra was the monster that we now know him to be... but then, why assign you to her personal elite guard? According to Eva, Uma summoned you with her elite guard when she would discuss sensitive information with them. Seven people in the world knew that we were planning to usurp the throne—by design—and yet, Uma believed that there should be eight."

"I—I swear I won't tell anyone."

"I know, I know. And I think Uma knew as well. I trusted Uma, and she apparently trusted you, so I will trust you, but it would help if you were being more honest with me."

Kandalanu aimed a level stare at Daniel. "Uma didn't trust you because you were mute or protect you because she had a soft spot for orphan boys. She had a gift for seeing what's important, and she definitely thought you were going to be important. I want you to tell me why."

Should I tell them? What if they think I'm a demon? Then again, they might not trust me if I don't tell them... Should I run away? If I tell them and it goes badly, I could probably run away, but I might be a fugitive, and if I bring Eva, then we'll both be fugitives. But maybe not if we don't hurt anyone when we escape. But considering everything that's happened, how likely is that? I don't know what to do. I don't know what to do.

Daniel grasped his forehead.

"Daniel," Kandalanu said patiently, "look at me. You're not in danger."

Daniel thought carefully for another moment.

"You're not."

"I think," Daniel began slowly, "I think I might... be a Weaver."

Kandalanu sat back in his chair and looked at Nabo with a smile. "I believe you."

"And you're not afraid of me?"

"Should we be?"

"Well, last night in the garden, before Ballit's men all... died... they were calling me a demon—Adad. They were all afraid of me."

"Adad, eh? Considering the state of the garden, I can see why."

"Yeah... I guess."

"You know, Weavers have always been rare, not quite as *mythical* as they are today, but always rare. It's natural for most people to be unaware of what they can do. Of what you can do, apparently. I'm sure there have been a lot of Weavers who abused their power, giving way to the stories of demons and djinn that maliciously influence humanity. But many were also known to have used their powers for the benefit of others. Healers who could weave were unmatched. Most healers repair damage or treat illness, but Weavers, they can *erase* injury and illness." Kandalanu shook his head.

"What happened to them?"

"Well, you know, people fear what they don't understand."

"Ah," Daniel said, looking down.

"People hardly considered them human, so they rarely had children—even with each other. What chance can a child have if they're labelled as a demon from birth?"

Daniel nodded.

"Weavers are not gods and they're not demons. They're just people who can weave. All people can be good, or not, but it's their choices that determine their alignment, not their heritage. Remember that."

"Ok."

Kandalanu smirked. "I'm glad your ability awoke at such a convenient time. This should give us a much-needed advantage over the enemy."

"Well actually," Daniel said, "that's not entirely true...."

Daniel and Kandalanu had talked until well after sundown. Questions led to more questions until Daniel had shared his entire life story, but Kandalanu wasn't the person he most wanted to talk to.

Daniel scanned the garden as he jogged into the silvery moonlight. A metallic smell still clung to the air, mixing with the green smells of plant life. Daniel pushed the memories aside.

I'm sure she's out here.

Finally, Daniel found her sitting on a bench near an empty flower bed.

"Hey, Eva!" Daniel shouted as he headed toward her.

Eva jumped in surprise.

"I'm sorry," Daniel said. "I didn't mean to scare you."

"No, it's my fault. I'm still not used to hearing your voice." Eva twisted slightly to face him.

"That makes sense, I guess," Daniel replied quietly, rounding the bench a few steps away.

Eva looked over the ground where they had fought the previous night. She stared at the patch of freshly overturned soil where layers of gore used to be.

"Can I sit with you?" Daniel asked.

Eva sighed.

Stupid. You're crowding her.

"I—I'm sorry. I'll go," Daniel said, walking away.

"No, wait," Eva said, "I'm sorry. I came out here to think because I wanted to be alone, but I think I'd rather have you here with me."

"Are you sure?"

"Yes, come sit." Eva patted the bench and peered out over the overturned ground in front of them where the lawn should be. Even places that usually held flowers and bushes were mostly empty beds.

I feel like I should say something. I never felt uneasy about silence when I couldn't talk, and now I feel like I'm obligated to say something. Especially about the state of this garden, which, of course, is my fault. I guess I should be glad it isn't like Mari.

"Apparently there was no way to salvage this part of the garden, so they just tilled the soil and replanted whatever was destroyed," Eva said.

Daniel sighed. "It's really crappy how everything played out. This was the area with the roses, wasn't it? I'm sorry about that."

"Yeah. Yeah, I think so. It's fine. I'm surprised you remember the roses."

"I remember most things... some things I wish I didn't."

"I know the feeling."

"Are you ok?"

"Yeah. I mean, I think so. It was just so intense. There was so much blood."

Daniel nodded. "Yeah, there was. They threw away my clothes."

Eva stifled a chuckle. "Mine too. I just can't believe everything that's happened. I mean, temple life was hard sometimes, but this... it was never like this. Everything that's happened so far—at what point can we say, 'Ok, we're there. This is officially the most ridiculous and dangerous and bloody that things can be', you know?"

Daniel nodded and allowed the silence to settle for a moment.

"And I'm a great fighter. Like really great. And Nabo and Kandalanu are *way* better than I am, but we got completely trampled, anyway."

"In your defence, though, there were like a hundred of them."

"Yeah, even so, we're up against the Assyrian Empire—an *entire empire*. How are we supposed to come out on the other end of that?"

"We'll find a way," Daniel said hopefully.

Eva searched his face and leaned forward, picking up a handful of soil and letting it crumble out of her hand.

Eva shook her head. "We shouldn't even be alive right now, but somehow you saved us? That's what everyone's saying. Somehow, you caused all of this."

"Well, apparently I'm a Weaver."

"You. You're a Weaver?" She searched his eyes.

"I would've told you sooner, but—" Daniel gestured to his mouth and shrugged.

Eva burst into laughter and shook her head. "You would've told me sooner."

Daniel grinned bashfully.

"You're so pleased with yourself. You make one good joke *ever.*" Eva shoved him playfully.

"Hey, I used to make lots of good jokes."

"You mean back when you couldn't talk?"

"Yeah, I used to make jokes all the time."

"We call those *pranks*, and most of those were hardly funny."

"You thought some of them were funny."

"Ok, so you had one good joke and one good prank. Clearly, you are the master of all comedy."

"*I* always thought I was funny."

"*You* would," Eva said, making them both laugh.

After a long pause, she looked at Daniel. "If you had this power to heal yourself all this time, why didn't you?"

"Well, I thought about it, but I figured you might stop spoon-feeding me."

"Come on, give me a real answer."

"Honestly, I just... didn't know I could, but when everyone was lying there, I realized weaving was a part of me. So, either I can weave—without hands—and we live, or I can't and we die. I wanted to live enough to try."

"I'm glad," Eva said, nudging him.

"Weaving on that many people turned out to be pretty horrible, though."

"You mean because of the gory hellscape you created?"

Daniel chuckled weakly. "I mean the experience of it. When you weave, you connect to someone, and once you're connected, you can feel the weight of their entire life; all of their memories and feelings and everything. You can feel their whole story."

"Wow, so then all of those guys you killed—"

"Yep. I knew—I still know—everything that ever happened to them. I know every justification for every decision any of them ever made, and the worst part about it is that most of them weren't evil. They didn't even want to be there. They were just regular guys following orders."

"That sounds so intense."

"It was."

"So... I guess you saw all of our stories."

"I did," Daniel said, shifting slightly. "I'll tell you right now, Kandalanu has had a wild life. That 'hapless old jester' act that he puts on was built out of necessity. He was a scary, scary man."

"So," Eva said, biting her lip, "what about my story? What did you learn about me?"

Daniel grinned, looking down. "Well, I saw you are strong and caring, but that wasn't really a surprise."

"Uh-huh?" Eva grinned.

"And I saw that you're deeply intelligent—which I also knew—but also that you're strangely analytical," he said, turning to her.

"Why *strangely*?"

"I mean, you seem so laid back. I'm just kind of surprised about how you think about things."

"So, you're saying I'm judgey," she said, fighting a smirk.

"Hey, your words, not mine," Daniel said, raising his hands.

Eva reclined and shook her head.

"I saw your village. It's exactly the way you described it, with the crystal clear water cascading over rocks from the mountain above, and the lush green valleys below. It was beautiful."

Eva pursed her lips and looked at the ground. "It's weird that you know everything about me, but you saved my life. So, I guess I'm glad you got to see it."

"Me too," Daniel said, smiling. Daniel caressed the pendant around his neck for a moment and looked over at Eva. "You know, I have something for you."

"Oh, yeah?" Eva said, straightening to look up at him.

"I've been wanting to give you this for a long time," he said, untying the pendant from his neck and placing the small stone in her hands.

Eva held the pendant delicately and looked up into his eyes. "Daniel, are you sure?"

Daniel nodded.

"Here, help me put it on." Eva turned and held her hair to the side.

"You know, I've always thought of it as good luck," Daniel said as he retied the straps.

"Really? This pendant?"

"That's what I like to think. Why not?"

"I mean, there could be good luck in this pendant, but honestly, I don't feel like you've seen a whole lot of it."

"Maybe it just didn't find the right owner. Didn't you tell me once that those pendants originally came from your village?"

Eva smiled and stared down at the pendant appreciatively. "Seriously though, it's beautiful. Thank you."

"I always thought it would suit you better than it suits me."

"I think you were right," Eva said, as she rested her head on Daniel's shoulder. "You know, this moment, this is something I would've talked to Ariel about. I miss her. I miss Uma."

"I know," Daniel said, putting his arm around her, "I miss them too."

Clacking wood vibrated the air around Eva almost rhythmically, overshadowing the shouts and grunts of her recruits. She and Nina had agreed that the girls from Nineveh had the right to learn how to defend themselves, and the training helped to take everyone's mind off everything that had happened.

Azra's unpredictable and he's fought us before... and now Azra is on the throne. If he sees us as a threat, the whole empire might be hostile to followers of Ishtar now.

Across the field, Nina ran drills with rows of new recruits, correcting their stance and posture while shouting theory over them. Meanwhile, Fatima was coaching another group through a sparring session. Sessions of every kind surrounded Eva at every skill level.

There are literally hundreds of women here, all learning to fight, and most of them aren't even from Nineveh.

Initially, it surprised Eva when a few Babylonian civilians asked to train with them, but she agreed. The next day, twice as many Babylonians joined them. Their numbers doubled again the day after that.

So, the training sessions are going really well, but we're getting a surprising number of requests from Babylonian citizens, Eva had reported. *Requests?* Kandalanu had asked in surprise.

Well, a lot of Babylonian women want to train with us... like almost double the number of people that came with us from Nineveh.

Kandalanu had chuckled. I can see why this concerns you, but don't worry. Babylonians are generally loyal to Babylon. If the women want to train, let them train.

And we definitely let them train, Eva thought with a smirk.

"You were not joking about your recruiting numbers," Nabo said, as he approached Eva and matched her stride.

"No, I was not."

"How are they coming along?"

"Not bad. I mean, a lot of these women have never picked up a weapon before, but they're all really motivated. You know? They *want* to learn, and that helps a lot."

"It certainly does."

"Do you not find that odd?"

"What do you mean?"

"Doesn't it seem odd that such a large population of women want to fight?"

"Why should it?" Eva asked with a laugh.

"Well, you know, they're *women*. I wouldn't think warfare would interest most women."

Eva nodded. "Imagine your life is filled with children, and cooking, and domestic life—sometimes under the hand of a violent husband or father. There are two options: you leave your family and live a lonely life defenceless against the world, or you stay and accept a life of humble domestic servitude. Now imagine someone offers you an opportunity—a third option— that not only empowers you but opens the door to an entirely different way of life. Tell me you wouldn't jump at that opportunity."

Nabo chuckled. "You basically described every young man I've ever trained."

"Oh, do many young Babylonian men have abusive husbands?"

"Not that I'm aware of," Nabo said with a smirk, "but I was referring more to the pursuit of adventure and a different style of life than that of a domestic tradesman."

"I'm glad I could provide some insight into the mysterious lives of women." She said, pushing her shoulder into him for a friendly shove.

A brief silence passed between them while they surveyed the trainees, causing a long-overdue question to nag at Eva.

"So," she began carefully, "Daniel was filling us in about his time at the temple... and his time with Azra. Did you know?"

Nabo clenched his jaw. "No. I had no idea."

"I'm sorry."

"Don't be. If anyone's to blame for Kaleb's death, it's me. I should've never agreed—I thought I was doing the right thing. Obviously, it's not always clear what that is. I will avenge my son soon enough," Nabo said, taking a moment. "Anyway, I didn't come here to talk about Kaleb. I wanted to ask you about Azra."

"Azra? What about him?"

"Did you know he was a Weaver when he stayed with you at the temple?"

"A few of us did."

"Did you know he was dangerous?"

Eva pursed her lips. "Uma never said anything specific to me or Ariel, except that we should be careful what we say around him and that he had a temper. In my experience, if someone warns you that someone with power has a temper, you should be extremely careful around them. We had a few close calls with him, but, you know, you follow your training and diffuse the situation however you can."

"What do you mean, *follow your training*? They trained you in diplomacy?"

"Of course. Some of Our Lady's ritual devotions involve sex magic and sometimes people would demand those services aggressively. Knowing how to be diplomatic could save your life."

"... and if that failed...?"

"Bo staff."

Nabo chuckled. "Fair enough. It wouldn't have defended you against Azra's weaves, though. That had to be frightening."

"What do you mean by that?"

Nabo gave her a doubting look. "I mean, you can't use a martial defence against magic."

"You really believe that?"

"Of course."

"That's funny."

"How is that funny? I was stating a fact."

"Because," Eva said playfully, "Bo Dancing was *specifically* developed to defend against weaving."

Nabo looked skeptically between Eva and the recruits. "You're joking."

"Nope. Uma introduced Bo Dancing *to the temple* as a nonviolent way of disabling attackers, but it's actually an ancient fighting style she brought with her from Egypt. According to the stories, they originally developed it to fight Djinn."

"Really?"

"Yep. Something about those fluid, sweeping movements allows a Bo Dancer to confuse the Weaver or prevent them from holding a target, basically dispelling the weave."

"That's... crazy," Nabo muttered, stroking his beard. "Why don't you have Daniel training with you? I'd love to see a demonstration."

"Oh, no. Absolutely not," Eva said with amusement.

"Why? Wouldn't it enhance your training significantly to spar against an *actual* Weaver?"

Eva sighed. "You'd think so, but I don't know. From what Daniel's told me, he's only ever done it a handful of times, and usually out of anger. It's too risky to pair him with someone right now. He's untrained, and if his emotions run high...? He would never intentionally kill someone in a training scenario, but until I'm confident he won't *unintentionally* kill anyone, I'd rather not risk an incident. Anyway, it might be too intense for him."

"Why do you say that?"

"Well, he told me it gives him this... insight into a person's full life story."

"Really?"

"Yeah. Keep that between us for now, but yeah. I wouldn't mark him down for any large-scale massacres anytime soon."

"Noted."

Nabo silently assessed the field for a moment, squinting against the sun. "You've really created a solid training ground out here."

"Thanks, it's just a little something I whipped up," she dramatized with a giggle.

Nabo laughed.

"In all seriousness, these ladies pour their heart and soul into this training. It has nothing to do with me anymore. I just like to come out here and see the progression they've made. There's something satisfying about it."

Nabo chuckled. "How would you feel about integrating my men into your classes?"

"What?"

"How would you feel about cross-training?"

"I don't know. I've actually never thought about it."

"Well, I think it could be valuable. We could train your fighters to use other weapons so they can defend against them. You could train mine to use bo staves and evade weaves."

Eva laughed. "If you think you have anyone agile enough, yeah, sure. We'll train them to fight."

"Ok, my guys know how to fight. We'd just be expanding a skill set."

"I guess we'll see when cross-training begins."

CHAPTER 15

SPARKS TO TINDER

~Several months later~

B lack clouds shone copper in the morning sunlight, revealing monstrous shapes lumbering across a grey-blue sky. Evaporating dew filled Daniel's nostrils. Intermittent caws from a crow perched on Daniel's shoulder broke the sound of over a thousand flapping cloaks. Black cloaked figures blanketed the front line, carrying scythes or spears. Behind them stood Babylonian and Median soldiers in black lamellar armour, swords or bows at the ready. Months of training and negotiations had led to this operation.

Eva stood beside Daniel, looking across the field toward the horizon.

Daniel smiled at her.

"Daniel, there's a battle out there. You need to focus."

But you're right here.

Daniel reluctantly turned his gaze to look at the field.

"Looks like somebody decided to avoid a siege," Eva said, pointing to the mass of figures marching toward them.

"Smart choice," Daniel said.

"Smarter than a siege, but still dumber than a surrender," Cyaxares said.

"Ready?" Eva said as she looked up at Daniel.

"Just like Larsa, right?" Daniel asked.

"Just like Larsa," Eva said, "Let's go."

Cyaxares barked orders to his archers, and Eva signalled her squad leaders to engage.

The frontline exploded into a silent sprint toward the enemy, pouring off of the hill and into the valley below.

The Arraphian soldiers roared and rushed toward them, while their archers sent a volley of arrows ahead of them, towards the front line.

Cyaxares ordered fire arrows loosed and Daniel wove the fire to spread and intensify until the sky burst into flames. Ash rained down onto the battlefield while Scythe Dancers spun and sliced, cutting down the Arraphians almost effortlessly.

A second wave appeared, supporting the Arraphians. Then a third.

The Scythe Dancers were becoming overwhelmed.

"Where are they all coming from?" Daniel asked, as he built seemingly endless weaves to resuscitate the fallen.

"Looks like Azra anticipated our arrival," Cyaxares said.

"Daniel, how easily are you able to keep pace right now?" Eva asked.

"Pretty easily."

"Ok, let's cut a path."

Daniel's glowing flames intensified, and he reached outward, triggering a flock of crows to emerge from behind him. Each of the birds carried a small bag in their claws, sprinkling seeds in lines across the battlefield, before circling the Arraphian commanders in the distance. Scythe Dancers in the centre of the field divided between the left and the right and continued pushing forward.

Daniel wove a line of trees on either side of him as thick as stone walls and so tightly spaced that even arrows couldn't penetrate them. The tree walls grew all the way up the field and then surrounded the Arraphian and Assyrian commanders, separating them from their armies.

"Shall we?" Cyaxares said, looking between Daniel and Eva with a smirk.

As they walked up the walled path, enemy soldiers caught inside rushed toward them, but Eva and Cyaxares disabled them without stopping until they reached the commanders.

"What—what do you want?" one of them asked as Daniel and the others approached.

"That should be obvious," Eva said. "We want you to surrender."

The commander looked nervously at the others beside him.

"This is ridiculous," another scoffed. "You are Assyrian. This whole rebellion is weakening your countrymen."

"Actually," Eva said, "we're Babylonian and the only thing that's weakening this country is the fact that people like you continue following that murdering pedophile usurper you call a king. We're offering you a chance to surrender and help us make things right."

"And if we refuse?"

"You die," Cyaxares said.

Deepening orange light saturated the air, turning the city of Assur's earthy mud-brick walls to a blood-soaked red.

Would my ancestors be ashamed of me right now?

Sin stared out at the city from a distance.

Bhodan, the King of Skuza, approached Sin from behind. "Any movement yet?"

"No, but I doubt they can see us from this distance with the sun at our backs."

"That's probably true. If only we could figure out a way to get past those walls. At this point, the day is nearly spent and we'll have to wait until morning to make a move."

"What if we go through the front door?"

Bhodan broke into laughter. "Boy, have you been drinking?"

"No, we could do it tonight. Right now, our forces are made up of horseback archers and melee fighters. No matter how we approach this wall, a lot of men are going to die, but what if we could avoid all that?"

"They're not going to let an army walk through the front gate."

"Look," Sin said, pointing east of the city, "people are still coming and going. That means that as far as anyone knows, we're still attacking cities to the south. Even if they've gotten word that we *could* be moving north, they haven't acted on it."

"That doesn't explain how you plan to get them to let us in."

"We let ourselves in."

"You *are* drinking."

"No, if we just get a small team inside, wait until dark, take out the guards and open the gates, we're in."

"How do you propose we do all of that?"

"We go in as merchants."

"Merchants with nothing to sell."

"We have tons of things to sell. Look around. We have food and weapons and armour. All it would take is loading some of it onto a couple of carts, add some guards and you've got a merchant caravan."

"If we get caught, we lose a lot of equipment and supplies."

"If we don't do this, we will anyhow."

Bhodan considered for a moment. "Fine, but you're going to lead them."

"Are you sure?"

"I'm trusting you, boy," Bhodan said, "get it done."

Seven soldiers dressed in bulky, multicoloured robes with long beige cloaks and head wrappings lined each side of the cart as it creaked along the road toward Assur.

The sun still peeked over the horizon at him as they approached the towering red walls.

A guard signalled them as they reached the gate and blocked their path. "Stop. What is your business here?"

Two other guards flanked the cart on either side, inspecting them.

"We're only merchants hoping to sell our goods at the market," Sin said.

"They have weapons here," one of the inspecting guards called out, "and Babylonian armour."

"Where did you get Babylonian armour and weapons?" the first guard asked.

"The battlefield is a precarious place to leave supplies lying around. Don't you think?"

"Are you lot thieves, then?"

"No. No, of course not. We bought these goods from a supplier in the south. I just mean that our supplier could have picked up these goods from almost anywhere," Sin said as he dismounted and pulled back the covering on the first cart. "In hard times like these, sometimes things go missing. It's just another cost of doing business."

The guard snickered and joined him, looking into the cart and then pulling out a well-made Babylonian sword. "I suppose it is impossible to avoid losing some of your goods in these... difficult times," he said, nodding to the other two guards to select something for themselves.

"It's nothing a small price increase can't fix at market," Sin said with a smile.

"Alright boy," the guard said, "enjoy your stay in Assur. I hope we cross paths again."

"You and I both." Sin mounted his horse and led the caravan forward.

As they crossed the threshold of the gate and entered Assur, night fell. Sin guided them toward the stables of the nearest inn and dismounted. In the shadow of the stable, they discarded their colourful garb, revealing tighter fitting black clothes underneath.

"Alright, grab whatever weapons you need and follow the plan. You all know where you're heading."

Seven black shadows slid towards the wall. As they approached a stairwell, two of the shadows disappeared into the darkness, removing the guard presence from the grounds. The buzz of nearby taverns drowned their short, muffled cries. A small group of soldiers gambled along the wall above.

Askuzai archers quietly cleared the guards along the wall on either side of the gamblers, and their bodies fell soundlessly in the darkness.

Bhodan's men really are expert archers.

Beside Sin, the archers coordinated their next shot. All five rose, taking aim in unison, and loosed. Suddenly, all the gamblers fell to the ground.

The silence was so abrupt that it was almost suspicious on its own.

The men waited and listened for any sign they had been noticed. Nothing. Silence.

"Ok, let's go," Sin whispered.

One man signalled the two below, while the others went to work raising the gates. Another waved torches from the top of the wall to signal Bhodan.

An army of shadows fluidly swept across the land toward the city and flowed in through the gate.

That was surprisingly easy.

Sin ordered the archers to guard the gates and hurried back to his horse. Bhodan was also on horseback when he caught up with him. The main street that led them to the palace was wide and tightly packed with tall brick buildings on either side. It seemed deserted aside from the lights and raucous laughter from the taverns.

"Not bad, boy," Bhodan said, clapping him on the shoulder, "you managed to sneak an entire army into the city. No one even knows we're here."

Sin's smile melted as he looked ahead. "I wouldn't say *no one* knows."

Bhodan peered ahead, where a blockade of shadowed figures awaited them. Even in the relative darkness of streetlamps, Sin could make out the faint shimmer of swords and shields held by the mass of soldiers ahead of them. Shadowed guards marched out from the alleys onto both sides of the street.

"They're on top of the buildings too," Sin said. "We're surrounded."

"Bhodan!" a soldier called, stepping out in front of the blockade. "How long has it been?"

"Not long enough," Bhodan said.

"Who is that guy?" Sin asked.

"He leads this Assyrian filth. His name is Nassir."

"I haven't seen you since I took control of your army. And here you are again, with a brand new army, delivering it to me. Just like old times. It's crazy how history repeats itself," Nassir said.

"Why are you here?"

"Isn't it obvious? King Azra entrusted me with protecting the ancestral capital. You could say I'm the governor of Assur, although, between you and me, I prefer thinking of myself as the king of Assur. I have my own palace, after all." Nassir laughed obnoxiously. "I didn't know I would run into you. I mean, I figured that your new allies would be along sooner than later, but I never imagined that you would personally come with them. It's just destiny."

"I'm going to kill you."

"Ah. That's too bad. I was going to offer you a chance to surrender for old times' sake, but—oh well," Nassir said as he walked away. "It was nice chatting--" he began, but an arrow through the throat cut his sentence short.

Sin stared in shock. Everyone around them froze. Suddenly, orders started flying off in every direction, calling for bows to be drawn and formations taken.

"Wait! Wait, everyone! STOP!" Sin boomed.

The entire scene froze.

"Listen to me," Sin shouted. "More than half of our army here today is made up of Askuzai archers."

He paused for a moment to gauge their reaction to the word "Askuzai".

"We don't need to fight," he continued. "Our only fight is with Azra. The people of Assur are not our enemy."

Sin rode toward Nassir's fallen body. "This man was not your leader. He was your oppressor and now he is dead."

Sin waited and listened to the murmurs of the crowd. Archers relaxed their bows.

A man threw off his helmet and stood beside Nassir's body. "What are you all doing? I'm taking command here. I can't believe you're going to let a *boy* talk you into surrender."

"You've all heard the legends of the Askuzai. If we continue this battle, there will be heavy losses on both sides, and very likely, we will still win. All of us here today can avoid further bloodshed," Sin shouted.

"Fine, show us the legends are true. If one of your archers can shoot me down before I end this sentence, then we'll surren—" An arrow lodged itself into the man's face.

Who is making these shots? Where are they even coming from?

The crowd boiled over with shocked gasps and whispers about the Askuzai legends.

"As you can see, the Askuzai legends are no exaggeration. The man that fired these arrows is standing in the darkness along your city wall. I doubt you have another archer that can match him today, but as allies, you could train with these legendary warriors. Be our allies. Let's put down our weapons and end this."

Clacking and muted clangs filled the air as thousands of swords and bows fell to the ground. As the dawn poured light back into the city, the blockade stood on either side of the road, making a path for Bhodan to reach the palace. Cheers rose from the surrounding crowd.

"Good work." Bhodan grinned at Sin.

"Thanks. I mostly just didn't want to die," he said, rubbing his neck. "I think we're going to need another cart to pick up all these weapons, though."

Bhodan laughed. "So we do. I have to ask, how long have you been studying archery?"

Sin gave him a sideways glance. "Most of my life. Why?"

"It surprised me a non-Askuzai could trace the trajectory of an arrow shot that far at night. You're full of surprises."

Sin swivelled his head to look along the wall and saw his original infiltration team climbing down the stairs.

No, he has to be kidding. Isn't he?

Sin shook his head.

I need to find a cart for these weapons.

"I've never seen bricks that colour," Daniel said to Eva as they passed under the walls of Assur.

"I can't believe this is your first time seeing the Red City since the road between Sippar and Nineveh runs right through here," Eva said, making a face.

"I guess I was asleep most of that ride."

The city was bustling. So many people were coming and going between shops that Daniel and Eva had to slow their horses down to a slow walk.

I wouldn't be able to see where we're going if I wasn't mounted right now.

When they arrived at the entrance to the palace, Sin greeted them.

"Hey! Long time no see," Sin laughed. "How was the ride from Arrapha?"

Daniel and Eva exchanged a glance and then laughed.

"Long," Daniel said.

"It's hard to go from constant battles to a peaceful open road," Eva said.

"I think the peace makes me more anxious than the battlefield now," Daniel said.

"Yeah, I guess you should expect more of that then. It's pretty peaceful here," Sin said.

"Almost suspiciously peaceful. How did you get the city back to normal so quickly?" Eva asked.

"That's a really long story I'll tell you about later."

"Alright."

"Where's your army?"

"Probably making the barkeeps in town very happy. We left about half of them in Arrapha though, to help Cyaxares restore order and rebuild the city," Daniel said.

"Oh, I thought he would come back with you."

"No," Eva said. "He wanted to resupply and check in on Media, apparently. His men could probably use a break, anyway."

"Yeah, that's pretty much what happened with Bhodan as well. He left with most of his men this morning."

"Have you heard anything from Kandalanu and Nabo?"

"Not for a few weeks now, but the last message said they were nearly at Palmyra. Apparently, Nebu's pretty excited about travelling with them."

"That's not surprising. This is his first actual mission, and he's been dying for people to stop treating him like a kid."

"Well, technically, he's the heir-prince now, so it's probably something everyone should get used to sooner than later," Daniel said, smirking.

"You're right, we should," Sin said, "when he gets back. In the meantime, who wants a tour of the castle?"

CHAPTER 16

SHIFTING WINDS

D aniel awoke to a loud shriek and shot up out of bed. A crow screamed at him from the window before hopping inside and gliding toward Daniel.

"You scared the crap out of me," he said.

"Message," the crow said.

Daniel looked the crow over, but there were no messages tied to its body.

"What are you talking about?" Daniel reached out to pet the bird, connecting to its lifethreads as his fingertips made contact with the soft black feathers on its neck and back.

Aerial views of the world unfolded before him. Daniel could remember the sensation of wind pushing up against his silky black wings and the intoxicating smell of death. In the distance, a strange noise caught Daniel's attention, and he swung around toward it. The sound slowly took shape, forming into loud drumming, and then pounding that grew more chaotic, the closer it became. Daniel swooped down for a better look and found himself gliding over thousands of men, all marching south.

Daniel released the weave. *Ah, shit.*

The crow hopped out of his hands and flew out the window.

Everything looks different from above.

The smell of baking leaves filled Daniel's nostrils, and the warm wind slid across his cheek. He breathed deeply, trying to absorb it all.

A horn sounded.

Daniel's eyes shot open. He instinctively kicked his legs outward, but instead of pushing himself into a sitting position against a tree trunk, he threw himself backward out of his chair. As he scrambled upright and looked around, he realized he was standing on top of the northern outer wall of Babylon.

Was I dreaming?

A nearby guard grinned at Daniel periodically as he kept watch and gossiped with another guard further down the wall.

Great. Daniel dusted himself off and picked up his chair.

The horn sounded again.

I definitely heard that. The guards definitely heard it, too.

The grinning guard was no longer grinning.

Daniel looked out and saw a shadow growing out of the horizon. It was much wider than the road, and it seemed to bubble and writhe as it got closer to the city walls.

Daniel shouted as he ran along the wall. "They're here! Sound the alarms! You," he pointed to the grinning guard, "go to the palace. Find Eva. Tell her Assyria is here. Go now!"

The guard ran to the palace while Daniel kept watch. After a few minutes, Sin and Eva arrived.

"Holy crap. They are here," Sin said, looking out over the wall at the approaching army below.

"They already sent two large squadrons south, likely to surround the city," Daniel said.

"It's just as we predicted." Eva exchanged a glance with Sin.

"You know," Sin whispered to Daniel, "you could wipe out this entire army before they get here and prevent the battle from ever happening."

Daniel said nothing.

"We've sent out messenger pigeons to Bhodan, Cyaxares and even to Egypt for Kandalanu. Daniel even wove a thick treeline wall around the city to put some distance between them and us. We've prepared for this," Eva said.

The three of them looked out at the dark waves of bodies approaching the city.

"So, what do we do now?" Sin asked.

"Now we wait," Eva said.

Daniel looked out over the city from the inner wall. The people below shuffled in every direction like lethargic ants.

It would almost look normal if you forgot everyone is terrified and all of us are trapped.

"You know," Eva said, approaching from behind, "when we were all getting assigned our roles here, I was pretty excited they made me a general, but now I'm thinking I should've held out for physician."

"Well, if no one gets sick, it's a pretty relaxed job."

"Yeah? So then, why is your face all scrunched up like that?"

Daniel smirked. "It's sunny?"

"It's sunny? Seriously?"

"I'm just thinking about everything going on right now."

"Yeah, well, you should stop that. It's my job to worry about all of this."

Daniel shook his head. "Why does that make sense to you?"

"Because it is. What are the other options? We have an absentee king, out on a diplomatic mission thousands of miles away. We have an exiled prince, who is a former enemy. And you, Doctor Face-crease, who is literally crumpling under the weight of responsibilities that are technically none of his concern."

Daniel frowned.

"Look, I've got this. Things are fine."

"I just worry, that's all."

"Really? You?"

"Ok, I definitely walked into that one."

"Lined it up perfectly," Eva chuckled, "but listen, seriously, I've got this. And jokes aside, you've had your hands full since the food stores ran out."

"It's not enough. It feels like I'm doing nothing."

Eva cocked her head at him in disbelief. "Look what you're doing right now. You're filling the fields with crops—daily. It's not nothing."

"But the crops are unreliable, just like a regular harvest. Sometimes they don't produce or come up right—"

"Yes, but that doesn't erase all the times that they do. And unlike a normal harvest, we don't have to wait for months to find out they're going to fail. If we get a good harvest, great. If not, we try again tomorrow. Simple as that. Don't downplay the good you're doing. You're keeping people fed, isn't that what's important?"

"Yeah. No, you're right."

"That's right, I'm right."

"I just can't shake the feeling that I should do more."

"No one looks down on you for trying to avoid a massacre."

Daniel shifted uncomfortably. "But Sin was right. If I just did what I need to do, then we could've avoided all of this and prevented things from getting worse."

"Is Sin offering *his* magic powers to save people?"

Daniel said nothing.

"My love, look at me," Eva said, gently turning his head. "No one is going to look down on you. You're doing the right thing."

"How do you know?"

"Because deep down, *you* believe you're doing the right thing, and that's all I need."

Daniel looked into her eyes. His lips pursed and then he exhaled, leaning in closer to her. "How did you get to be so awesome?"

"I think I was just born this way." Eva pulled him down into a kiss. Then she turned, pressing her back against his chest, and draped his arms around her like a cloak. Without realizing it, the two of them swayed gently from side to side as they stared out over the city. "Seriously though, it's weird. I feel like I've been training my whole life for something like this."

"Leading an army under siege?"

"Yeah. Well, not under siege specifically, but yeah, leading everyone this way. I'm really good at it."

"You are really good at it," Daniel said, squeezing her gently. "Maybe Uma *was* training you for it. You were really close with Uma. Maybe she was training you to replace her."

"I thought about that. I guess it makes sense. I just feel like she would tell me."

"I doubt that. Uma never struck me as someone that was *forthcoming*. About anything."

"Yeah, I guess," Eva said, pausing thoughtfully. "You know, she told me once that information should be handled like a puzzle. Every piece has a time and place."

"Hmm," Daniel said behind a contented smile, "Just like you and me."

Eva smiled and rested her head back on his chest. "I wish I could just stay here with you all day."

"Then stay."

Eva giggled. "We both know I can't. I have to go hold a kingdom together. Dinner later though?"

"Definitely. I'll make you that lamb dish you like."

"Oh, now you're saying all the right words."

"Am I?"

Eva snatched another kiss. "I love you."

"I love you too."

Eva spun to smile at him as she walked away.

The old tree pulls and creaks. Leaves rustle loudly overhead, dislodging themselves and leaving holes in the canopy. Sunlight beams warmly onto Daniel's face, but the warmth ignites into fire. Blue flames spread over his entire body, searing every nerve. Daniel screams. He falls from his branch, numb to the impact, and rolls to put out the flames.

But they won't go out.

Daniel stands up, crying and screaming, blue flames obscuring his view, and he runs. Daniel runs as fast as he can, but the air only seems to fan the flames. Relief pours over him as he falls into a pool of black mud, extinguishing the fire, but panic grips him once more. He can't climb out of this pool. He's sinking. Daniel struggles helplessly to escape. Instead, he sinks deeper and deeper into the murky pool while the black water rises higher and higher, spilling out and devouring everything. Devouring Daniel.

Daniel gasped for air in the darkness. Eva lay beside him, still asleep.

I need to clear my head, Daniel thought, walking out of the room.

The smell of spiced lamb lingered strongly as Daniel travelled down the corridor, and his footfalls echoed past him like ghosts.

As he walked, he could hear a distant pounding grow louder. A few days prior, the Assyrians had rammed the main gates while shielding themselves from arrows with a plated mobile canopy. Daniel reinforced the gate with bramble vines as thick as trees when the battering began, but the pounding persisted, day and night.

They're relentless. Am I making the right choice? Am I being selfish by trying to avoid facing a little pain? I guess it's not exactly 'a little' pain. Their lives are so vivid when I connect with my weaves. How does Azra do it so easily? Is he broken? Or maybe he's just pure evil? That can't be it. I used to think of him as a father. He cared about people at the temple... didn't he? Maybe he didn't and I just couldn't see it because I was just a kid.

The corridor opened to the ramparts, giving Daniel a view of land blanketed in darkness, below a brightening sky. The sun would soon peek over the distant mountains and bleach away the shadows. Daniel had seen a lot of mornings in Mari when he would start his farm chores.

Things are so screwed up now. I used to live on a farm. Now I'm helping a rebel force take control of the empire. Technically, the rightful prince is on our side, so can they even consider us rebels? It all seems so... inflated. If Azra wasn't trying to erase us, none of this would matter. Eva and I could've run away and become farmers. And we wouldn't be so invested in this stupid war.

Daniel sighed, as he slumped forward onto a crenellation square, and hung his head. Sunlight glowed against his eyelids, causing him to open them. The darkness had evaporated aside from the stretched shadows, shrinking back against the walls of the outer city below. The city was silent and at peace.

Wait, why is it silent? When did the pounding stop?

Daniel raced along the ramparts toward the main gates.

The sound definitely stopped. Where did they go?

Daniel kept an eye for patrols and posted guards, hoping to gauge any reaction from the men along the outer wall.

No guards. No enemies. Did everyone just call it a night? Wait, is it Ankl? No, it can't be. Everything is too colourful. What's going on?

Men yelled from below, directing others that came pouring in from semi-hidden holes along the outer wall.

Shit! Shit! Shit!

Daniel reached out to the plants around that section of the wall, but their threads carried no vibrations. Daniel refocused, weaving layer after layer of vines against the inner gates and curving the tendril tips back toward the enemy to prevent climbing, before running off to raise the alarm.

Smoke hung thickly over the city of Assur like a black, foreboding cloud.

"They burned all of our fields," Sin said quietly, looking out at the low, smouldering fires.

Where the soil was once a rich black, it now appeared to be grey and sparkle in the sunlight. Hundreds of men were still dumping the granules out of baskets while wagons straddled the field at both ends, allowing the men to refill.

"Why are they pouring sand onto the fields?" Eva asked.

Sin shared a glance with Daniel. "It's not sand, it's salt."

"But why?"

"So that nothing will ever grow there again," Daniel muttered.

Behind the fields, men continued pouring in from tunnels along the wall and joining a line with others that came before them.

"I'm counting way over a thousand men in that mass. Maybe two," Sin said.

"I would've guessed more just from looking at them," Daniel said. "How were they even able to build a tunnel while we have men on that wall all day and night?"

"It's likely that we didn't," Sin said, "but you're going to have to put that on the list of tomorrow's problems because their next move is to breach the inner gate."

"Yeah, I saw them directing men that way when I first spotted them. The inner gate was the first thing I reinforced."

"It's a basic strategy. You keep the momentum and element of surprise by breaching both walls in rapid succession. They probably wouldn't have even revealed the tunnels tonight if they didn't think they could get through the inner gates immediately after."

"So I guess we wait."

"You want to wait for them to break down the door?"

"What more can we do?"

Eva rested her head on his shoulder. "He's right. We've done everything we can do. I've reinforced the archers along the walls. Daniel can't really weave any more vines than he already has. We just have to wait until they make their move."

"General!" A guard jogging towards them, escorting another man in Assyrian battle gear. The Assyrian carried a large sack of some sort.

"Stop!" Daniel yelled.

"Sir, this man arrived at the gates, saying he has a message for the king."

"My message comes from King Azra. My orders were to hand-deliver my message to the king of Babylon," the Assyrian said.

"The king isn't here," Eva said, "but I'm in charge."

The man looked Eva over for a moment. "You'll do," he said and then threw the sack at her.

Daniel snatched the bag out of the air. *This must be a trap! Actually, it just feels... lumpy. Is this a bag of potatoes?*

Suddenly, the Assyrian stole the guard's knife and slit his own throat before collapsing onto the ground.

"What... just happened?" Eva said.

Sin shook his head. "Have someone deliver the body

back to them."

The guard nodded and dragged the body away, leaving a bloody trail behind him.

Daniel focused his attention fully on the bag as he opened it.

"What is it?" Eva asked.

"It's a bag of dead birds—wait," Daniel said as he pulled one out. "Look at the leg, these are messenger birds."

Sin knelt beside Daniel, and the two of them pulled messages out of the bag.

... we require immediate aid..., Daniel read silently.

This handwriting is so familiar, he thought.

... I realize that our alliance is new....

"Does this handwriting seem familiar to you?" Daniel said as he showed the message to Eva.

"Oh, no. No, no, no...." Eva whispered.

Sin frowned for a moment and studied the messages in front of him. Suddenly, his face smoothed with realization and disappointment. "It's not a bag of messages, the bag *is* the message."

Daniel looked down at the messages again.

What? Who would send so many messages just to make one statement?

Eva put her hand to her mouth. "Skuza and Media... never got our calls for help. They're not coming."

Sin shook his head. "These are all the messenger birds we've sent out since this whole thing started. They've been shooting our messages out of the sky."

"No one even knows we're being attacked?" Daniel said.

Eva slowly walked to the edge of the wall, staring idly at the enemy below.

Daniel joined her, putting his hand on her shoulder. "I'm sorry."

"Do you see that?" Sin asked.

Daniel followed Sin's gaze as he squinted at one of the breach points along the outer gate.

"I think something just trampled an entire squad of guys."

Daniel watched for a moment, but nothing happened. Until finally a figure plowed forward, tossing men to each side and then leapt back. As he disengaged, the figure unfolded into the shape of a man, arms outstretched, with an enormous battle-axe in each hand. The man looked up into the sky and roared. Hundreds of men ran at him, weapons raised.

"That's Nabo! Sin, we have to help him," Eva said.

"Eva, that's suicide," Daniel said.

"He's right, that's way too dangerous. We can't help him," Sin said.

"No, I can't just leave him to die. I won't. I have command of the entire army of Babylon. I'd never be able to forgive myself if I don't try."

"That's true, but you'd be leading all those men to their deaths. Do you think you'll forgive yourself, then?" Daniel said.

Eva looked back at Nabo and shook her head. "Fine, I'm going alone."

"Eva—" Daniel said.

"—No. I'm going. If you stop me from going and he dies, his death is on your hands." She grabbed a scythe and a bow and jogged off towards the vines blocking the inner gate.

Sin sighed. "I have to go with her."

"But why? Why are you all throwing your lives away?" Daniel said.

"I think the real question is, how could you let things go this far?"

"It's not like that."

Sin gave Daniel a disgusted look, but said nothing.

This is my fault.

Sin slung a quiver across his back and selected a bow and a scythe from the nearby racks.

And now they're all going to die.

"Goodbye, Daniel," he said coldly and then jogged off toward the vines where Eva had climbed down.

Because of me.

Eva shot two arrows from the top of the vines before tossing down her scythe and scrambling to the ground beside it with inhuman agility. Sin was close behind, with no difficulty keeping up. The two fired arrows with near-perfect precision, thinning out enemies along a path between the two gates. All the while, Nabo used his axes in a spinning cleave to cut down seemingly endless waves of enemies, only stopping to block an attack, or impale and toss a man.

Daniel stood over the gate, gripping the edge.

When Eva and Sin ran out of arrows, they tossed their bows and leapt off the vines, executing the flowing liquid dance of the scythe perfectly. The two of them sliced through the crowd of soldiers, leveraging each other's attacks until they were within sight of the old giant.

"Nabo!" Eva called.

Nabo looked around in confusion.

"Nabo!"

Nabo turned and saw Eva and Sin cutting a path toward him. "Eva? Sin!" he yelled, cleaving the endless stream of Assyrians. "What are you doing out here? You have to go!"

"No, I'm not leaving you behind. We're going to fight our way out of here together," Eva said.

"No! You need to get out of here! Sin, take her back!"

"Look out!"

Nabo turned to face his assailant, but not before the man buried his sword to the hilt into Nabo's torso. The man tried to pull the sword out, but Nabo snapped his neck and tossed him into the crowd before he had the chance. Then Nabo lifted his axes, rotating while shifting his stance against the crowd that was slowly closing in. Eva used her scythe to vault in beside him, and Sin used the distraction to slide in from below.

The three of them took a stance, rotating together, anticipating where the first attack would come.

There was no first attack. Instead, the entire courtyard charged at them simultaneously, with those behind pushing those ahead. The circle closed in on them so quickly, and so completely, that it wasn't a battle anymore. It was a drowning.

As time slowed to a halt, the despair and reality-altering pain froze tightly on their faces.

Daniel climbed down the vines, standing at the shore of the black lamellar ocean. He looked out at his friends sadly.

Ankl appeared beside Daniel. "You know, I have seen some of the most dramatic displays of friendship, kinship and self-sacrifice in all of human history. And it never ceases to amaze me."

Daniel said nothing as he studied the tableau of horror before him. Nabo's head was down, his shoulders slumped. Eva and Sin were looking upward.

Eva looks like an angel, reaching up to the sky. And Sin, he looks so tired.

"Be careful now, if you look too closely you'll see into their souls and the price of admission—as you know—is quite high."

"You always show up like this, and we have our little talks, but I always feel like you're talking to yourself more than me."

"I'll let you in on a little secret. This separateness you hang onto—you, me, them—it's all an illusion. It's all temporary. Yet here you are torturing yourself... over what? Being good? Over choosing one life over the other? I mean, humanity *as a whole* matters. I don't dispute that. But this whole thing you're doing, placing an inherent value on individuals, as if the universe is begging you to protect every individual you come across. Why?"

"Are you seriously lecturing me about morality right now? You don't care about people. At all. You literally told me to abandon everyone I knew."

"I actually did not tell you to abandon anyone. I proposed you cut ties with these people that cause you distractions because it draws everything out. And can you guess how that time gets filled? Meaningless interpersonal drama. And, by the way, I do have quite a few people I care about. You *used* to know that."

"You have people you care about?"

"Of course."

"Who—"

"*And* what makes them important isn't who they are in the world or what they've experienced, it's who they are to me. Well, technically, everyone I care about *is* genuinely important to the fabric of the universe, as far as humanity is concerned. But for you, right now, as *Daniel the human*, it seems like a person's value is defined by their proximity to you. So, you want to go through life making tight interpersonal connections on an unpredictable roller coaster of emotion? Have at it. You want to treat every passing stranger with unconditional kindness and respect, even though it will rarely be repaid, and may often be resented? You do you. But if you think it's responsible to intensify the weight of every human life beyond the limits of normal human comprehension, and then—somehow—attempt to appreciate the value of all of those lives *simultaneously*, then you are an idiot of the highest order."

"So as long as I care about my people, your way, then it's fine, but if I care about them my way, then I'm stupid."

"See? This is what I'm talking about. The human brain can only process so much, and when you try to pack in more, stuff just falls out. My way is better because it's bite-sized and easy to digest. Yours is literally beyond mortal comprehension. It's just not healthy. You're torturing yourself over preserving the lives of people that literally don't matter to you at all. Remind me, why didn't you erase this army before they ever had a chance to mortally wound your friends over there?"

"Because they're people. A lot of them have wives and children and people that care about them. They carry dreams and wishes—"

"Ok, *dreams and wishes* aside, it sounds like you're getting hung up on the fact they have families and people they care about."

"Don't they?"

"They do, but why do you care? Everyone has children and family ties. It's literally humanity's primary defence against extinction."

"I just see someone's wife in their memories and I can't help but think of Eva. I see mothers and I'm reminded of my mom. I can relate to so much about their lives that killing them feels like I'm killing myself. Like hurting the people they care about is the same as hurting the people I care about."

"That's probably the most human thing I've ever heard."

"Are you making fun of me?"

"No, I'm saying where you're coming from is very human. I was asking you to go against something more fundamental than I initially realized."

Daniel looked back at his friends' faces, twisted in various degrees of pain. He looked at the Assyrian soldiers packed tightly around them. Above them all, smoke hung in place like a passing cloud, providing a dramatic accent to the scene below.

How can something so horrible be so beautiful?

"I know what I have to do, but I still don't think I can do it."

"Could you live with the regret if you don't? Look at your friends. Think of Eva. Would you honestly regret their deaths *less* than the deaths of a few thousand strangers?"

Daniel's heart wrenched. "I—" he began, but Ankl was gone.

Daniel sighed and then climbed carefully onto the shoulders of his enemy. He kept his head down to avoid seeing their faces. All the while whispering, 'I'm sorry' as he hopped across them. When he reached his friends, there was nowhere to climb down, so instead, he climbed over Nabo and stood on his shoulders. Then he took one last look around and drew air deeply into his lungs one last time.

Blue sparks flew in his mind and blue flames burned coolly against the skin on his hands and face. Daniel paused for a moment, feeling his heartbeat steadily against his chest. Then, in one fluid motion, he raised his hand and drew a circle in the air above his head.

A layer of surrounding soldiers smeared into a dense mist that hung in the air around the empty floating armour that marked where a ring their bodies used to be.

Daniel immediately flinched and his hands shook. He let out a groan with the intensity of a scream through clenched teeth.

He drew air in harshly and exhaled slowly, forcing his body to relax.

Again, he raised his hand and drew a circle in the air. Another ring of bodies transformed into red mist and again, Daniel screamed and his muscles clenched. Screaming evolved into laughing, and laughing turned to crying.

Daniel looked into the sky and took deep shaky breaths, trying to calm himself and regain control.

He raised his hand and then hesitated, letting it drop.

You can do this. You've gotta do this.

Daniel struggled to suppress a cry. He shook his head and exhaled six times fast.

You can do this.

Daniel filled his lungs and then shot his hand in the air, tracing circles as fast as he could. Primal calls of agony clawed their way out of Daniel's throat. He changed hand positioning, reaching out, connecting to all the men Azra had sent against them. Daniel's voice became hoarse and his tears blurred his vision, but he could still see the threads clearly in his mind. He pulled the threads upward.

One breath. Two breaths.

Then he screamed again as he slammed the threads against the ground.

A shock wave radiated outward from Daniel, transforming the black lamellar ocean into a crimson fog.

Daniel struggled to breathe, and his knees crumpled beneath him, causing him to fall onto the grass. After a moment, he rolled over and found himself looking up into Nabo's unreadable, statuesque face.

Did I do the right thing?

CHAPTER 17

A Moment of Silence

Somehow,
today feels like a perfect day.

S unlight streamed into Azra's newly renovated
solarium, painting its gentle light onto tiny green
seedlings.

He sprinkled water across their little shoots and leaves.

"Come," Azra said, responding to a knock at the door.

Ballit entered the room and stopped a few paces away.
"Good morning, sire."

"Good morning Ballit. Is it not a beautiful morning?"

"It is, sire."

"Have you come to enjoy the garden, or is there some
other purpose to which I owe this visit?"

"A messenger has arrived with several updates
concerning the state of the empire. Should I direct him
to the throne room until you are ready to receive him?"

Azra chuckled. "Frankly, that depends on the news. You know what? Show him in."

"Right now, sire?"

"Yes, Ballit. Here, in the solarium. I'll listen to his updates as I water my plants. A king is like a gardener to his empire, after all. And I challenge anyone to spoil my mood." Azra chuckled to himself.

Ballit left for a moment and returned with the messenger.

"Ah, good morning, sire," the man mumbled, looking around the room nervously.

"Good morning! I hear you have some news from around the empire."

"Ah, yes, sire."

"You may read it to me now."

"Now? Here?"

"Yes, now. Come all the way in. There's no point lingering by the door. I wouldn't be able to hear you anyway," Azra said over his shoulder as he continued to tend his plants.

Azra shook his head. *They always stand by the door.*

"Y-yes, sire."

"Well?"

"Well, it appears that Lord Necho will finally assume the role of Pharoah."

"Finally, indeed."

"Well, due to the... unusual nature of his father's death, there was some suspicion cast upon Lord Necho, but that has obviously since dissolved."

"Excellent. Ballit, please arrange a message of congratulations and a gift of some sort. A token of our renewed friendship with Egypt."

"I'll see it done."

"Alright messenger," Azra said with a smirk, "tell me another."

The man coughed, and his eyes darted nervously to the door. "Uh, well, sire, as you know, our initial reports concerning the siege of Babylon appeared to be quite favourable by all accounts. Our last communication showed our forces had breached the outer wall and were launching a decisive attack to take the city by morning."

"I wouldn't exactly call that news. It's the same report as yesterday," Azra chuckled.

"Yes, well, all reports from the front lines have stopped."

Azra paused thoughtfully. "That *is* strange, but I expect they're on their way back. The stupid bird probably got lost on its way home."

"Ordinarily I would agree. However, no one has seen your men along any road or passing through any cities returning to the capital. It seems as if they've disappeared entirely."

"Come on now. How does a platoon of over 2000 men just disappear without a trace?"

"I am unsure, sire, but some reports seem to indicate Babylonian merchants have returned to their usual trade circuits."

Which means they are no longer in Babylon either.

Azra sighed and watered a row of plants sitting on an island in the centre of the room. "Alright. What else have you got for me?"

"Media continues to rebel against you and expand his borders along the Zagros Mountains."

Azra slammed his watering can onto a table beside him. "Did we not send an army—twice as many men as we sent to Babylon—to crush him?"

"We did, sire."

"And?"

"They have not returned either. We believe the Medians may have had some outside help."

"Outside help? From who? Where?"

"There's a strong possibility of an alliance between Babylon, Media and at least one other—"

"For fuck's sake. Is there anything else I should know about?"

"There is."

"Is it good news?"

"Not exactly, sire —"

"Ok, how about this? Whatever you're about to say, spin it so that it sounds like you're actually giving me good news. Can you do that?"

"Yes, I think so."

"Fine then. Go on with whatever *good* news you have left for me."

"Yes, sire. It seems that you have been relieved of one of your prisoners and now that site will have expanded availability."

"Expanded availability."

"Yes, sir."

"So my guards killed a prisoner?" Azra rounded a planter, putting his back to the messenger.

"Well, yes and no."

"Yes and no?"

"Two prisoners were being relocated and one died in transit."

"So one died and the other one...?"

"He was relocated successfully, sire."

"Where?"

"We are still finding that out."

Azra stopped working, leaned on a planter, and stared at the wall ahead. "Ok, can you tell me *who* was responsible for this relocation?"

"My lord?"

"Who? Who was the guard that authorized the prisoner's transfer?"

"No one, sire. He—uh—transferred himself."

Azra threw his head back and sighed. "So he escaped?"

"Yes, sire—"

"The word you chose to describe an escape was *relocation*?"

"I thought—you asked me to finish the report with a positive—"

"You're an idiot. Just give me a name."

"Sorry?"

"His name—the name of the prisoner—what was it?"

"It—it was General Nabo, sire."

Azra reached out and broke the man's neck with a weave. "I think that'll be enough news for today. Ballit, I have some serious concerns about your hiring process. It seems to lack the ability to successfully attain competent staff."

"Admittedly, the royal messenger has become a difficult role to fill, sire."

"Why not just fill the role yourself? It is *your* information being read to me, after all."

"I appreciate your confidence in me, sire, but I am certain I would be a terrible fit."

Azra scoffed. "And how would that be?"

Ballit glanced down at the corpse on the floor and then back into Azra's eyes. "Dying doesn't suit my skill set."

Azra narrowed his eyes and then broke into laughter. "Dying doesn't suit your skill set?"

Azra shook his head as he returned to his gardening. "That's genius. Alright Ballit, find yourself a new messenger. Maybe someone with more competence than the last one. While you're at it, I want you to find out everything that Nabo may have overheard during his stay and who let him escape. I want to know exactly what happened. Also, find out who killed the jester and have that man tortured. Actually, just have all of them tortured. It's time we refresh the guard detail there, anyway."

"Very good, sire." Ballit bowed and turned to leave.

"Oh, and Ballit?"

"Yes, sire?"

"Send someone to clean up this mess. This is a palace, not a graveyard," he said, waving his hand dismissively.

"Understood, sire," Ballit said, and then he slipped out of the room and closed the door behind him.

Screams echo in Daniel's mind. Smoke fills his nostrils, and familiar despair fills his heart. The muddy, trampled earth below him is cool against his shins, and silvery daylight washes the colour out of everything around him. Daniel looks out over an eerily empty battlefield. Bodies litter the ground, and blue fires dance across overturned wagons and straw rooftops. A boy holds his dead father, cradling his head in his arms.

Is that Nabo? Daniel draws closer.

"Kaleb?" Daniel calls to the boy, and the boy turns to face him.

Something's not right.

Daniel rounds the body and stops directly in front of the boy. "Are you Kaleb? Or Nebu?"

The boy looks up at him, his eyes piercing Daniel with a familiar ferocity. "Does it matter?"

Daniel sat up out of bed and palmed his forehead.

A crow flew onto Daniel's bed and hopped up onto his leg.

"No rest for the wicked, eh?" it squawked in Ankl's voice.

Daniel sighed, as he placed his arm under the crow's feet and placed it on his shoulder. "Well, *you* never sleep, so I'm starting to believe that might be a hard and fast rule."

Ankl laughed. "Someone's coming."

"I know," Daniel said, gently scratching the crow's breast.

Footsteps stopped in front of Daniel's door, and the visitor knocked.

How many days has it been since I've talked to another person? Twenty? Thirty?

"Well, you've never been one to turn down an opportunity to wallow in self-pity," Ankl squawked.

"Shut up," Daniel said quietly before calling out, "Sin, you can just come in."

"How did you know it was me?" Sin asked, cautiously grabbing a chair from the wall and setting it beside the bed for himself.

"I'm just trying something new with weaving."

"Ah, think about keeping that a secret. It actually makes things *more* creepy."

"I'll try to remember that. Just don't forget my 'creepy' weaving saved your life again."

"How could I? As much as I appreciate you saving my life, I didn't realize that weaving also gave you my entire life history."

Ankl hopped onto Daniel's lap and he pet the crow instead of responding.

"I wasn't sure if you were feeling up to having visitors."

"I'm sorry about that. It's been kinda hard since... that day."

"Yeah. I can imagine." A drawn-out silence settled between them, but Daniel could sense Sin's anxiety simmer and his need to unburden. "Look, Daniel, I'm really sorry."

"Don't worry about it."

"No, just listen. I shouldn't have pressured you over and over to—to do what you did. I didn't know it affected you this way. That's too much to put on one person. I should've never asked. I just shouldn't have."

"Sin, it's honestly ok. Really. I always had the chance to say no and stand by it. And technically, I did stand by that decision for a long time, but in the end, I changed my mind. That's not on you. And that's not on Eva. You made your choices, and I made mine, and I think if I had to, I would do it all again."

Sin nodded but allowed the room to go silent again, while Daniel continued to stroke the giant black bird on his lap.

"So, you have a pet crow now?"

"Yeah, I guess so."

"Actually, *I* have a pet human. If you want to be accurate. Stupid human."

"Any particular story on how that came about?" Sin asked.

"I think it's kind of a Weaver thing—"

"It's not," Ankl said flatly, "it's a *you* thing."

"Or maybe not," Daniel chuckled weakly, stroking the bird.

"Yeah, he doesn't seem to think so either," Sin laughed.

Daniel peered at Sin. "Can you hear him?"

"What? No, he just squawked," Sin said, "Wait, can you talk to birds now?"

"I don't really know. Maybe just this guy."

"That's—You know what? Let's just circle back to that another time."

Daniel smirked. "Ok, fair enough."

"So, how are you doing? You know, aside from talking to animals you happen to find."

Daniel chuckled weakly. "I mean, it took me a while to put myself back together—but to be honest, I'm actually better than I thought I would ever be again. What happened that day... was probably one of the most intense and *horrific* things that have ever happened to me. And that's not an easy bar to raise. Yet somehow, it was also weirdly cathartic."

"So, you don't feel all of those deaths anymore?"

"Well, no, obviously I still do. I will probably mourn every one of them to some extent for the rest of my life. But the feeling of all of those lives crashing over me, over and over and over... even though it was agonizing, there was a certain point where the pain couldn't get any more intense. It was as if my brain couldn't mentally register another level of intensity if it tried. In that moment, I realized it didn't matter whether it was a few hundred or a few thousand lives I took, it would feel the exact same way. And I guess that—" Daniel interrupted himself with a chuckle, shaking his head, "I guess that made it all *bite-sized*."

Sin frowned at Daniel.

"Sorry, I guess it's sort of an inside joke."

"It's pronounced *valuable life advice*," Ankl said.

"Whatever, stupid bird," Daniel said, scratching Ankl's chest feathers.

Sin shook his head.

"You were right, though. If I would have taken action from the start, we could've avoided everything that happened, and you guys wouldn't have almost died."

"True enough, but look at all the memories we shared because of it."

"Heh, yeah. Literally *all* the memories."

"And I have all these new experiences to draw on now. I used to wonder what it feels like to be stabbed multiple times by an overwhelming number of enemies."

"Now you don't have to."

"Exactly, AND as an added bonus, my *other* near-death experience probably just made a friend, so there's a pretty solid chance that now I'll alternate between *two* hellscapes at bedtime instead of reliving the same nightmare over and over."

"At least you'll get a little variety."

"Right? And who knows, maybe they'll really hit it off and make themselves a little nightmare baby."

"Sometimes I wonder why you don't have your own talking animal friends."

"Maybe I should get one. I'll see what other kinds of animals we have lying around and go from there."

"Seriously though, don't worry about me."

"I wasn't. You usually bounce back. I'm more worried about Nabo."

Daniel glanced at Sin and sighed. "Yeah, so is everyone."

"You're being creepy again, but yes. He is the focus of a lot of people's concern."

"Sin... Something happened to him. Something bigger than yesterday. I'll be honest with you, he's in a pretty dark place. He and Kandalanu went through a lot at the end of their journey—one sec, Eva's at the door."

"What?"

Suddenly, Eva entered the room.

"Creepy." Sin crossed his arms and glared at Daniel.

"What is?" Eva asked.

"Daniel can tell the future now, apparently."

"No, I can't tell the future. I'm just trying something out with weaving."

"Meaning what?"

Daniel sighed. "Basically, I'm using weaving to sense people who are nearby. I can tell when they come and go from a pretty good range."

"So, doesn't that mean you are technically inviting yourself into a person's head without them knowing?"

"Technically, I guess, but the point isn't to collect everyone's dirty little secrets. I'm just—I've said it before. weaving can be very overwhelming, and if I can learn how to deal with absorbing that much detail about people, who knows?" Daniel shrugged.

Eva nodded, taking a seat beside him on the bed. "Then you can prevent what happened during the siege?"

Daniel nodded.

"At least you're up and talking again," she said, lacing her hand in his.

Daniel smiled at her.

"How are you doing, anyway?" Eva asked, turning to Sin.

"It's a lot to process. I mean, we almost died—again— but somehow it feels less traumatic than last time. If that makes any sense."

"Like the fear of dying is less," Eva said in agreement.

"Yeah, basically. But the question is, do you think that means we're becoming less afraid of actually dying or more confident we'll never die?" Sin asked.

A long silence settled between them and they chose three radically different focal points to stare into during those passing minutes.

"So, before you came in, we were talking about Nabo," Daniel said, looking up at Eva.

"Yeah. What happened to him?"

"So," Daniel said with a sigh, "there's a reason Nabo came back alone."

"Oh no," Eva said, covering her mouth.

Sin frowned at the floor.

"It looks like Azra captured them on the way to Egypt."

"How far did they get?"

"They didn't even make it to Palmyra, but that's not the worst part. Once they were captured, Azra's people imprisoned them separately and tortured them almost continuously. Nebu... couldn't take it."

"The fact that you know means that Nabo knew. How did he find out?" Sin asked.

"Wherever they were being tortured was close enough to Nabo's cell that he could hear what was happening pretty clearly."

"So he heard it happen?" Eva asked.

Daniel sighed. "Yeah, he knew right away. That was hard for him. Eventually, Kandalanu stole a guard's key and broke Nabo out. Their escape path took them through a sewer or storm drain system of some sort and it ended up becoming quite a maze. Azra's men didn't take long to realize Kandalanu and Nabo were missing, and soon the guards caught up to them. Kandalanu, probably realizing they were about to be recaptured pushed Nabo through an iron gate, locked the door behind him, and tossed the keys through the bars to Nabo's side to buy him time to escape. Nabo wanted to stay and drag Kandalanu out but he demanded Nabo run. Eventually he agreed. Nabo didn't stay to witness it, but he was certain they killed Kandalanu. When he finally made it out of the sewers, he just followed the roads until he ended up here."

"How did he know we were in Assur?"

"He didn't."

"So, when he charged into the siege—" Sin began.

"—he didn't expect to survive. He didn't want to." Eva whispered.

"Yeah. So obviously, all of this is kind of sensitive, but—"

"—but you think we should keep an eye in case he's looking for other opportunities." Eva nodded and folded her arms.

"That would probably be best."

"What does all of this mean for our alliance with Egypt?" Sin asked.

"Pretty much what you'd assume, but worse. Kandalanu expected talks to go well, but they never actually reached Egypt. Then Phraortes died and his son basically hunted them down and handed them over to Azra." Daniel allowed the silence to settle for a moment.

"That man needs to die," Eva said.

"Azra and Necho both deserve to die, but I'm realizing that Azra's not the entire problem. It's the empire. They founded it on war and oppression. There's no room for peace here."

"The elders always said you would know the world is about to end if Assyria ever lost a war. There was a prophecy about it," Sin said.

"So you're saying we may have caused the end of the world?" Eva asked.

"That's the prophecy."

"There's actually something else we need to talk about," Daniel said.

"More important than the end of the world?"

"Maybe more urgent than more important. You'll want to hear this."

"Ok...?"

"Kandalanu officially has no heir."

"What?"

"When they took Nebu with them, there was no contingency plan. Ariel was Kandalanu's only child, and since he has no other living relatives..."

"So everything we've been fighting for—" Sin said.

"—Was for nothing." Eva finished.

Silence compressed the room.

"So, what are we going to do?" Eva asked.

"Well, it turns out that just before he died, Kandalanu wrote a decree naming Nebu as his heir. It's hidden in Babylon and written on papyrus. I've already sent a crow to retrieve it," Daniel said.

"So? How does that help us now?"

"Very few people alive today ever knew Nebu. Even people who met Nebu in passing probably couldn't pick him out of a crowd because he didn't matter back then. He was only the son of a soldier."

"Why does that matter?" Sin asked.

"Because he could look like anyone," Eva said.

"He could even look like Sin," Daniel said, as he and Eva stared at Sin.

Sin reddened. "You're kidding, right?"

"I'm not."

Eva paced between Sin and Daniel. "I guess that makes sense. You were already raised to become the king of Babylon, and you have no allies in Assyria."

Sin looked at the ceiling.

"I know. I would've never expected this either, but you're the right choice. You know that," Daniel said.

"But could this even work? People may not be able to pick Nebu out of a crowd, but they know me," Sin said.

"Not as well as you might think. The only person alive who knew Nebu really well—other than Eva and I—is Nabo. And despite his current state, I'm sure we can still trust him. People don't know you're a deposed prince because you've mostly been with us in hiding. For all anyone knows, you're a servant of some sort. So if we reveal your 'real name' is Nebu, rightful heir to the Babylonian throne, they'll assume that we were hiding you in plain sight," Daniel explained.

"So, what do you think?" Eva asked.

Sin sighed. "It's... a lot."

"Just think about it. We're still waiting on that decree, so you have some time," Eva said.

"Ok, I'm going to go. I need to process all of this. I'll talk to you guys later."

"See you later, Sin," Eva said.

Daniel nodded and Sin left the room, closing the door behind him.

Eva flopped onto the bed beside Daniel and leaned against his chest. He wrapped his arms around her and kissed her head.

"I'm glad you're back, my love."

"Me too."

After a moment, they began to sway from side to side in unison.

"So Nabo's a husk of his former self, Kandalanu and Nebu are dead and Sin is the new king," Eva whispered.

"Yep," Daniel replied, matching her tone.

"You're like a really depressing messenger pigeon."

"All in a day's work, I guess."

Eva gave a brief chuckle, and they continued to rock in silence for a long time. "Kandalanu was always kind to me. I don't know if I just reminded him of Ariel or what, but I always felt like he was someone I could trust. Like Uma. And now they're gone."

Daniel nodded, but remained silent.

"You know, the craziest part about all of this is that it seems normal now. Like I miss him and I miss Uma. It still bothers me that Ariel and Nebu died, but it doesn't *surprise* me anymore. That's scary to me."

"That would be scary for anyone, but look at everything that's happened to us. It makes sense that you are feeling numb to it. And who knows? Maybe one day we'll find ourselves in a quiet house in Beit Jinn, trying to start our little family, and suddenly—all at once—it hits you. Everything you felt numb about just pours over you like a forgotten memory—"

"I stand by my pigeon comment."

"—BUT, I'll be there for you when it does. Just like you were for me."

Eva tilted her head up and smiled at him. "What scares you most about all of this?"

"You mean if I had to pick just one thing?"

Eva laughed. "You know what I mean. What's something that keeps you up at night?"

Daniel sighed. "I think what probably scares me most is that I almost let *this*—you and me—almost slip away because I kept running from myself. I was too scared to do what I needed to do to protect everyone. You could have died and it would've been my fault."

"You wouldn't have let me die."

"But what if I hadn't done what I did?"

"I *always* knew you would make the right decision."

"How could you know when I didn't even know?"

Eva smiled as she laid her head on Daniel's shoulder. "I guess maybe that's *my* special power. You're not wrong that attacking Azra's army early on would have avoided a lot of tough decisions later, but I stand by what I said before."

"Which was?"

Eva hit him playfully. "Come on, like you don't memorize every word I say."

"I don't."

Eva sat up and eyed him critically.

"I don't *intentionally*," Daniel smirked without making eye contact.

Eva put her head back on his shoulder.

"I knew no one would look down on me for trying to avoid the massacre, but the issue for me was less about what everyone would think and more about what I would think of myself. I didn't know if I could live with myself after killing that many people."

"And what about now?"

"I still don't know if I was right or wrong. I mean, we didn't know if anyone was coming to save us and if they had, it would've been a completely different situation. But after you and Sin ran off to save Nabo, I realized it would be harder for me to live with myself if I let the people I care about die. And in the end, I did what I did because I couldn't imagine living in a world without you."

Ankl squawked from the table.

"So, I couldn't help noticing you have a pet now."

"Yeah, he just sort of appeared one day. To be honest, I wasn't sure if he was real until Sin asked me about him."

"Why, did your bird friend tell you a funny joke?"

Daniel gave an insincere laugh.

"Wait, do you hear him talk to you?"

"No more than my other animal friends."

"All this time and still, somehow, you think you're a comedic genius. This is my fault for not telling you how bad your jokes were from the beginning."

"You haven't been?"

"No, because I am too kind to tell you and you are way too delicate to take that kind of criticism."

"Too delicate?"

"*Way* too delicate."

"All I can say is, don't be surprised if my animal friends give you the cold shoulder for a bit because they are definitely hearing about this tomorrow."

Eva rolled her eyes and laughed at him. "No matter how crazy things get with your powers or the war or whatever is going on, we deal with it together, ok?"

"No matter what, we stay together."

CHAPTER 18

SEALS UNBROKEN

Colourful banners and flags fluttered from every wall and parapet in the White City. Musicians and entertainers paraded the streets, showering the road in colourful grains. Inside the palace, the celebration carried a more formal tone.

The grand reception hall hung the banners of every ally nation, and kings and representatives from nearly every nearby state mingled in the finest silks, furs and jewels. Polished gold statues of gods and former kings mingled with living guests, poised for conversation and dance.

As Daniel and Eva milled around the room, Cyaxares emerged from the crowd in a fine red robe with gold embroidery and a tall, cylindrical, golden headdress.

"King Cyaxares," Eva called out to him, "it's good to see you here."

"Are you kidding? I would never miss an opportunity to judge my future son-in-law."

"About that," Eva said, lowering her voice, "sorry about the deception. We had to hide Sin's—Nebu's— true identity for his safety."

Cyaxares chuckled. "I understand. To be honest, though, I'll probably always think of him as Sin the humble serving boy. First impressions are powerful."

"That they are," Daniel said.

"Well, I need to keep moving. I have to make time for most of the leaders here—including Bhodan. Hopefully, I have the time."

"You might not have a chance before the coronation, but definitely after. We're aiming to get started as soon as we can find our king-to-be," Eva said.

"I thought Skuza and Media had resolved their feud already," Daniel said hastily.

"Indeed, but diplomacy is a needy mistress," Cyaxares chuckled. "I had better get going. See you after the ceremony."

After Cyaxares walked out of earshot, Eva leaned her head in toward Daniel. "So, how are you doing so far?"

"Surprisingly well. It's almost as if not murdering everyone takes the edge off the entire process," Daniel said, prompting Eva to shove him playfully. "It's still intense, but I'm taking it slow, screening one at a time like we talked about. It seems ok so far."

"Good. If that changes—"

"I know, I know."

"You better."

"... But now that I'm in, I have quite a bit of juicy gossip here. Any burning questions you'd like me to answer?"

Eva elbowed him lightly. "Just one, and you already know what it is."

"I haven't been through everyone here yet, but so far everyone seems to be here for Sin. They're genuinely excited for him and ready to come together as a new allied force. That alone is pretty crazy because a lot of them are old enemies, but apparently, they're willing to set it all aside for something better."

"Wow," Eva said.

"Yeah, like I said, pretty crazy."

"Maybe it is the end of the world after all."

In the far corner of the room, Sin wove his way through the crowd, greeting guests and tugging at the gold tassels on his ornate white robes.

"He looks so... regal," Eva commented.

"He looks uncomfortable," Daniel said, catching Sin's eye.

Sin came to them, shifting his eyes nervously. "Hey. So how much danger are we in?"

"None, Sin. You can relax. Everyone here so far is a genuine ally," Daniel said.

"If that's true, then they've all left themselves open to assassination just to see another fraud take the throne."

"You're being way too hard on yourself."

"He's right Sin, these people are all here to celebrate you becoming king, and it's important that they're here to support you. It shows your strength as a leader."

"I guess..."

"You're going to do a good job. You've trained to be a king your entire life. You've already proven yourself in battle a bunch of times. You were literally born for this," Daniel said.

Sin nodded, glancing under his brows at the nearby guests.

Eva straightened his robe. "Listen, I've seen you speak to the leaders here. You speak well. You look great. You just need to believe in yourself—and stop tugging at your clothes. Your tassels are an extension of your wealth and influence, not tiny pull cords."

Sin snickered. "Ok. Hey, thank you, by the way, for learning the coronation ceremony. I'm sure that was frustrating."

"It was actually no problem at all. I spent a lot of my time in a library when I was young. It was kind of nostalgic to bury myself in research like that again."

"I can't tell if you're being sarcastic."

"He's not. Trust me." Eva said.

"Well, I appreciate it anyway. Apparently, this is something a trusted high-ranking official would usually carry out."

"Ouch. You remember I am the Royal Physician, right?"

"Alright. This has been a good talk. I'm going to slip out the back, but if anyone asks about me, just tell them I died."

"Ok, come on now."

Daniel reached out and put a hand on Sin's shoulder. "Look at me. You're going to be fine. You've practiced this ceremony with me. You've studied to be a king since you were a kid. You are ready."

"Right."

"That's not very convincing. Tell yourself that you're ready."

"I'm ready."

"You're going to be fine. Ok?"

"I'm going to be fine. I can do this."

"Ok. Let's make you a king."

Murals ran the length of the walls and banners hung under thick, elaborately carved candles affixed to the alabaster pillars of the throne room. A polished marble floor, inlaid with gold, ran the length of the room. Colourful rugs paved the path from the main doors to the throne dais, where Sin now sat stiffly upright, awaiting the ceremonial "Master of the Household". Sin found out that Master of the Household had been Tavis' official title, but he had been killed the night of the Garden Massacre and never replaced. Luckily, tradition allows any trusted high-ranking official—such as a Royal Physician—to fill the ceremonial role in situations like this.

Finally, Sin thought, as the three loud knocks came from the procession door.

"Come," Sin called.

The oversized door opened with a loud creak, allowing Daniel to enter the room.

"My lord?"

"Daniel, bring me Media."

"Yes, my lord."

Daniel left the room and returned with Cyaxares. "My lord, King Cyaxares of Media."

"King Cyaxares, join me at the throne."

Cyaxares approached the throne and then bowed before taking his place on one side of the dais, facing the door.

"Daniel, bring me Skuza."

Daniel left and returned with Bhodan, who approached the throne, paid respect, and stood to the other side of the dais. One by one, each of Babylon's ally states followed the same ritual actions until the last of them had gathered around Sin, completing a semi-circle.

"My lords, the king is dead. Return to me your seals of office, so that I may appoint those best suited to carry out my will."

Each of the lords produced a seal from within their robes and then knelt, placing the seal on the floor in front of them.

"My lords, placed before each of you is a seal, representing an office specifically attuned to your abilities. Will you choose to accept the office before you and serve me in the court?"

"We do, lord," they replied, in practised unison.

"Then take up your seals as a symbol of your allegiance to the throne of Babylon."

After each of them had regained their seal, they stood again.

"You may now properly welcome your new king, King Nebuchadnezzar of Babylon," Daniel stated formally.

Raucous cheers and congratulation surrounded Sin, breaking up the earlier formality. As he descended the throne to join them, they began clapping his arms and back while slowly ushering him to the reception hall beyond the enormous throne room doors.

Music and laughter saturated the air as fully as the smells of the feast laid out before them on an enormous long table at the centre of the room. Hundreds of attendees filled the room, moving, flowing, and rocking like a sea of colourful finery. Dancers spun and mingled with the crowd like smoke, fluidly passing from group to group, encouraging some patrons to join them.

Sin waded through the crowd, wineglass in hand, taking it all in. He leaned against a pillar to steady himself for a moment.

It's just like when I was a kid—except they're celebrating me. I'm the king.

"Why so sad, my king?"

Sin stared into his goblet, and the warmth in his face intensified as he looked up into Cyaxares' smiling face.

Sin chuckled weakly. "I'm ok. It just takes me back to when I was a kid. Big state gatherings, tons of food—and now I'm realizing—endless wine."

Cyaxares laughed. "So far, that's been my favourite part."

"Yeah, me too. Maybe I should water mine down."

"Let me take care of that for you. Right now, you need to be thinking about your speech."

"Speech? What speech?"

"I thought you've been to state gatherings?"

"Yeah. I also said I was a kid. We stayed for the food and then we'd take off with other kids."

Cyaxares smiled, but a mild sympathy touched his eyes while he looked over Sin. "I can't say I was any different as a young princeling, but, as one king to another, these occasions are always used to make a political statement. And why shouldn't it be? You're a new king and the country is in turmoil. Everyone here wants to hear something that reassures them they've made the right choice backing you."

"I never considered that. What do you suggest?"

"You need something big. You need to promise something achievable that no one thinks you can do."

"Well, that really narrows it down. Thanks."

"Come on, now," Cyaxares said patiently.

Sin took a deep breath and exhaled slowly. "What if I just don't give a big speech?"

"You have to. Now think, what would be a grand gesture to the people that their new king is strong and competent and—"

"Wait, I have it! Actually, no. Nevermind."

"What?"

"Forget it, it'll never work."

"Why?"

"Because it'll never work."

"Why?"

"Because the civilian losses would be too great."

Cyaxares stared at him. "What? What's the plan?"

"Nineveh."

"What?"

"We siege Nineveh, and eventually, when Azra's starving and weak, we take him out."

"That's a brilliant plan."

"Except that a ton of innocent people living in the city will probably starve to death while we smoke Azra out. And it's Azra. We're talking about marching an army to his door so he can presumably weave them into ground meat. I don't want to prove I'm a good king by killing our own people."

"What if you could take Nineveh without any loss of life?"

Sin met his gaze. "What do you mean? How is that possible?"

"Anything is possible when you have a Weaver," Cyaxares said with a smirk.

"I don't know...."

"Listen, we don't have to plan every detail right now. All you need to do is ask yourself, "is it possible?""

"Ok."

"So? Do you believe it's possible?"

"Well, yeah—"

"Then make your speech and leave the rest for the strategy session," Cyaxares said.

Sin ground his teeth as he exhaled. Then he emptied his wine on the floor and clanged his cup against the pillar. Music stopped and the murmur of conversation ceased. The entire room now focused on Sin.

Warmth flooded Sin's face, but he pressed on. "Thank you, everyone, for coming to celebrate my coronation."

Cheers burst from the crowd, but Sin clanged his cup again. "Hold on, hold on. I appreciate your support, but I want to say a few things. I know this war has gone on for far too long. For some of you, this war has been going on for generations. We have all felt loss. Wives have lost husbands to this war, and husbands have lost their wives. Children have lost their fathers, just as I have lost Kandalanu, our king."

Sin paused dramatically, soaking in the head nods and mumurs of agreement.

"But the time for loss has passed. The time for tyranny and defeat at the hands of monsters has passed."

The crowd rumbled with excitement. Every promise sang like music to their ears.

"Today I ask you to join me in looking ahead towards victory and towards a new empire. Today I ask you to join me in taking our first step toward purging our land of monsters by reclaiming Nineveh from Azra the Pretender!"

Cheers erupted from the crowd, drowning out the musicians. Sin beamed, raising his glass, and glanced down at Cyaxares, who gave him a nod.

Maybe I am cut out for this.

CHAPTER 19

WILDFIRE

B lue light lifted the darkness off of the dew-soaked grass and rolled it back into the western sky.

Daniel stared out at Nineveh as the morning bloomed. *For a moment every morning, the whole world is the colour of those walls, and every day the blue light recedes, leaving the blue walls to stand alone. In and out, empty and full, just like the tide.*

Daniel breathed the morning in deeply and sipped the bitter coffee he held casually in front of him as he stood at the entrance of their base camp tent.

Another beautiful day for trading the lives of strangers, for the lives of friends and allies, he thought sadly.

Thousands of men stood before him in reddish lamellar armour, swords drawn and shields ready. Behind them, thousands of black hooded cloaks flapped against the shadowed faces of women carrying scythes. Further back, archers with conical hats and colourful, tight-fitting robes awaited orders on horseback.

Eva walked toward Daniel from behind and wrapped her arms around his waist.

"Hi, my love," he said, putting an arm around her, gently rubbing her arm.

She gave him a squeeze and then quietly appreciated the view beside him for several minutes. "It's really beautiful out here this morning."

"It is."

"Are you ready?"

"As ready as I can be, I suppose," he said with a weak chuckle.

"Alright, well, Sin's waiting for you inside, to go over the plan as soon as you're up for it."

Daniel emptied the contents of his cup onto the ground. "Now is as good a time as any."

Eva and Daniel ducked into the tent and approached the large table where Sin sat with Bhodan and Cyaxares.

"Daniel. Thank you for joining us," Sin said.

"Eva has assured us you are comfortable with the plan and you understand what we're asking of you," Cyaxares said, leaning over the table.

"I understand."

"I only ask because, according to Eva, you've never done anything of this scale before—or at least nothing requiring this level of finesse."

"I understand your concerns, but I believe I can do it."

"With all due respect, we don't need you to try. We need you to succeed," Bhodan said, leaning back into his chair with crossed arms.

"With all due respect to you, your highness, I can't offer guarantees on something I've never done before. You're asking me to pacify one group while sending the other into a blood-crazed frenzy, all the while keeping them separate. So I can only offer to do my best."

"Bhodan, are you suggesting we abort the plan and go with a more traditional siege approach?"

"No, but we need result, and Daniel's responses leave me wondering if he truly appreciates the gravity of the situation."

"I can assure you, I do," Daniel said flatly, "but if you doubt me—"

"Alright, everyone needs to cool down. Now, we promised the people we would retake Nineveh without losing a single fighter. Daniel has agreed to try and make that happen, despite the great personal cost. I am extremely grateful that Daniel would even agree to take on this mission," Sin said.

"Thank you," Daniel said.

"However," Sin said, levelling a stare directly at Daniel, "I need you to remember that your mission has three priorities, not just capturing Azra. You *need* to prevent both allied casualties *and* civilian casualties. I've seen you basically perform miracles in the past, so I'm trusting your judgement here, but if you don't think you can successfully accomplish all three goals, I think we should abort."

"That choice is yours, my lord, but I believe I can do this."

Sin kept his eyes locked on Daniel's for a long time and then scanned the room before he spoke again. "Alright, good enough for me. Are we ready to begin?"

"Just keep everyone back, ok?" Daniel said as he exited the tent.

He closed his eyes and breathed in deeply. When he opened his eyes, he could feel the blue fire bursting out of them and engulfing his hands. He reached out, making thousands of connections, manipulating their vibrations simultaneously.

A scream rang out. Then it was followed by another. And another, until the screams mingled with cries and shouting, echoing in endless waves across the horizon.

"That doesn't sound right. What did you do?" Sin said.

"I wove the guards into a frenzy. They should be killing each other right now."

"And everyone else?"

"They should have no concept of where they are or what's going on around them."

"I don't know, Daniel."

"It's fine. Just trust me."

Sin shook his head. "Fine."

Daniel and the others waited silently for over an hour before the screams faded.

"Ok, I'm going," Daniel said.

Eva held a tight smile as she glanced at him.

"Don't worry," he said.

Then he approached and passed through the gates of Nineveh without a trace.

Inside the city, people laughed and screamed as they darted through the streets, chasing each other, covered in blood.

A man sprinted toward Daniel, knife in hand, but he immolated the man instantly. Then a woman came, and Daniel waved again, reducing her to ash. More and more crazed townspeople ran at Daniel.

Holy shit. They shouldn't be running around. Maybe I made them a little too carefree? I'll check for the guards—and Azra—and then release the weave.

Daniel wove a wall of fire on either side of him that carved a path through the city to the palace.

Ok, that should at least deter—

Townspeople began throwing themselves into the fire, sometimes running out and darting into the nearby houses, spreading the flames. Daniel began to walk up the road toward the palace and tried to mitigate the fires as he passed.

Seriously, people? What the hell?

By the time Daniel reached the palace, fire engulfed the entire city, causing ash to rain down from the sky. Daniel reached out and felt the surrounding threads, but there were no nearby signs of life—except for one. Daniel groaned at the loss of life.

I have to worry about that later. For now, I'm coming for you Az—wait, you don't feel like Azra.

Daniel followed the man's lifethreads to a room on the second floor. He opened the door and stepped into the room. A trail of blood traced a path to the man Daniel had been tracking. The man sat on the floor with his back propped against a wall, one hand attempting to cover a gash in his side.

"Who are you? Where's Azra?"

The man looked up at Daniel and laughed weakly.

Daniel knelt in front of him. "Can you stand?"

He chuckled and tried to prop himself up. "No, boy, my back is broken. You should leave me and get out of here while you can."

"Here, I can help," Daniel said, extending a hand. "Don't be afraid."

As his eyes and fingers ignited into tiny blue flames, the man recoiled, but Daniel connected to the man's lifethreads before he could protest.

A monsoon of new information washed over Daniel, transforming a million old assumptions into facts. "You're Ballit."

An oily smirk shaped Ballit's lips. "So the rumours are true."

"What rumours?"

Ballit said nothing.

Daniel struggled to focus. "Azra's not here. He never even told you where he was going when he left."

"That's right, boy."

"I imagine he didn't tell me where he was going for just this occasion. No, you've been with him for a long time. Where do you *think* he would go?"

"You know everything I know. Where do *you* think he would go?"

Daniel couldn't take his eyes off of Ballit. Rage was bubbling up in Daniel.

"So you're not going to help me?"

Ballit laughed. "Help you? No, definitely not. I'm fairly certain Azra choreographed this whole situation as a distraction to buy time."

Fire peeked into the room, prompting Ballit to burst into laughter again. "Looks like time is running out for all of us."

Daniel stared at him for a moment as flames danced across the floor around them. "You killed so many of the people I cared about. People my friends and family cared about."

"Yeah? Please, go on. Read me a list of my crimes so you can bring me to justice. Unless you have somewhere better to be?"

Seconds seemed to stretch out endlessly while Daniel considered his options.

"The way I see it, boy, you can either kill me now or heal me, bring me back to your—"

"Goodbye Ballit." Daniel made a crushing gesture with his hands and twisted. Ballit's body instantly compacted into a dense ball, spraying blood into the flames.

As Daniel walked out of the city, the wooden frames of the gate collapsed into ashes behind him. Eva and Sin ran to him.

"What happened in there?" Eva asked.

Daniel closed his eyes, allowing the blue flames to fade. "Looks like Azra was in another castle."

"What do you mean?" Sin asked.

"When I was in there, I ran into Azra's second in command. It looks like Azra left days ago—most likely to Harran, based on their conversations—and has probably been waiting there for Egyptian reinforcements. We need to get to Harran before his reinforcements do."

"Ok, and what about Ballit?" Eva asked.

"He's dead," Daniel said, walking past them, toward their troops.

"Wait, Wait, Wait. You killed Ballit? He was a high-ranking soldier, he could've been valuable alive."

"I know how it looks, but he was already dying. He wasn't going to help us and if you knew what I know, you wouldn't have spared him, either. So, yes, I killed him, but it was quick and probably more merciful than he actually deserved."

"*Do* you know how this looks? Explain to me why the city is on fire, and by that I mean *razed to the ground*. Where are the townspeople?" Sin said.

"By the time I could release the weave on the townspeople, most of them were already dead."

"But why wait *that* long? I thought you were just weaving to create an opening for yourself to enter the city and search for Azra. What happened?"

"That's exactly what I did," Daniel shouted, and then

exhaled sharply before beginning again. "Look, you weren't in there. It was chaos. People were coming at me from every direction, and I had to defend myself. Some of them may have caught on fire, but I got the information we need to stop Azra. That's what matters, isn't it?"

"You're not seeing the whole picture here."

"I get it. I made a mistake. I got completely sidetracked with Ballit and used the wrong weaves, to begin with—"

"NO! You don't get it. This isn't about what weaves you used. We could have waited them out. Some of our people may have died, but it wouldn't have been a massacre like this fucking nightmare you've created behind me. That's how a siege works Daniel, we had the advantage," Sin said.

"You were the one concerned about your promises and preventing a prolonged siege. As it turns out, it was the right call. Azra *lured* us into this seige. He built this whole ruse to buy time for Egyptian reinforcements. If we would have waited them out, we might've saved a few lives, sure, but then what?"

"How many civilians did you set on fire today, Daniel?"

"Only the ones that weren't smart enough to stay inside."

"You wiped out the entire population of Nineveh. Not the army, the entire population. I've never seen a slaughter like that. That wasn't the plan."

"Well, some things just don't go as planned, do they?"

"This was a completely unacceptable loss of life and I think you know that, but you're too fucking proud and thick to let it sink in. This could've all gone differently."

"Taking brutal, decisive action is better than being indecisive until circumstance decides for you. Remember that you were the one who suggested I turn an entire army into mist back in Assur?"

"I've never asked you to turn anyone into mist."

"You asked me to take them out. What the fuck did you think that even means?"

"You know what? I don't know. I don't fucking know, but I didn't expect that, and I certainly didn't expect all of this." Sin gestured to the ruined city, before stomping away.

"Then you should be careful what you fucking wish for," Daniel shouted after him.

"Daniel," Eva said gently, "I don't want to pile on, but you know he's right."

"We took the city without a single loss."

"And no one's disputing whether our soldiers are safe, but look at this. Think about how many innocent people died. Didn't you tell me once that Sin had people he cared about still living in the city?"

Roohangiz. Roo Roo... and her granddaughter.

"Think about how he's probably feeling right now."

Daniel sighed. "I'll go apologize later, but I know I made the right choice. The goal was to minimize *our* losses, and we did that. We didn't get Azra, but we got a lead on his whereabouts and we took away his advantage of time."

Eva slumped sadly onto his chest, and the two of them swayed from side to side as they stared at the smouldering city. "Don't let yourself flake away until there's nothing left. Save a piece for me, ok?" she whispered.

"You already have all the pieces of me that matter," Daniel said, kissing her on the head.

Chapter 20

A Mixture of Ashes and Water

Small hearth fires dotted the landscape south of Nineveh, where the allied armies had set up camp. Smaller tents near the fires acted as sleeping quarters and temporary stables, while a cluster of large tents at the centre stood for Eva, Cyaxares, Bhodan, and Sin.

Muted conversation lingered on the air, broken intermittently by bursts of laughter or argument.

Except for a small radius around Daniel.

As he made his way to Sin's tent, hushed silence marked his path, along with stares from nearby soldiers.

These men are alive because I prevented a protracted battle. They're alive because of me.

A crow swooped down and landed on Daniel's shoulder.

"I made the right choice, didn't I, Ankl?" Daniel said as he stroked the bird's chest.

"It's definitely what I would've done," Ankl squawked.

"It sounds like everyone's already here."

"—Egypt has to be stopped, but we also need to go to Harran before Azra can make any more moves," Cyaxares said.

"That may be, but if we don't keep a presence in these newly captured territories, we could leave ourselves open to rebellion. Especially if we neglect to repair the damage we've caused," Bhodan said as Daniel pulled back the flap and entered.

Everyone suddenly became silent, with some exchanged glances. Eva signalled for Daniel to join her, while Sin glared at him.

"To be honest, I think Cyaxares is right," Eva said, drawing Sin's glare to her. "I think we need to send as many of our warriors as we can to Harran. Azra is not an enemy to take lightly, and I don't think we can afford to wait."

"We don't need to delay the entire army for what I'm proposing," Bhodan said.

"How many men would you need?" Sin asked.

"Maybe a quarter of our combined forces," Bhodan said.

"That's a pretty considerable amount," Cyaxares said. "I still say we should attack with our full force now and rebuild after we defeat Azra."

Sin considered his options. "I think Bhodan's right. Since we would outnumber an enemy that will be under siege, we can spare the men. We should leave a force behind to rebuild and keep order."

"So, what do we do about the Egyptians?" Eva asked.

"What if we meet them head-on? If we send a small specialist force east and extend our borders along the coast toward Egypt. That would force them to travel further on foot, slowing them down," Daniel offered.

Sin pursed his lips.

"That could work, actually. Ally with anyone we cross, conquer everyone else. If we do it right, we could force them to turn around entirely," Cyaxares said, pointing at the map.

"He's right. Then, when we finish with the Egyptians, we can regroup with the main force at Harran and help end the siege," Eva said.

One by one, each general looked toward Sin, assessing his reaction while Sin considered his options. "Fine. Bhodan, you will stay in Nineveh to rebuild, but with half the men you originally requested. You will need to request additional men from Babylon to make up the difference. You will also need to develop a patrol schedule to secure the entire region from here to the southern border."

"Yes, my lord."

"Cyaxares, how secure is the eastern border?"

"Very, my lord."

"Good, arrange your top generals so it stays that way, then ready all the men you can spare and accompany me to Harran for the siege."

"Yes, my lord," Cyaxares said with a smirk.

"Eva, you're most familiar with the western region. I want you to gather every available Scythe Dancer. You'll also be responsible for half of our Askuzai archers and half of our Median forces. Your army will expand east and slow the Egyptians down."

"What about Daniel?"

"He's coming with me to Harran," Sin said, focusing a hard stare in his direction.

"That's not going to work," Eva said bluntly.

"What? Why?"

"Daniel goes where I go."

"Fine, you and Daniel will accompany me to Harran. Cyaxares, you will command the Scythe Dancers—"

"The Scythe Dancers also go where I go," Eva said, locking eyes with Sin.

Finally, Sin sighed and palmed his face. "Fine, you and *Daniel* will travel west, but Daniel will not engage in battle. You'll set up a command center and he will stay there at all times." Sin turned to Daniel. "You're not there to fight. Got it?"

"Got it."

"Ok. No more massacres. Let's do this right. Questions?" Sin said, surveying their faces.

"What do we do with Nabo?" Daniel asked.

It had been several days' ride since Daniel and Eva's group had disguised themselves as a merchant caravan and split off from the main army. Crows came and went frequently as Daniel used their aerial memories to navigate. Each time, he would give Eva an update on their location, but he was otherwise silent.

"How's it going over here?" Eva asked, riding up beside him.

Daniel gave her a confused look. "Good. Why do you ask?"

"Because you're brooding."

"I'm not brooding."

"Then why are you giving me the cold shoulder? Are you mad at me for taking this mission?"

Daniel scratched his head and sighed. "It's not like that."

"Then tell me what it's like."

"I'm just... thinking."

"... about?"

Daniel looked at her and sighed again.

"I'm going to get an answer. You know I am, so why not save us some time and just tell me what's on your mind?"

"It's dumb."

Eva stared at him until he rolled his eyes and started again.

"It's just that I keep running into all of these obstacles—all the way back to Mari—and when we got attacked in Assur, I had this grand revelation that a lot of it was my fault. Maybe even all of it."

"How was any of it your fault?"

"Inaction. Sometimes it was from taking half measures or choosing an alternative because I was too afraid to do something I should've done. But either way, it was always because I was running from doing everything I can. After the siege, I decided I would never back away from doing something difficult to protect the people I care about. I absolutely believe that's the lesson in all of this." Daniel paused for a moment.

"And then Nineveh happened, and people started doubting you."

Daniel nodded and let the silence sit for a long time. "At Assur, Sin told me to literally massacre an army before they even got to the gates and when I finally did it, he thanked me for saving his life. I turned every Assyrian that breached the wall that day into a fine mist, and Sin *reassured* me I did the right thing."

"For Sin, soldiers go into every situation *expecting* to die."

"And at Nineveh, it wasn't just soldiers, right?"

Eva pursed her lips into a sympathetic frown. "I think, for Sin, it was just so shocking to see civilians die in such a brutal way—to actually witness it—it's hard for him to even consider it might have been an accident."

"I really didn't want civilians to die. I made a mistake and then tried to fix it with another mistake and then eventually I just told myself that as long as I could get Azra, it would all be worth it."

"I know you didn't mean for all of that to happen. I know that deep down you were trying to do the right thing. I think Sin knows that too, even if he won't allow himself to admit it right now."

"I'm just tired of everyone doubting me, and I'm tired of constantly doubting myself."

Eva nodded. "Back when I was at the temple, maybe a year or two after I got there, they started having me perform rituals and devotions by myself. Now, I didn't know it at the time, but I was ready. I was knowledgeable enough and competent enough to perform those rituals and say those prayers. I had trained so hard and I was ready, but I didn't think I was, and it wasn't because of all the nervousness and inexperience—not really. It was because everyone kept telling me I wasn't ready. That I wasn't good enough. That I shouldn't even be there. And every day I would cry and cry because being a temple slave was the only thing I ever trained for in my life and everyone said I was bad at it."

"So, you're saying I should cry every day?"

"No, and I also didn't say I was finished," Eva said with a look that betrayed her smirk.

"I'm sorry," Daniel said, smirking back as he looked down.

"So, one day Uma asks me to join her on a walk around the temple. As we walk around, she's pointing things out she likes or that she thinks are interesting and asks me for my opinion about those things, and we just have a light chat for a while. And then she asks me, 'how have things been going?'. Suddenly, I start crying and she puts her arms around me and strokes my hair. Eventually, I calm down a little and she asks me what's wrong, you know, 'why are you crying?'. So I tell her what everyone's been saying, and how I feel stupid and useless—I just tell her everything—and she just listens quietly until finally, I say, 'I just don't know what I'm doing wrong'. I remember that clearly because of what she said next."

"Which was?" Daniel said, arching an eyebrow.

"She pushes me back a little and kneels in front of me. Then she looks me in the eye and says, 'What you're doing wrong is that you're listening to everyone. There are only two people in your whole life you need to listen to; who you were and who you want to be."

"I guess good advice can't be *good* if it isn't super cryptic."

"It's kind of like what you're doing with the crows. You're sending them out and then pick out memories that show you what's immediately ahead of us. They're helping you keep track of *where you want to go*, but in order to do that, they need to fly back so that you can read those memories and follow their flight path. In order to tell you where to go, they literally need to remember where they came from."

Just as Eva finished speaking, a crow swooped down and landed on Daniel's shoulder. Daniel scratched the crow's breast gently as he sifted through the animal's memories. Suddenly, his heart ached and his whole body stiffened as he came across a familiar feature on the landscape.

"I think you're right," Daniel said.

"Of course I am," Eva said with a smile.

"Do you mind if we take a slight detour?"

"You're the navigator. Do what you need to do."

Daniel altered their route to dip a little further south. They arrived on the bank of the Euphrates in the early afternoon a few days later. The river was so wide that the distant shore looked like an island stretching across the horizon.

Daniel dismounted and reached into a pouch on his belt, pulling out a handful of seeds. Leaving his horse, Daniel walked to the edge of the bank and threw the seeds outward around him. Then he reached out to the little seeds, felt the life inside of them, and coaxed them to grow. Suddenly, enormous trees grew out of the bank, twisting and wrapping around each other as they stretched out across the river into the bank on the other side. Branches shot out of the bottom of the trees like support beams, and their large roots thickened into a stable anchor. Finally, the upward-facing side of the trunk reshaped itself into a flattened platform.

As Daniel walked back to his horse, he noticed that some of the newer soldiers stared, open-mouthed, at the woven tree bridge, while others snickered at them.

"Ok, let's go."

It took until late afternoon to get everyone over the bridge, partly because of the soldiers' apprehension about crossing it. Eva decided they would make camp and leave again at dawn. Now Daniel and Eva stood a few paces from the edge of the bank, standing hand in hand, as they watched the camp take shape.

"Are you alright getting everyone set up if I go— um—," Daniel said.

"That's why we're here, isn't it? Go, I'll be fine. Just come back before dark. We don't know who else is out here," Eva said.

Daniel smiled. "I love you."

"I love you too."

I won't need crows for this.

He walked away from the camp and away from the river. The vegetation started off really familiar, but as he walked, everything became less familiar. Trees and bushes turned to low grasses, and low grasses transitioned into new growth vegetation. Eventually, all of it gave way to blackened earth. At the centre of the blackness stood a stout elderly man, clothed in simple brown linens. His white unkempt hair wrapped around his head, leaving the top bare. Daniel followed the old man's line of sight to the tall stones that marked the spot where he had awoken from the ashes only a few years prior.

"Hello?" Daniel said, approaching the man.

The old man twisted slightly to face him. "Hello, young man."

"What brings you to a place like this?"

"I was from Mari before it... before it looked like this. I was out of town at the time, and when I came back... well, you can imagine the rest. Life goes on, though. You move on, start again. It's like being born a second time in a lot of ways."

The old man was quiet for a long time, staring distantly before turning back to Daniel. "What's your name, young man?"

"It's Daniel."

"Ah Daniel, a sound name. You can call me Omar. What brings you to the Ruins of Mari, Daniel?"

Ruins. I guess it is a ruin now.

"I lived in Mari when I was a kid."

Omar smiled and gave Daniel a long look. "Yes, it feels like a lifetime ago. I think I remember you, though. Your mother was an herbalist, wasn't she?"

"Yeah, she was."

"Yes, I remember your family. Good people, all of them. Your father was an honest man, very proud. Your sister was the sweetest little girl. Always running. She probably left more footprints on this land than the wildlife. And you. You were so curious, always exploring, always asking questions. Did they make it...?"

"Ah, no. No, I'm the only one that survived."

"Hmm," Omar grunted with a nod.

Silence stretched between them.

Daniel surveyed the blackened ruins. *What am I doing here?*

"It's so strange," Omar said.

"What is?"

"That flower," he said, pointing his curled finger toward the ruins.

Daniel tried to follow his line of sight. A tall stone stood straight ahead, with a shorter boulder several paces away.

Where is it?

Then a thin mauve splash of colour reached out to him from the blackness. Daniel rubbed his eyes and focused again. A lone lily bowed its head bashfully before them.

Omar twisted stiffly toward Daniel. "Those stones out there, they were foundation stones. They've been there since before The Sundering when Mari was a kingdom, rather than a small, forgotten village. Like echoes of a past life. Mari has been destroyed a lot over the generations."

Daniel shook his head. "I had no idea."

"Well, it was, and every time, people return and build upon the foundations of the past. But that little flower, it's breaking the mould."

"How so?"

"Look where it is. The foundation stones on either side of that lily were monumental buildings in the centre of town, and a road passed between them. A road that ran right over that lily. If Mari hadn't been levelled so completely, it would be impossible for that little flower to grow in that exact spot at this particular moment. Now, I'm not saying the lives of every person lost in the fire were worth the bloom of one tiny flower. What happened here was a devastating, irreversible tragedy. But if I'm going to be asked to endure it, it's nice to know that it enabled something so beautiful and impossible to exist. It's like having the land itself tell me 'I'm truly sorry for your loss', but also 'thank you for your sacrifice'."

Daniel reached into his belt and felt the small grains within. He dug out a handful and knelt a few paces behind the lily, at the centre of the old road. Then he poked a small hole in the ground and filled it with seeds.

"What are you doing there, young man? Daniel?"

"This lily could've grown anywhere. It could've found somewhere greener and safer to bloom, but here it is. Its path intersecting with ours, against all odds." Daniel stepped back and blue flames ignited from his hands and eyes as he wove the little seedlings into an imposing tree. Then the flames receded and Daniel headed back toward the old man, who now stared at him, mouth agape.

Daniel clasped the older man gently on the shoulder as he walked by. "The least I can do is make sure its life was not in vain. Peace be with you, Uncle."

Almost a month had passed since Daniel and Eva had left Mari, but the roads had been relatively peaceful. The rolling savannah stretched out in every direction, displaying its lush beauty. In the distance ahead, a mountain range crowned the horizon.

"Have you ever seen anywhere this beautiful before?" Daniel asked Eva.

Eva faced forward and said nothing.

"Eva?"

Still nothing.

"What's wrong?" Daniel asked her, frowning.

"Nothing. Why does something have to be wrong?"

"Well, it's not that something *has* to be wrong, you just had this face—"

"What's wrong with my face?"

"Nothing. Forget I said anything."

A few more days passed. They found themselves camped outside of Damascus, waiting for a resupply run to return.

Daniel gently touched Eva's arm as he approached her.

She turned and gave him a small smile. She wrapped her arms around him and rested her head on his chest. Daniel replied with a gentle hug. Soon stillness became a sway, and Daniel kissed her on the head and rubbed her back.

"I love you, you know," Daniel said.

"I love you too," Eva whispered.

"I know, but I also know that something's bothering you and you won't tell me."

"No, it's nothing. I'm just thinking about the battle ahead."

Quiet passed between them for another moment.

"You see that mountain on the horizon?" Daniel asked.

"I—I hadn't noticed it."

"Some people say that it has the freshest water anywhere. They say that it flows down the mountain from heaven."

Eva cleared her throat. "What else do they say?"

"I've heard," Daniel began slowly, " that many years ago when the world was still new, there was a magician king named Solomon. He was so powerful he commanded an army of Djinn."

"Oh, yeah?" Eva whispered.

"Yeah. And one day, the magician king ordered the Djinn to find the most beautiful women in the land and bring them back to his palace. So, the Djinn went out in search of the most beautiful women any man had ever seen—and they found them. But along their journey, the Djinn had fallen in love with the women."

Eva sniffed. "What did they do?"

"Well, instead of bringing them back to the magician king, the Djinn settled down at the base of a nearby mountain. *That* mountain right there."

Eva sniffed and tried to wipe her eyes covertly. "I can't believe you remember all of that."

"I remember most things."

"Do you still want to settle down in Beit Jinn when all of this is over?"

"Of course, but Eva, I see you. I know you're not suffering right now because you suddenly miss your hometown."

"Aren't I? How could this be anything but selfish homesickness? I mean, look at it? I wanted to see it one more time for so many years, and here we are, just a few days' ride away. It just makes sense that old feelings are creeping up on me."

"Eva, I don't think it's that at all."

"How could you know how I feel better than I do?"

"Because I know you, and because I had all the same thoughts and feelings when I realized how close we were to Mari. I needed to see it one last time. Why would I feel like that? I'm probably able to wipe out any standing army in the world with a wave of my hand. But I don't think it's about knowing or not knowing you have the advantage. I think it's about being human. It's about being anxious before you fight a huge battle and it's about wanting that one last reminder of where you came from—*just in case*. I know you try to stay strong for everyone. We both know you've supported me over the years more than any one person deserves. The least I can do is convince you to take this one detour for yourself. Taste that super-fresh spring water and remember where you came from so that you can go into battle with no regrets and a reason to come back out in one piece."

Eva nodded. "I suppose I could set up a command center in Beit Jinn just as easily as anywhere else."

"You deserve to do something for yourself sometimes, and what better time than now?"

"I love you," she said, looking up at him.

Daniel wiped her tears with his sleeves. "I would be empty without you."

Eva pulled Daniel down into a long, soft kiss. Then she rested her head back on his chest and they swayed back and forth, watching the sun sink behind Mount Hermon.

Beit Jinn seemed unchanged from the memories Daniel had imprinted from Eva's mind. Colourful square houses lined a cluster of roads that branched off of the main road running alongside a freshwater stream. Most of the houses were abandoned, so Daniel and Eva arranged for the Scythe Dancers to fill them a few weeks prior when they had arrived.

Eva barely held it together when we rode into town.

Daniel leaned back against the post behind him and closed his eyes while the stream babbled peacefully beside him.

Eva's right about this place, though. I could see myself staying here forever.

"Don't forget we eventually have a war to fight," Eva said as she stood over him.

"How could I forget with all the constant reminders?"

Eva pulled his leg to the side so she could sit between them, leaning against his chest.

"What if we just stay here?"

"Are you serious? Daniel, we can't. Sin is expecting us to meet him in Harran."

"Eventually."

"Sooner than later."

"Nah, they'd hardly miss us."

"I doubt that."

"What if we just never showed up? They might not even notice."

"Yeah, that's how real life works. For. Sure."

"Why not? Maybe they'll forget about us."

Eva sighed and smiled despite herself. "You always choose to be ridiculous at the most ridiculous times."

"How about this? You and I stay right here, just like this for the rest of the day?"

"What about food? Are you saying you won't move from this spot, even for meals?"

"Even for meals. We can have the crows bring us food."

"No, thanks."

"Fine, no meals at all. Just you and me sitting here, starving together, enjoying the peace."

Eva smirked. "Fine, we'll see how long that lasts, but if anyone comes with any news—"

"I'll have my birds create a perimeter."

Almost immediately, a crow swooped down beside Daniel.

"Shoo," Daniel whispered, blowing at the bird.

"You shoo. I flew really far and came back to deliver this stupid message to you." The bird lifted its leg, gesturing to the dangling message container.

"You're supposed to be on my side. Did Ankl teach you guys how to be sassy? That's really annoying."

"I don't know who Ankl is. Can you please take your stupid message?"

Daniel peered at the crow.

"Who's Ankl?" Eva asked.

"Just one of the crows," Daniel muttered, as he removed the tiny paper from around its leg.

"What's the message say?"

Daniel held the message in front of them. "I guess the vacation's over. We're heading to Megiddo."

"You mean *I'm* heading to Meggido?"

"Nope, the letter is really clear that I need to be there."

Eva snatched the letter from his hands.

"See?" Daniel said, after a prolonged silence.

"Shhh. I'm reading."

"It's not that long of a message—"

"Shh!" Eva repeated.

"—maybe two or three sentences max."

Eva stood up and stared into the distance while she gently unfurled the message over and over, allowing the paper to roll back up as her fingertips passed the end.

"So are you against meeting Josiah?" Daniel asked.

"No, but Sin's orders were really clear."

"So order the Scythe Dancers to conquer them."

"I can't. He's offering to join us willingly."

"Either his conditions are too much, or they're not. You don't have time to send a message to Sin and then wait for a response by the sounds of it."

"I know. He says they're only a few days away from them."

Daniel went to Eva and rubbed her arms. "Listen, you were a trusted leader long before we were a rebel army. Right now, this is your call and no matter what you choose to do, everyone here trusts that it will be the right one."

Eva frowned as she glanced up into Daniel's eyes, and then looked down at the message as she slowly unfurled it again. Finally, she exhaled slowly, punctuating her breath with one word. "Okay."

"Okay?"

"Okay. *We're* going to Meggido. Help me spread the word. Everyone needs to be packed and ready to move in one hour. We only take what we need. We'll be back before we head to Harran."

"Got it."

"Make sure you send a crow ahead of us. Tell Josiah, we're on our way."

Daniel and Eva took four days to arrive at Meggido with the Scythe Dancers. Their encampment sat upon a hill overlooking a wide valley below. The largest tent, where everyone now stood, had a clear view of the valley and a large hill beyond it.

Daniel sent a crow to survey the grounds while they met with the King of Judah.

"Your Highness," Eva said, greeting him with a bow.

"You must be General Eva. Welcome," Josiah said, before eyeing Daniel. "And you must be Daniel."

"Yes, your Highness, thanks for meeting us."

"Curious hobby you have with those crows. I've seen that kind of training done with hawks, but never crows."

"Crows are really intelligent birds. It's only their personality that makes it difficult for most people to train them."

"But not you."

"Your Highness, you requested we come to meet you here, and we're here. We're here as allies."

"They say your army travels with the blessing of Ba'al Hadad. They say he follows you. I wanted to see for myself if the rumours are true."

"Do you see Ba'al Hadad travelling with us?"

"I haven't decided, but I will tell you, this is the land of the One True God. Those vile creatures that wander the earth as enemies of the One True God will be destroyed without mercy."

"Your Highness, I'm not a demon."

"We'll see."

"Do we have any idea where the Egyptians are?" Eva asked.

The crow returned and landed on Daniel's shoulder. Daniel turned and looked out across the valley as he read the bird's memories.

"They should be here any day now," Josiah said.

"Actually, I think they're already here," Daniel said, pointing to the hill on the horizon.

A grainy shadow crested over the top of the hill. Daniel squinted into the distance until the dark mass took on the shapes of individual men.

"I think they're taking on a battle formation," Eva said.

"Then so too shall we."

Chapter 21

The Fog of War

An orange sun hung low ahead of Sin and Cyaxares while they rode side by side and chatted. Dried grasses crunched beneath hooves, dulling the impact into a deep basso percussion. The air buzzed with the sounds of soldiers talking across the blockade camp, shrouding Sin's conversation, but they spoke in hushed tones, anyway.

"It's been four days and yet, things seem so... quiet," Sin said.

"Yes, but this is potentially normal for a siege," Cyaxares said.

Sin twisted around to look at the camp encircling Harran, noting the wide buffer of grass between his men and the city walls.

Cyaxares chuckled. "You don't need to twist around like that. The horse will spin for you if you guide it."

"I figured, but why make the horse walk in circles when I can just turn my head?"

"You're a strange king, my lord."

"Are you making fun of me?"

"I don't mean any offence. It's been a long time since we had a king that would care about the horses."

Sin rode silently for a moment before speaking again. "Do you not think... King Ashur was a good king?"

Cyaxares gave him a sidelong look. "Your father, you mean?"

Sin nodded with a frown.

"I didn't know King Ashur well or on a personal level. He seemed to be an effective king. Although, I will say humility and diplomacy were certainly qualities some of our predecessors could have benefited from."

"I'm assuming you're not talking about *your* father."

"No, I am not."

"My father wasn't a tyrant."

"Are you asking me or telling me?"

"I'm just saying. Everyone seems to think he was an evil man, but he was only doing what he thought was right for his people. You must have seen that to some extent."

"As I said, I never actually met your father. I met a man named Madius, though, who claimed to represent him."

"It doesn't sound like he left a good impression."

"I killed him. Brutally."

"What? Why?"

"He killed my father and burned our city to the ground, all in the name of your father."

"I'm sorry. I didn't know that happened."

"It was a long time ago."

Sin nodded. "It's strange hearing all of this. It's not how I remember him."

"No man is perfect, but a boy rarely realizes his father is only a man until he, too, is a man. There is a reason that people believe your father was a tyrant, but there is also a reason that the same men who follow you once rebelled against him."

"What reason is that?"

"Because you are not him. All of us have seen you lay down your life and join the battle. The men trust you as a warrior and brother in arms. They would follow you anywhere now. Your father never earned that kind of respect from his men. You did."

Sin nodded and stared ahead as they rode. A tall black figure appeared to notch the orange ground directly ahead of them. Sin shielded his eyes and squinted to make out who approached them until he realized he was looking at Nabo sitting in the distance.

"What do you think he's doing?" Sin said.

"Let's find out."

Sin dismounted as they reached Nabo. "Hey, Nabo."

Nabo turned slowly toward him with a hollow gaze. "My lord."

Sin sat beside him as Cyaxares watched from behind. "What are you doing out here?"

Nabo snorted. "I'm analyzing the enemy."

"Ah. So you just wanted to get a closer look?"

Nabo turned toward Sin and met his gaze. "With all due respect, I am not a child. Kandalanu would never have questioned my motives."

"I just wanted to make sure you're ok and we're so close to the wall here—"

"What did I just say!" Nabo shouted.

"Rein it in Nabo. He has a right to ask."

"Then let me ask you something, *my lord*. Why did you save me?"

"Wha—what?"

"Back in Assur. Why did you save me?"

"Technically, it was Daniel..."

"We both know Daniel might not have intervened if you hadn't—"

"We both know Daniel *would* have."

"Answer the question. Why didn't you let me die?"

"I thought it was the right thing to do."

"Well then, who am I to stand between a king and a good night's sleep?"

"Are you kidding me?"

"Watch your tone, boy."

"Watch *your* fucking tone. Even if I wasn't the king, you're still way out of line. I've lost people too. My whole family got wiped out. Do you know why? Because you and Kandalanu and Uma thought it would be a good idea to overlook *that* fucking guy," Sin said, pointing toward Harran. "So fuck you. I tried to save your life."

"No one asked you to," Nabo said, as the sun sunk below the horizon.

"You used to be someone I admired. I looked forward to you and Kandalanu visiting the castle. What a mistake that was for all of us."

Gears shrieked with strain, drawing their attention toward the city.

Cyaxares mounted and galloped across the camp, shouting for the men to take positions. The camp broke into a clamouring scramble, but soon the cacophony turned to dead silence as men made formation and waited.

Enemy archers topped the walls, standing with bows ready, but darkness shrouded everything inside of the gate, keeping whatever enemies lying beyond it hidden.

A few moments passed with no sign of attack.

Sin took stock of his men and tried to glimpse Cyaxares' position, but he was out of sight.

Suddenly a whinny broke the silence, and a mounted horse galloped out of the darkness towards them.

"Stand Ready!" Sin shouted.

Nabo rose to his feet, grasping his axes.

A single, flaming arrow flew down from the city walls and immediately buried itself into the rider, causing him and the horse to burst into flames. The horse screamed and panicked.

"Ready your arrows!" Sin shouted, but the Harran archers were faster than his men.

Arrows rained down from the wall, falling onto the horse in a tight circle. The horse collapsed into a smouldering heap, still struggling to take weak breaths.

Nabo walked up to the horse and buried his axe in its neck. Then he beheaded the rider and walked back.

"They didn't shoot you!"

"They weren't looking for a fight. It looks like they killed the rider themselves. They gagged and tied him to the horse before they were both doused in oil," Nabo said.

"Why?"

"They were sending a message. They would rather set their own men on fire than surrender."

Shadows filled the valley and deepened with each passing hour. Flags and cloaks whipped loudly across an otherwise dead-silent forest of armoured bodies. Scythe Dancers stood in a wide front line ahead of the Judean main force, their black hooded cloaks and scythes contrasting sharply with the colourful tunics and shields of the warriors behind them. Ahead, the

Egyptian formations cascaded down the hillside, clearly outnumbering them.

Daniel looked out over the battlefield, his eyes instinctively drawn to Eva. *I won't let you die.*

Eva looked back at him as if reading his thoughts, before focusing her attention back on the hill ahead where a horse rode down toward them. Josiah sat ahead of his allied army, waiting.

Daniel squinted, trying to make out the figure meeting with Josiah. The newcomer wore a kilt wound around the body with a pleated section drawn to the front, and a lion's tail hung from his belt. His chest was bare aside from the leopard skins that hung over his shoulders.

The two men spoke for several minutes before returning to their armies. Daniel heard the rider yell something in a vaguely familiar language as he rode away, but Josiah remained quiet.

"What happened? Who was that?" Daniel asked.

"That was Necho."

"The *Pharoah?* Why is the Pharoah personally leading his army?"

"It's just their way. The Egyptians are a proud people and there is a lot of prestige in saving your allies from a crushing defeat at the last possible moment."

"Won't they be surprised...," Daniel said as he drew his black cloak over his head, shielding his eyes from view.

"We don't even register as a threat to them, nor should we. Their army outmatches ours three to one, at least."

They think.

Daniel was now reaching out to everyone on the battlefield, and he could feel Josiah studying him. Daniel heard the dirt shift beside him as Josiah took in the field.

"Looking out at your fighters, there is no doubt about the strength and fierceness of your army. However, the forces of evil are strong in this world, and I have pledged myself against them. If I detect, even for a moment, that the forces of evil have made themselves at home in my country—on this battlefield—my opponent will no longer be the Pharoah alone. Are we clear?"

Daniel did not turn or reveal his face, instead kept his gaze locked on Eva. "Yes, your majesty."

Josiah walked behind Daniel to the tent and gave orders to his men before taking a seat.

As long as he's observing the battle from behind me, I should be able to weave without being seen.

Trumpets echoed across the valley, disjointed and out of sync like songbirds in the morning. Scythes and spears pounded the ground until the air vibrated with their rhythm. Eva shouted something to her Scythe Dancers, raising her scythe in the air. Everything became still. Only the sounds of cloth whipping in the wind broke the silence. Eva looked over her army and spoke.

She's giving them a speech of some sort. A motivational speech.

When Eva finished speaking, she raised her Scythe into the air once more and the Scythe Dancers joined her and roared. The sound of a thousand roars and screams spread across the entire army until even the Judeans joined them.

The Egyptians showed no interest in their display, but Daniel could sense their fear. They thought the Judeans had joined forces with something *mythical*.

It seems so long ago when they were just civilians looking for a means to defend themselves. Now they're feared warriors defending a nation.

As the allied army's roars died down, the Egyptians advanced. Rhythmic marching and chanting rolled over the valley like a cresting wave, carrying the clang of swords beating against metal Egyptian shields.

Clacking wood seasoned the air as archers nocked their arrows.

"Hold positions!" Allied leaders shouted, each regiment taking a rigid formation.

The Egyptians continued to march forward.

"Hold positions!" the orders came again.

Bows creaked and archers took aim.

"Hold!"

Clanging and chanting dominated the air, as the Egyptian infantry came within a few paces of the Scythe Dancers.

"Fire the arrows!" Josiah ordered.

At the same moment, Egyptian forces loosed their own barrage of arrows.

Arrows darkened the sky, landing on either side of the valley.

The Egyptians raised their shields, dominating the noise with their clatter. The Scythe Dancers spun and twisted, evading most arrows. Daniel subtly healed those who got hit, giving them an element of surprise when Egyptian forces attempted to walk past them.

"They feigned injury? What an advanced strategy. Who trains your army?"

"Eva trains them, your majesty."

"It's spectacular. Look at how they've outmatched the enemy! Have there been many losses so far?"

"No losses, your majesty."

"No losses? From an unshielded infantry? That's... remarkable."

"Eva would appreciate hearing as much when the battle concludes."

"Yes, I'd imagine she would."

Black cloaks now saturated the Egyptian side of the valley, swirling around the golden fighters like muddy footprints in a riverbed. Behind them, Judean forces held the line, preventing the Egyptians from passing.

Arrows came in waves from either side. Daniel continued healing Scythe Dancers and Judeans, preventing casualties from each barrage.

Slowly, slowly, the difference in numbers levelled out. Scythe Dancers and even a few Judeans had climbed the hill toward the enemy's camp.

"Victory will be ours," Josiah said.

Soon enough.

Egyptian trumpets cut through the noise and echoed across the valley.

"What are they doing? Daniel, order your soldiers to pull back. Their support troops are too far away. They're going to be surrounded."

Daniel stopped listening and reached out.

Oh no, he thought, as he searched frantically for Eva.

He spotted her fighting on the Egyptian hill. The surrounding battle was a sea of movement and flashing weapons, and barrelling towards it came a fleet of chariots.

What do I do? If I take over, I can't move or fight as fast as she can.

Daniel sent his crow. It swooped down toward the valley and then up toward Eva.

You just need to pass her line of sight. Just flash past her.

The crow was just a few paces from Eva, lining up its path.

Just draw her attention up the hill. You can do it.

The crow was almost in front of her.

Please, Eva, look at the crow.

The crow was just flying through her line of sight.

Look at the crow Eva. Please see it.

Eva spun and faced the opposite direction, deflecting and slicing an opponent in half, missing the crow entirely. By the time she spun around, the crow was flying up the hill toward the chariots.

Daniel reached out to the crow, *Ok, turn around and make another pass....*

Black feathers exploded in the air as the crow and a newly embedded arrow plummeted to the ground.

Daniel reached out for another crow, but it was too late.

Screams and shouting rolled down the hill as chariots crashed into allies and enemies alike. Ground troops began running back toward Daniel while he flash-healed as many of the injured as he could, but casualties were climbing.

I can't keep up. We're getting decimated.

Scythe Dancers and Judeans scattered in every direction back down the hill, trying to avoid being trampled or cut down. Eva spun, evading the first chariot, and narrowly missed the second, but when she jumped backward, she positioned herself too close to the third. His crescent blade swooped down, slicing Eva at the neck. A thin red line quickly became a gushing flow of blood that washed over Eva's body, and she fell. As her body hit the ground, her head rolled down the hill, resting in the arms of the dead.

The candlelight flickered inside the tent as a stray wind blew past.

Sin shivered.

"Are you alright, lord?" Cyaxares asked, looking up at him from across the table.

"Y—yeah. It was just an icy breeze for this time of year. Continue what you were saying, Nabo."

Nabo shot a glance at Cyaxares and gestured to the map in front of him. "Our forces encircle over three-quarters of the wall. The remaining quarter is where the river comes in and out of the town."

"So we send in a small team through the river channel, infiltrate the city and open the doors. It could work, but we need to disable the archers along the walls," Cyaxares said.

"Exactly. And if we can find something flammable to distract the guards, it may be enough to get us into the city." Nabo said.

"Assuming we can even get a team into the city. How do we know they don't have a guard detail along those river entrances?" Sin asked.

"Because we're dealing with Azra," Nabo said. "He's too arrogant to even look for vulnerabilities like that, let alone reinforce them. He believes no man in the world would dare oppose him face to face, so he probably doesn't consider our forces a threat even if we get in."

"That's a pretty big gamble."

"Trust me. If he has anticipated this play, he dismissed it just as quickly. He'll never know we're there."

Sin studied the map for a moment. "This is not ideal. I still feel like we should wait for Daniel and Eva."

"Ordinarily I would agree, my lord, but this is an opportunity we need to exploit," Cyaxares said.

"We waited for so long to avoid getting within range of Azra's weave, and now here we are, charging toward it."

"Azra can reach us, yes, but if we can surround and ambush him quickly, our weapons will reach him first.

He's powerful, but he's still just a man and all men can be killed," Nabo said.

"I can't disagree," Cyaxares said.

Sin sighed. "Ok. Cyaxares, assemble a team, whoever you think is appropriate—"

"Hold on. This is *my* plan, and these were my men long before you were even born." Nabo growled.

Sin shot a level stare at him. "They're *my* men now."

Nabo sighed aggressively. "What I'm saying is, I know them better than you or Cyaxares. I have no doubts that either of you can put together a good team, but I can build a *great* team if you let me."

Sin looked to Cyaxares' expressionless gaze. "Who's leading this team under the wall?"

"I am."

"I don't know Nabo—"

"Can you not trust me to do it?"

"Can I trust you to come back alive?"

"This is not a suicide mission. There are many moving parts, sure, but the goal is to come back alive. I'll disable the archers, open the gates, and join your main force when you storm the city."

Sin contemplated. "... Fine. Get it done."

"Thank you, my lord."

It feels like putting my skin back on. The studded black Babylonian leathers hugged Nabo's body in the familiar way they had when Kandalanu was still alive.

Nabo chuckled to himself as he picked up his swords. They felt so light in his hands; the grips, so foreign.

It feels like I haven't touched them in decades, like I'm rediscovering my childhood training weapons. Except that they're more practical in battle. I guess I'll bring them.

Nabo sheathed his swords, strapped his battle axes onto his back, and left the tent. Four men in similar black leathers waited for Nabo outside. They were chatting quietly as he left the tent and went silent as he approached.

Nabo inspected his team. *Toma, Amjad, Ruel, Natan. How many times have we fought side by side?*

Nabo sized each of them up before asking, "Do you all have everything you need? Does everyone understand the plan?"

All nodded.

"Let's go."

The five men jogged to the riverbed, staying in the shadows of the moon. One by one, each of them climbed into the river, creating barely a ripple. They crouched low so that the water was level with their mouths and kept near the shore, using the reeds to obscure their position.

Slowly they waded up the river while always watching the wall for patrolling archers, walking at a quarter normal pace and stopping only while patrols passed.

As Nabo reached the mouth of the aqueduct under the wall, he took a quick look on the other side and began flagging the team to join him one at a time.

"That seemed... almost too easy," Toma whispered once they had all gathered.

"It definitely smells like a trap," Natan agreed.

"Nothing's impossible at this point. Just stay cautious and stay in the shadows. We're not looking to confront anyone unless absolutely necessary. Got it?" Nabo collected their nods and checked inside the wall. "Go."

One at a time, they climbed out of the river and ran into the shadow of a nearby building. Ruel peeked around the building and gave the sign for all clear. Nabo nodded and then signalled the team to make their way to the gatehouse.

They could only access the gatehouse from above along the ramparts.

The team shadow hopped from building to building until they finally reached the stairs. The stairs themselves were in the moon's shadow and the guards' chatting echoed from a distance. Ruel took another look around and directed the team to climb, one at a time.

Nabo ran a headcount when they reached the top.

"Too easy," Toma whispered.

Ruel punched him hard.

"Keep your report for after the mission," Nabo whispered. "Toma, you're on gate duty. Ruel, Natan, you take left. Amjad, you and I go right. We meet back here or evacuate via the river. Got it?"

Nabo collected nods. "Let's go!"

Amjad led them forward along the rampart, sliding up behind his victim, like a perfect shadow, slicing his throat and gripping him for a slow crumple to the ground. One after the other, the darkness swallowed guards along the wall.

Toma was right. This is almost too easy. The guard detail here is sparse, Azra, you arrogant dick.

"Looks like we got here first," Amjad said as they reached the north gatehouse.

We shouldn't have, though. The other wall is shorter.

"Alright, the others should be here shortly. Start raising the gate and I'm going to head back to the south gatehouse and do the same," Nabo said.

Amjad nodded.

Nabo jogged to the other gatehouse, but as Nabo came closer to the south gate, he looked out at the allied army.

They haven't moved. They never got the signal.

Nabo clung to the shadows in a low crouch as he reached a doorway. It was dead silent.

Nabo peeked inside the building. It was empty.

Where is everyone?

Nabo made his way to the gate controls. There was still no sound aside from his own footfalls, but that sound had changed shape, from a grind to a splash. His feet were still wet from their entrance into the city, so he crouched to touch the brick floor. It was slippery. Nabo raised his fingers to his nose, and the smell of iron flooded in.

Blood... but is it Toma's?

Nabo walked through the gatehouse to the other entrance and peeked down the rampart. It was clear.

I don't have time for this. Just survive somehow guys, I'm bringing reinforcements.

Nabo searched the gatehouse until he found the supplies to light a torch. Large ceramic casks of oil lined one wall. Wood and cloth lay on shelves elsewhere in the room. Then he searched for the crank to wind open the gate.

There you are.

Gears creaked and strained loudly as Nabo cranked the gate open. Crank. Crank. Crank. The gate rose a few inches at a time with each pull.

Suddenly, guards shouted from below. Nabo pulled twice as fast, putting his weight into it.

Come on, you stupid gate.

The sound of hurried steps got closer and louder.

Almost there.

Men gathered outside the entrances on either side of him.

Shit, I might have to break my promise, Sin, but you can thank me later.

"Get him away from the gate controls!" one man yelled.

Guards began pouring into the gatehouse. Nabo stepped back from the controls and pulled his axes from behind his back.

"Where's the rest of ya!" he roared, and then barrelled toward them, cleaving and spinning, impaling and chopping, as each successive wave crashed against him. One of them tried to run around him toward the release lever, but Nabo tossed one of his axes, splitting him from his skull to his collarbone. Then, in a fluid sweep, he swung his axe through several opponents, cutting them down.

A mound of corpses had formed around him, forcing him back against the wall. And fatigue was setting in, but Nabo ignored it. He cut through another wave, deflected oncoming attacks, and threw his axe to stop a runner from calling reinforcements.

Nabo drew his swords.

Ah, much better.

The lighter swords allowed Nabo to spin, thrust, and parry with renewed energy. They were like an extension of his hands.

Nabo danced circles around the younger soldiers. They were no match for his mastery of the sword. As Nabo looked around the room, he noticed there was only one man left, now running toward the door. Nabo casually tossed his sword, not caring to watch as it buried itself into the man's chest.

Nabo huffed. Every breath was on fire.

I hope that's the last of them.

Suddenly, the sound of footsteps returned.

Nabo went to work, rolling an open ceramic drum to each door that left a trail of liquid behind it and dumped them onto the rampart walkways. Then he dragged several bundles of wood and stacked them with the oil drums. Soldiers sloshed their way up the ramparts on either side of the gatehouse, just in time to see a surge of fire rush toward them. Nabo gave them a wave and jumped down through a large kill hole to the ground below.

He landed in a squat and looked out at Sin's men, clamouring into formation beyond the wall. Then the gate crashed down in front of him.

Shit.

Nabo spun back toward the city. Hundreds of soldiers had gathered at the gate. Hundreds of eyes locked onto Nabo.

Shit! Shit! Shit!

Nabo crouched into a defensive stance, weighing his options. The sight of Azra, emerging from the crowd, demolished his train of thought because behind him followed a dirty, barefoot boy, wearing a simple stained tunic, with eyes downcast.

Azra, you monster! You have no shame! That boy could easily be the same age as—

And then the boy looked up, passing an empty stare through Nabo that cut him to the core. He dropped his sword and dragged himself toward the boy.

"Nebu?" he said, reaching out toward him.

Azra grinned. "Hmm. It seems we have a lot to talk about."

"Daniel, order your soldiers to pull back," Josiah called. "Their support troops are too far away. They're going to be surrounded."

Daniel stood motionless, facing the field. His stillness resisted the passage of time.

"Daniel, tell them to pull back! Daniel?"

Daniel reached into his pouch and grabbed a handful of seeds and tossed them over his shoulder, before coaxing them into a restraint around Josiah.

"Daniel, what are you doing?" Josiah demanded, struggling against the thick vines. Daniel pushed his hood off and threw his shoulders back, shedding his cloak as he walked onto the battlefield. As the cloak fell to the ground, blue flames engulfed his hands and extended upward from his eyes, becoming visible from behind, like two fiery horns hovering over his head. The flames spread further with every step until they covered his entire body.

He made a sweeping upward gesture as he walked as if he were scooping silt from a riverbed. Suddenly, the bodies of the dead convulsed violently. Loud snapping sounds amplified the ambiance of the battlefield. Their necks broke at the collarbone and became thick with unnatural muscle tissue. Elbows and knees bent backwards to support the skyward-facing torso. Ribs snapped apart from their adjoining sternum, tearing the flesh open and exposing themselves as teeth in a gaping alien maw. Then, taking a wolf-like stance, the creatures released a trumpeted scream as loud as a howling storm wind.

The howling beasts rose all around Daniel, leaping at Necho's army, blocking attacks and clearing a path towards the pharoah.

Josiah watched Daniel, engulfed in blue flames, cross the valley while he raised an army of howling beasts.

He is a Demon! This cannot stand. A demon and a false god in open combat, in the land of the One True God? How dare they defile this place with blasphemy and demon magic? I invited this calamity. I allowed the same evils to enter this land that I swore I would defend against. Assuming that the faithful can only triumph over the enemies of God, I arranged this battle. Please Lord, let this great deception yield a mighty purge in your honour!

Howlers continued to rise as quickly as bodies hit the ground. Chaos swept through the battlefield as the clang of metal was replaced by the crack of bones and yells were replaced by screams. Soldiers tried to flee in every direction as the Howlers leapt upon them indiscriminately.

Josiah struggled harder against the vines, screaming and flexing, until finally, one branch broke, crumbling away from his arm. Josiah grabbed his sword and hacked at the tendrils wrapped around his other limbs until they, too, cracked and fell away.

Time to slay a demon.

Josiah threw off his cloak, picked up a second sword, and ran into the valley after Daniel. At first, Judeans and Egyptians alike ran past him, more concerned with their lives than the battle itself, allowing Josiah to run toward Daniel with minimal dodging. Suddenly, an Egyptian soldier lunged at Josiah. Josiah ducked, causing the man to somersault over him. Another Egyptian followed, forcing Josiah to whirl and putting him under the sword of a third opponent. Josiah blocked with one sword while slicing the man's abdomen with the other. Another Egyptian came at him from behind. Josiah rolled and came up facing his assailant, slicing him as he spun and continued his pursuit. Three more ran at him. Josiah stood and charged toward them.

Josiah ducked, evading the first swipe, spinning and then slicing off the first man's arm. Then he spun in the opposite direction and buried his elbow in another man's face, extending his arm as he hopped backward, drawing his blade along the man's throat. The Egyptian gurgled and fell to the ground, grasping at the open wound. The last man lunged at Josiah. Josiah evaded and brought his hilt down onto the man's wrist, disarming him, and then impaled him with both swords. Josiah put his foot on the Egyptian's chest, withdrawing his swords and knocking the man onto the ground to bleed out.

Where are you, demon?

Josiah searched the valley for the telltale blue flames.

There you are.

Josiah ran at Daniel, throwing his swords toward him. The swords buried themselves into Daniel's back, below the ribs. Josiah picked up two more swords without stopping and tossed them again, burying them under Daniel's shoulder blades. Daniel stopped advancing toward Necho and stood motionless. Josiah picked up two more swords, sprinting toward Daniel. Just as Josiah reached him, Daniel sunk to his knees.

Josiah wound his arms back as he slid to a stop and beheaded Daniel in one scissored sweep.

As Daniel's head rolled off his shoulders and his body dropped to the ground, an arrow blew through Josiah's windpipe and lodged itself into his spine. Josiah grasped at his throat and collapsed to the ground.

My lord, I banished the demon. What is happening? I can't breathe. Save me, lord, for cleansing this land. I still have a blaspheming false god to kill. Save me. Please save me. Am I finished? Is this my reward? Lord, can you hear me?

Nabo sat leaning up against the crenelation wall, bleeding, with his limbs broken at odd angles, while Azra stood a few steps away, looking out over the darkened landscape. Nebu stood behind Azra, eyes downcast. Nabo couldn't help staring at the boy, wondering how he's changed.

"I have to admit, Nabo, you really live up to your reputation." Azra cast a downward glance toward him.

"And what's that?"

"You're a veritable giant. Tough as stone."

"I guess I should take the compliment," Nabo said, spitting blood to one side.

"I would. I've tortured many, many men—and women, I guess—and all of them died long before they experienced anything near the pain you just endured. It's genuinely impressive."

"Is that why I'm still alive?"

Azra laughed. "Oh no, I still have to find out what your little band of rebels is planning. I guess I don't really *have* to since it's impossible for you to defeat me, but knowing would certainly allow me to crush you faster."

"What do you mean? You just used weaving to torture me. For hours. How can you not know everything about me?"

Azra turned and peered down at Nabo for a moment before bursting into laughter. "So, you actually believe that Weavers can read the minds of their targets?"

"You can't?"

Azra chuckled again. "I am genuinely surprised at you, Nabo. It's a myth—a fireside tale your rebels tell my soldiers to try to intimidate them. I mean, Weavers are more powerful than you could probably ever imagine, but we definitely can't read minds."

"That's too bad. I'd love for you to know what I'm thinking right now."

"I'm sure you would. To be honest, I'm glad I can't."

"Why?"

Azra shook his head and sighed. "Most people are an incredible mess of emotions and melodramatic reactions. It's all nonsense, really. I find it much less chaotic to tell other people what to think. Teach a man to fish and he may choose not to, teach a man to fear and he will do whatever you ask."

"You don't understand anything about people."

"I disagree. Take our current situation, for example. Those men out there seem to believe I have this tiny little radius around me, and anyone outside of it is safe from my weaves."

"You don't?"

"I'm sure I have *some* sort of distance limitation, but it's quite far. So far, in fact, that I've never had a practical reason to explore how far it actually is."

"Great."

"So, I find it amusing that your men think *they* know how far my reach extends. So amusing, in fact, that I've developed a game for those days when I'm particularly bored."

"A game?"

"It's simple. All I have to do is pop a few heads near the front lines, then I wait. The remaining soldiers will move back. When no one dies for a little while, a few will get curious and try getting as close to the arbitrary line as possible. If they cross it, there's a fifty-fifty chance I'll snap my fingers and make their heads explode, or pretend to, so nothing happens. I'll only kill people within a certain radius to make it seem like that's the extent of my reach, but then pop, pop, pop, some heads explode further back. 'How is this possible?' they wonder, and then panic sets in, but then you stop again, and they come to feel comfortable and believe it was a fluke. They tell themselves, 'He can't reach us here'. Then I explode a few faces a little farther back than before and let the panic work its magic again. It doesn't matter how many times I do this, they will always do whatever they can to adjust to the new line between safety and danger. They would rather believe that they are discovering my limitations than believe that none of them are safe and I'm manipulating them."

"How is this a game? How does this even have anything to do with what we were talking about?"

"The game is about making your enemy trust you. Against their better judgment, they always will eventually. People think they're complex, but they're not. They're faces with levers and the man that pulls those levers is their god."

"You consider yourself their god?"

"Why not? I control whether they live or die. Meanwhile, their lives are of no consequence to me. I would think the power disparity alone should qualify me."

"Do you think they view you as their god?"

"Probably not. Probably never will. I'm certain they lack the comprehension to truly appreciate my power."

"So then, why kill them?"

"Boredom."

"You murder people, en masse, out of boredom?"

"Why not? Their lives are inconsequential anyway."

Nabo shook his head and glanced over at his son.

No reaction to any of this. I wonder if he's even aware of where he is anymore.

Nabo turned to Azra, leaning against the wall, head propped by one palm until he lifted his free hand as if to snap his fingers.

Are you kidding me right now?

"If you're so bored, why don't you fight me?" Nabo said hastily.

"Fight you? Why?"

"Why not? It could fill the time until Egypt gets here."

Azra chuckled, looking him up and down. "You're a cripple. You can't even stand."

"Then fix me. You're a Weaver."

"Hmm. So I heal you, and then we fight?"

"Yeah. Hand-to-hand combat. Unless you're worried, I'll outmatch you without your powers."

Azra's smirks soured. "Fine. Hand-to-hand combat. I've got nothing better to do."

Azra angled himself and pointed a hand toward Nabo. Nabo expected to see the blue flames that always ignited from Daniel, but none appeared. Instead, Azra's fingers seemed to twitch and pluck at the air, with no sign anything was happening. Until the pain began.

Wounds aggressively sewed themselves shut. Joints relocated themselves. Broken bones sprung back into place and fused together. Nabo didn't even realize he was screaming until the process had finished.

"Just rest for a moment while I prepare," Azra said. Then he stripped off his clothing and handed the carefully folded pile to Nebu.

Azra stood for a moment, looking down into his open palms, and then his fingers plucked the air again.

Suddenly, the muscles on every limb of Azra's body exploded in size. His back grew broader and his chest grew thicker. His skin shredded open across his entire body, unable to contain the explosive growth beneath. Another twitch of his fingers resealed the open wounds while the skin gained a healthier elastic look. A younger look.

"You can reverse aging?"

"Of course. I told you before, I am a god. Nothing can kill me," Azra said, redressing. "Are you ready?"

"As ready as I'll ever be."

"Good," Azra said, and immediately charged at Nabo.

Nabo locked palms with Azra, standing his ground. The two men strained against each other, grunting with exhaustion. Nabo tried to disengage, but Azra maintained an iron grip on his hands and pulled him back into position.

I have to break away somehow.

Nabo resumed his grip and pointed their arms to the ground before ducking low and charging at Azra's legs. He connected. Then he stood upright, launching Azra behind him.

Azra released his grip as he somersaulted clumsily and landed on his back. Then he hopped back onto his feet. "Clever trick."

"It wasn't a trick. I just couldn't get you to stop holding my hand."

Azra smirked and ran at Nabo, throwing a punch at the last moment.

Nabo evaded and jabbed Azra's right. Azra brought his arm down on Nabo's and punched him in the face.

Nabo staggered back before taking a run at Azra. Azra dodged, but Nabo expected it. He spun, hammering a backhanded fist into Azra's face.

Nabo kept up the pace, launching blow after blow, crunching Azra's ribs and cracking his collarbone. Suddenly, Azra ducked away. Nabo connected with the wall, causing a brick to crack and shift outward.

Azra lunged, throwing his momentum into Nabo's kidney. Nabo groaned and grabbed Azra's arm, pulling him in for a downward strike to the temple.

Azra staggered.

Nabo lifted him, delivering a headbutt, but missed the follow-up punch, causing him to lose balance.

Azra seized the moment, grabbing his arm and twisting it behind his back before punching him repeatedly on the exposed side. Nabo roared as his ribs snapped under the assault. Azra threw him hard against the wall, head first.

Nabo turned to face Azra, partially leaning against the wall, while Azra wiped his mouth and took a low, ready stance.

"I have to admit," Nabo began, between breaths, "I genuinely thought this would go differently."

"You honestly thought I would fight you as a feeble old man?"

"There was a chance."

Nabo tried to take a readied stance, but Azra rushed with a three-punch combo that ended in a knee to the ribs.

Azra lifted him by the hair and leaned toward his face. "Let's be honest, there was no chance. I would never agree to your rules if I didn't have the advantage."

Azra backhanded Nabo, knocking him down.

Nabo chuckled as he lifted himself to a crawl. Azra launched a running kick and stomped his head. Nabo coughed and spit, but as he pushed himself upright again, the cough transformed back into a pained chuckle.

"Why are you laughing?" Azra demanded with a nudge.

"That's not why I thought it would go differently," Nabo said, as he stood.

"What?"

"What you said before, that's not why I thought this fight would go differently."

"Then why? Why would you think that?"

"I genuinely—and you'll love this—I genuinely didn't think I would get hit this much," Nabo said, doubling over slightly and wincing as he tried to laugh.

"How—" Azra began with a laugh, but he was interrupted by the impact of his back hitting the ground after Nabo pulled his legs out from under him. Suddenly Nabo swung Azra's entire body over his head with one arm and slammed it into the ground on the opposite side of him. Then he smashed Azra's body against the top of the wall, cracking it into an odd shape before slamming him to the ground again.

"You may have mirrored my size, but you never gained the advantage," he said, and then launched Azra over the wall.

Nabo immediately ran to his son. "Ok, Nebu, we don't have much time. We have to go."

"No. This is my place. I must wait for Master Azra," he said flatly.

"What?"

"This is my place. I must wait here for him to return."

"No, Nebu—your name is Nebu. You remember that, right?"

Nebu remained silent, focussed on a fixed point on the ground.

Nabo fought back the rising emotion that threatened to take him. "Listen. Your name is Nebu. You are my son. We need to leave this place."

"No, Master Azra is my father. He told me so."

Tears welled up in Nabo's eyes. "Listen, I will explain everything to you. I owe you that, but you need to come with me right now. It's not safe here."

"I must wait for my Master."

Nabo nodded and then took Azra's robes and immediately shredded them into strips.

"What are you doing? Master Azra will be mad!" he said, genuine fear colouring his voice.

Nabo tied the boy's hands and feet. "We have to leave this place. Stop talking and just let me save you."

"No! I won't let you take me! You can't take me! Guards! Guards!"

"I'm sorry son, I promise you will understand soon." Nabo shoved a cloth gag into the boy's mouth and secured it with another strip tied around his head.

Then he hoisted Nebu onto his shoulders like a lamb and ran for the gates.

The slow hoof falls of Sin's horse provided rhythm to an otherwise silent night. Sin had yet to see a signal from Nabo's team.

Was that fire in the gatehouse the signal? If it was, then where is Nabo?

Sin reached down to pat his horse and noticed its ear rotate and twitch. Sin halted and listened. Heavy footfalls were coming from the wall. As he peered into the darkness, he saw something large heading toward him.

Is that a horse?

Sin strained to see until he saw the shape of a large man with a body draped across his shoulders.

Holy shit! That's Nabo!

Nabo looked over his shoulder and sprinted harder.

A chill ripped through Sin.

He's not running to me, he's running away from—

Sin's horse vibrated. Horrifying alien noises shook out of its mouth, and panic clouded its eyes. Sin suddenly fell, feet first through horse-shaped visceral, which rained around him a moment later.

What the hell?

"Run! Run now!" Nabo yelled.

Sin looked up and saw a fusillade of arrows climbing into the sky and then arcing downward in his direction. Something hit him hard in the chest, shoving him onto his back several feet away.

It was Nabo.

The arrows dug in all around them, but none hit Sin. Sin gasped and struggled to breathe.

"Nabo. Nabo? Let me up."

Nabo wheezed and rolled onto his side, allowing Sin to wiggle out from under him. Arrows densely tacked the ground around them, except for the void where they laid. Instead, the missing arrows were lodged deep in Nabo's back and legs. Nabo coughed and spattered blood on the ground beside him.

Cyaxares is with the north wall troops, and my men are too far away to hear me. I have to get him back to camp myself.

"Did Nebu... make it?"

Sin looked around them and then saw the body of a boy lying a few feet away, arrows sticking out of him.

Nebu was alive. This whole time, he was alive.

Tears welled up in Sin's eyes, but he fought them.

"Sin? Did Nebu make it?"

"No, Nabo. I'm sorry."

Nabo coughed out short howls of grief. "I tried. I tried to bring him home. He fought me, but—"

"You did everything you could."

Nabo cried and pounded the ground. "Nebu!"

"Listen," Sin began carefully, "we need to get back to camp. Can you move?"

"No, I can't," he said, struggling to pull himself together. "You should just go."

"No, I can't leave you here. I'll just drag you." Then he grabbed Nabo by his armour and tried to pull him, but Nabo only screamed in pain. He didn't budge at all.

"Stop! Stop," Nabo pleaded between gasps. "Just—just stop. I'm too big for you to drag anywhere, boy."

Sin felt panic and helplessness replace the surrounding air. "No. I don't accept that. Am I your king?"

"You are, my lord."

"Then get up. At least help me move you."

"I can barely move. I think I'm going to have to stay."

Sin choked. Tears burned the dust from his eyes. "No. This wasn't supposed to be a suicide mission."

"I'll tell you a secret my lord," Nabo said, straining to look up at Sin. "They're all suicide missions, but I really had planned to come back this time."

What do I do?

"I—I don't know what to do."

Nabo smiled and looked up at Sin. "You do. Go. Go be the king you were always meant to be."

A single arrow buried itself into Nabo's temple. His face sagged, and the life drained away. Sin looked back to see the archer and found Azra tossing a bow aside casually.

Sin couldn't swallow. He couldn't breathe. Panic rose inside of Sin with every step that Azra took until invisible needles pricked every inch of his sweat-soaked skin.

"Hello, young princeling," Azra said, standing over him with a twisted smile. "I was just thinking about you."

"Get away from me. I have Askuzai archers in range to shoot you down. All I have to do is say the word."

"Oh my. Askuzai, you say? I'm much too close."

"That's right. Now I'm giving you a chance—"

Azra snapped his fingers and screams rang out in the distance. "There. That should put us at a safe distance."

Sin spun his head around to stare, open-mouthed, at his shattered front line, now in chaos. Then he turned to face Azra, still unable to speak.

"Any other concerns I can help you with?"

Sin shook his head.

"Alright, get up. We're heading back to the city. You will follow me or I will carry you."

"Why?"

Azra snapped his fingers, causing another burst of screams.

"Okay, okay. Please stop. I'll go willingly."

"Excellent. All things considered, you should thank me. You're about to get a much better view of the show."

CHAPTER 22

THE SECOND SEAL

E choes of dripping water surrounded Daniel, filling
the shapeless void with sound. Cold, damp rocks
pressed against his feet and a musty mineral
smell pressed into his nostrils.

Am I in a cave?

Daniel slid his feet forward and reached out into the
darkness. A rocky wall met his fingertips. He sighed
in relief, allowing the wall to guide him away from...
wherever he was. Time passed without measurement as
his feet gently patted the ground and his fingers silently
dragged against the wall, sensing a path through the
cavern. Finally, dim shadows took shape, revealing forms
in the darkness. Warm light reflected off the dampened,
meandering walls ahead and trickled toward Daniel. He
drifted away from the wall, allowing the growing light to
guide him until the passage opened into a large chamber
with no exits. Long stalactites hung overhead, sometimes
merging with stalagmites reaching up from the edges of
a deep, luminescent pool that replaced much of the floor.

Daniel crept toward the water and stood at the edge. The pool was too bright to cast a reflection of the dark ceiling above it, but occasional droplets ringed the otherwise still surface of the water. Below, a cloudy, blue mineral hue deepened proportionally with the depths of the pool.

Daniel leaned forward, bracing himself between two pillars to get a better look into the pool. Despite the cloudiness, he could see hundreds of feet down. Grasses grew along rolling hills and valleys. Rocky features thrust upward in some places while dropping sharply in others. At the top of one rocky mound, a plateau had formed with smaller structures poking up uniformly across it. Daniel studied the plateau appreciatively.

It's so flat and the rocks on top are almost in perfect lines. Or maybe even rectangles—wait, is that a building?

Daniel leaned in closer, but one pillar broke away, throwing him forward into the water. He struggled to swim back to the surface, but he sunk quickly as if he were free-falling from the sky. After a few seconds, Daniel finally hit the grassy mud on his back, painfully forcing all the air from his chest and leaving him in a daze. A tiny, involuntary cough triggered a gasp for air. Daniel panicked momentarily until he realized he was breathing rather than drowning.

What is happening? Where am I?

Daniel stood and looked around. Grassy, windswept fields and lush forests matted the ground in every direction, interrupted only by the vast, wandering rivers that cut across them on either side of the mountain plateau where he now stood. And the walled complex beside him. Daniel looked up. No cavern and no sign of the pool, aside from the familiar blue hue that canvassed the sky.

I guess I might as well investigate the only man-made structure for miles.

The white walls soared above Daniel and stretched across the width of the plateau where he stood. An ornately carved ivory gate shone in the sunlight as it cut through the centre of the wall. As Daniel approached the gate, he could make out tiny human forms in the intricate filigree carvings, and noticed gilded silver vines painted along the bars and handles. No one stood on the other side. Daniel pushed the gate forward, and it opened soundlessly, with no resistance.

Why would someone leave this gate unlocked and unguarded?

Daniel passed the gate, passing between the thick walls, and climbed several steps to reach a grassy lawn that filled the gap between the outer wall and a newly visible inner wall. White marble paved the path below his feet and carved a straight path ahead. He kept going, past the inner wall, up more steps and out to a large pavilion. Marble paved the pavilion, which led up to an arched colonnade cutting across Daniel's path. Daniel craned his head to take in the intricate gilded silver vines painted along the columns and the detailed carvings of people reaching out to each other along the frieze. The colonnade opened up into a large courtyard with a raised temple in the centre.

I can't believe I've made it this far without seeing another person. Wait, is that humming?

Daniel climbed the steps to the temple, and the humming got louder.

I recognize this voice. I think I recognize this song, too.

As Daniel reached the top of the steps, he noticed familiar dragons and lions and suns alongside other symbols embossed on the walls. Silver gilding crept under the vaulted ceilings. Daniel traced a path across tightly fitted mosaic tiles and mysterious geometric designs to the back of the room. A man in white and blue robes leaned against a raised platform as if waiting for someone. After four or five steps, Daniel could see the man's eyes were closed and his chest heaved whenever he ran out of air from humming.

"H-hello?" Daniel said louder than intended.

The man opened his eyes. "Ah! You've finally arrived!"

"You were waiting for *me*?"

"Of course."

Daniel looked the man up and down. "Who are you? Do I know you?"

"I would hope so."

Trinkets hanging from the man's braided hair caught Daniel's eye. Each hung from a different braid, each appeared to glow a different colour.

"You're not Ankl," Daniel croaked.

He smiled. "My name is Raziel. We knew each other long ago."

"Raziel! I'm sorry. My memories have been weird since I got here." Daniel's eyes settled on the platform Raziel was leaning against—but it wasn't a platform. It was a giant well of glowing water, about 10 feet across. "Where am I?"

"Can't you tell? This is Earth's Lifestream."

Daniel took a moment to reach out to the lifethreads, but instead of sensing nearby life, he connected to the essence of all living things, at every point in time. "I can sense... *everything*."

"Well, that's the Lifestream. If every living thing were a droplet in a rain shower, you're connecting to the puddle where that rainwater pools. Except the puddle is an endless ocean, and that rainstorm happens across all eternity."

"I feel like that should be harder to understand than it is."

"That's one benefit of being dead—your comprehension has no limits."

Daniel nodded solemnly. "You know, I always thought I would be with Eva when I died, and in a sense I kind of am. I can feel her everywhere, but it's like she's both here and not."

"Having a consciousness in this place can definitely be both a curse and a blessing. Any answer to any question you've ever had is here, but there's no reason to discuss it anymore."

Daniel sat on the edge of the glowing well, looking into it intermittently while he talked. "I keep sensing things out of place here. It's like there's a mark on the flow of time. Did I make some kind of mistake?"

"Not exactly. In a manner of speaking, it's *Humanity's* mistake—they created a perfect utopia. A world where everyone coexisted harmoniously with every other creature on the planet. We are here to aid in the correction of that mistake."

"That doesn't sound like a mistake."

"It wouldn't until you factor in what happens when people are happy and healthy and well-fed with no conflict or external threats."

"Which is?"

"Complacency. They live such contented lives that they lack the drive to push boundaries and make advancements. Not all advancements, obviously, but certain technological advancements only come from war. Like space travel."

"And without it..."

"And without it, their fates were tied to the planet. You remember. Humanity tried everything to preserve the peace they had achieved and still prevent the extinction event, but in the end, no amount of change was fast enough. They were simply too far behind to save themselves. So, in their desperation, they chose another route."

"But how was anyone able to change the past at all? I thought they didn't have the technology."

"That part is more complicated. When a community is *that* unified—almost single-minded—in their desire for something, that intention reaches out into the universe. It searches for a solution and materializes that solution into the reality that we know. Here, an alternate, less evolved version of ourselves—humanity—summoned us to go back to a key point in our mutual past and give them a second chance to survive."

"I remember agreeing to come here. And... I remember being called Azazel. Ankl used to call me Azazel."

"That never really leaves you. You technically *are* still Azazel. But you're also still Daniel. And many other reincarnations, both before and after him. It's just different perspectives, with different names."

Daniel paused thoughtfully. "And I will experience those perspectives again. Am I reading that right?"

"You are."

"Does that mean I have a destiny?"

"It's probably more accurate to say you have a purpose. Your choices are still your own while you play out your intended role."

"What *is* my role?"

"You tell me."

Daniel thought deeply for a moment and then allowed his head to drop. "I'm not going to see Eva again for a long time, am I?"

"In the next time around, maybe. You usually run into each other. Eva always appears when you need her strength to fulfill your purpose, but your purpose was never about meeting Eva or settling down with her."

"Yeah. I'm seeing that now," Daniel said, meeting Raziel's gaze. "It wasn't even about Azra. Not really."

"In a manner of speaking. Do you remember the pact?"

Daniel nodded. "Our pact. It was never exclusive to Ankl and me. It never even started in Mari."

Raziel nodded. "Our pact was in place all along."

"Why didn't he tell me?"

"It wasn't relevant."

"I have to go back."

"You do, but nothing will be the same. You've touched the lifestream now. You died."

Daniel paused thoughtfully. "Daniel died, but the world doesn't really need Daniel, does it?"

Raziel shook his head. "Whether they know it or not, the world needs Azazel again. Go be Azazel. At least for a little while."

Daniel nodded and then hoisted himself up, straddling the well. "We will see each other again, Raziel."

"Until then, take care, old friend," Raziel said, smiling.

Then Daniel hopped, feet first, into the well, swallowed into its blinding light.

As the sun sunk below the horizon, shadows blanketed the oozing bodies piled along the valley of Meggido and lining the hills on either side. Entrails, limbs and bits of flesh littered the blood-soaked field and the only signs of life were the crows calling as they gathered and circled overhead.

Streams of crows coalesced from every direction into a vortex of feathers that grew until it covered the sky completely. Suddenly, squawks and calls became shrieks and frenzied screams as crows darted at each other from every direction. Blood and feathers began falling from the sky with a hail of crow carcasses that covered Daniel's corpse and soaked the surrounding earth.

Suddenly, his body twitched. Then it happened again. And again. Until the twitching became convulsions, and his body rocked violently before coming to a complete stop.

Fingers began to feel along the inside of his skin from his legs, up toward the torso and stopped at the neck. Slowly, a glistening, worm-like tentacle poked out of the open neck of Daniel's corpse. It slid along the ground, sensing and caressing the bloody landscape until it reached Daniel's head. As it felt along Daniel's face, a second tentacle emerged from below the head, wrapping itself around the first. Both stopped moving. A moment passed and then a flurry of tentacles burst from both ends of the neck, darting toward each other, and violently entangling as the body and head drew together.

Daniel's body inflated and his wounds healed. Then Daniel stood. He held out his hand and a small stream of blood flowed into it, travelling up from the ground along his body and forming a crystalline red sword. When he lifted his other hand, blood bubbled up from the ground in front of him, hardening and shaping itself into a horse with glowing red eyes and a whinny that sounded like a thousand terrified screams carried in the wind. Daniel mounted and spun the steed around, gesturing to the corpses on the battlefield. One by one, they cracked and reshaped themselves into howling beasts, anxiously pacing as they awaited his commands.

The smell of blood and war was everywhere. It called out to him. He raised his sword and pointed it north, galloping at full speed while crows darkened the skies ahead and thousands of Howlers followed at his heels.

CHAPTER 23

ASCENSION

Blueish hues coloured the countryside, giving everything the depth and visibility only twilight can. Only the orange glow of cook fires broke the monotone veil. The sounds of men were everywhere. Men shouting. Metal clanging. Wood scraping. Sin couldn't draw his eyes away from the buzz of the morning at this vantage.

"It's amazing how a better view changes everything, isn't it?" Azra said from his side.

Sin passed a sideways glance. "Back in Nineveh, there was this one window on the third floor of the palace that looked out over the lower city. The room was always empty, so I liked going there to think."

"The one at the southeast corner of the building?" Azra asked.

"Yeah, how did you know?"

"That was my room growing up."

Sin turned to him. "You grew up in the palace?"

"My father was the royal physician, at that time."

"Was that why you were my father's physician... before everything?"

"Technically, I suppose."

Sin considered this for a moment, but a question bubbled up, cracking the silence. "Why did you kill everyone?"

"I haven't killed everyone. There are obviously quite a few people left in the world," he said, gesturing to the army beyond the wall.

"That's not what I mean."

Azra sighed. "Power rightfully belongs to those strong enough to take it."

"But you lived with us *for years* before you slaughtered everyone. Years. If you could have just killed us all instantly at any time, why wait?"

Azra cleared his throat and shuffled uncomfortably for a moment. "Your father was always meant to die— not by my hand specifically, but he was always meant to die. I guess, as time went on, I was reminded more and more of our childhood bond. A part of me pitied him. Maybe even wanted to save him."

Sin allowed the revelation to absorb, reconciling new information with old. Finally, he looked up at Azra, unable to smooth a tightening frown, "What changed?"

Azra did not meet his gaze. "A witch unclouded my eyes."

Sin wanted to ask more, but his thoughts were interrupted by trumpeting in the distance.

"What was that?" Sin asked.

Galloping hooves drummed in the distance and the wind howled strangely as it carried the second trumpet blast.

"It sounds like the Egyptians have arrived," Azra said smugly.

Rumbling footfalls rolled in from the south, behind Sin's camp. Soon the golden Egyptian army—now silver in the twilight—rose over the horizon and poured down onto Sin's men. Shouting. Panic. Chaos.

Sin's army fought desperately to find a formation and defend against the rear assault.

I have to do something. They're getting wiped out.

"I know what you're thinking, but it's a waste of time."

"Even if I could just help them organize—"

"Even if you could, they would survive this battle to die a more gruesome death by my hand later."

"Then why even call the Egyptians at all? If you can just snap your fingers and kill hundreds of men, why even have allies or a standing army or any of that?"

"Because I want an empire, and one man alone cannot stand as an empire. Power without subjects to rule is meaningless. And besides, I don't want an empire where I have to do everything. People aren't as useful when they find out they're dispensable. I'm disappointed that I have to explain that to you."

"Another manipulation. You're—"

"I didn't bring you up here for casual chit chat or morality lectures. Do you know what's happening down there right now? History. If I had left you down there, you would've died and missed all of this. Now you're here and we're both missing it because you won't shut up."

Sin looked out at the battle, where his friends and allies were being brutally cut down. *How could he think I would ever regret not seeing this?*

Suddenly, the sky darkened as black clouds rolled in from every direction. As the clouds grew closer, they took the shape of crows, the cawing now audible over the sounds of battle.

"Do you... see that?" Sin asked.

"I've never seen anything like that in my life," Azra said, his mouth slack with surprise.

Otherworldly howls cut across the landscape. Men stopped fighting and turned toward the horizon. The howls came again, but this time creatures bounded over the hill and plowed into the battle, targeting only Egyptians as they ran toward Harran. Crows began dive-bombing Assyrians along the walls, scratching, biting and sometimes impaling their victims. When the enemy fell, their bodies would convulse, violently reshaping into terrifying four-legged creatures, and announce their resurrection with the same howl of agony, before leaping after their former countrymen.

In the distance, a single rider galloped toward the castle, passing through the battle as if it were smoke. Sin and Azra leaned over the walls to watch the rider enter the city and calmly dismount. Then he unsheathed his sword and looked up at them with glowing blue eyes.

Is that... Daniel?

Fires erupted all around him as soldiers ignited into flames which spread to the nearby buildings. Without looking away, Daniel dumped something out of his hand, which erupted into a wooden platform, carrying him up to the walls.

"This is impossible. I was told you were dead," Azra said.

The fire sprung up from the platform and spread along the floor.

"Daniel?" Azra said shakily.

"The Daniel you knew is gone. I am Azazel."

Goosebumps rose along Sin's arms at the sound of his voice.

It's like a thousand echoes.

"If you aren't Daniel, then why are you here?"

"You called me here. Your actions put events into motion that summoned me here. A complex ritual."

"So you're my ally, then? Good. Help me wipe out—"

"I am not your ally. I am the avatar of everything you created. All of this... War."

Sin ducked to avoid a flurry of crows, diving toward the ground. When he stood again, he noticed fresh scratches across Azra's cheek.

"People think that war is a rivalry or a competition. It can be used for those things, but war is a confident party trying to take something from another party. It can be a resource or political control, but usually, it is something that should not be taken. You have taken many things that should not have been taken."

"Do they not say, 'to the victor goes the spoils'?"

"Some, of course, would, and in practice, this is true. But before conquest, there is War, and War is the great leveller. Before there are spoils, there are screams, and confusion, and uncertainty and loss."

"So, what do you want?"

"I am here to end your world."

"You're joking."

Daniel only stared back with glowing eyes, motionless, with no sign of his thoughts.

Azra shifted uncomfortably, scratching at his hands. "So, what will you do now?" Azra said, attempting to break the silence.

"I will erase you."

"No. No, surely you don't have to. Killing me serves no purpose."

Daniel said nothing, only stared while the carnage raged all around them.

Suddenly, Azra lashed out with a weave, slicing clean through Daniel's body.

Sin couldn't move his limbs or turn away. He couldn't even speak. Instead, he just watched as Azra seemed to exhale a long sigh of relief, and the top portion of Daniel's body slid and fell off of the bottom, but the cleaved portion turned to dust before it touched the ground, spinning and reassembling itself back onto Daniel.

Azra sent another attack. And another. He kept cleaving and amputating parts of Daniel's body, but they always melted into a fine dust that the wind whirled and carried back to its original place.

Daniel slowly advanced toward Azra. Unreadable. Cold.

Panic layered across Azra's face, deepening creases while widening his eyes and mouth with every failed attack. "Look, Daniel—"

"Daniel isn't here."

"Azazel then. Azazel? Azazel, listen, I'm sorry. I can be useful to you. Surely someone that has tasted the power of a god like yourself can be a worthy partner."

Daniel continued to advance.

"Or servant. I could be your servant. Clearly, someone such as yourself can appreciate the value of a servant."

Daniel showed no reaction and continued to advance forward.

"Ok, please! Wait! Azazel? I'm begging you to have mercy and spare my life. I will do anything. I will forever be in your debt. Please!" Azra babbled as he cried.

Daniel stopped in front of him and placed his hand on Azra's shoulder. Azra searched Daniel's face, his fear giving way to a relieved optimism, but that optimism faded as the moment stretched too long. Now Azra's entire body expressed one emotion in perfect synchronicity—dread.

"The war you started is complete. There is no longer a purpose in your being alive. In fact, it would be detrimental."

Azra's shoulders slumped, and he looked up at Daniel's empty eyes, confirming the finality. Azra's voice became small and childlike. "I don't want to die."

"It doesn't matter what you want."

Suddenly, Azra burst into bright blue flames. Azra screamed with intense pain, arms flailing until the flesh melted away from his body. The muscle crisped and flaked away. Finally, the skeleton crashed into a pile, then exploded into a fine dust that scattered in the breeze.

"Daniel?" Sin said, feeling the dryness rasp in his voice. "Am I going to die?"

Daniel turned to Sin and smiled before a sharp wind swirled around them, disintegrating Daniel's body into smaller dust devils and carrying it away. The bloody horse followed, releasing one last haunting whinny. One by one, all the howling creatures spontaneously erupted into ash, and the crows dispersed in every direction away from Harran, allowing the morning sun to shine through and cleanse the world in its yellow light.

EPILOGUE
THE ETERNAL RIPPLE

Seven years later.

A gentle spring breeze swept across the colourful flowerbeds and lush green lawns before rising slightly and caressing the hanging plants and dangling vines that layered the Gardens of Babylon. The breeze swirled around a young girl, dancing playfully between strands of her fine brown hair, as it carried the sounds of the girl's laughter to Sin's ears and the sweet smells of roses to Sin's nose, where he sat just a few paces away.

Beside him, a woman in a regal purple silk dress laced her fingers with his and rested her head on his shoulder while the young girl danced and chased butterflies across the lawn.

"You know, Amytis," Sin began quietly, "sometimes I think about all the loss and the pain and all the horrible things that led us to this moment. And I know I could never truly regret any of it, because undoing a single thing could erase our beautiful Kashshaya from existence. I could never risk that."

Amytis smiled and rubbed his hand. "I know, my love. I couldn't either."

A guard approached from behind and bent low to whisper in Sin's ear. "Sire, there is a young man here seeking an audience with you. Should I send him away?"

"Is this about the Sippar restoration?" Sin whispered.

"No sire, he is a young princeling named Daniel—"

"Daniel?"

"Yes, my lord, he was gifted to you by the land of Judah as a peace offering."

"Bring him here. I would like to meet this boy."

Several minutes later, the guard returned, presenting a teenage boy wearing a fine linen tunic with piercing blue eyes and groomed light-brown hair that fell in large ringlets around his ears.

Amytis called Kashshaya to join her on the bench as soon as he arrived, but Sin studied the boy for several minutes before finally addressing him.

"Your name is Daniel. Is that correct?"

"Yes, your highness."

"Do you know why you're here?

"I am here to advise."

"You were sent to me as a gift—a peace offering. You are a promise of loyalty from a new king so we can move past the betrayals of the old one. Do you know what the Pharoah Psamtik sent me? Gold."

"My people value knowledge more highly than gold."

"I already have scholars in my court. I've been well educated myself. What can you offer me that I don't already have?"

"A man's dreams can inform a man's future. I can interpret those dreams."

Sin exchanged a long glance with Amytis and stroked his chin before he locked eyes with Daniel once more. "Go on."

Modern day.

Tiny particles drifted in and out of streams of sunlight that slipped between the shutters on the attic window and painted onto the half-filled cardboard boxes and warped wooden floors. The smell of mothballs mingled with the almond-vanilla scent of old newspapers, which were stacked everywhere.

"Lucian? Are you done up there?"

The question made Lucian drop the old leather bound book he had been reading, sending puffs of dust into the air on either side of him.

"No," he said, barely getting the word out before he sneezed.

"Well, what are you doing? Are you filling boxes?"

"Yeah. There's just lots of stuff up here."

"Ok, well, your mother wants to get going soon so I need you to hurry, ok?"

"Ok, dad."

Lucian shuffled himself closer to an old leather-strapped chest, dragging a half-filled box behind him. Inside the chest were empty glass bottles, leather-bound packets, and stacks of small manila envelopes.

Why did grandpa keep all of this stuff?

Lucian popped open an envelope and dumped its contents in front of him. Photos, printouts of historical texts, and newspaper clippings sprawled across the floor.

Great, more newspaper.

"Lucian," his dad said unimpressed, as he poked his head into the room, "I thought I told you to help clean out the attic. Instead, it looks like you're making a bigger mess."

"I *am* cleaning, dad, but a lot of this stuff is junk. I found this chest, and it's full of glass bottles and stuff. And look at these pictures. Was grandpa in the war?"

"He might've been. I know he took pictures, like a reporter," his dad said, walking over to him.

"He was a reporter?"

"He was later, but back then most of the people taking pictures on a battlefield were soldiers just recording the war for the government. What's this?" he said, picking up the leather bound book Lucian had been reading moments before.

"It's a storybook grandpa was writing, I think. It's about this guy who can control fire and talk to crows and stuff. It's really cool. I want to keep it."

"Ok, buddy."

Lucian picked up a clipping of a man aiming a rifle over some kind of barricade. "This soldier looks really young. How old did you have to be to be a soldier?"

"You were *supposed* to be around 17 or 18 to join, but sometimes they weren't much older than you."

Lucian looked over the picture again, imagining what it would be like to be a soldier until a mark on the picture caught his eye.

"Hey dad, look at this. They had soldiers on horseback."

"I don't see it."

"Right there in the background."

Lucian's dad squinted at the photo and lifted his glasses. "Oh yeah. Wow, he's so tiny, but that's definitely a guy on horseback. I didn't think they had cavalry units."

"Hey look, there's a horse guy in almost all of these," Lucian said, handing his dad a stack of pictures. "And the rest just have this rock with weird writing on it."

"Hmm. Maybe he travelled with a cavalry unit and caught them in the background by accident."

"But then, what about the rock pictures?"

"Those look like cuneiform tablets—if I remember my anthropology correctly—but I'm not sure why he would've collected pictures of them. And I wouldn't ask your mother right away. She was really close to your grandfather, and she doesn't need you badgering her with questions about him right now. You can try to look it up when we get home, but we have to finish up here first. Try to hurry, ok?"

"Ok," Lucian said, shoving the clippings back into the envelope, "and dad?"

"Yeah?"

"Can I keep this chest?"

He sighed, "Sure, buddy. Just clean up around it, ok?"